R BEN.
WAYS.

WITHDRAWN

ONE

I'm told that the day I was born, Uncle Paolo held me against his white lab coat and whispered, "She is perfect." Sixteen years later, they're still repeating the word. Every day I hear it, from the scientists or the guards, from my mother or from my Aunt Brigid. *Perfect*.

They say other things too. That there are no others like me, at least not yet. That I am the pinnacle of mankind, a goddess born of mortal flesh. *You are immortal, Pia, and you are perfect*, they say.

But as I follow Uncle Paolo to the laboratory, my bootlaces trailing in the mud and my hands clutching a struggling sparrow, the last thing I feel is perfect.

Outside the compound, the jungle is more restless than usual. The wind, lightly scented with orchids, prowls through the kapoks and palms as if searching for something it lost. The air is so damp that drops of water appear, almost magically, on my skin and on Uncle Paolo's pepper-gray hair. When we pass through the garden, the heavy-hanging passionflowers and spiky heliconias brush against my legs, depositing dew onto the tops of my boots. Water is everywhere, just like every other day in the rainforest. But today it feels colder—less refreshing and more invasive.

Today is a testing day. They are called the Wickham tests, and they only come every few months, often by surprise. When I awoke in my glass-walled bedroom this morning, I expected the usual: reciting genus and species lists to Uncle Antonio, comparing algae specimens under microscopes with Uncle Jakob, followed, perhaps, by a long swim in the pool. But instead, I was greeted by Mother, who informed me that Uncle Paolo had decided to hold a test. She then breezed out the door and left me scrambling to get ready. I didn't even have a chance to tie my shoelaces.

Hardly ten minutes later, here I am.

The bird in my hands fights relentlessly, scratching my palms with his tiny talons and snapping at my fingertips with his beak. It does no good. His claws are sharp enough to break the skin—just not *my* skin. That's probably why Uncle Paolo told me to carry the bird instead of doing it himself.

Indestructible it may be, but my skin feels three sizes too small, and it's all I can do to keep my breathing steady. My heart flutters more frantically than the bird.

Testing day.

The last test I took, four months ago, didn't involve a live animal, but it was still difficult to pass. I had to observe five different people—Jacques the cook, Clarence the janitor, and other nonscientist residents—to calculate whether they contributed more to the welfare of Little Cam than it cost to feed, pay, and keep them. I was terrified that my findings would result in someone being fired. No one was, but Uncle Paolo did have a talk with Aunt Nénine, the laundress, about how much time she spent napping compared with the time she spent keeping up with the wash. I asked Uncle Paolo what the test would prove, and he told me it would show whether my judgment was clear enough to make rational, scientific observations. But I'm still not sure Aunt Nénine has forgiven me for my report, rational observations or not.

I look down at the sparrow and wonder what's in store for him. For a moment, my will—and my fingers—weaken only slightly, but it's enough for the bird to jerk free and launch into the air. My enhanced reflexes make a decision faster than my brain: my hand reaches out, closes around the bird in mid-air, and draws him back to me, all in the time it takes the eye to blink.

"Everything all right?" Uncle Paolo asks without turning.

"Yes, fine." I know he knows what just happened. He always does. But he also knows I would never be so disobedient as to let his chosen specimen fly free.

I'm sorry, I want to say to the bird.

Instead, I hold on tighter.

There are two lab buildings in Little Cam. We arrive at B Labs, in the smaller one, and Mother is waiting inside. She wears her crisp, white lab assistant's coat and is pulling on latex gloves. They snap against her wrists.

"Is everything ready, Sylvia?" Uncle Paolo asks.

She nods and leads the way, passing door after door. We finally stop in front of a small, rarely used lab near the old wing, which was destroyed in a fire years ago. The door to the ruined hall is locked, and from the rust on the doorknob I can tell it hasn't been opened in years.

Inside the lab, metal shelves and cabinets and sinks line the walls, and they all catch and distort my reflection. In the center of the room is a small aluminum table, with two chairs on either side and a metal cage on its surface.

"Put subject 557 inside," Uncle Paolo says, and I release the bird into the cage, which is just large enough for him to fly in a tight circle. He throws himself at the metal grate, then lands, wings spread awkwardly, on the bottom. After a moment he launches up again, beating his wings determinedly against his captivity.

Then I notice the wires snaking from the cage to the table, down and across the floor, to a small generator under the emergency eyewash station.

I miss a breath, then glance at Uncle Paolo to see if he noticed. He didn't. He's filling out some forms on a clipboard.

"All right, Pia," he says as his pen scratches away. The bird lands again, takes off, clutches the side of the cage with his small talons. Uncle Paolo hands me the clipboard. "Take a seat. Good. Did you bring a pen?"

I didn't, so he gives me his and pulls another from his coat pocket. "What do I do?" I ask.

"Take notes. Measure everything. This particular test subject has been given periodic doses of a new serum I've been developing with suma."

Suma. *Pfaffia paniculata*, a common enough stimulant, but there are probably dozens of uses for it we haven't discovered yet. "So . . . we're testing to see if the subject handles the . . . stress of this test better than an untreated control subject."

"Right," he says with a smile. "Excellent, Pia. This serum— I call it E13—should kick in when the bird has exhausted the last of its strength, giving it another few minutes of energy."

I nod in understanding. Such a serum could prove useful in a myriad of medicinal ways.

"No computers today," Uncle Paolo tells me. "No instruments. Just rely on your own faculties. Observe. Record. Later we'll evaluate. You know the process."

"Yes." My eyes flicker to the bird. "I do."

"Sylvia!" Uncle Paolo snaps his fingers at my mother, and she flips a switch on the generator. I feel the electricity before it hits the cage, a low vibration that sizzles through the wires by my feet. The hairs on my arms begin to rise as if the electricity were pumping into *me*.

The cage begins to hum, and the bird shrieks and jerks into the air, only to collide with the metal and get shocked again. I lean forward and watch and *see* the moment the bird realizes he can't land. His pupils constrict, his feathers flare, and he begins wheeling in tight, dizzying loops.

I feel nauseated, but I dare not let Uncle Paolo see. He leans back, hands folded on his own clipboard. He isn't here to observe the sparrow.

He's here to observe me.

I bow my head and force myself to write something down. *Ammodramus aurifrons—yellow-browed sparrow, usually found in less dense areas of the rainforest.* I look up again, watching the bird. Watching Uncle Paolo watching me. I keep every muscle in my face perfectly still and draw each breath deliberately, slow and even. I can't let him see me wince, or gasp, or anything that might indicate my emotions are hindering my objectivity. The bird tries to land again, and I hear the snap and sizzle of the electricity. Already weary, the helpless sparrow resumes his frenetic circling.

In flight for 3.85 minutes, I jot down. *At 9.2 wing beats per sec =2097.6 beats . . . flight for 2.4 minutes . . .* The numbers are all reflex to me. The scientists like to tease me about it, saying I spend too much time with them. Once I responded, "Who else is there?" They never replied to that.

The sparrow is beginning to make mistakes. His wings grow clumsy, earning him more frequent shocks. At one point he seizes the metal bars in his talons and flattens himself against the side of the cage, tiny body shuddering with electricity.

I know Uncle Paolo's eyes are on me, searching for any sign of weakness. It's all I can do not to wince.

I can't fail this. I *can't*. Of all my studies, the Wickham tests are the most important. They gauge whether I am ready to be a scientist. Whether I'm ready for the secrets of my own existence. Once I prove I'm one of them, my real work can begin: creating others like me. And that is everything. I am the first and only of my kind, and I've been the first and only for sixteen years. Now, there is only one thing I want: someone else who knows. Knows what it is to never bleed. Knows what it is to look ahead and see eternity.

Knows what it is to be surrounded by faces that you love, faces that will one day stop breathing and start to decay while your own will remain frozen outside of time.

None of them know. Not Mother, not Uncle Paolo, not

any of them. They think they can understand. They think they can empathize or imagine with me. But all they really know is what they can observe, such as how fast I can run or how quickly bruises on my skin can fade. When it comes to the hidden part of me, the inner, untouchable Pia, all they can really know is that I'm different.

They cannot possibly imagine how much.

Suddenly the E13 serum must take effect, because the bird takes off again, circles and wheels, and I note every move, though my hand begins to shake. I see a look of triumph in Uncle Paolo's eyes as the bird beats its wings with double the vigor it had when the test began. One, two, six more minutes, and the serum-induced energy begins to wane. The bird starts to falter again.

I want it to stop, but I can't look to Mother. She'd only side with him, as she always does. Uncle Paolo's pen scratches and scratches. I want to see what he's writing down about me, but I have to concentrate on holding myself together.

The sparrow can't keep it up much longer or his heart will stop. *Surely you won't let it go that far.* I glance at Uncle Paolo's face, but he remains as impassive as ever. The perfect scientist.

"I think . . ." I pause, lick my lips. My mouth is dry. "I think I have enough data."

"The test isn't over, Pia," Uncle Paolo says with a frown.

"Well, it's just that . . . in another minute, his heart will—"

"Pia." My name is severe on his lips, and the wince I've been holding back finally escapes. Uncle Paolo leans forward. "The test is not over. Get your emotions under control, Pia. Keep your eye on the goal, not the steps you must take to reach it. The goal is everything. The steps are nothing. No matter how difficult the journey is, the goal is always worth it."

I open my lips to protest further, but then slowly sit back and relent. *He won't let it go that far. He won't.*

The sparrow lands clumsily, takes off again, seeking not escape now, but rest.

He won't.

The bird doesn't stay aloft for more than three seconds before crashing again. He struggles, but can't summon the energy to take off. Instead, he hops raggedly, eyes glazing.

The electricity sizzles and pops.

Will he?

My lips part, and I gather my breath—

But finally Uncle Paolo speaks. "Enough. Turn it off, Sylvia."

My mother shuts off the generator, and the bird slumps with relief.

So do I.

Uncle Antonio finds me in my room. I sit cross-legged on my bed, holding the sparrow in my hands. He's too exhausted and traumatized to struggle now, and I stroke his feathers absently as I stare out at the jungle.

Three of my bedroom walls and even the ceiling are made of glass. Since the little house sits on the outskirts of the compound, by the western fence, I have an almost 360-degree view of the rainforest. My room used to be a greenhouse. When I was born the scientists decided to convert it into a bedroom for me, and the rest of the house—botany laboratories—was renovated into another bedroom and bath, a living room, and a study to accommodate my mother.

They've often discussed replacing the glass of my room with plaster, but I've fought them on it every time, just as I fought to have them remove the cameras that once watched me night and day. I won on both accounts, but barely. Since the glass house sits only yards from the fence and my bedroom faces the forest, I am hidden from the rest of Little Cam but still have a panoramic view of the jungle. It's almost like not having walls at all. I love waking up and seeing the trees overhead. Sometimes I'll sit on my bed for hours, staring out to see what animals will pass by my window.

And sometimes I even imagine what it would be like to stand on the other side of that fence. Looking in, instead of looking out. Being able to run as far as I want.

But that's ridiculous. My world is Little Cam, and even if I were out there in the jungle, I'd have nowhere to go.

Uncle Antonio walks to the glass wall and stands with his back to the jungle, hands in his pockets, and watches me.

Of all my aunts and uncles in Little Cam, Uncle Antonio is my favorite. Unlike everyone else, he never calls me perfect. He calls me "Chipmunk" instead, though I've never seen one, except in zoology books. Neither has he, for that matter. Like me, Uncle Antonio was born in Little Cam.

"I passed," I say to his unspoken question, and his eyes fall to the sparrow cupped in my hands.

"And him?"

"I'm supposed to put him back in the menagerie."

Uncle Antonio's lips are pressed tightly together, hidden in

SSICA KHOURY

the thick growth of his beard. He disapproves highly of these tests, but he never says so. Uncle Paolo calls all the shots in Little Cam, and there's nothing Uncle Antonio can do about that.

"I'll walk with you," he says. I nod, glad for his company.

We leave the glass house and make our way to the menagerie. Ten rows of horizontal bars, webbed in between with electrically charged chain link, surround the glass house and the rest of the research compound we call Little Cam, where we're hidden beneath the rainforest canopy like ants in a patch of grass, safe and secret. There are thirteen buildings here. Some are laboratories, some are dormitories, and one is the social center, where the gymnasium, pool, lounge, and dining hall are. Twenty-four scientists, a dozen guards, and several maids, maintenance men, cooks, and lab assistants make up the population of Little Cam. I'm the reason they're all here, and I'm the reason no one can know this place exists.

"How many more tests do you think I have to pass before I'm ready?" I ask.

Uncle Antonio shrugs. "Not something Paolo discusses with me. Why? Are you in a hurry? Of all people, I'd think you'd be the last one in a hurry."

Because you've only got forever, I know he must be thinking. I look up at him, wondering—not for the first time—what it must be like to know that one day you could suddenly just *end.*

Uncle Antonio scratches his beard, which is thick and curly and makes him look like a woolly monkey. "What did he say? After it was over?"

"What he always says. That I was perfect and that I passed."

"Perfect," he snorts.

"What? You don't think I'm perfect?" I can't resist, because he gets so riled whenever I bring it up. "I can run up to thirty miles without stopping. I can jump six feet in the air. There is not a material in this world sharp enough to pierce my skin. I cannot drown or suffocate. I am immune to every illness known to man. I have a perfect memory. My senses are more acute than anyone else's. My reflexes rival those of a cat. I will never grow old"—my voice falls, all smugness gone—"and I will never die."

"Perfect is," Uncle Antonio whispers, "as perfect does, Pia."

I almost laugh at him for sounding cliché, but his eyes are so solemn I stay quiet.

"Anyway," he says, "if you're so perfect, Chipmunk, why does he keep testing you?"

"That's not fair and you know it."

"Did you ever consider . . ." He stops, shakes his head.

"What? Consider what?"

His eyes flicker over his shoulder before he answers. "You know. *Not* passing."

"Failing on purpose? Why? Just so I don't have to take any more tests?"

He spreads his hands as if to say, *Exactly*.

"*Because*, Uncle Antonio, then I'd never be allowed to join the Immortis team. I'd never know how they made me the way I am." *And I'd never be able to help make others like me.* "You know as well as I that I'll never learn the secret of Immortis until I'm part of the team. That is"—I give him an encouraging smile—"unless you want to tell it to me?"

Uncle Antonio sighs. "Pia, don't."

"Come on. Tell me. I know all about the elysia flower . . . but what about the catalyst? How do they make Immortis?"

"You know I won't tell you anything, so stop asking."

I watch him closely, but he can be as impassive as Uncle Paolo when it suits him. A moment later we reach the menagerie, but instead of going inside, I stand and stare at the door.

"What's the matter?" asks Uncle Antonio.

I look down at the sparrow. His wings are splayed over my palms and his head is abnormally still. I feel the beat of his tiny heart in my palm, so faint it's hardly there at all.

In this moment, I suddenly find myself not caring about being the perfect, obedient scientist. It's an irrational whim, and I'll probably regret it in less than a minute, but I open my hands until they're flat, lift the sparrow up, and gently thrust him into the air. Surprised and disoriented, he drops a full foot before spreading his wings. Then he hurls himself skyward, climbing high above the roof of the menagerie to disappear into the darkening sky.

TWO

I wake the next morning to thunder.

Above me, the branches of the trees shudder in a strong wind, and every few seconds lightning flares over them, like hot white branches of some larger, celestial tree. The thunder is so deep I feel it in my ribcage.

For a moment, I just lie in bed and stare. I love thunderstorms. I love the raw, unpredictable power shattering the air, shaking the jungle, searing the boundary between earth and sky. The lightning fills my room with bursts of light, making my pale skin seem even whiter. Outside, the vines of lianas in the trees thrash like snakes.

After several minutes, I drag myself from bed and yawn my way into the bathroom. As I brush my teeth, the lights above my mirror flicker. The storm must be interfering with the power, but I ignore it. It seems like every other thunderstorm that rolls overhead knocks the power out for fifteen minutes or so, before Clarence gets the backup generators running.

There's a flashlight in my sock drawer just in case, but it's light enough outside that I won't need it.

After showering and dressing, I jog to the dining hall and snag a bagel and a banana from the kitchen. It's not raining yet, but judging by the thickness of the clouds, it won't be long off. I clamp the bagel between my teeth as I peel the banana and head for the gym. There's time for a couple of miles on the treadmill before my lessons with Uncle Antonio.

Uncle Antonio's main job is my education. We alternate subjects every day, according to a curriculum Uncle Paolo writes out. Yesterday, after the Wickham test, was mathematics (we studied combinatorics—easy). Today is microbiology. Tomorrow could be botany, biomedics, zoology, genetics, or any of the various fields represented by the residents of Little Cam. Uncle Antonio really only tutors me half of the time. The rest of my studies are done under the scientists themselves, with Uncle Antonio monitoring my progress and reporting it to Uncle Paolo at the end of each week.

The gym is empty when I arrive. As I run, the slap of my sneakers and the hum of the treadmill echoing in the deserted room, I try not to think about yesterday's experiment. Mother told me after the last Wickham test that the best thing to do is just to move on. Force the mind to look forward and not backward.

To keep my mind from slipping into the past, I mentally run through the day's schedule. *Two hours with Uncle Antonio. Lunch. Five more hours of studying. Dinner. Painting with Uncle Smithy. Run a few more miles. Swim. Read. Sleep.*

It's a wonder I fit everything in, but even if I had free time, Uncle Paolo would be sure to fill it in with something.

He says the mind is a muscle like any other, and letting it sit unused will make it weak and slow. There's plenty to do in Little Cam. There's the gym, the pool, the library filled with science and math books, the lounge with games like chess and backgammon. There's usually some kind of interesting experiment being conducted in one lab or another, and the scientists always let me drop in and watch or even help. And there's the menagerie of animals that are constantly in need of feeding, grooming, exercise, and attention.

The lights flicker again, and the belt of the treadmill jerks. Anticipating it, I slow down, then speed up once the electricity settles again and the belt resumes its steady roll.

I glance at the screen on the treadmill. Twelve miles. Not bad for half an hour, though I usually go faster. I hit the stop button, and, instead of waiting for the belt to slow, I vault over the handrail and land lightly on the tile floor. I wipe away the few beads of sweat that are on my brow and head outside. Rain begins to fall as I jog to my room, but I make it indoors before my clothes get soaked.

As I wait for Uncle Antonio, I start pruning my orchids. I have ten different species of them, each one specially cultivated for me by Uncle Paolo, who likes to dabble in botany in his spare time. One of the species, which he named *Epidendrum aureus*, is genetically manipulated to be the only one of its kind.

"Completely unique, just like you," he told me when he gave it to me, three years ago. "And see? I've specially designed it to have those flecks of gold. It almost looks like elysia."

That is the Uncle Paolo I know best. The detached scientist who sticks birds in electric cages is a rare side of Uncle

Paolo that I admire for its cool reason and objectivity, but I'm glad he's not always that way.

Outside, the clouds are disintegrating, and no more thunder pounds at the glass around me. The storm is over. Thin tendrils of sunlight creep through the trees as if embarrassed for having been so long absent.

It's time to meet Uncle Antonio for lessons. I quickly spray the orchids with a diluted formula of potassium, calcium, and nitrogen, then grab my bag of textbooks and head down the hall, twisting my hair into a ponytail as I walk. It's smooth as water in my hands. I have my mother's dark, straight hair, though she cuts hers short. I pause at the kitchen and grab the molding around the doorway, letting myself swing into the room. Mother is sitting at the kitchen table, doing sums.

"I'm going to meet with Uncle Antonio."

She looks up. There is a brief moment in which anger flashes across her face before her features smooth silkily back into her accustomed composure. I ignore the anger; she always does that when I interrupt her. "Don't forget you have your monthly MRI with Paolo this afternoon."

I tilt my head to the side and frown at her. "Forget? Me?" She might forget, or Uncle Antonio. But not me. Never me.

"Yes," she says, her eyes scanning me from head to toe. "That's right. You're *perfect*."

As I wave to her and head for the front door, I feel a sudden coldness in the bridge of my nose, right between my eyes. Of everyone in Little Cam, my mother is the only one who never smiles when she says that.

• • •

Later, after my lessons and MRI—which showed nothing new—I am sitting in the menagerie, brushing Alai, when the alarms go off. Alai is a two-hundred-pound jaguar that Uncle Paolo gave me for my ninth birthday, when Alai was just a cub. He hates everyone in Little Cam except me, Uncle Antonio, and the cook, Jacques, who brings Alai cookies every morning. Alai is mad about cookies.

The alarms blare in two short bursts. Behind me, the monkeys start screaming in response. They like to think they run the menagerie, but I won't have any of it.

"Oh, shut up, you dummies," I say, rising from the ground and turning to shake Alai's brush at them. The Grouch, a huge orange howler monkey, stares straight at me and lets out an obnoxious roar. The howlers used to scare me when I was little, but now I just roll my eyes at them.

"Come on, Alai!" I say, heading for the door. The menagerie is a long, low cement building with dirt floors and wide picture windows in every cage. Most of the animals are there for experimentation—which means we have several immortal residents—but Alai is not allowed to be used for any tests. He is completely mine.

After pulling the heavy metal door shut behind me, I start running. Alai lopes at my heels, his huge paws all but silent on the path. I have to circle most of Little Cam before I finally reach the gate. My heart is racing, not because of the run, but from excitement. Two alarms means the supply truck is here.

We only get a delivery every few months, so it's always a special occasion when one arrives. Uncle Timothy, a huge, muscular man with skin as dark as obsidian, is in charge of making the trek through the jungle to the Little Mississip, the nearest river to Little Cam. I don't know what comes after the Little Mississip, but it must be a long journey since every supply run takes him nearly two months. Once I asked Uncle Paolo to show me a map of Uncle Timothy's route, but he told me to never ask him or anyone else that question again.

The gate is the only entrance or exit from our compound, and now it is swinging open on mechanical tracks to admit the trucks. There are three of them, huge, growling, angry things with canvas tops and wheels drenched with mud. Belching and rattling, they pull into the wide dirt drive in front of the dining hall and shudder to a stop. Uncle Timothy jumps out of the lead truck, his bald head glistening with sweat. He has a handkerchief tied around his mouth and nose, and as I come running up, he pulls it down and smiles. He has the whitest teeth of anyone I know.

"Hey, little miss! Come give your Uncle T a hug, yeah?" He spreads his arms, but I wrinkle my nose and dodge aside. He smells like the Grouch.

"You're disgusting! What did you bring? Where did you go?" I race around to the back of his truck and climb onto the high bumper so I can peer inside. "Did you trade with some natives?" Ever since I first heard of the jungle dwellers whom Uncle Timothy calls the "natives," I've been fascinated by the possibility of seeing one. I've not had the chance yet, since he usually goes to their villages whenever he needs to trade for fresh fruit. Often the scientists go with him to ask the natives how they use certain plants for medicine.

"Get down from there, Pia!" calls my mother. She and a crowd of people are gathering around the trucks, and everyone looks excited, since delivery days are our only contact with the outside world.

I eye the boxes and crates eagerly, wondering what they hold. I start to reach for something with the word *Skittles* across it, with a picture of a rainbow and what look like pieces of candy, when suddenly someone pops up from behind the crate. Startled, I jump backward and land on the ground beside Alai.

It's a woman. She's squinting and yawning as if she just woke up, and her rumpled clothes suggest that she just did.

"Oh, hi," she says with a sleepy smile. "Is this Little Cam, then?" Her accent is clipped in a way I've never heard before. Her hair is as shockingly orange as a howler monkey's, and it frizzes out in every direction.

"This is Little Cam," I reply warily. "Who are you?"

"Dr. Fields!" says a voice, and I turn to see Uncle Paolo striding toward us. "Welcome! So good to meet you!" He helps her down. She's very tall and thin, and her white shirt is stained with brown spots.

She must have seen me staring, because she laughs and pulls at her shirt. "Coffee," she explains. "I must have drunk a gallon of it in Manaus and another pint on the Little Mississip. What a name for a river! Who's the Yank responsible for that one?"

Suddenly everyone grows silent.

"Where's Manaus?" I ask.

She stares at me with a funny smile. "What do you mean, 'Where's Manaus?' You *have* to go through Manaus if you want to get anywhere in this jungle—"

"Dr. Fields," interrupts Uncle Paolo. "I'm sure you must

be exhausted. Come inside, we'll get you something to eat and show you to your room."

"Sounds brilliant. Whoop! Wait just a tick—" She clambers onto the truck and bends over the tailgate, rooting around for something inside. I notice Uncle Paolo, Uncle Antonio, and a few other uncles observing how her rear bobs up and down while she searches. I scowl, not too sure about this *Dr. Fields* woman. No one told *me* she was coming.

"Ah! Got it!" She holds up a large metal canteen as if it were a cure for cancer she'd just discovered. "My coffee!"

"Excellent, excellent," says Uncle Paolo. He offers her a hand down, but she ignores it and jumps clumsily, nearly breaking her ankle when she lands.

"Whoop!" she hollers. "I'm such a klutz! Ha! Oh, great Scott, a jaguar! Hello, beautiful!" She bends down and makes a kissy noise at Alai. I wait for him to growl and snap like he does with everyone else, but instead he pads right up to her and starts purring as she scratches his ears. Finally she declares she's ready for dinner and some hot coffee, and, chattering all the way, she leads a cluster of men into the dining hall. Each of them is shoving the others to extend a handshake and their names. They disappear inside, leaving the crowd around the trucks much smaller in number. Alai rubs against my leg, still purring.

"Traitor," I hiss. With a yawn, he flops onto the ground and starts licking his paws.

"What a dope," I say to Uncle Antonio. "Who invited her, anyway?"

"What's your problem, Chipmunk? She seems nice." He

stares at the dining hall wistfully, and I sigh. At least he hadn't joined the welcoming committee.

As if in direct response to my relief, he adds, "I better see if she needs help with her luggage." And off he goes.

"What about the supplies?" I yell. "Who's gonna unload those? Me?" I point at the trucks, but he ignores me. Uncle Timothy comes over and slaps me on the shoulder, laughing.

"Looks like our new ginger's got plenty of help, eh, Pia? She's a nutter, that one, and she talks enough to make a sloth want to run the other way."

"Who is she?"

"Dr. Harriet Fields, a biomedical engineer. Come to replace Smithers, I think."

"Uncle Smithy's leaving?" The ancient, white-haired scientist has been in Little Cam longer than anyone else. Some say he was here when the Accident happened, thirty years ago. Besides being a biomedical engineer, he's a painter, and he always keeps a brush close at hand.

"It's what I heard." Uncle Timothy shrugs. "So, did I hear you volunteering to unload everything? Sounds great, I'm bushed."

I don't rise to the bait. I'm too disturbed by this new biomedical engineer. It's been years since someone new has come to Little Cam. The last new arrival was Clarence, the janitor, when I was eight.

Deciding that I am tired of talking about Dr. Harriet Fields, or, as I'm already calling her in my head, *Dr. Klutz*, I ask Uncle Timothy if he's brought my dress.

"Dress? What dress?"

I slap his massive arm. It's as solid as steel, but he makes a show of pouting and rubbing the spot. "Oh, *that* dress."

I have to wait until a crew unloads the trucks, hauls everything to a warehouse, and starts opening boxes before we find it. It's teal blue, and the bodice is studded with tiny crystals. "Oh," I breathe when I see it. Mother comes over and takes it. She holds it up to me, her face uncharacteristically cheerful.

"Lovely," she says. "Chiffon and silk . . . and it even matches your eyes. I'm surprised at you, Timothy! I thought surely with *you* doing the shopping, you'd come back with a jaguar-print toga or something hideous like that."

"Mother!" I gasp, and I reach down to cover Alai's ears. "You've offended him."

"I didn't pick it," Uncle Timothy protests. "I had that Fields woman find it. Send a man like me to shop for a party dress . . . *pah!*"

"Go try it on," Mother urges.

"No, it's for my party. I won't wear it until my birthday." Two more weeks. I can barely stand the wait. Ever since I found out about parties, I begged for months for a real one. Finally everyone agreed, though most of them were grudging about it. Tuxedos are scarce in the middle of the rainforest. Luckily Uncle Timothy already had a supply run planned, so one of the boxes scattered around the warehouse has to be stuffed with party clothes. Uncle Paolo still grumbles at me about the cost and the inconvenience of it all, but only halfheartedly, or he'd never have agreed to it in the first place.

"Here," says Uncle Timothy, handing me a little package. It's the one called Skittles, and he's already ripped it open and started munching on a handful. "Try those."

I expect chocolate, since they look like M&Ms (which Uncle Timothy brought me last time), but instead I taste a burst of fruit. "They're good!" I dump half the bag into my mouth and decide I want Skittles instead of birthday cake at the party. Mother wanders off to help inventory a box of syringes and other medical supplies, and I trail after Uncle Timothy as he oversees the unpacking.

"Uncle T," I say, trying to be as nonchalant as possible, "what's Manaus like?"

His back is turned to me, and I see the muscles in his shoulders tense. As he turns around, I put on my most determined face. "Well? Is it true you have to go through Manaus if you want to get anywhere?"

He looks around, but no one heard my question. He leans over and puts his dark face inches from mine. "Now don't you be asking me questions like that, Pia. You know it's against the rules. Do you want to get me in trouble?"

I frown, and beside me Alai raises his hackles slightly. "I won't tell anyone you told me. Come *on*, Uncle T! I know all about protozoons and mitochondria, and I can tell you the genus and species of all the animals in the menagerie, but all I really want to know about is my own jungle!"

"No, Pia." He turns away and pretends to be busy moving some boxes around.

I watch for a while, but not even the prospect of more of those Skittles interests me now. Delivery day is ruined. I leave the warehouse with Alai at my side, angry at Uncle T, angry at Mother, angry at Uncle Antonio, and angry at that Dr. Klutz for ever mentioning Manaus.

The rules. The stupid rules that have been in place for over thirty years. A list of them hangs in the lounge, in huge print, so that no one can forget. No books, magazines, or movies from the outside, unless they're science textbooks, and even those get edited by Uncle Paolo. I have biology books full of blacked-out paragraphs and defaced photos. All music played must be instrumental only, no lyrics. No one can talk about the outside world, at least not when I'm around. No maps. No radios. No photographs. Anything deemed by Uncle Paolo, as the director of Little Cam, to be a "corruptive influence" is seized and locked up somewhere, probably in Uncle Timothy's room, until its owner retires. And that's if the item isn't destroyed altogether.

I know why the rules exist.

Two words: the Accident.

THREE

Uncle Antonio tries to run on the treadmill and read from his quiz sheet at the same time. Not a good idea, but I don't say anything. We're in the gym, doing a microbiology lesson. There's no one else in the room, which is unusual in the early afternoon, but I know where everyone is: helping that Harriet Fields settle in. She was all anyone talked about at dinner last night, and her table was crowded with scientists vying to awe her with their intellects. I sat in a corner with Mother, the pair of us watching with dark looks over our tuna salad. I don't think Mother's any fonder of Dr. Klutz than I am.

Uncle Antonio's voice is husky from running. "Typhus fever is contracted by *Rick—*"

"*Rickettsia prowazekii*," I finish.

Uncle Antonio hits the stop button on his treadmill and jogs to a halt. He's panting heavily, and there are more sweat stains than dry spots on his blue tee. After he catches his breath, he says, "That wasn't the question, Chipmunk. I was *going* to ask, what animal carries—"

"Lice. *Pediculus humanus.*" I crank the speed of my own treadmill up a notch, my stride lengthening to match the whir of the belt.

"Hey, who's doing the teaching here?" Uncle Antonio comes around to the front of my treadmill and throws his arm over the safety rail. His other hand grips his water bottle as if it is the only thing keeping him alive. He looks at the digital display on the machine and shakes his head. "You're something else, kid."

"Why is everyone so worked up over that new woman?" I ask, my tone more than a bit terse. "What's so special about her?"

His eyebrows lift quizzically. "Why, Chipmunk, are you *jealous?*"

"No!"

The amusement in his eyes makes me more irritated. "I think you are. You're jealous of the attention she's getting."

"I am not," I reply. "It's not like I want everyone hanging all over me all day."

"No?" He sits on the weight-lifting bench that no one ever uses. "Because it seems to me that's the normal order of business."

I glare, but he only laughs.

"She's new and different, Pia. That's all it is. Couple of months and she'll be one of us, just another regular face. But you'll always be you, immortal and special. So don't worry. No one's taking your place."

"I don't see why we need her, anyway. Soon I'll be part

of the Immortis team, and then we'll make more immortals. What do we need Harriet Fields for?"

The smile leaves his face, replaced by a strange, shadowed look. "I don't know."

"Do you think they'll stop bringing in new scientists once I'm in charge?"

"I don't know." Still that grim look in his eyes. Maybe I'm pushing the Dr. Klutz thing a little too far.

"You're wrong," I say. "I'm not jealous of the attention she's getting. But do you think . . . do you think she's here because Uncle Paolo doesn't believe I'm ready? Does he think we need someone as backup, in case I don't pass the next Wickham test?"

Uncle Antonio stares at me. "No," he says softly, but I wonder if he said it just because it's what I want to hear.

"So, where do you think she's from?" I ask, trying to lighten the conversation.

"Dr. Fields?" He shrugs. "Doesn't matter."

"Oh, come on, Uncle Antonio." I stop the treadmill to retie my ponytail, which came loose while I ran. "You're just as interested in her as everyone else. I saw you last night, hovering at her elbow all through dinner."

"I was not *hovering*."

"You were so."

A smile plays on his lips. "Well. Maybe a little."

"It's strange, isn't it? These new scientists who come here, they have whole other lives outside Little Cam. Do you ever think about it? About where they must come from? Who they were before they came to the jungle?"

He gives me a guarded look. "Why? Do you?"

"It's a natural question. And I'm a scientist. It's my *job* to ask questions. Uncle Antonio." I sit beside him and chew my lip a moment, then ask in a hush, "Do you ever . . . you know . . . wonder what it would be like? Out there?"

Uncle Antonio stares at his hands. "Out where?"

"You know what I mean. Outside . . . the fence."

When he finally meets my eyes, his lips are a thin, taut line. "No. I don't."

Without another word, he stands up and leaves.

I stare at the door as it swings shut. I don't believe him. Not for a minute.

When I go to my laboratory for my weekly checkup that afternoon, I pass Harriet Fields in the hall. She says hi and gives a little waist-level wave, and I give her a little jerk of my chin in response. I feel her eyes on my back as I pass her.

I call it *my* laboratory because it's the one entirely devoted to me. It's like a second bedroom, and I'm quite proud of it. I keep a row of potted orchids along the window sills, and there are pictures of me all over the walls. They're kind of boring, having been made to chart things like the development of my facial bones, but still.

Uncle Paolo is waiting for me as usual. He sits by my metal examination table, thumbing through a stack of past checkup reports.

"Morning," I say to him, and I pause by a glass cage in the corner. The fat, sleepy rat inside wiggles his nose at me. "Morning, Roosevelt."

Uncle Paolo smiles. "Morning, Pia," he says as I take

my place on the exam table. "Find anything good in the delivery?"

"Skittles." I swing my legs back and forth under the table and watch him make some notes on a clipboard.

"Ah, yes." He pulls out a stethoscope and takes my heartbeat. "I haven't had Skittles in years. I'll have to get some."

"Too late. I got dibs already. They're for the party."

"The party," he repeats. "Still planning for your fairy-tale ball, eh? Open."

I open my mouth, and he swabs the inside of my check with a cotton wad. "It's not a fairy-tale ball. It's a real party, like the ones they have in cities."

"And what would you know of cities?"

"I read about them in the dictionary. 'An urban area where a large number of people live and work,'" I quote.

He only grunts as he deposits the saliva sample on a microscope slide.

Then, just to see what his reaction will be, I add, "I know that Manaus is a city."

Uncle Paolo drops the cotton swab. "*Damn.* Open again, I'll have to get another."

I wonder if that *damn* was for the lost saliva sample or my lucky guess. "So it *is* a city!"

"Pia." He sets the second sample on a small metal tray and starts pulling off his squeaky latex gloves. "Never bring up Manaus again."

"Why?"

His hands pause with one glove half off, and he draws in a sharp breath before continuing. "I have told you many times,

Pia. It's dangerous out there. Those people wouldn't understand you. You would frighten them with what you have, and they would soon grow jealous. You cannot die, but that does not mean they can't hurt you."

"Those people," I repeat softly.

"Yes. The ones out *there*. They don't see things as we do here, Pia. They would put you in a box and never let you out, don't you see?"

I nod my head, thinking of the sparrow and the electrified cage, imagining myself in the place of the bird. I shiver.

"Do not bring up Manaus again." He speaks in the tone he usually reserves for testing days, but then his face softens. He covers my hand with his own. "You're safe here. For now, this is where you belong. One day, Pia, you'll see the world. Don't doubt that. But until the world is ready to see *you*, I'm afraid Little Cam will have to suffice."

"All right," I respond meekly.

He smiles and squeezes my hand. "I was here the day you were born, you know. I was the first one to hold you. I was the one who chose your name."

"You were?" He's never mentioned it before.

"Yes. *Pia*, because it means reverent, and that's exactly what I felt when I saw you."

His eyes, locked on mine, are warm and earnest, and I find myself smiling.

The rest of the examination goes as usual. It doesn't take long. I'm so used to the exam that I could do it myself. Heartbeat, saliva sample, eyes, ears, and nose, check, check, check, and we're done. Uncle Paolo gave up on taking blood samples years ago. No matter what material the needles are made of, and no matter how hard he presses, nothing punctures my skin.

"All done, Pia. Go and work on planning your party or something."

"I need to water my orchids."

He nods and does a few more little tasks around the lab before he leaves.

I am watering the first flower when I hear footsteps and turn to see what Uncle Paolo forgot. But it isn't him. It's Dr. Klutz.

"What do *you* want?" I ask.

She raises her eyebrows in surprise. They are as red as her hair. "Relax, why don't you? I just want to chat. We didn't get to properly meet one another yesterday."

Great. I turn back to my orchids. "Hi. Nice to meet you."

"Nice to meet you too," she returns in an equally blank tone. "Good heavens, girl, at least give me a chance before you decide to make an enemy of me. Here, let me help."

She tries to take the watering can from me and ends up knocking it over and pouring water all over my shoes.

"Oops!" she says, and as I stare openmouthed at the mess, she finds a towel and hands it to me. I sop up the water, biting my tongue to keep from snapping something I'll later regret. Dr. Klutz perches herself on the examination table and looks around.

"Terrible pictures," she says as she studies my portraits on the wall.

I normally wouldn't throw it in someone's face like this, but I can't help it. The woman rubs me the wrong way. "They're *perfect.*"

"That's right," she says thoughtfully, eyeing me. "I hadn't even had a chance to wash the dust from the road off my face when your Doctor Paolo Alvez had me cornered. I got the whole Pia talk, oh, yes."

"The Pia talk?" My curiosity bests my stubbornness for a moment, and I step closer. "What's that?"

"You mean you didn't get it too?" She draws a pack of cigarettes from her pocket and lights one. I hate cigarettes. They are the only thing in the world that make me ill, though Mother tells me that I just don't like the smell and that I'm not really ill at all. "Yes, I was properly backed into a corner, with Alvez breathing down my blouse about secrecy and signing contracts and consequences and all sorts of spookiness. And at the center of it all"—she inhales deeply and blows a stream of disgusting smoke toward me—"was you."

"Well," I reply stiffly, "I *am* the reason this place exists."

"I must confess, I had no idea what I was getting into when I took this job. Thought I was coming down just to study the cell structures of mosquitoes, maybe clone a few rats. They told me this was a research center that targeted the 'big ones'—cancer, heart disease"—her face goes suddenly still, as if she's looking at something far off—"cerebral palsy. Though I did think it odd I had to sign on for a minimum of thirty years, but . . ." Her cigarette seems forgotten between her index and middle fingers. Its thin tail of smoke curls across her face. "Well, let's just say the deal this place offered was very convincing."

Her eyes refocus, finding me and then narrowing suspiciously. "And *then* there was all the cloak-and-dagger stuff on the way here. That giant moose of a man, Timothy, wouldn't tell me *any*thing. And what do you think but the first thing he asks me is if I can go buy a dress for a seventeen-year-old girl?" She shakes her head, and I notice for the first time that her wild red frizz is tamed into a braid over her shoulder. With the hair under control, she's quite pretty, and younger than I'd first thought.

"The dress was all right." I shrug. No need to tell her I love it. I don't want her thinking we're friends or something.

"It's weird, having a black-tie party in the middle of the wilderness."

"You just say whatever pops into your head, don't you?"

"Always. Without question. That's the only way I know I'm being truly original."

"Why did you come to Little Cam?"

"Didn't you hear? To study tapirs and three-toed sloths."

"What did Uncle Paolo say about me?"

"That you're *immortal*." I can tell from the twitch of her lips around her cigarette that she doesn't believe it.

"I am."

"Huh. He also said you were perfect."

"I'm that too."

"Psh. Sure, honey."

"I *am!*" I'm bristling like Alai now. "Watch."

I pick up a scalpel from Uncle Paolo's tray of tools. Dr. Klutz's eyes widen. "Pia . . ."

"Just watch." I run it down my arm, pressing as hard as I can. It stings, but only mildly. I *can* feel pain, but not as intensely as other people. A faint white line is the only evidence of the blade's touch, but it disappears in seconds.

Dr. Klutz gapes, her eyes wide, cigarette forgotten between her fingers. "My sweet, giddy aunt . . ."

That seems like an odd thing for someone to say, but I feel strangely pleased with her response. Setting the scalpel down, I reach into a drawer, pull out a rolled-up chart, and spread it on the exam table beside her. She watches my every move with rapt attention.

"What's that?"

"This," I announce with no small amount of pride, "is my family tree. Did Uncle Paolo tell you the story behind Little Cam, me, all of this?"

"He said we'd cover that in orientation tonight, but"— she leans forward and whispers—"I'm rather an impatient woman. So go on. Tell me."

"Well," I begin, thrilled to have an audience. I've never had the chance to tell someone my story before, not like this. "It all began one hundred years ago, in 1902. A team of scientists were going through the jungle in search of new plants to use for medicines. They went deeper than anyone else from the outside had gone before and met natives who had never seen people with white skin and mustaches. They were led by a biologist and botanist named Heinrich Falk, who heard of a plant in the very heart of the jungle that could extend human life. Everyone else thought it was a myth. Stories like these were more numerous than the leaves of a kapok tree, and none of them had ever been proved. But Dr. Falk found it. *Epidendrum elysius.* Elysia, he called it. In all of the rainforest—and in all of the world—it's found in only one place. Falk's Glen. It's not far from here, I'm told, though I've never been there myself."

"So what did this magical flower do, then, eh?" she asks.

I can hear the skepticism creeping back. That's fine. I'm not done with my story yet.

"It's not magic. It's science. And it kills you within minutes if you eat it or drink the nectar that pools in the cup of its petals." I have never seen Falk's Glen, but I have seen elysia. Uncle Antonio brought me a stem once, a single stem of the precious plant that is the basis of my existence. It is a deep purple, and the tips of its petals are tinged with gold. It doesn't look much different from some of my orchids in the window. I tried to replant it, but it died. I wasn't the first to try it. One of the Little Cam scientists' greatest hopes is to figure out how to replant elysia. So far, no luck at all. It wouldn't be such an issue if we knew how it reproduced, but that's another mystery. The same flowers that grow in Falk's Glen now are the exact same blossoms Falk and his team discovered. The life cycle of elysia has never been discerned; for all we know, it *doesn't* reproduce."

Dr. Klutz snorts and remembers her cigarette. Before she inhales again, however, she says, "Sounds like some bully magic. So that's what happened to Falk, then? Shows up bold as brass, names the flower, names the place after himself, and then promptly eats the bloody thing and drops dead?"

"No, that's not how it happened at all. They set up camp and began experimenting on rats, that's what they did. The camp moved here and there and finally *here*, where we are now, and then it became permanent. I think it was Dr. Falk's successor, Wickham, who finally named it Little Cambridge." And who developed the Wickham test, designed to evaluate new scientists before bringing them into the project. I wonder what Dr. Klutz's Wickham test was.

"So what's the chart about?"

"I'm getting to that. Will you be patient?" I brush my hair behind my ears and draw a deep breath. "So, they experimented on rats. They figured out how to add the nectar of another flower to elysia to counteract its lethality and make it safe to inject into rats and humans alike. I've never seen the other flower, but Uncle Paolo tells me it's just called the catalyst. It must be rare because I can't find it in any encyclopedia or database anywhere. Anyway, they started injecting the rats, but nothing happened. They lived their normal little rat lives and died when they got old. End of story."

"Is it?"

"Is it what?"

"Is that the end of the story?"

"Of course not!" The woman may be a biomedical engineer, but I begin to think she might also be a certifiable idiot. "Because something happened that no one expected. The scientists had been injecting the rats' offspring and the offspring's offspring with Immortis—the nonlethal form of elysia made with the catalyst—never quite believing that anything would come of it. The rats lived, the rats died, and they never showed a sign of anything abnormal. Until . . ." I cross the room, lift the lid of a cage, and pick up the rat inside it. "Until Roosevelt."

I hold him up to Dr. Klutz, hoping that—doctor of biomedicine or not—she might scream and cringe. Instead, she plucks Roosevelt from my hands and coos over him as if he were a kitten. A little surprised, but oddly pleased that she seems so taken with him, I continue, "Roosevelt was born in 1904."

She nearly drops him, and he squeals indignantly. "You're lying!"

"I certainly am not. Roosevelt is over a hundred years old. Most rats don't live more than two or three."

Dr. Klutz stares at Roosevelt, then stares at me. "What happened then?"

Ah. I have her attention again, and this time I know she's hooked for good. "Well, Roosevelt here revealed a few more surprises. He was the only rat to be born in his litter, which is unusual in itself. When Dr. Falk went to inject him with Immortis, the needle of the syringe snapped. So did the other dozen or so he tried to use. Yes, Roosevelt's skin is as thick as mine. That is to say, it is completely impenetrable. And what is more, Roosevelt is faster and more agile than any other rat. Uh-huh," I nod when she looks at me questioningly. "Me too. And most important of all, three, four, twenty years pass, and Roosevelt goes on living as happily and healthily as you could wish for. So of course Dr. Falk runs dozens of experiments on hundreds of rats and discovers the secret."

I pause, relishing the way Dr. Klutz is hanging on my every word. Finally, I say it. "It comes down to the gradual alteration of the human—or rat—genome. It takes five generations, no more and no less, of periodic injections of Immortis for the immortality gene in the flower to assimilate into the genetic code of the rat or the human. Dr. Falk returned to the outside and found thirty-two of the most healthy, athletic, brilliant, and beautiful young people society had to offer. He brought them back to Little Cam, which is when this place really started to boom, and began injecting them. They had children, their children had children, *their* children had children, and those children had me."

I take Roosevelt back and stroke his soft fur, feeling the pattering of his heart in my palm. "And precisely as everyone had hoped during those hundred years of research, experimentation, and selective breeding . . . I am immortal."

FOUR

"**S**o," says Harriet as she grinds her cigarette onto the exam table and flicks it in the trash, "that's it then? Here you are, immortal, perfect Pia. Seems like the end of the road. Or is there an immortal, perfect hunk around here somewhere?" She looks around as if she expects one to be lurking behind the refrigerator full of saliva samples.

"What do you mean?"

"Well, the way I hear it, the purpose of this place is to create a new race of *ubermenschen*—"

"Uber what?"

"Immortals. But all I see is one scrawny girl with an attitude bigger than her bra size—"

"I am *not* scrawny," I say, throwing my shoulders back and glaring at her.

"Yes, yes." She waves a hand dismissively. "You're perfect, I forgot. Anyway, my question is this: Where's *Mr.* Perfect?"

I nod in understanding and draw a deep breath. "Well,

once I'm finished with my studies and become part of the Immortis team, we'll make one." Saying my dream out loud like that makes my heart flutter in anticipation, and I smile proudly.

For some reason, she busts out laughing. She leans on the exam table, head in her hands, and every third laugh comes out as a snort. When she looks up again, she must see the look on my face, because she stops. "Sorry, Pia. Sorry, I just . . ." She nearly cracks again, but gets herself under control. "To hear you say that . . . I'll bet you're the first kid in history who can honestly say something like *that*."

"There's nothing wrong with what I said!"

"No, no."

I can tell she's still trying not to laugh, and I'm getting angrier by the minute. "I wish you would stop that."

"Stop what?"

"Stop making fun of me. Everything I say, you act like it's . . . it's stupid."

She frowns and comes toward me. I flinch as she takes my hand in hers. "Oh, Pia. I don't think you're stupid. But you have to understand. I just got here a day ago. I came here under the impression I'd be doing routine research and documentation. But instead I find *you*. A young woman of astonishing beauty who tells me she's immortal. And perfect. And she can prove it, to boot! It's a lot to take in."

I see by her face that she's telling the truth, but I'm still angry. "It's not your business, anyway. Like you said, you're here to do routine research. Not study me."

"No?" She cocks her head. "I once studied a white tigress at the San Francisco Zoo that had as much attitude as you.

Beautiful creature, extremely rare, and she knew it too. Wore it like a badge on that snowy coat. I never knew an animal could be disdainful until I met Sasha."

I think she might be making fun of me again, but I'm not sure, so I ask instead, "What's San Francisco?"

"What did you say?" asks a different voice.

We both turn in surprise to see Uncle Paolo standing in the doorway. I know immediately that Harriet Fields is going to be in *trouble*. I give Uncle Paolo a huge smile. "Hi! Doctor Fields was just telling me about San Francisco."

She swivels her head and gives me a look to burn wet kapok wood. "I most certainly was *not*, young lady!" She looks back at Uncle Paolo. "I wasn't."

"Doctor Fields," he says coldly, still watching me. "May I speak with you in my office?"

She groans and throws up her hands. "Oh, come *on*! I'm new here! Cut me some slack already!"

"Dr. Fields, *if you please*." Uncle Paolo is not happy. Not happy at all. I decide to pull out of this one and keep my mouth shut tight. Dr. Klutz gives me a dirty look as she leaves the room. Uncle Paolo lingers a moment longer. There's a look on his face that reminds me of Alai when he's hunting a mouse in the menagerie.

"Pia, it would be best if you didn't speak to Dr. Fields for a few days."

"Is she in trouble?" I ask.

The *look* grows even colder. "Please go to your room."

Well, now I'm just mad. "No!"

"Pia. Your room. Please." The *please* sounds more like a warning than a request.

I can't face that look any longer, so I relent. "Fine." I stalk from the room. If I had a tail like Alai, or that white tigress of Dr. Klutz's, it would be twitching.

In my room I sit on my bed with my legs crossed and back stiff, hugging a pillow while I stare at the outside world. Beyond the iron bars and electric fence, the jungle is still, as if waiting for something. Or someone. For a wild moment I imagine it's waiting for me.

I have only been outside that fence once. I was seven, and it was a delivery day. The gate opened, the trucks came in, and I darted out. Thirteen steps. That's as far as I got before Uncle Timothy scooped me up like a bag of bananas and dumped me back inside the fence. I got at least five lectures from five different people, most of them containing grisly stories of people getting lost in the jungle and swallowed by anacondas. It didn't take me long to realize that even a girl who can't bleed can still be swallowed whole. Needless to say, I never did it again.

But as I stare out the window into the shadowy teal and blue and green of the rainforest's depths, I think about that day and those thirteen steps. It's about thirteen steps from the glass wall of my bedroom to the fence.

"Pia, time for dinner!" my mother calls from the living room.

Shaking myself from my reverie, I join her on the walk to the dining hall. It's still a little early, so the room is mostly empty. Thanks to the delivery, we have steak and shrimp. Both are rare treats, and I usually dive face-first into meals like this. But I can't stop thinking about that day when I almost made it into the jungle. I remember the excitement and the euphoria that came with those thirteen steps of freedom as if it were yesterday, and the memory leaves me with a haunting emptiness no amount of food could fill.

One scientist sits at a table in the corner, and my mother and I join him. I call him Uncle Will, but if I wanted, I could call him Father—because he is. I don't see him much. He lives in the dorms with the others and spends nearly all of his time tucked away in his lab, where he studies insects my Uncle Antonio gathers in the jungle. Uncle Will is nuts about bugs.

Both he and my mother were born in Little Cam, as were their parents, and *their* parents before that. Each generation of my family tree is stronger than the last, a result of the elysia assimilating into their genetic codes. My parents each have unusually high IQs and nearly perfect immune systems, but already their cells have begun to deteriorate—as mine never will. According to Uncle Paolo's calculations—drawn from observing the various immortal animal species in Little Cam—once I'm around twenty years old, my cells will continue to regenerate, instead of deteriorating like those of normal humans. I'll stay young forever.

Unlike Uncle Paolo, Uncle Timothy, Uncle Jakob, and the others, who all came to Little Cam from the outside, my parents—as well as Uncle Antonio—were born in the compound and have lived here their entire lives. They were educated by the scientists just as I am now, and they have taken on roles in Little Cam that were once filled by scientists brought in from the outside world.

Uncle Paolo told me once that the scientists hope to discover a way to create immortals without resorting to organic reproduction. Forty years ago, they began using in vitro fertilization, which apparently made the whole process run smoother. But until they discover a way to successfully nurture an embryo outside the womb, there will continue to be mothers in Little Cam.

I'm glad they haven't found a way to replicate gestation yet. I like knowing I came from real, breathing human beings and not from some glass vial in a lab. Though I never knew my grandparents, their names are all on the genealogy chart I showed to Dr. Klutz. It's my lineage. My family tree.

If you were to trace the lines of the chart, starting with my parents and moving up one and over two, you'd find Alex and Marian. The ones who died too young.

I think about Alex and Marian as I stab at my shrimp. They were the only ones of their generation—which included my grandparents and Uncle Antonio's parents—who opted not to use in vitro fertilization. Unlike their contemporaries, they chose one another as lifelong companions and wanted to reproduce naturally. I've heard Aunt Nénine talk about it to Aunt Brigid, about how they *loved* each other. I study my parents, wondering why they never fell in love. They hardly speak to one another, and I'm surprised they're even sitting at the same table. At best, their relationship could be described as tolerant.

Alex and Marian left Little Cam together over thirty years ago, and they never came back. I don't know where they were trying to go or why . . . but I do know they never made it.

I'm told the scientists discussed starting from scratch to replace that generational line, which would have meant bringing in sixteen new couples and starting to treat them with Immortis. Since at that time no one knew if the Immortis project would even succeed, they decided to wait until I was born. And they're still waiting, to see what I'll become.

To see if I can pass the Wickham tests.

"Dr. Fields got in trouble today for telling me about San Francisco," I say.

My parents stop eating and look up at me, then around the room. We are still alone. Mother looks mildly angry, but Uncle Will smiles.

"That's a city," he says. "Dr. Marshall told me about it once. He said it's in the United States in America."

"United States *of* America," Mother corrects, and I'm surprised that she knows that. Out of all of us, she is the one *least* interested in what lies outside the fence. As the top mathematician in Little Cam, she is completely absorbed in her work and often says that numbers are the same no matter where you are, be it in the jungle or on the moon.

"I *thought* it was a city!" I say to Uncle Will. "It must have even more people than Little Cam." I picture another Little Cam with all the same buildings in different places.

"She shouldn't have said anything," my mother mutters. "I don't like the looks of that Fields woman. She's wild and unpredictable."

"She's not a math problem. You can't subtract the parts of her you don't like." Even as I say it, I wonder why I'm defending Dr. Klutz. I don't like the looks of her either.

Uncle Will laughs at that. Mother frowns now and stabs her knife in his direction. "And *you* shouldn't be saying anything either. Paolo won't like it." She looks around again. The cook is putting out a bowl of hot dinner rolls, but he's too far across the room to hear our conversation.

"Why shouldn't he say anything?" I challenge. "Maybe I *want* to know about San Francisco."

"You don't need to worry about anything except your studies," Mother says firmly. "When the time comes, you have to be ready to take over Dr. Alvez's work."

"Uncle Paolo's not that old. He'll be here for years and years."

They are training me to eventually assume Uncle Paolo's role as director, so that Uncle Timothy will never have to bring another head scientist to Little Cam again. I'll be in charge. Forever. Fulfilling the destiny of which I've dreamed for years: creating others like me. My own kind. Immortal, perfect people who will in turn help create even more of us. In time, we'll no longer be an isolated group hidden in the jungle, but a *race*. Thinking of that day almost brings tears to my eyes, I want it so badly.

It's all part of the plan that Dr. Falk wrote out a century ago. Well, most of it's part of the plan. The Accident wasn't anywhere in the plan, but it happened anyway.

If it wasn't for the Accident, Alex and Marian would have had a baby girl. When they ran from Little Cam, Marian was pregnant. That baby girl was supposed to have been bred to my Uncle Antonio, and *their* son would have been my "Mr. Perfect," as Dr. Klutz put it. Then we would have started the new race together. So much for Dr. Falk's great plan.

Alex and Marian died, and my immortal mate died with them. So now I have to wait for Uncle Paolo to make one from scratch. And he can't do that until he decides I'm ready to help. Which means I must pass more Wickham tests. The thought destroys the little appetite I had, as I remember the quivering heartbeat of the sparrow in my palm.

"I'd like to see San Francisco," my father says dreamily as he plays with a shrimp on his plate.

"That's ridiculous," says my mother. "You're never going to see San Francisco. Your place is here, in Little Cam."

I look from one parent to the other, wondering suddenly if they ever looked out their windows the way I look out mine. I wonder if they hate the fence like I do, and if the jungle calls to them too. They have been outside, of course. My father sometimes goes with Uncle Antonio to collect specimens, and my mother has even been as far as the Little Mississip. One day Uncle Paolo will let me out too, but it's so *hard* to wait.

"Uncle Will," I say as I help myself to some fresh plantain, "have you ever seen a map of the world?" I ask him and not Mother because I already know what she'll say. *Of course not, Pia. That's ridiculous.*

But I see that even Uncle Will is growing anxious with the turn of the conversation. "No, Pia. No." He says nothing more, but he wipes his mouth, throws his napkin on the table, and stands up. "I have some tests to run in the lab."

I watch him go, wishing I had a lab to run off to. All I have is my glass room. It's times like these that I almost wish I hadn't stopped them from plastering my walls, however fond of the view I am.

My glass room is wonderful for looking out, but not very good for hiding.

FIVE

oday I am seventeen years old.

Seventeen birthdays down. An eternity of them to go.

Evening falls, and I take out the dress Dr. Klutz picked for me. When I stand in front of my mirror and see it on me, I feel breathless. No matter what I think of Dr. Klutz, I can't deny that the dress is beautiful. It does match my eyes, like my mother said. My eyes are the same blue-green of the rainforest. I pin strands of my hair above one ear and let a few fall across the sides of my face.

I would never have known about parties were it not for Clarence the janitor. One night while I ate dinner in the dining hall, he forgot I was sitting nearby and began recounting what his life had been like before he came to Little Cam. No one is supposed to talk about their past lives. That's the first rule here, the one that everyone must read and sign on the day they arrive. But sometimes they forget, and I hear stories. Clarence talked about the day he met his wife at a party with

dresses and tuxedos and cake. After his wife died in a car accident, he left everything behind to come here.

It was a sad story, but it made me dream of parties. When
I asked Uncle Paolo for a party with dresses and cake, he
wanted me to tell him where I heard such stories. I told him
that I'd read about it in the dictionary, which was a lie, but he
let me have the party. Sometimes I wonder why everyone else
seems so timid around him, because Uncle Paolo's softer than
he lets on.

I catch my image in the glass wall facing the rainforest and
spin slowly to see the full effect of the gown. The reflected
color nearly blends in with the jungle beyond, as if I'm dressed
not in fabric but in leaves.

I walk to the window and press my hands to the glass. It
is a perfect night for the perfect party. I look up, and through
the gaps in the canopy of trees, I see a clear, starry night. A full
moon shines above the kapoks and the palms, but the leaves
and vines are so thick that its rays hardly reach the jungle
floor. Yet I see one place where a column of faint silver light
filters down through the canopy and tinges the lower foliage.
It dances across the leaves, creating a path over the undergrowth, a road of moonlight that would be invisible by day. If
I were a butterfly, I would follow that path into the heart of the
jungle, perhaps even to Falk's Glen, where the elysia grows.

For a moment, I don't want parties or cake or dresses.
Those things seem suddenly hollow and silly. I want instead
to follow that silver path until it ends and never look back.
Pressing my hands against the cold glass, I stare at the jungle
and wonder what secrets lie in its shadows.

Suddenly I notice movement in the leaves, and a

coatimundi emerges from the undergrowth, his long black tail pointing straight up at the sky. He sniffs the fence, and for a moment I'm horrified that he'll touch it and shock himself. The electric pulses in the fencing are generated every 1.2 seconds, and only at enough voltage to deter intruders, but to a small animal like the coatimundi, the fence could do serious damage. But he must smell the danger, because he shakes his head and turns around.

He disappears into the leaves, and my insanity disappears with him. I laugh out loud at my own crazy thoughts—really, running off into the jungle at night?—and hurry to find my party.

The center of Little Cam is a garden. It includes one large plot where we grow vegetables and fruits, but the rest is made of pathways and ponds and flowerbeds. I smell the orchids before I even reach the garden. They smell sweetest at night, to attract the moths that spread their pollen through the jungle.

I find a crowd waiting for me. They cheer when they see me, and I can't help but laugh at how they look. Most of the men are in suits they brought when they came to Little Cam years ago, and I can tell that this is the first time they've worn them since arriving. They are all wrinkled or don't fit right. Some of them have tuxedos, including my father and Uncle Paolo, which they must have had Uncle Timothy bring from the outside. My mother is wearing a silver dress, and there are orchids in her hair. She looks nothing like the serious, stern woman who normally runs around in a tank top and shorts. I've never realized how beautiful my mother is until now. The few wrinkles on her face seem to have vanished, and she is smiling and holding Uncle Paolo's arm.

When she sees me, she sighs and lets go of Uncle Paolo to take my hands.

"Oh, Pia." Her fingers brush the delicate sleeves of the dress. "Turn for me."

"Why? What's wrong with it?" I ask as I spin slowly. Leave it to my mother to find something to criticize.

But when I face her again, it isn't scorn I see in her eyes— but tears. I try not to gape. Tears? *My* mother? Unheard of.

"Are you . . . okay?" I ask uncertainly.

She smiles. "You look so grown up. My Pia. Seventeen years old." Suddenly—as if the moment were strange enough already—she pulls me into a hug. A *hug*. The last time my mother hugged me I couldn't even walk yet. I freeze in astonishment, then slowly return the embrace. I stare at Uncle Paolo over her shoulder and the look he gives in return is just as surprised.

When Mother pulls away, I feel warmer inside. Maybe I don't know her as well I thought.

"Come, Pia," she says. "Your party's waiting."

There are torches thrust into the ground all over the garden. Their flames sway sinuously, dozens of tiny orange and white dancers creating silent fire music with their bodies. I am momentarily mesmerized by them and feel the urge to dance their dance. The torches are an extravagance, a special indulgence I hadn't asked for. When night comes in Little Cam, we leave as little light on as possible. Uncle Timothy told me once that the outside world has eyes in the sky, satellites flung so far from the earth they hang in space, watching everything below. By daylight we are hidden beneath the many palms, kapoks, and capironas that grow between the buildings. But at night, even the dense canopy cannot keep light from reaching the sky.

"Pia, you look beautiful," says Uncle Paolo. He hands me a glass of punch. "Seventeen years," he says, raising his own drink. Everyone raises theirs with him. "Seventeen years of perfection, Pia. Most of us remember the day you were born, and what an unforgettable day that was. One day, your birthday will be celebrated not by a small crowd like this, but by the *world.*"

His eyes burn brightly, filled with torchlight. "The day you were born marked a new era in the history of man, and an entire race of immortals will someday rise to honor you. But let's remember that it all starts here. It all starts with us." His eyes shift to the people of Little Cam, and he sweeps his arm wide. "All of us are a part of this. We have altered the course of history, my friends, but most important of all . . ." He looks back at me, takes my hand in his. "Most of all, we ourselves have been altered. By you, Pia. By the fierce, unquenchable fire of life that burns within you. Happy birthday."

I can't help it; I smile, my eyes meeting his with equal light.

"To Pia!" he says.

"To Pia!" everyone else choruses, and then they all drink.

"Now," Uncle Paolo says, "come and look at your cake."

He leads me to a long table covered with food, and everyone gathers around and behind us. There are mostly native fruits, yumanasa berries, aguaje, and soursops. But there are also strawberries and apples and my favorite of all, watermelons, all brought by Uncle Timothy from the outside. Then there's the cake.

It's enormous, three tiers of pink and white icing, and cascading with deep-purple orchids and—I can't help but grin—multicolored Skittles. I gasp and clap my hands, too delighted for words. Everyone else starts clapping too, and Jacques the cook takes a deep bow before he starts serving it. I get the first slice and dive right in. When I taste it, I force myself to slow down and savor each bite. Lime and vanilla and cream . . . I swear I'll never eat anything else after this. Nothing else could compare.

"Happy Birthday, Pia!" someone yells from behind me, and the words spread from mouth to mouth. My parents each hug me, then Uncle Antonio and Uncle Paolo, Aunt Brigid, who runs the medical center, Aunt Nénine, Uncle Jonas the menagerie keeper, old Uncle Smithy, who accidentally stabs my foot with his cane, and dozens more. Everyone wants to hug me, even the ones I rarely speak with, like the maintenance men and the lab assistants.

Uncle Antonio starts grumbling and pulls me away from everyone just as a beaming plumber named Mick steps up for his hug. Mick shouts indignantly at us, but Uncle Antonio ignores him and leads me to the wide tile floor that usually holds tables and chairs for people to eat lunches outside. A great Brazil nut tree rises from an opening in the center of the floor, its trunk rearing a staggering hundred feet before it bursts into a wide, umbrella-like canopy. There are several torches burning around its trunk, and at its base sits a skinny, freckled lab assistant with a CD player in his hands. He seems half-asleep, and Uncle Antonio kicks his leg.

"This is supposed to be a party, Owens! Get that music cranked or I'll put you in charge of mucking the menagerie for a month!"

Owens hastily punches a button, and the music pumps through two large speakers sitting on either side of him. It's the kind of music called jazz, I think. We don't listen to music much in Little Cam. Uncle Paolo says it's extraneous and distracts from our real work. The music fills my ears and my veins, and even the flames of the torches seem to alter their swaying to match the beat.

"May I have this dance?" asks Uncle Antonio, bowing low. I laugh at him. "I don't know how to dance!"

"Let me show you then!" He sweeps me around in a circle, and I can't stop giggling, it's so ridiculous. But soon other people join in, and I feel less silly. My mother dances from Uncle Paolo to my father. Aunt Brigid dances with Uncle Jonas. The cook dances with the laundress. Soon nearly everyone is dancing, but I suddenly realize someone is missing. "Where's that Dr. Fields? She didn't seem like one to miss a party."

"Right here," someone says, and I turn to see her standing behind me. She's wearing a very tight red dress that starts low and ends high. Her long legs are tipped with enormous red heels that would have me falling onto my face, but she navigates around me with ease.

"May I?" she asks.

I stare at her until Uncle Antonio interrupts. "Ahem. You may indeed."

He puts a hand around her waist and pulls her close. Laughing, she changes the position of his hands so that *she's* leading them across the floor. When she dances, I must admit, she's not klutzy at all. I go to the table and fill a cup up with punch, then lean against the Brazil nut tree, watching them as they dance circles around everyone else. The freckly lab assistant Owens is sitting a few feet away from me, and he stammers something that sounds like an invitation to dance, but I wrinkle my nose at him and shake my head. Dance with *Owens?* I've seen him pick his nose when he thought no one was looking, and there's no way I'm letting those hands touch me.

He turns red and finds something fascinating to fiddle with on the radio.

Uncle Antonio and Dr. Klutz dance like twin fires. I'm not at all sure I like him dancing with her, but all the same, they're enchanting to watch. I notice a few other people admiring them too. There is something between them I can't name, a light in their eyes when they look at each other. It's not a light I see in my mother's eyes when she looks at my father. I think of Alex and Marian and wonder if this could be love.

Love is not something that Uncle Paolo or the other scientists encourage, though even they can't stop the flirting that goes on among some of the younger members of Little Cam. I remember something Uncle Paolo said to me about love: "It's a phenomenon, Pia, but it's dangerous. Look at Alex and Marian, for example. Love makes you weak. It distracts you from the important things. It can make you lose sight of the objective."

"What objective?" I asked.

"The new race. That's what it's all about, Pia. That's all it can ever be about for you and me. The others . . . they can play at love and romance. But you and I have work to do, and we can't let ourselves be distracted."

I wondered then if that was why there were no boys my age in Little Cam. Owens is probably the youngest person here besides me, and he has to be near thirty. He came to Little Cam when he was just a toddler with his father, Jakob Owens, one of our biologists, and all I've ever seen him as is the skinny, freckled, nose-picking guy who spends most of his time playing poker with the guards. No danger of distraction there.

As I watch Uncle Antonio and Dr. Klutz dance and laugh, I wonder if they might be in love. The thought makes me strangely sad . . . and a little envious. *Strange.* Love is nothing more than elevated levels of dopamine, norepinephrine, and other chemicals. But the way Uncle Antonio's face lights up as they dance . . . I wonder what it would be like to feel that. To let the chemicals of romance take over for just a little while.

Then I remember that I'm immortal and that my body doesn't work like everyone else's. Who knows if I even *can* feel love?

As I stare at the dancing people, I wish the night could go on forever. They all seem infected with a vivaciousness that isn't common in our compound, and there are more smiles on their faces than I've ever seen at once. And yet as I watch them, I feel more intensely than ever the knowledge that I'm not one of them. For these mortal humans, birthdays are a kind of countdown to the end, the ticking clock of a dwindling life. For me, birthdays are notches on an infinite timeline.

Will I grow tired of parties one day? Will my birthday become meaningless? I imagine myself centuries from now, maybe at my three-hundredth birthday, looking all the way back to my seventeenth. How will I possibly be happy, remembering the light in my mother's eyes? The swiftness of Uncle Antonio's steps as he dances? The way my father stands on the edge of the courtyard, smiling in that vague, absent way of his?

The scene shifts and blurs in my imagination. As if brushed away by some invisible broom, these people whom I've known my entire life disappear. The courtyard is empty and bare, covered in decaying leaves. I imagine Little Cam deserted, with everyone dead and gone and only me left in the shadows.

Forever.

No. It won't be that way. I'll never be alone, because I'll have my other immortals. I'll have someone who will look at me the way Uncle Antonio looks at Harriet Fields, only he'll look at me that way for eternity. My abdomen tightens with longing. I want to run to Uncle Paolo and demand that he tell me the secret to Immortis, beg him to start the process of creating my Mr. Perfect. I think of the five generations it will take before he's born, and I want to scream. I want someone *now.* I want someone who will look into my eyes and understand everything behind them.

To distract myself, I go hunting for more punch. No one is at the food table; they are all on the dance floor. I find an empty cup and fill it up and then hang back. I consider trying to join the dancing again, but my earlier excitement has vanished, replaced by a melancholy that I cannot seem to shake.

No one seems to notice I'm not dancing. I abruptly set down my cup and slip away. I make my way through the

gardens to the menagerie. My long dress catches on the flowers I pass, so I scoop up the fabric around my knees.

The menagerie is dark, and I don't want to wake up the
Grouch and start him howling, so I fumble around until I find
the small electric lantern Uncle Jonas keeps on top of the bar-
rel of macaw feed.

Following the circle of light cast by the lantern, I pass the
cages silently. A few birds twitter at me, and the pregnant ocelot Jinx peeps down from the high branch where she likes to
sleep, her eyes two yellow lanterns of their own.

Alai is awake, as if he was expecting me. I open the door
of his cage and slip in, leaving it open behind me. After hanging the lantern on a hook on the wall, I sink down beside the
jaguar and wrap an arm around his neck. He rubs his head
against me, enjoying the smoothness of the silk.

"There you are," says a voice from the darkness.

SIX

It's Dr. Klutz. She walks right into the cage and plops down across from me. She groans as she yanks off her heels and then crosses her ankles. "I don't know what idiot decided we had to choose between beauty and comfort, but I'd like to drive this heel through his eye."

I say nothing, but watch her as warily as a mouse eyes an ocelot.

"Then again, I guess not all of us have to make that choice. You'd look great in a couple of palm fronds held together with duct tape, I imagine." She makes a pouty face. "Not fair at all. Most of us have to work for our looks."

"What are you doing here?"

She raises her brows. "Hey. Easy. I just wanted to give you your present."

I notice then the small package she's holding. "Oh, yeah. Presents."

"If there's one thing you should never, ever forget about,

it's the presents." She tosses it to me. Anyone else might have missed, but my hands leap up automatically and snatch it from the air.

"I didn't *forget*," I tell her as I turn the package over in my hands. "What is it?"

"It's not a viper or a poison dart frog, if that's what you're asking. Good lord, child, just open it, will you? Before someone finds us."

"Why? Is it a secret?"

She bites her lip before answering. "Yes . . . of sorts. That is, you probably wouldn't want your *Uncle* Paolo finding you with it."

That catches my interest. The package is wrapped with plain white paper and tied with string, and it only takes a few seconds to unwrap. Inside is a large piece of paper that's been folded many times over. "What is it?" I ask again.

"Better not unfold it here; it takes hours to get it back down to that size. And whatever you do, don't open it in front of everyone. I'll lose my contract, my career, and my pretty salary if that gets traced back to me. So my life is pretty much in your hands, missy. I'll thank you not to throw it into the nearest trash bin."

"What am I supposed to do with it?"

"For starters, don't go brandishing it around in public." I look around, then hide it in the straw where Alai sleeps. "Good," she says. "Now, you going to skip out on your own party or what? From the grumbling I heard, this whole place bent over backward putting this thing together for you. It'd be a crying shame for you to throw it all back in their faces. A downright tragedy."

Something in her tone makes me ask, "What would *you* do, if you were me?"

She shrugs and tweaks Alai's tail, which he thrashes irritably at her. "Me? I'd leave the whole lot of 'em to their terrible dancing and worse small talk—honestly, that plumber thought I *wanted* to hear about the alarming increase in blocked toilets around here—and I'd find myself a quiet, secluded corner in which to study my totally wicked birthday present from an equally awesome redheaded biomedical engineer." Then she sighs and shakes her head. "But yes, you should probably go back to your party and open the rest of your presents."

"I guess you're right." I open the door and step outside, Dr. Klutz behind me. Just before I reach the door of the menagerie, I pause.

"About Uncle Antonio . . ." I start.

"Yes?" She looks genuinely intrigued. "Do tell."

"He's my favorite uncle, you know," I finish clumsily. "I just . . . he—"

"Don't worry, kid," she says gently. "I'm not going to break any hearts."

"Right. Yeah." I shuffle a bit, wondering what to add, then give it up and flee.

Hours later, after the party finally ends, I stop by the menagerie on the pretense of bringing Alai with me to my room, where he often sleeps. Dr. Klutz's mysterious paper, which I slipped down the front of my dress, seems to burn through my skin, and I can't wait to open it. Back in my room, I turn on a small lamp by my bed and kneel on the floor, pulling the paper from my dress. Alai pads softly to the chair in the corner, where he usually sleeps, and loses all interest in me and my contraband.

As I start unfolding the paper, my heart begins to race. Could it be . . . ?

It *is*.

I gasp and rise to my feet, staring wide-eyed at the paper. It's so large it covers most of my bed. With trembling hands, I turn and shove a chair against the door, since there's no lock. This could get me—and Dr. Klutz—in more than just trouble. I don't know what Uncle Paolo would do if he found out, but I know it would be awful. As if sensing my agitation, a bristling Alai ghosts to my side.

"It's all right, boy," I whisper.

Still hardly believing my eyes, I force myself to kneel again and spread my hands over the paper, smoothing the creases.

"It's a map of the world, Alai." He's already lost interest, but I'm completely enthralled.

I've never seen one before. There's not a single map in all of Little Cam that isn't locked away from view, except for the one hanging in plastic in the maintenance building, but it just shows the area inside the fence.

This map shows continents and oceans and countries and mountains, an entire world. *The* world. My world.

My fingers trace the outline of the land masses. Europe. Africa. Australia. Asia. Beautiful names, mysterious names. I know there must be millions of other words behind those names—people, places, stories.

I'm overwhelmed by a strange new thirst, as if I've been dehydrated my whole life and am only now starting to realize it. With all my heart and soul I long to know the words and names and stories, to know everything. I want to leave right now, this very minute, and scour every inch of this map with my own eyes, to feel the soil and trees with my own hands and taste the air of every corner of the planet.

I wonder where I am right now. Little Cam wouldn't be marked; Uncle Paolo would never allow that. My eyes sift through the names that *are* there: New Guinea. Sudan. India. Alaska. More oceans and seas than I can count. There are dozens, no, scores of areas outlined in black. Cities? Countries? I want to run through Little Cam screaming for Dr. Klutz to come and teach me.

Looking at the map, I'm struck by how little I know. Which is alarming, because I feel like I've learned so much. I can quote the periodic table backward. Show me an animal and I can tell you its kingdom, its species, and everything in between. I know the name of every plant in the rainforest and how they can be used. Give me a disease, I'll tell you how to treat it.

But ask me to name five countries, and I draw a blank. Ask me where the supplies Uncle Timothy brings are manufactured, and I couldn't tell you. I can point to the west, but I don't know what ocean lies in that direction or how far away it is. I know what lions and kangaroos and grizzly bears are, but I don't know where they live.

The more I learn about the world, the less I seem to know.

I raise my left hand to see what it's covering, and my eye catches some words that I can tell were drawn with a pen. I bend closer, squinting to read the tiny handwriting. *Little Cambridge, Amazon.*

My stomach twists; it feels like a flock of butterflies are

trying to flutter up my throat and out my mouth. Little Cam. *My* Little Cam.

It's little. *Very* little. Dr. Fields didn't outline a large area. She didn't even make a fat dot. Instead, she drew a tiny, *tiny* little speck of red. I blink at it. Surely that's not Little Cam. Maybe the speck was an accident, a brief brush of the pen to paper without meaning.

Surely Little Cam is not *that* small.

I circle the little speck with my finger, then start making bigger circles. My finger spirals outward from Little Cam, and it's only three loops before I reach other dots. These ones have names. Peru, Colombia, Brazil, Bolivia. A network of blue lines spiderweb across all of these, and each of them is connected to one main squiggle. *River*, my mind tells me. I have to squint again to read the words printed above it. *Amazon Rainforest. South America.*

"Amazon," I say very softly. Then, a little louder, making Alai flick his ears at me, "Amazon."

I realize I've heard this word before. I realize it in the way you might realize there is a spot on your shirt: you see it every time you pass a mirror, but until you really *look*, it doesn't register in your brain. I've heard of this *Amazon* in the whispers of the maintenance men at dinner. I've heard it slip from the tongue of a careless scientist. I've seen it scratched on different research documents, field notes, and labels on jars of specimens. *Amazon.*

"The Amazon rainforest," I whisper, looking up to see it for my own eyes. This part of the world, at least, is mine. Outside, the dark jungle looks as it always has, but I am struck by the difference I feel when I see it. *A name is a powerful thing. It sets one apart and gives significance.* The rainforest has always been the whole of my world, but the *Amazon* — while it makes the trees and the lianas and the animals lurking behind its leaves seem special to be part of a place with a name, it also makes it feel smaller. Which is strange. After all, I've never seen the edge of the rainforest. If truth be told, I've never really been *in* the rainforest.

"If I've never been *in* it," I ask Alai, "and I've never been *out* of it . . . where have I been all this time?"

In reply, I hear a knock on the door.

My heart leaps into my mouth like a monkey up a tree. I crumple up the map, not bothering to refold it in any way. Alai paces to and fro at the door and growls softly.

"Pia? Are you in there?" It's Mother.

I hurriedly stuff the map under the bed, drag the chair aside, open the door, and try to look innocent. "Yes?"

She glances around the room. "Can I come in?"

"Oh." My heart beats faster. "Okay."

She brushes past me and sits on the bed. When I turn to face her, I see a corner of the map sticking out, right between her feet. I swallow and try not to stare at it. "What do you want?"

"To give you your present." She hands me a small envelope.

Well. She is full of surprises tonight. Trying not to look too stunned, I take the envelope and open it. Inside is an old photograph of three children, two boys and a girl. I look up at her. "You and Uncle Will and Uncle Antonio?"

She nods. "It was before . . ."

Before the Accident. I look closer at the picture. The three of them are no older than ten, arms around each other's shoulders and smiling. I've never seen a picture of them when they were young. And I've never seen such a smile on my mother's face. The girl in the picture looks carefree and happy, words I would never use for my mother. I've always known her to be aloof and objective, the kind of scientist Uncle Paolo so prizes, which is why he has her assist on most of his experiments.

"Who's that?" I ask, squinting at a blurry form in the background.

She takes the photo and studies it, then turns pale. "That—it's no one."

"What do you mean, no one?"

"It's . . . your grandfather. I didn't realize he was in the shot, or I wouldn't have . . ."

I grab the photo back and stare. "My grandfather." When I look up, I see her face is strained. "You told me he and the others of his generation left Little Cam to start lives in the outside world."

"I did. Yes, I did." She stands and runs her hand through her hair. "This must have been before that."

She goes to the door, then turns back. I step sideways so my foot covers the exposed corner of the map. Mother holds out her hand. "Give it back."

Shocked, I automatically jerk the picture away. "What?"

"Give it back. It was a stupid gift. Emotional. Paolo wouldn't approve. I didn't know Fa—your grandfather was in the picture."

"It's *mine*. You gave it to me. I'm keeping it."

"Give it to me, Pia!" Her voice is harsh and cold.

Half disbelieving my ears, I slowly give her the photograph.

Now this is the mother I know. Demanding. Stern. Though I admire her cool head in the laboratory, when we're at home in the glass house, it can be grating. Sometimes I wish my father lived with me instead of my mother, but I've never told her that.

She tears it into shreds. "This party, the dancing . . . it wasn't a good idea. It made me lose my head for a while. I shouldn't have shown you that."

I stay silent, my teeth clamped angrily shut.

She tucks the pieces of the picture in her pocket. "Good night, Pia."

I shut the door behind her and stand there a moment, wondering what just happened and why I feel so upset. I wish she hadn't shown me that picture. It was very unlike her to exhibit such sentimentality, and it's true, Uncle Paolo wouldn't have approved.

Even so, I wish she'd let me keep the picture.

I sink against the door, kneel on the carpet, and hug Alai around his furry neck. "Too close. Way too close." In response, he licks my cheek, his tongue as rough as gravel.

I crawl forward and tuck the corner of the map back under the bed, then change my mind and pull it out. Dr. Klutz wasn't exaggerating. It takes me ten minutes to fold the thing back up.

Looking around for a hiding place, I wonder if it might be better off under the bed. My room is pretty sparse. There's the bed and a small table beside it on which sit my clock, lamp, and a botany book I've been working my way through. On the one plaster wall hangs my mirror above a dresser holding clothes and some of my research notebooks. They're mostly all on biology, which is the subject Uncle Paolo has me studying the most. Alai's chair in the corner of two glass walls. The shelf in the other corner with my orchids.

My dressing room isn't much better. The clothes are all hanging, and I briefly consider hiding it in one of my shoes, but then I think that if *I* were looking through this room for a hidden map, that would be the first place I would look.

Nothing seems right. I even lift the back off the toilet, but it's too wet to put anything in there, unless it were a frog, maybe. I remember doing something like that when I was around three.

Finally I pry up the carpet in the corner of the room where Alai's chair sits. Hauling the chair aside proves cumbersome; it's huge and overstuffed, and unfortunately "extra strong" is not an added perk of being immortal. But the carpet comes up easily, and I'm able to slide the map under it. After I shove the chair back in place, I plop down in it and wait for my nerves to stop humming, while Alai stretches on the floor below me.

That's when I see the hole in the fence.

SEVEN

A medium-sized ceiba tree has fallen from its stand several yards outside the fence. It fell toward the rainforest, and I see where its roots were yanked out of the ground. The chain link was buried at least a foot into the earth, but where the roots have been pulled up, the fence has come with them. Beneath the mangled chain link is an opening about three feet wide and two feet tall. It is nearly invisible behind the bromeliads that grow along the fence, but from my vantage point I can just see it.

Hardly believing my own movements, I rise to my feet and get my flashlight from the top drawer of the dresser. I keep it there for the times when a storm puts out the electricity until Clarence can get the generators running again.

"Come, Alai."

What's gotten into you? I ask myself as I tiptoe down the hallway of the glass house. My room is the only one with actual glass walls, and hence the reason for calling it *the glass house,* but there are windows everywhere. As I pass them, I can see the glow of the torches reflecting off the buildings toward the center of Little Cam, where a handful of late-nighters are still dancing. Only B Dormitory, its dark windows indicating that nearly everyone inside is asleep, stands between me and the remains of my birthday party, and it would only take a few steps to bring someone within view of the house.

Holding my breath, not daring to stop and consider the consequences of this mad course of action, I open the front door and slip outside. The night is cool and the air so crisp it makes my senses as acute as Alai's. As if encouraging my madness, shadows cling to us and cover our trail. I don't need the flashlight yet. I know every inch of Little Cam as well as I know my own reflection.

Stray notes of jazz escape the confines of the gardens and find their way to my ears. The music is lively, but beneath the airy melody is a steady, relentless drumbeat. These are the notes I hear best, perhaps because they seem more like an amplification of my own pounding heart. My palms are sweating, and I wipe them absently on the chiffon of my dress, passing the flashlight from hand to hand.

It doesn't take long to circle the glass house, though I go slowly, watching every shadow for sign of my mother or Uncle Paolo. Everything is quiet; I hear nothing but the wind in the trees and the constant humming of cicadas, which I am so used to that I only hear it when I think about it directly.

Once behind the house, I kneel at the hole in the fence and push the heavy leaves of the bromeliads aside. The gap is still there; a part of me had hoped it was just a trick of my mind. But it's there, and, as terrified as I am, I'm not stopping now. I've never wanted anything in my life as badly as I want to be on the other side of the fence. It shouldn't be like this, I know. I lack nothing in Little Cam. In the jungle there's only darkness; I don't know what I think I'll find in the trees and leaves.

Hesitating, feeling the dampness of the ground through my dress, I fight the impulse. But it's strong, stronger than it's ever been before. *Go! Go! Go!* my heart screams at me, low and steady and irresistible. It is the drums pounding beneath the jazz. It is the thrashing of a wild, savage inner demon I never knew I had inside me. Uncle Paolo says there are no such things as demons or angels, so perhaps it is simply another Pia. The Pia who gets bored with her own birthday party and hides maps of the world under her carpet.

As if spurning my hesitance, Alai suddenly darts forward and slips through the hole, not a single hair touching the fence. He stops on the other side and turns to watch me with moonlike eyes. I turn on the flashlight and inspect the gap. I can fit if I crawl on my belly. The dress will be ruined, but I'll probably never wear it again anyway. The fence is tangled and bent, but nowhere have the wires been severed by the uprooted tree, which must be why the alarm in the guard house wasn't triggered. Straggly roots hang down like hair from the larger tubers of the fallen tree, creating a tangled, dirty curtain. When I lean back, the hole disappears behind the plants around it. I wonder that I saw it at all.

Alai paces back and forth, urging me with his yellow gaze to follow.

Go now or lose your chance forever, Wild Pia's voice whispers in my head. She frightens me with her fierceness, but I obey.

I toss the flashlight through the gap. Its beam shines back at me, illuminating my way. Now I must hurry; if anyone wanders near this spot, they couldn't miss the light if they tried, much less the girl in the teal gown clawing her way through the fence like a capybara grubbing for seeds.

I'm careful not to let the fence snag my skin as I crawl. It won't hurt me. Not *me*. But I don't want to set off the alarm by brushing against the wires and triggering a shock.

Once I'm on the other side, I fluff the dirt with my hands and straighten the bromeliads I crushed in my escape. When I am satisfied that my exit has been well hidden, I pick up my flashlight and turn to face the jungle. Beside me, Alai roars.

"Sh!" I clamp my hand over his muzzle, and he shakes his head irritably before bounding a few steps forward. With the jaguar to guide me, I start for the trees.

I have only gone a dozen steps when Little Cam disappears behind me and a wave of dizziness and breathlessness drives me to my knees. I cling to the jaguar and fight the stars that dance tauntingly in my vision.

What are you doing, oh, what have you done? They'll find you, they'll catch you, you stupid, stupid girl! I stand and turn around, ready to go back, finished with escape and madness and the dark. But I don't take a step. I stand there, eyes wide, flashlight aimed at the ground, just breathing.

After a few minutes, I feel my nerves calm. Turning again toward the trees, forcing my feet forward, I tell myself, *Only an hour. No more. Back in one hour, and I'll tell someone about the fence. They'll fix it, and I'll never be tempted again.*

Wild Pia whispers that she has no intention of doing so, but I ignore her as best I can. She's brought me this far, and that is enough. I will explore the immediate area and no more. I doubt I will find much to interest me anyway. I've seen all the plants and animals of the jungle. They've all been brought into Little Cam for research. The scientists say there are hundreds of species not yet discovered` in this place I now know is called the Amazon, but if so, surely they won't be lurking this close to Little Cam.

My flashlight strikes off the trees. I see mighty kapoks rising to unfathomable heights. Lianas crisscross every level of the rainforest, creating a network of narrow roads traveled by all manner of monkeys, reptiles, and insects. Every now and then I see a pair of eyes glint in the darkness. I wonder what they belong to. The largest animal in the Amazon is the tapir, but the most dangerous is the anaconda, at least for me. The thought of the giant snake, capable of swallowing a man whole, is the only thing about the rainforest itself that terrifies me. The poisonous snakes can't puncture my skin, so I don't fear their venom. The diseases carried by mosquitoes have no effect on me. But anacondas . . . I have little desire to be strangled and swallowed alive. I can't suffocate or starve, which would mean an eternity trapped in—*I'll stop that line of thought right there.*

Suppressing a shudder, I try to focus on the beauty around me. I can only see what my flashlight falls on, but that is enough to take my breath away. Flowers as big as my head blossom full beneath the moon, whose faint light is rare this close to the jungle's floor. The soil here is too poor to sustain much life, so the trees spread their roots above the ground in great fan-shaped buttresses draped in moss. The frequent rains are the trees' main source of water; the larger the roots, the more rain they can catch, and the taller the tree. I see plants with leaves the size of umbrellas, their tops thick and smooth, their bottoms laced with red veins.

Alai lopes in ever-widening circles around me, and I realize this is his first time in the wild too. He must feel what I feel—perhaps more. He is a creature of the jungle, after all. His head turns right and left, his tail is rigid behind him, and he misses nothing.

Beneath my feet, the moss and leaves are as thick and lush as any carpet. More so, for every step I take sinks an inch as soon as my full weight is on it. The soft, moist earth receives my steps silently, as if reluctant to allow an outsider like me to interrupt the rainforest's nocturne. Frogs and birds and other insects chirp along with the perpetual hum of cicadas. When I stop and close my eyes to listen, I'm struck by how *noisy* it is. At first the jungle seemed as silent as it is dark, but in truth, the sounds are almost cacophonous.

As I concentrate now on the way ahead, the noises fade again into the background. I am getting wetter with every step; the leaves that brush against me are damp, and little droplets of water splash off of them onto my dress and my arms. A spider monkey swoops across my path, swinging at head height and chortling with monkey laughter. Alai snaps at it. My flashlight just happens to catch its round yellow eyes, which stare straight into my own for a brief moment. Startled, I stop until it melts into the darkness.

The jungle enchants me. I'm unable to turn around and go back. Every sound, every glimpse is a breath of sweet, fresh air. Instead of filling me up, the rainforest empties me, leaving me thirsty for more. The more I see, the more I want.

My nerves and will are stronger now, my fear is less. I am committed. Little Cam is out of my reach, so whatever is happening there, I cannot stop. If they've already discovered my absence—so be it. Uncle Paolo can't forbid what's already been done.

Flooded with this conviction, the last of my inhibitions flee, and I quicken my pace. Soon I am nearly jogging, my razor-sharp reflexes preventing me from tripping over the numerous roots and rocks abounding across the jungle floor. There's too much; I can't take it all in. But I keep trying. My eyes hardly blink, they are so intent on seeing every detail. My ears fill with sounds that, though I've heard them my entire life, suddenly feel new and exciting. Even the scents of the jungle are stronger out here—moist soil, ripe fruit, flowers, water, and a faint, woody smell like smoke.

The outside! I've done it! I found a way out and I took it, and I only looked back once. I have never realized how much I wanted this until now.

Freedom. It's as intoxicating as any drug, a rush of adrenaline through my body. Wild Pia and Timid Pia merge; fear is overwhelmed by heady exhilaration. I am one. I am whole. I am free.

I am so captivated by the emotions inside me that I don't even see the boy until we collide.

EIGHT

He yells. I yell. We both hit the ground, him on his back and me landing smack on top of him. For a moment all we can do is stare, astonished, at one another. His eyes are startlingly blue and as wide as papayas.

The hair on the back of my neck stands on end, like Alai's hackles.

A boy.

Our noses are inches apart. I feel very warm from head to toe, and my abdomen clenches as if I've swallowed one of the torches from my party.

A *boy*.

I have never seen such blue, blue eyes.

I bolt upright, every muscle tense and alarmed, ready to flee in a heartbeat, as Alai springs from midair and lands atop the boy, pinning him to the ground. The boy is chattering away in a strange language that's nothing like English, but when he sees the jaguar's fangs inches from his nose, he falls silent.

"Who are you?" I demand, my voice shaking.

He's still gaping at the jaguar when I shine my flashlight right in his face, and he winces and holds up a hand between himself and Alai—as if that could protect him if Alai decided to bite.

"Jaguar," he gasps. "You have a jaguar!"

"I asked, who are you?" I hold my flashlight with both hands, angled at him like a gun.

The boy, still holding up his hand and never taking his eyes from Alai, replies, "Call away the cat, and I will tell you."

I hesitate a moment, then call for Alai. He hisses, spraying spit across the boy's face, then slips to my side.

The boy climbs slowly to his feet, keeping a watchful eye on the jaguar. "My name is Eio. Who are you?"

"Pia." I take a step back as he reaches his full height, my flashlight still aimed at his face. "What do you want with me? Where—where are you from?"

"You're the one who crashed into *me*." He is taller than me, and though he is thin, he is very muscular. I can tell because he's half-naked. He's wearing khaki shorts and a cord around his neck from which hangs a tiny jaguar carved into jade, but nothing else, not even shoes. His skin is the color of a shelled Brazil nut, light, warm brown, the brown of days spent in the dappled sun of the rainforest. His hair is as black as the night around us and thick with tangles. There is something vaguely familiar about his face, but I can't think of what it is. That's very disconcerting for me, since I forget nothing. If I had seen this boy before, I would remember it. And not just because my memory is perfect. I'd remember those eyes . . . that sculpted chest . . . the definition of his abdomen. . . .

I snap my eyes up to his face, whipping my thoughts back into line. My initial fear gives way to anger. "What are you doing out here, anyway? It's the middle of the night. Where are your clothes?"

He replies, remarkably calmly, "You've wandered far from your cage, Pia bird."

"What?" I ask blankly.

"The dress," he says, nodding at it. "It makes you look like a bird. The kind we Ai'oa like to keep on our shoulders. But that's not a good thing to be running around the jungle in."

I look down at my torn dress. "It's my birthday." Furious, I glare at him, refusing to let him distract me. Again. "Ai'oa? What is that?"

He presses a hand to his bare chest. "We are a *who*, not a *what*."

"Are you a native?"

"I'm Ai'oan. Only the scientists call us *natives*." He cocks his head curiously. "Are you a scientist? I think you must be, because you are of the Little Cam village."

"No. Yes. I mean, I will be soon. How did you know where I'm from? Have you been to Little Cam?" Fear had turned to anger, but my anger now transforms into fascination. I've never spoken with anyone from outside Little Cam. Harriet Fields doesn't count because now she's from Little Cam too.

"I've seen it," he says, "but only from the trees. It is no place for the Ai'oa. Kapukiri says there is evil in the village of the scientists."

"Little Cam isn't evil," I reply, bristling. "What do you know about it?"

"Only what Kapukiri says." He kneels and stares curiously

at Alai. "He obeys your command and follows where you go. Incredible. Truly, you are blessed to have such a companion."

His words soften me, and I warm a little. "Is your village close?"

Eio's eyes narrow suspiciously. "Why? What do you want with Ai'oa?"

"I want to see it," I say on a whim. "Show it to me."

"I don't know. . . ." He frowns.

"That smoke I smell, is it from Ai'oa?" I close my eyes and breathe deeply. "It's coming from . . . that direction." I open my eyes and start to follow the scent. When I look back, Eio is staring at me with wide eyes.

"You . . ." He runs to catch up with me. "You can smell it from *here*?"

"Ah . . ." I swallow and backpedal a bit. "Well, can't you?"

Uncertainty plays openly across his face. "I guess . . . if you promise not to wake everyone . . ."

"I swear."

"Well . . . okay." He still seems uneasy. I take it that visitors aren't often invited to Ai'oa.

I follow him over fallen logs made soft with mosses and under low-hanging vines and limbs. I wonder how he'll see where he's going, but he seems to feel his way rather than see it. I thought *I* moved silently through the jungle, but Eio seems to float over the ground rather than walk on it. He moves as sinuously as a snake and as lightly as a butterfly. Alai stays between us at all times, showing his mistrust in his hackles and rigid tail.

Before long I smell smoke; then I see the fires from which it comes. They burn low, more embers than flames, several dozen of them. Around the fires are huts made of four poles and thatched with palm leaves. They have no walls. When we reach the edge of the village, Eio stops me.

"They are sleeping. It is never good to wake what is sleeping. Stay here and look, but don't wake them."

"You're awake," I point out.

"I couldn't sleep. I heard a jaguar and went looking for it." He looks down at Alai.

I remember Alai's roars as we escaped through the fence. "Is it a good idea to hunt jaguars? Seems to me they'd end up hunting you."

Eio sits on a mossy rock, arms crossed over his bare chest. "Not to catch one! To see it. It is a powerful sign, the glimpse of the jaguar."

"I see a jaguar every day," I say, reaching down to rub Alai's ears.

"It is a thing unheard of." He shakes his head. "In the jungle, the jaguar is king. He follows no one but himself, and we Ai'oa fear and respect him and call him guardian."

"Alai's just a big baby, really."

Eio gives a short laugh. "Of course. That's why he tried to bite the nose off my face!"

"How do you know English? Uncle Paolo told me you natives were ignorant about everything outside your own villages."

"I'm not *ignorant*," Eio objects. "It is you who are ignorant, Pia bird. My father taught me English."

"Your father?"

"He is a scientist like you, in Little Cam."

"Really!" I blink and stare at him with astonishment. *Well,*

well, some*one's been hiding a really big secret. . . .* "Who is it? What's his name?" I think of all the scientists, wondering who it could be.

"To me, he is only Papi. He comes and teaches me English and math and writing."

"What does he look like?"

Eio shrugs. "Ugly, like all scientists."

I frown. "You think *I'm* ugly?"

"Of course," he says, staring toward his village.

I feel my face flush with anger. "That's the meanest thing anyone has ever said to me! I'm not ugly! I'm . . ." I look down at my muddy, bedraggled dress, and my voice falls to an embarrassed whisper. "I'm perfect."

"Perfect? Is that why you're running around in the jungle, making noise like a tapir running from the spear, in a dress?"

"I—it's my *birthday.* . . . I wanted to see the jungle. I've never been outside Little Cam before. I wanted to feel what it was like to be outside, in the wild."

"Are you a prisoner, Pia bird?"

"No," I say, startled.

"Why have you never left, then?"

"I—they say it's dangerous. Anacondas."

"Anacondas! I have killed an anaconda."

"You have?"

"Yes. It was as long as I am tall, and I am the tallest Ai'oan in the village. I made its skin into a belt for Papi."

"I've only seen an anaconda once. It was dead too. Uncle Timothy shot it."

"With a gun?"

"Of course with a gun!"

"I don't like guns. I hunt with dart and spear and arrow. These are silent and will not scare away your prey like a stupid gun."

I wouldn't have thought it possible, but the night is growing even darker. "I should go back now." It's been much, much longer than an hour. My delirious rush of adrenaline leaves me weary and nervous. I want to get back, to change and shower before my absence is noticed. If it hasn't been noticed already.

"I will take you back," Eio announces, rising to his feet.

"I can find the way," I say.

"I will take you back," he repeats in a firmer tone. "It's not good for a woman to walk alone in the jungle without a man to protect her."

He thinks I'm a woman. I stand a little taller. "Well, all right. If you want."

As we walk, he begins telling me all the names of the plants we pass. I already know their names, but I don't tell him that. He seems to think that scientists always want to know the names of things, and so I guess he thinks he's being helpful. Anyway, I like listening to his voice. It's deep and a little hoarse, as if he's been yelling all day, and his accent makes every word sound new and exciting, as if he's speaking another language I don't have to strain to understand.

"Here is annatto, for repelling insects and curing snakebites. The girls say it makes a love potion, but I don't believe them. They have all tried it on me, and I don't love any of them."

"Why? Aren't they strong or beautiful?"

He gives me an odd look before answering. "Some, I guess.

Look, here is suma. It helps the blood and the muscles and the memory, very good to eat. Curare, to poison our arrows. It is a strong poison, but not as strong as *yresa*."

Unlike the others, that name is unfamiliar. "What's *yresa*?"

"There is none here. In all of the world, there is only one place were the *yresa* grows. That place was very sacred to the Ai'oa, but we cannot go there anymore. The scientists forbid it with their guns."

I now have a feeling I know what this *yresa* is, but I don't say so. There is no warmth in Eio's voice when he talks about the scientists taking the flowers from his people, and I don't want him to think it was *my* decision. For some reason, I want this strange, wild boy to think better of me than that.

I watch his every move with fascination. Questions surge to my lips, batter at my teeth. I want to know everything about him. Where does he sleep? What does he eat? Has he been to a city? Does he have friends? But I feel unusually shy and don't know what to say. Or even how to say it. In just the minutes I've known him, he's shown himself to be entirely different from anyone in Little Cam.

"Look," Eio says, stopping by a tall, slender tree. "Know what this is?"

I tap the bark. "*Mauritia flexuosa*."

"No." He looks at me like I'm crazy. "It's aguaje."

"That's what I said."

He shakes his head. "Wait here. I'll get you some."

Before I can say a word, Eio grabs the branch of a different tree and hauls himself up. Within seconds, he's twenty feet in the air and still climbing. I watch him with wide eyes, waiting for him to slip at any moment and crash to the ground.

Soon he's lost to sight, hidden by leaves. I stare for a long minute and start to wonder if he changed his mind about walking me home and just abandoned me in the middle of the jungle. Then I hear a rustle and a shout behind me, and I whirl to see him sliding to the ground on a thick liana. He lands lightly, knees bent, with a string of aguaje draped over his shoulder.

With a smile that can only be described as cocky, he deftly skins the fruit and hands it to me. I discover I'm grinning like a monkey.

"Thanks, I guess," I say. The fruit is mildly tangy, not my favorite of the local produce, but what can I say when the boy climbed a hundred feet to pick it? "Aren't you going to eat some too?"

He laughs. "No! Aguaje is for girls. If a man eats too much of it, he starts to look like a woman."

"That is the most unscientific thing I've ever heard."

"Then you haven't met my cousin Jacari." Eio swings the string of fruit back and forth. "Too much aguaje. Now the mothers use him as a wet nurse."

My mouth freezes in mid-bite, and I stare at him. "You're teasing me."

A smile tugs at the corner of his mouth. "Maybe."

I throw the aguaje pit at him, and he laughs again and catches it. His laughter is infectious. I can't stop smiling. Everything he does, each movement, each word, is so vivid and strange. I feel like I've discovered some fascinating new species. *Homo ferus*: wild human. *An unpredictable, nocturnal creature usually found in trees. Caution: may cause bewilderment and disorientation. Also, prone to teasing.*

He picks another aguaje from the vine and tosses it up and down, watching me with his head tilted and his eyes curious. "How old are you?"

"Seventeen. How old are you?"

"Almost eighteen."

"Do you have brothers and sisters?" I've always been enchanted by the idea of siblings. As a rule, the members of my family tree could never have more than one child, for the sake of population control—though that rule backfired on them when the Accident happened.

"Not by blood," he says. "But by heart."

"What does *that* mean? If not by blood, then they're not really siblings."

He frowns and catches the agauje again, rubs his thumb over its scaly skin. "Shows what you know about family."

"I've spent months of my life studying genetics," I say. "I think I know all there is to know about family."

"Genetics," Eio repeats thoughtfully.

"It's the study of—"

"I know what it is. But that's just a part of what family is, at least in Ai'oa. And it's a very small part."

I open my mouth, shut it again. My brain does a somersault and lands with its fists raised. "It's *everything*. My genetic heritage was handpicked, designed by the best scientists in the world—" I stop before I go too far and tell him what I really am.

Eio gives me a sad smile. "You really are a scientist. Whenever we contradict one of you, that wall comes up in your eyes. We have a word for it in Ai'oa. *Akangitá*. Head like a rock."

My mouth drops. "Head like a *rock*!"

I clamp my jaw shut, whirl on my heel, and march off toward Little Cam in a huff.

At first I hear nothing behind me, and I almost slow and stop, but then I hear Eio hurrying to catch up. I wipe the smile from my face before he sees it. He skips around me and blocks my path.

"Sorry. If it makes you feel better, everyone in Ai'oa calls me *Akangbytu*."

"What does that mean?"

He thinks for a moment. "Head full of wind."

My indignation, already thin, shatters. I laugh. "Head full of wind! Perfect. How do you say *mouth*?"

"You say *îuru*." He frowns. "Why?"

"So if I called you *Îurubytu* . . ."

He gives me a dark look. "Mouth of wind. Ha ha. *Îurukay*."

"What's that?"

"I said you speak with fire, Pia bird. Your words scorch."

I smile. "Teach me more."

As we walk, I name words, and Eio tells me their Ai'oan translation, which I file away in my memory. He is stunned by how quickly I remember things and how easily I string the words together into sentences.

"It took me years to speak English this well," he says. "You speak my language as if it were planted in your heart."

I smile and wonder if he can see the warmth in my cheeks.

Suddenly the fence appears, and we're not far from my escape hole. I see the fallen ceiba only a few dozen yards to the right. The heat melts from my face. I wish I had walked slower.

"Thank you for walking me back," I say, because it feels like the right thing to do.

"Pia . . ." He looks down at his feet suddenly, seeming almost embarrassed. "I must tell you something. I told you a lie."

"You didn't kill an anaconda after all?"

"No!" he retorts indignantly. "*Îurukay*. I *did* kill the anaconda! I lied when I said you were ugly. It is not true. You . . ." He scrubs at his hair, and his discomfort makes me smile. "You are in fact very beautiful. More beautiful than any girl I know. Because I lied to you, I must give you a gift. It is the Ai'oan way. I took the truth away from you; now I must give something back." He extends his hand, and I see he is holding a flower. It's as big as both of my hands, a lovely pink and purple passionflower.

I stare at it as my heart tumbles over itself and my tongue turns into stone.

"Will you come again?" he asks. "In the daytime? You are not like the other scientists, who come and try to bully us, showing off their guns and motorboats." He snorts. "If it wasn't for us, your scientists wouldn't know half of what they know about this jungle. But you are . . . still young and not so ugly. I can teach you more of my language. And I can show you Ai'oa."

I swallow the shard of ice that's formed in my throat. "I . . . can't, Eio."

"What are you so afraid of?" He stares at me defiantly, his blue eyes cutting right to my heart.

I repeat my promise to myself to never leave Little Cam again, but my thoughts get muddled, and all I can think of is the jade jaguar on Eio's necklace. The words come out of their own accord. "Okay . . . I will."

A slow smile spreads his lips, revealing a row of beautiful white teeth. He nods and turns to Alai, bends from the waist, and says, "Farewell, guardian."

Then he is gone, blending into the dappled night like smoke.

NINE

The next morning, when I look at the syllabus Uncle Paolo wrote for this week's studies, I can't help but smile. Today, instead of the usual routine with Uncle Antonio, I get to work with Uncle Will in the bug room. Then again, I could be scheduled to give the Grouch a bubble bath and I wouldn't mind. Last night's adventure—though I'm awed and a little terrified that it happened at all—has left me giddy and lightheaded. It doesn't feel quite real, and if it weren't for the passionflower I hid in my nightstand drawer, I might dismiss the memory as a wild, vivid dream. Before leaving my room, I peek at the flower one more time, just to be sure it's still there. The sight of it sets butterflies loose in my stomach, and I wonder if it's because it came from the outside—or because Eio gave it to me.

The entomologist lab is located in A Labs, and there are boards covered with insects all over it. Butterflies, spiders, caterpillars, you name it, Uncle Will has it. The nastier and bigger the bug, the more fond of it Uncle Will is. He's pretty much the only one, however. Everyone in Little Cam does their best to avoid Uncle Will's lab. I don't mind it so much; there's only one member of his collection that I don't care for, and I hope it won't make an appearance in today's lesson.

Uncle Will looks up from his microscope as I enter the lab and gives a little smile.

"Pia," he says, and that is all. My father is the quietest person in Little Cam. He rarely spends time in the lounge or gym, choosing instead to keep to himself. There are many cliques within the population of the compound, but I've never known Uncle Will to be in any of them. He seems to enjoy the company of his bugs more than that of other people. Sometimes I imagine a day when everyone leaves Little Cam to go back to the outside world, leaving all the buildings empty and dark. Except for Uncle Will. I can't imagine him anywhere except right where he is now, and I think even after the rest of us have left he'll still be here, pinning beetles to Styrofoam.

"Uncle Paolo sent me to study with you. Didn't he tell you?"

Uncle Will nods absently. He's already glued his eye back to his microscope. I slide onto a metal stool, its blue cushion cracked and leaking yellow foam, and wait.

After several minutes, Uncle Will looks up again and smiles. "Pia."

"Um . . . yes?"

"Today we will study my little pet." He opens the lid of a terrarium and takes out the most terrifying creature in Little Cam. It's a beetle larger than my hand, dark, shiny black, and fitted with a ferocious pair of pincers. My heart sinks. So Babó is to be the lesson after all. I'm normally not squeamish, but the sight of this abnormally huge beetle makes my stomach turn. When I was three, Uncle Will gave me a titan beetle, thinking it a perfect pet. It escaped its cage one night, and I found it two days later—under my pillow. They told me years later that my terrified scream reached every ear in Little Cam.

"Oh . . ." I shake my head. "Can we just study butterflies? Or ants? Or even worms? Please? Anything but *that*."

Uncle Will looks hurt. "Babó won't hurt you, Pia. He's gentle, see?"

He sets the monster on the metal table beside me, and I automatically lean away from it. It scrabbles across the papers and petri dishes, knocking things over and making a general mess of everything.

"He looks hungry," I comment.

"No, no. Babó doesn't *eat*. He's a male. Male titan beetles don't eat, they just fly around looking for females to breed with."

I know all of that, but Babó is Uncle Will's favorite subject. My father rarely says more than three words a day, but if you mention the beetle, he can get as talkative as Dr. Klutz. Either we talk about Babó, or I'm in for a very quiet lesson.

"Charming," I say.

"I know, I know!" Uncle Will bobs his head cheerfully, pleased I've caught on to the joys that come with titan beetles.

He starts babbling on about Babó as the grotesquely huge beetle attempts to climb up the microscope. Uncle Will scoops it up, keeping his fingers well out of the way of its pincers.

"See how strong he is?" He picks up a pencil and dangles it in front of Babó's head. The beetle looks far more interested

in escaping Uncle Will's grasp than in the pencil, and I frown
dubiously.

Suddenly Babó snaps his pincers around the pencil, which
cracks clean in half. I yelp and leap off the stool, then feel like
an idiot as Uncle Will laughs.

"It broke it in two!" I press myself against a terrarium filled
with ants, unwilling to go an inch closer to the beast.

"You want to hold him?"

"No!" I rock backward on my heels, and the ant farm
behind me sways.

Uncle Will gives a wordless cry, drops Babó to the floor,
and rushes at me. Stupefied, I wonder what's gotten into him
and then realize that the ant farm is about to tip off its stand
onto the floor. My father throws himself on it, steadying it until
it's still again. Sweat beads his brow, and I see he is shaking.

"Uncle Will? I'm sorry, I didn't mean to upset the ants—"

"Not just *ants*, child!" He peers into the terrarium, nearly
feverish. "*Eciton burchellii*. Or they were *Eciton burchellii*
before the experiments."

"Experiments?"

Uncle Will chews his lip. He seems unwilling to talk
about it, but I stare pointedly at him, waiting for an answer.
Babó has disappeared to the far corner of the room, where I
hear him rooting through a pile of discarded Styrofoam.

"I . . . have been developing a formula, mainly with *Ilex
paraguariensis. . . .*"

"A steroid," I remark. I see some of the leaves scattered
across the table.

"Yes. Sometimes it has no effect. Sometimes it makes the

subjects race in circles until they die from exhaustion. But this time . . ." His eyes are grim. "This time was different."

I look from him to the ants. They are large, but not freakishly big like Babó. The terrarium isn't filled with sand and dirt like most ant farms; it has leaves and sticks to simulate the rainforest floor. I realize there are many, many more of the insects than I first noticed. What I took for topsoil lining the bottom of the terrarium is actually a living carpet of ants. "*Eciton burchellii* are army ants," I say. "Carnivorous, hunting in swarms."

He nods. "Just so. But there was a mistake. I cut my finger on a broken vial when I was making the formula. I thought I cleaned it all up, but I found later that a drop had made it into the mixture." His voices trembles, and he continues hoarsely, "The ants . . . they have a thirst for human flesh."

"*What?*"

He clears his throat, but his voice still shakes as he holds up a finger wrapped with cloth. He unwinds the bandage, and I gasp.

The finger looks as if he dipped it in a jar of acid. The skin is red and mangled, evidence of a hundred tiny jaws at work. "They attacked me. I reached into the terrarium to change their water, and they just . . . attacked me."

Man-eating ants. I've read of species of ants that can devour human beings, but never of any that specifically target them. "If they were to escape—"

"I have prepared for that unlikely event." He points at a white box on the wall. Inside the box is a wide red lever.

"The emergency alarm," I say, recognizing it immediately.

There is one in every building in Little Cam, even in the glass house. If pulled, the lever will set off a series of loud alarms all across the compound, signaling everyone to evacuate immediately. As far as I know, the alarms have never been set off.

"And I have this," Uncle Will adds. He opens a metal cabinet under the terrarium. It's filled with cans of aerosol insecticide.

I tap the side of the terrarium. Instead of scattering, the ants pile on one another, trying to bite through the glass to get at my finger.

"Let's hope we never have to use it," I say. "Why don't you get rid of them *before* they break out and eat everyone?"

Uncle Will retrieves Babó and returns the beetle to its cage. "There's still so much to learn from them," he says, a little sheepish. "It's worth the risk."

As he tidies the mess Babó made on the counter, I absently touch a petri dish of water, watching the ripples undulate on the surface. My mind is filled with the memory of last night, particularly with how uncannily blue Eio's eyes were when I shone my flashlight in his face. Suddenly I'm struck with a thought.

"Uncle Will?"

"Hmm?"

"When was the first time you left Little Cam?"

His forehead crinkles as he brushes flakes of Styrofoam into a wastebasket. "I guess when I was nine. I went out with Dr. Sato for an hour or two to collect spiders."

"Nine! *That* young?" I sit up straight in indignation.

"Things . . ." He stops, his mouth contorting into a wince. "Things were different then."

I do my best to quell my irritation at the unfairness of it. I have a different reason for asking the question. "You mean, before the Accident?"

"Yes."

"So have you ever seen any of the people who live in the jungle?"

"Natives?" He shrugs. "A few times. Why?"

"What are they like?"

"They keep to themselves, unless we're trading." He frowns. "Wait. I don't know if Paolo wants me to tell you all this."

"Forget Uncle Paolo," I say. "Tell me more."

He shakes his head guardedly. "I think I better not."

"Uncle *Will*—"

"Pia, please." His eyes scrunch pleadingly. "Let's just get on with the lesson, okay?"

I watch him silently as he sorts several plastic boxes of specimens, wondering if he ever dared sneak out like I did. Would he even tell me if he had? No. He's too timid, too lost in his world of titan beetles and army ants. I can't imagine him cheating at checkers, much less sneaking out of Little Cam and into Ai'oa.

Maybe Uncle Will won't answer all my questions . . . but I'm fairly certain now that Eio's not my brother.

To my surprise, I realize I'm smiling.

After my time with Uncle Will is up, I go out and discover that the rain is coming down in sheets, battering the gardens and making the fishpond overflow. A goldfish has been swept out onto the path, where it flops feebly in an inch of water. I dart through the rain and scoop it up, then toss it back into the pond.

Clarence and Mick are in the courtyard, wearing yellow ponchos and picking up the remnants of last night's party. Bits of uneaten fruit, napkins, and dropped silverware litter the ground, mixed with leaves and branches blown down by the storm. I bow my head against the rain and hurry past them, glad the task didn't fall to me. By the time I reach my house, I'm completely soaked.

After I change and dry my hair, I shut the door and spread out on the floor in front of the glass wall facing the jungle. My head is propped on Alai's side, and his purring vibrates through me. The few patches of sky I can see are colored charcoal with clouds, and the rain shakes the leaves of the trees as roughly as any wind. Though my wall is partially sheltered by the overhang of the roof, wet trails of water still streak the glass. Through them the world outside seems like the other end of a kaleidoscope, multiplied and magnified in an explosion of green and black and brown.

A quiet knock at my door reminds me that I didn't put my dirty laundry out for Aunt Nénine this morning. I open the door and find her standing with a huge, dripping umbrella in one hand.

"Sorry, Aunt Nénine," I mutter, racing around my room to pick up everything in need of washing. When I pull my party dress from under the bed, I gape at the mess it's in. Mud, leaves, and two or three tears are plain evidence of my night out. It hadn't seemed that bad last night, but then, I was too overwhelmed by what I'd done to really notice.

It's too late; Aunt Nénine has seen it.

"Pia! What have you done to your beautiful dress?" she gasps, taking it from me and inspecting it with dismay. She slips her finger through a tear and shakes her head. "I can mend it, but it will take several washes to clean."

"I . . ." My mind is utterly blank.

"Did you not think, Pia, before running off to the menagerie in this? See what that jaguar's claws have done?" She clicks her tongue disapprovingly.

"Oh . . . of course. The menagerie!" I sag with relief and play it as repentance. "I'm sorry, Aunt Nénine. I guess I didn't think."

"I'll see what I can do," she sighs as she shuffles out, my laundry in a sack over her arm.

Once she's gone and I can relax again, I unfold a section of my map and pore over the Pacific Ocean. My mind devours the names of the islands strewn like Skittles across the blue, but after a while, my thoughts begin to wander.

I retrieve my passionflower from the drawer in my nightstand, where it's been floating in a shallow dish of water, and set it beside me on the carpet, studying its intricate structure. Few flowers are as complex as the passionflower, and even fewer are more beautiful. I think of the time I held elysia in my hands and decide that it and this blossom are the two most beautiful I've ever seen. *The life flower and the passionflower.*

Of course, I can't look at the flower without thinking of Eio. Of his jade jaguar necklace against his bare chest. Of his jungle-blue eyes.

I wonder again who his father is. I've ruled out Uncle Will.

It might not even be an actual scientist; it could be Clarence or Jacques for all I know. I decide I'll ask Eio next time I see him for a description of his Papi.

The next time I see him.

"When did I decide I was even *going* to see him again, Alai?" The moment I swore I would? Why had I done that? I can't go back out there. Last night was dangerous enough. . . .

What are you so afraid of?

Uncle Paolo. Mother. Even Uncle Antonio.

What can they do to you? You, the girl who cannot bleed.

What *would* they do? Take away what freedom I have? The thought troubles me. I've never really looked that closely at the question before. Just what *do* I have that they could even withhold?

It's not like they'd lock me up or something.

Would they? I shiver.

As long as I don't go back into the jungle, I can still think that the possibility is always there. Like hiding the map under my carpet. Even if I left it there, never took it out again, I would still know it was there if I really needed it.

And you are content with that? Content to die of thirst when a glass of water sits within your grasp?

I don't know! I don't know. I turn and bury my face in Alai's spots. I've never been so confused in my life. It was simpler before. Study your biology, Pia. Eat your dinner, Pia. Go to sleep, Pia. Let Uncle Paolo check your pulse and your saliva and your eyes and ears and nose, Pia.

Run, Pia.

I don't understand this urge I have to run away. It doesn't make sense. Over the past few weeks, it has been getting stronger. Maybe if I hadn't found that hole in the fence, the feeling would have passed. Maybe it's just a phase.

Maybe it's not.

A new feeling takes hold of me now: guilt. If I'm so committed to my purpose here in Little Cam, then why did I enjoy my brief freedom so much? *You're not here to run around the rainforest,* I tell myself, *filling your head with wild jungle boys.* Uncle Paolo is right. I'm not ready yet. I'm too undisciplined, too easily distracted. I need to get myself under control.

I want the freedom of the jungle. I want to create someone who is like me. My dreams are tangled around each other like plants vying for the best spot in the sun. They strangle each other in their attempt to get the better of my reason. I *know* which one I truly want—I've wanted it all my life. But I'm being overtaken by a new desire, a raging, unpredictable dream that could destroy everything I've worked for.

What do I see in that boy, anyway? I remember the deep loneliness I felt last night at my party and the urge to have someone who understands what it's like to be eternal. Eio isn't that person. Can't ever be that person. He's just like the rest of them: brief, evanescent. A fire that burns brightly, yes, but a fire that will one day go out.

I remember Clarence talking about his wife, about how she died in a car accident. I remember the pain in his eyes and the tremble in his hands when he spoke of her. I realize I'm terrified—*terrified*—of losing someone that way. I imagine Uncle Antonio or Mother suddenly *gone*, taken from me by a force I will never understand. *Death.*

I shudder.

I may as well shackle my wrist to a bolt of lightning as

attach myself to a mortal. The muscles in my shoulders tense, and I hunch over, face in my hands, staring but not seeing.

But oh . . . the moment I looked into his blue, blue eyes . . . it wasn't like shackling lightning.

It was like eating it. A bolt of electricity to my stomach.

I thought I left my wild self in the jungle or at least appeased her appetite for a time. But it seems that feeding her only made her hungrier. *Makes* me *hungrier*, I remind myself. The last thing I need is to develop some kind of psychological disorder like schizophrenia. *There is only me, one Pia. Wild Pia and Timid Pia are the same.* But that doesn't make me feel any less torn. If anything, it confuses me more.

Uncle Paolo tells me that as complicated as DNA or the ecosystem or even a single cell can be, in the end, science makes everything simple. A formula can make sense of the most complicated numbers. There is no *maybe* in science, except in a hypothesis. And you don't treat hypotheses as truth, you treat them as springboards that launch you into careful analysis, experimentation, and documentation. Only then can you find truth, and once that's done, then everything is simple again.

Uncle Paolo says that in the end, everything comes down to science. There is nothing that the scientific method cannot solve. We are limited only by the questions we haven't yet thought to ask. And he has never been wrong before, so there must be truth in what he says. After all, he helped create *me*. If there's anyone I can trust, it's Uncle Paolo.

If I go back to the jungle, I'll be encouraging everything in me that's most unscientific. Instead of moving toward my goal, I'll be regressing. I know I'm close to the end. I *must* be. I've been training my entire life. Can I really afford to be distracted now?

I run my fingers over my arms, imagining Eio—*no, not Eio*—someone else, another boy, a boy with unbreakable skin like mine. An immortal boy. *Mr. Perfect.*

My mind is made up. I'll tell Uncle Paolo everything: about Eio and his Ai'oa, about the hole in the fence, even about Wild Pia. Then he will draw some charts, maybe some equations, pull out a psychology book, and explain it all scientifically. Everything will be simple again.

Everything will be just as it was.

TEN

Leaving Alai to sleep, I pick up the dish with the passion-flower floating in it and go outside without once glancing at the hole in the fence. A row of heliconias grows outside the kitchen, and I toss the flower behind them, where it will decay and turn into earth.

Then, strong with purpose, I walk through Little Cam looking for Uncle Paolo. He's always very busy, and no one ever knows where he'll be at any given time, so I have to search for a while. At last I find him in my lab, wearing his long white coat and latex gloves. Mother is with him, and in her hands is Roosevelt, the immortal rat.

"Pia!" Uncle Paolo seems surprised—and not happy—to see me. "What do you want? Why are you here?"

His greeting makes me pause a moment and glance from him to Mother to Roosevelt with uncertainty. "I want to ask you something."

"Can it wait? We're in the middle of an experiment."

"With Roosevelt?"

His left eyebrow arches sharply. "Obviously."

"Can I help?" After all, pretty much any experiment run on Roosevelt will eventually be run on me. We have a shared destiny, Roosevelt the rat and I.

"I don't think that's a good . . ." But he stops and seems to reconsider before saying slowly, "On the other hand, maybe you should. After all, it will be you heading up these tests one day. It's time you got more involved in the actual process. Books and theory can only take you so far. Get a coat and some gloves."

My confession momentarily forgotten, I set down the dish and practically skip to the small metal cabinet that stores a row of crisp white lab coats. I slip one on, pleased that the arms aren't too long, and pull on a pair of squeaky latex gloves.

"What's the experiment?" I ask as I join Uncle Paolo and Mother, who hasn't stopped frowning at me since I entered the room. I ignore it.

"Care to explain, Sylvia?" Uncle Paolo extends a hand.

Mother sniffs and says, "We're going to give Roosevelt a taste of elysia."

A chill runs through me, even though the room has to be over 25 degrees Celsius. As usual, my mind automatically runs the calculations: *25 degrees Celsius times 1.8 plus 32 makes it 77 degrees Fahrenheit.* I shake my head, brushing aside the numbers. I want to be completely alert for this.

"Is that . . . hasn't it been done before?" Surely someone's tested it. But when I stop and think, I can't recall ever reading of such an experiment in any of the notes on Roosevelt's medical history. Or in the notes on mine, for that matter.

"It hasn't," Uncle Paolo confirms. "And the test is long past due. We've tried every kind of disease and dozens of poisons, including curare and the secretion of poison dart frogs. But never elysia."

I feel strangely numb as Uncle Paolo picks up a syringe filled with a clear liquid that must be elysia extract. I don't ask if it's pure or diluted; I don't really want to know. I wish I'd never asked to join them. I wish I was back in Uncle Will's lab, feeding pencils to Babó.

Uncle Paolo nods to Mother, and she holds up Roosevelt. The plump rodent is so used to human touch by now, he doesn't even squirm. He looks about as happy as a rat can be; his eyes are bright and alert, his nose is quivering as it picks up the scents in the room.

Uncle Paolo hesitates only the briefest of moments before he squirts one drop into Roosevelt's mouth. The rat's tiny jaws work rapidly as he tastes the elysia, and I watch with fascination. What must it taste like? If Roosevelt has an opinion on the matter, he doesn't share it.

Mother sets the rat down on the same exam table I usually sit on. Roosevelt sniffs her fingers, then the table, then starts trundling around like he usually does in his cage. He seems completely unaffected by the elysia.

Inside me, several knots of tension begin to relax. I almost feel my muscles giving individual sighs of relief. *Truly immortal.*

An uncharacteristic grin bursts onto Uncle Paolo's face. "Would you look at that! The mortal rats, dozens and dozens of them, all died immediately! Not so much as a squeak. They just *went*, like a breeze through a window. But look at our

Roosevelt! So much life. We've done it, Pia, my angel, my darling, my exquisitely perfect girl!" He grabs me by the hands and we spin in a circle.

I can't help but laugh with him. I've never seen him—or anyone—so excited. I didn't even know Uncle Paolo had it in him to twirl. His joy is catching; my pace quickens with a thrill of heady exhilaration.

"We did it! We did it! We did it!" we chant in unison, though of course it was really Dr. Heinrich Falk who did it and not us at all, but we don't care. "We did it!"

Finally Uncle Paolo lets go of my hands and stops to catch his breath, still with a smile the size of one of the watermelon slices we'd had at my party. "We did it," he repeats softly. "Life, Pia. Life without death. *Immortality.* Thousands of years in human history, thousands of theories, attempts, myths, dreams . . . but *we,* we have done it. Cheated death. Pia, I have lied to you. I told you there were no gods. But there *are,* oh yes, there are. We are gods, Pia, you and I and Roosevelt. Yes, ha! Roosevelt, the rat god! We have created life! And so we have become gods in our own right." He closes his eyes for a long minute, basking. Then he opens them again and smiles at me. "Now, what was your question for me?"

I draw a deep breath and remember my conviction. *Can't afford to be distracted.* The success of this experiment is just further proof that Little Cam is where I need to be, with all my attention focused on the Immortis project. "Last night, after the party, I went to my room to . . . just be alone." No point in getting Dr. Klutz in trouble too. "Anyway, I was sitting and staring outside when I saw a—"

"Paolo?" Mother's voice is so soft I almost don't hear it.

"Yes, Sylvia, what is it?"

"Roosevelt."

We turn as one to the rat.

Roosevelt is lying on his side, his tiny body heaving as he gasps for air. His tongue hangs out, startlingly pink against his dark brown fur. His eyes are glassy.

Uncle Paolo turns white. He rushes to the exam table and scoops the rat into his hands. "No. No, no, no, no, no, no. . . . Roosevelt! *Roosevelt!*"

It's useless. Roosevelt keeps gasping, his breaths coming too quickly, too sharply. Uncle Paolo turns him over, holds him upright, lays him down again, but nothing helps.

"Stop it, Roosevelt! Stop it, you stupid, *stupid* rat!"

"Uncle Paolo!" I run to him and grab his arm. "Stop yelling at him! It's not his fault!"

"Get off of me, girl!" He shakes me away and turns back to Roosevelt. I stare at him in shock, bewildered and blindsided by his sudden rage.

"Come on, buddy," Uncle Paolo coos to the rat. "Come on, old friend! You and I have been through too much together. . . . Come back to us, little god-rat. Come back now. . . ."

Roosevelt's breaths start to slow again, but they don't return to their normal, healthy pace. They keep slowing until they become *too* slow. Soon his sides are barely moving, and his eyes grow even glassier.

Uncle Paolo, his eyes bright and wild, whirls on Mother. "*Do* something!"

Mother gapes at him and steps back. "I . . . I . . ." She trails off, her hands spread helplessly. Uncle Paolo slams his fist onto the counter, making the syringes and vials rattle, and curses low beneath his breath. His eyes catch mine, and I'm chilled by what I see in them. I've never seen him this angry, this . . . dangerous. Not even during Wickham tests. Stunned, I drop my eyes and swallow hard.

"Well," he says softly. "Now we know."

He sets Roosevelt on the exam table, then wipes his hands on his coat. His face has gone cold and distant. My mother hovers behind him, her concerned eyes on Uncle Paolo and not the rat. All three of us stand very still as Roosevelt weakens before our eyes. My gaze flickers to Uncle Paolo uneasily, wondering if he'll explode again. It's extremely unnerving, seeing him so undone. The Paolo Alvez I know is always cool, always calm, always self-controlled.

"Enough," Uncle Paolo says at last. "Pia, clean up this mess and ice the body. We'll examine it later. Sylvia, I'll need your help with the paperwork."

I gently pick up Roosevelt. He doesn't even have the strength to twitch his whiskers as he usually does. Around his nose and on his paws, numerous hairs have turned white. *That's odd.* I didn't know elysia did that to its victims.

I wrap him in a small towel, but there's little more I can do. He shudders once in my hands, then falls still.

Roosevelt, the immortal rat, is dead.

For some reason, I expect all of Little Cam to go into an uproar. But it doesn't.

No shouting or wailing haunts the compound. No one tears at their hair or clothes in hysterics. After all, he was only a rat.

I sit in one of the rockers by the goldfish pond, just rocking, my knees pulled up to my chin. Of everyone in Little Cam, I am the quietest right now. But inside, I *want* to tear my clothes and run screaming through the compound. I want everyone to hear the turmoil raging in my thoughts.

Roosevelt is dead. Elysia, the very substance that immortalized him, killed him.

It could kill me.

Uncle Paolo is locked in his private office. He won't talk to anyone. At first no one could understand what was going on, and they kept asking what was wrong, what happened, why was Dr. Alvez so upset? But Mother must have talked— it certainly wasn't me—because now, instead of asking me questions I won't answer, everyone tiptoes past and tries not to disturb me. I can't blame them. I wonder if they suspect the hurricane of emotions roaring in my head and if that's why they're so careful to avoid me, not wanting to set it loose. They must think I'm completely terrified that what happened to Roosevelt will happen to me. Even *I* think I ought to be terrified. After all, my whole life I've been under the impression that I couldn't die. And here I am, finding out that I can after all.

But when I shut my eyes, it's not Roosevelt dying on the exam table that I see. It's not the syringe filled with the deadly poison that could take my life far more quickly than it gave it to me. I don't even see myself writhing and gasping to death, which would make sense after what I witnessed.

What I see instead is Uncle Paolo and the look in his eyes when he realized that Roosevelt was dying. I hear his triumphant shouts just before it happened. *We are gods, Pia. We cheated death.*

But we didn't. *He* didn't. Does he think his entire life's work is a waste now? Surely there is still much to be proud of. After all, I am still immortal. So long as I never do something as stupid as drink elysia, I'll still live forever. I'll create a race of immortals, my own race, and Dr. Falk's and Uncle Paolo's and my dream will come true. Once the immortal race is self-sufficient, we can destroy all the elysia, and we will truly be completely invulnerable to death. We'll live on and on, repro-ducing and growing our eternal numbers, until the world is full, and then we'll stop. And live. And live. And live.

I try to focus on that thought, on the image of my immortal race with me at its head. An immortal boy to love. Immortal friends my own age. But my mind keeps blurring back to Uncle Paolo's face and the wild desperation in his eyes as he fought to bring Roosevelt back from death's door.

Uncle Paolo was supposed to make things clearer, not muddle them up even worse. My earlier convictions crumble in light of this new fear, a fear I've never felt before. Fear of the man who created me, named me, raised me . . .

I decide I *will* go back into the jungle.

And I'll go again. And again. And again.

I'll go into the rainforest until the memory of Uncle Paolo's eyes in that moment of Roosevelt's death is gone, washed away by the cleansing rain of the jungle.

An hour after night falls, I am on the other side of the fence.

ELEVEN

Eio steps out from behind a kapok, startling me. I've never met anyone who could sneak up on me like that, and it makes me nervous.

"You came," he says, looking me up and down and giving Alai a long stare, which the jaguar returns coolly. "And no dress this time."

I'm wearing a black tank and camouflage cargo pants. Over my arm is a dark raincoat, just in case. There are only a few clouds in the sky, but it takes only minutes for that to change.

"Of course I did. I made a promise." I don't mention that only a few hours ago I fully intended to break that promise.

"I thought you were afraid."

"I'm not."

He sizes me up dubiously, and I do the same to him. He's wearing exactly what he wore last night. Maybe those are the only clothes he has. The only difference is that today he wears face paint: three red lines on his forehead, two white dots on each cheek, and a blue line down his chin.

"What does your face paint mean?"

He touches a finger to the three red lines. "The mark of the Jaguar claw." His finger moves to the white dots. "The spots of the Jaguar." Finally he points at his chin. "The Sighting."

"Sighting?"

His fingers brush the streaks on his face, and he nods at Alai. "It is good luck to see a jaguar."

I stare at Alai and wonder what everyone in Little Cam would say if I painted my face too. *Going native, Pia?*

"I will show you Ai'oa," Eio announces, "if you are not too afraid, little scientist."

"I'm not a scientist yet," I reply mildly. "And I'm not afraid. Will they be asleep?"

"No. They wait for you."

Waiting for me? I feel a nervous flutter in my stomach. "You told them about me?"

"There are no secrets in Ai'oa."

I let him lead the way, since my path the night before took me in a wild zigzag through the jungle. Eio takes me straight to his village, or as straight as you can go in the rainforest. We have to circle giant trees and nearly slide on our backs down steep, leafy hillsides. Even so, it only takes about half an hour to reach Ai'oa.

The village looks much different tonight. The fires are bigger, and I see that Ai'oa is larger than it seemed the night before. Open-walled, thatched huts stretch in two long lines. They are barely taller than I am. Each hut contains anywhere from five to twenty hammocks, all of which are empty now.

Colorful strips of fabric flutter from the poles supporting the roofs, and brightly painted pottery hangs from vines strung between the hammocks.

The fires march in a perfect row down the aisle between the huts, and I am struck by how perfectly parallel everything is. The more I look, the more I see it. The structure and placement of the huts, the way the hammocks are hung, even the cloths tied to the poles—they are all placed with meticulous care, maintaining aesthetic balance as much as possible.

I must take all of this into account in mere seconds, because the Ai'oans demand the major part of my attention. They emerge from the huts and the trees, gathering around the fires and waiting, I assume, for Eio and me.

I'm amazed at how slight the Ai'oans are. None of them is as tall as me. They wear a strange assortment of traditional and modern clothes. Some of the Ai'oans wear the same shorts and tees that are common in Little Cam, while the rest wear next to nothing. One woman wears a shirt with the words I LOVE NYC on it (I wonder who NYC is), and beneath that she wears a skirt made of long grass.

Eio leads me down the row between the huts, and soon I am surrounded by Ai'oans. I stare, and they stare back. There are murmurs and whispers all around, but whenever I turn to see who is talking, I see only still faces, and the voices slip behind me again. They seem more fascinated by Alai than by me.

It takes me several minutes to sort the men from women. I finally discern that women wear their hair to the waist and flecked with parrot feathers, while the men wear theirs to the back of the neck. They all have the same flat bangs down to their eyebrows. Except Eio.

My guide is an anomaly. I look at him once, and he seems to blend right into the crowd, with his face paint and bare chest. But when I look again, he seems as out of place as I am. His hair, unlike the rest of the tribe's, is too curly to stay in the neat bowl cut they favor. The Ai'oans have flat noses, and their eyes slant slightly at the outer corners, but Eio's features don't match. He has a face that could easily appear in Little Cam, due, no doubt, to his mixed parentage. He is also head and shoulders above his people, and even when the Ai'oans press around me and separate us, I can easily spot him by simply looking over their heads. He is watching me closely, an amused smile on his lips, and I ask him what's so funny.

"They think you are ugly," he says. "Like all the other *karaíba*."

"I am not ugly! What's a *karaíba*?"

"It means *foreigner*, and it's all right. They think I am ugly too, because of my Papi's blood."

I can't help it. I laugh at that. "Well, you *are* ugly!" I say, just to annoy him.

Suddenly the Ai'oans start to laugh with me. I don't know why until Eio shoves his way back to my side and tells me, "Most of them speak English, you know. Papi taught them too."

"Oh!" I stare at the faces around me. "Well, then . . . um . . . hello."

I hear a few *hellos* murmured back, and there is more laughter. My nerves stop humming so violently, and I start to feel less apprehensive. A little girl dressed in a pair of blue shorts and a necklace of fresh flowers appears at my elbow and stares up at me. After a moment, she rapidly chatters something in their native tongue and disappears again. Laughter ensues, this time raucous and uncontrolled. When I look at Eio for a translation, he only shakes his head as his face turns pink.

"I will translate," offers a pregnant, bright-eyed woman in traditional Ai'oan dress. I stare at her swollen belly in fascination. I've seen pregnant animals, but never a pregnant woman. I realize my hands are feeling my own stomach curiously. *Will that happen to me?* I'm so mesmerized I nearly miss the woman's translation. "She said, 'An ugly bride for the ugly hunter.'"

"What!" I whirl until I find Eio, and I pin him with a wild look.

He waves his hands. "No, no! It isn't . . . I didn't . . ."

"In Ai'oa, little *karaíba*," continues the woman, "it is the custom for the hunter to bring back a wife from another village, but only if she accepts him. But Eio is so ugly, perhaps no girl from the Awari tribe or the Hatpato tribe wants him, so he must find an ugly scientist girl for his wife."

"I'm not going to be anyone's wife," I reply hotly. And I think Eio is far from ugly, but I don't say it. Even so, I feel warmth in my cheeks.

"No," agrees Eio. "I did not bring Pia here to be a wife, Luri."

"Why did you bring her then?" asks Luri. "Look at her. She has no questions to ask about how we use annatto and suma. No paper and pens. Nothing to trade with us like the other scientists."

"I brought her," replies Eio, drawing himself up, asserting his height, "because last night I heard the jaguar, and when I went to look for it, I found *her*, the girl who commands the jaguar. Don't you see? It is a sign. The spirits made the jaguar call, to send me looking, so that I would find her and bring her back."

This is met with silence. I wonder if they will laugh at him again, but their faces are straight and solemn. Then Luri says, "This is a matter for the Three."

The others murmur their agreement in both English and Ai'oan. The Three? I don't have long to wonder who they might be, because the crowd in front of me falls away until there are only three people left standing there in a row.

The first is a man elaborately garbed in a heavy collar of parrot feathers, animal teeth, and beads. He holds a spear taller than himself with feathers tied around it. Next to him is a plump woman with intricate facial tattoos and piercings in her lips and nose. Her arms are also tattooed. She is so elegant and confident that I hardly even notice she is naked from the waist up. Beside her is a man so old he is bent double, and the skin on his face hangs in folds. His hair is white and thin. Ropy vines hang over his shoulders and around his waist, and from them dangle bundles of herbs, carved bits of wood, and multicolored beads and gourds.

I know instinctively that these must be the leaders of the Ai'oa.

The oldest one watches me with eyes that belong in a younger man's face. They are bright and sharp, and I find it difficult to meet his gaze for long. I feel as though he can read the thoughts in my head. I look instead at the woman, who seems softer. There is a small smile on her face, but her look is inquisitive and searching, flicking from me to Alai. The man on her other side simply stares at Eio.

They all seem to be waiting for someone to speak, and I hope it isn't me. I've no idea what to say. I don't know what Eio meant. They should be asking him.

Finally the oldest one speaks. His voice is soft as a sigh, but every word is clear. Unfortunately, he speaks in Ai'oan, so I have no idea what he says. Luri steps close and softly interprets for me.

"The sign of the jaguar is a powerful sign. If the Farwalker heard the call, then it must not be ignored. The foreigner girl must have a powerful magic, to be heralded by the spirits and to have the respect of the mighty jaguar."

"I heard the call," Eio confirms.

"I don't have any magic! Tell him I don't have any magic." Except immortality, of course, but that isn't magic, it's science.

"It is not good to go against a spirit man like Kapukiri," Luri says. "I will not tell him. What he says must be true. If Eio Farwalker heard the jaguar and went looking and found you, the spirits must want you here among us."

"I can't stay with you. I have to go back to Little Cam."

"Go back or stay," she replies with a shrug.

Kapukiri steps closer to me. He stands straight, unfolding himself from his bent posture, and sticks his face only inches from mine. I expect Alai to object to the man's proximity, but to my surprise, the jaguar merely watches calmly. My impulse is to back away, but the Ai'oans form a barrier behind me, and there is nowhere to go. I am forced to stare down at the shriveled little man as he pierces my eyes with his own. What is he looking for? My "magic"? I don't believe in these natives' spirits and signs—that wouldn't be scientific—but I cannot doubt the sincerity in their gazes. They are all waiting for Kapukiri to make some sort of announcement, I guess.

Suddenly the medicine man steps back, his eyes wild. He begins shaking from head to foot in spastic, jerking motions. I wonder if he's having a seizure. Then he pulls a small gourd from one of the vines around his body and begins shaking it. It rattles noisily. He shakes it above his head, from side to side, and at his knees. While he shakes the gourd, he moans and chants in Ai'oan, eyes rolling, body trembling. Beside me, Alai makes a strange sound, half-growl and half-whine deep and low in his throat.

"What's the matter with him?" I ask. "Does he need help?"

Luri shakes her head and puts her hand on my arm, motioning for silence. The other Ai'oans watch their medicine man raptly. When he finally stops shaking and moaning, he lifts his hands to clasp both sides of my face. I don't try to pull away, but wait nervously to see what will happen.

"The Farwalker heard the call," he announces as Luri hastily translates, "and I, Kapukiri, have seen the mark in the foreigner girl's eyes."

"Mark?" I ask, and Luri shushes me.

Kapukiri continues. "I have seen the sign of jaguar, mantis, and moon. This foreigner girl is . . ." Luri stumbles in her translation, her eyes wide and fixed on mine. *"Tapumiri."*

A murmur goes through the crowd.

"Jaguar, mantis, moon," whispers Eio. "The Ones Who Were but Are No More. *Tapumiri.*"

Kapukiri removes his hands from my face and picks up my wrists, turning them over so that the pale blue veins beneath my skin are showing. He traces them with his gnarled fingers as gently as a butterfly's touch.

"In these veins flow the tears of Miua," he whispers.

Silence falls over Ai'oa. I feel a chill and credit it to the cool night air. Kapukiri's words mean something to these people, something that strikes them dumb with awe or fear, I cannot tell which. They stare at me with long faces and wide eyes, and I don't know whether it's revulsion or worship in those looks. Uncomfortable, I try to avoid their gazes. Even Luri has stepped back and melted into the crowd of faces.

"*Jaguar, mantis, moon*," they whisper in Ai'oan, the words already branded into my memory, thanks to Luri's translation. "*The* Tapumiri, *who are no more. The tears of Miua flow again. Jaguar, mantis, moon.*"

At first the whispers are jumbled and incoherent, but gradually they blend into one voice, a unified chant that makes my blood crawl. I don't know what it means or what it has to do with me, but I feel I'm missing something big and important.

"Eio," I whisper, "what are they saying?"

He alone is not chanting; instead, he's staring at me with a calm, searching gaze. "That you have come to save us."

TWELVE

"**S**ave you?" I repeat. "Save you from what?"

But Eio doesn't answer. He grabs my hand and pulls me to the biggest of their fires and makes me sit, with Alai stretched at my feet. The Ai'oans start bringing banana leaves and pottery filled with food. Much of it I recognize, since Little Cam often trades with the Ai'oans, earning fruits and meat in exchange for clothing. But there are other dishes that are strange to me, and I don't want to touch them.

Everyone is watching expectantly, urging me to eat, so I try each dish as it passes by. I don't know what else to do. Eio is on my right, looking absurdly smug for reasons that escape me, and Luri sits on my left. The Three sit across the fire, seeming apart from the others despite the fact that they're surrounded by Ai'oans. They watch me quietly, and after a while I decide to just ignore them as much as I can. After that, I begin to enjoy some of the food. After I've tasted everything, the Ai'oans begin to eat too, even though it must be around midnight.

I know I should go back home, but I can't tear myself away. This village and its people are so alive and strange and different from everything I've ever known. I'm terrified, bewildered, and completely enchanted. I wonder if this is how my father feels when he researches a newly discovered beetle or how Uncle Paolo feels when he makes a breakthrough discovery on one of his experiments.

For whatever reason, they have made me the guest of honor. It must have to do with the "jaguar, mantis, moon" mark that Kapukiri claims he saw in my eyes. What they think I'm supposed to save them from, they do not say. But it's hard to dwell on that while they are draping garlands of orchids around me. Children press close to me and ask shy questions in a mixture of English and Ai'oan, and they don't seem to mind when I can't answer. They try to pet Alai, but he warns them away with a snarl.

The children fascinate me. I've never seen anyone younger than me before; growing up, I was the only child in Little Cam. The children's games and laughter and the way they move—as if they weigh less than flowers drifting in the wind—enchant me. They are so small and so free, my heart almost aches from watching them.

One day, when my immortal race is complete, there will be no more children. There can't be or we'd risk overpopulating the earth. As often as I've dreamed of creating my immortals, for a moment, the thought only makes me shudder.

I have to move back a few yards when a circle of Ai'oans begins twirling around the fire. This is nothing like the rigid, methodical dancing at my birthday party. The Ai'oans move wildly, unpredictably, as swift and vivid as the fire. Several sit and beat drums or play on slender wood flutes, and the dancers add their own rhythm with their bodies. No two move alike. I stop eating and just gape, probably looking like an idiot. But I can't help it. It's captivating.

"Come." I look up and see Eio standing over me, his hand extended.

I shake my head. "I don't dance. Trust me."

"*Come.*"

Reluctantly I take his hand. It is warm and strong, and he pulls me up and whirls me around before I can change my mind. Then there is no escape; I am trapped in the ring of dancers as if drawn by some magnetic force. But I don't care. In fact, I soon forget everything and just feel the music, the fire, the swirl of small, lithe bodies twirling around me, pulling me onward, around. Eio is right by my side, still holding my hand. He and I move as if we are two flames on one torch, like Uncle Antonio and Dr. Klutz when they danced. But we are wilder, and every step we make is purely spontaneous, springing from some primeval impulse I never knew I had.

I forget I am immortal and that I'm not supposed to be here. I forget about Uncle Paolo and poor Roosevelt. I forget that the years will roll by, and all of these people will die, and I will live on. For now, for these few precious minutes, I belong in this dancing ring. I belong to the jungle and to the Ai'oans and to their intoxicating fires. I'm not Pia. I'm not anyone. I'm just another body, lost to the drums.

Lost in Eio's arms.

He spins me and catches me, and everywhere I turn, he's

there. His touch is like fire, light and effortless, but searing. The tips of his fingers burn on my wrists and my shoulder. *Don't stop*, I think. *Don't you dare stop.* My own thoughts terrify me, or at least they terrify that other Pia. Tonight I am Wild Pia, and nothing can scare me, not even the tingle that runs down my spine every time my eyes meet his.

But even if I can dance all night, Eio soon grows exhausted. We spin out of the circle and collapse, laughing, to the ground, where children flock to me with more fruit and flowers. I take a roasted plantain skewered on a long stick and smile warmly at the little girl who gave it to me. She smiles back before giggling and running away.

"Eio, what did the old man think he saw in my eyes?"

"Kapukiri?" Eio is still breathing heavily. He lies back, eyes shut. "He saw the sign of jaguar, mantis, and moon. The mark of the Kaluakoa."

"But what *is* it? Last I checked, my eyes were no different from anyone else's."

Eio waves at the fire in front of us. "There is your answer. The mark is only seen by fire. Are there no fires in your village of scientists?"

I'd give anything for a mirror right now. Though I'm not totally sure I believe him, I know the only way to find out is to see for myself. "What did you mean when you said they think I've come to save them? Save them from what?"

He sits up and shrugs. "Who can say? Maybe it hasn't appeared yet. But why else would the spirits send an undying one?"

Startled, I pull away, eyes wide. "Undying one . . ."

He returns my stare evenly, his blue eyes fixed on mine. Something inside me, something that came alive in the light of the Ai'oan fires, begins to crumble. "But . . . how did you know what I am?"

"I didn't. It's like Kapukiri said. I only followed the call of the jaguar, but Kapukiri saw the mark of jaguar, mantis, and moon. It is the mark of the Kaluakoa, and of the *Tapumiri.* The undying ones, who do not know death."

I feel oddly sad, and the roasted plantain I'm holding no longer looks so delicious. So Eio knows what I am, and once more I am immortal, perfect Pia. Completely unique. Completely different. *Completely alone.* The word reverberates through my body like a shard of ice, bouncing off my ribs and settling in my stomach.

But . . . I've always been alone. Hence my dream of creating more immortals, so that I *won't* be. So why does the word strike me so deeply in this moment and in this place? It has never . . . *hurt* like it does now.

Alone.

Then I see it.

I came to the Ai'oans as a scientist and a foreigner, but that was the extent of the difference between us. When these wild, vivacious people of the jungle swept me into their dance, I left even that behind. I became something different, someone new. Someone who could blend in instead of stand out. Though I hardly know them, and they hardly know me, these Ai'oans and I—we were connected. And for a short time . . . I belonged.

But then the truth fell like a knife, severing the tenuous

connection. I am an immortal among mortals, and I will never belong. Not here. Not in Little Cam. Not with any kind but my own.

Suddenly Eio decides he wants to dance again, and though I resist at first, he pulls me to my feet. I try to lose myself in the dance of the Ai'oans. We whirl and pound drums and someone's pet monkey leaps from shoulder to shoulder, screeching and pelting an irritated Alai with berries.

But no matter how fast and furiously I dance, I can't shake the word from my mind.

After we dance a few more rounds, Eio pulls me out of the circle and away from the village. Alai trails behind, escaping his simian tormentor. We are within sight of the dancers, but here the jungle sounds take precedence, and Ai'oa becomes part of the background. There is only enough light from the fires to illuminate Eio's nose, forehead, and cheekbones. His eyes catch flecks of light in them, like fireflies trapped in glass jars.

"Come. I want to show you something."

"What is it?"

"Just be quiet! They'll hear, and then they'll follow us." He takes my hand and starts for the jungle.

"But where—"

Suddenly he stops, faces me, and presses a finger gently to my lips. "Sh," he whispers. "You talk too much, Pia."

His face is mere centimeters from mine, a slight, almost mischievous smile playing at his lips. Caught off guard by the closeness of him, I nearly forget to breathe.

I nod, and he drops his finger, takes my hand again, and leads me on.

Questions shoot like sparks through my head—*How far? What is it? Why are you still holding my hand?*—but I don't ask them. Instead, I let him sweep me through the dark rainforest, my heart hammering.

The ground slopes downward; we're moving away from Ai'oa, in the opposite direction of Little Cam. We half walk, half slide through thickets of ferns as high as my waist. High above, the call of the potoo—eerily similar to a human whistle—seems to follow us, starting high and smooth and sliding down a scale of eight notes. My ear picks out each one. The potoo is only one of the many nocturnal birds singing tonight. The trees seem to nearly vibrate with their song.

Less than five minutes after leaving Ai'oa, Eio slows. My hand is still in his, and our palms are slippery from the humidity. But neither of us lets go.

When we emerge from a thick stand of palms and come to a halt, I gasp in wonder. Eio has brought me to a river. *The* river. This must be the Little Mississip.

The water is still and silent; if it weren't for the gentle waves brushing the bank, I'd never even know it was flowing. When I look up, I see more sky than I've ever seen before, because the river is so wide that the canopy cannot stretch over it. The exposed band of night is laced with stars. The river, too, is full of them, ten thousand reflections glittering down its dark blue-gray length.

There's no one here but us. Us and the stars and the river. We walk to the edge, until the water nearly licks our feet. Alai crouches on the bank and drinks.

"I never . . ." I stop, the words turning to cotton in my throat, and shake my head. It's too much. I can't put words to what I see. I dare not try, lest my inability to articulate some-how lessen the enchantment.

Eio watches me curiously, and I can tell he's surprised at my reaction. "You've really never been outside that fence, have you?"

I shake my head. His fingers brush my face; he's wiping away tears. I didn't even know they were there. "It's beautiful," I whisper. "It's . . . it's almost too much. What's down there, I wonder?" I point to where the river bends away. "Where does it end?"

"The sea," he replies. "And the city. I've been to the city, you know."

"You have?" My eyes grow wide. "What's it like?"

He shrugs. "I didn't go in. Just to the edge. Papi told me to find it, so I went, saw it, and came back."

"Why would he want you to do that?"

"He said it was part of a plan, but he wouldn't say more. I was glad to do it. No Ai'oan has ever gone that far, so after my journey, they called me Eio Farwalker."

"That's a . . . nice name," I say, since he seems quite proud of it.

"The Three did not want me to go, but when it comes to a choice, the father must be obeyed first. Burako, the headman, was afraid it was a trick to make me a foreigner like my Papi. All my life, the Three have worried about this, since I look more like a foreigner than an Ai'oan, and in the past there have been Ai'oans who left the village and never came back. The scientists promised to take them to cities, to let them ride in airplanes and trains, and they listened and turned their backs to Ai'oa and disappeared into the outside world. I have never known an Ai'oan who did this; these ones left long ago, before I was born, but Burako feared that if I left, others would desert too, and the village would lose many more. I'm not allowed to talk about the journey, or the city, in Ai'oa. Burako wants me to be completely Ai'oan." He tosses a pebble into the river. It skims the surface and nearly makes it to the other side. "But no matter what rules he makes, I'm still half-*karaíba*."

"I see." *Eio is an outsider in his own village, like I am an outsider in mine.* "Where is your mother?"

"She died when I was little. I don't remember her well. Achiri became my mother, as she does for all the motherless in Ai'oa. It's her job, as Third of the Three."

"It's amazing," I whisper. "Your world. It's so close to mine, and yet it's so different."

He stares up at the stars. "It is wrong, Pia. They shouldn't keep you trapped like a pet bird. You should have seen this long ago." His gaze falls to the river. "We call it *Ymbyja.* Star-water."

"*Ymbyja*," I repeat softly. The word is filed into my memory, where it will never be forgotten.

"Look," Eio says. He takes my hand and holds it up against the sky. "See there? That group of stars?"

I nod.

"We call that the hunter. And there"—he shifts my hand so that I'm pointing at another cluster of stars—"that's the armadillo." He lowers my hand, but doesn't let go. "We have a story in Ai'oa, about how the hunter chased the armadillo through the sky until the armadillo hid in a hole. When the hunter dug into the hole to find it, he dug too deep and broke through the bottom of the sky and fell to the earth, where he found the river and the trees. He led his tribe down to the earth, and they became the first people."

Hardly a scientific explanation for the origin of mankind, but out here in the night jungle, under the starry sky, the story is enchanting instead of ridiculous. Uncle Paolo might laugh at it, but it fills my heart with a sudden mysterious longing, as if some part of me wants to believe it's true. "So is that the Ai'oa? Do you believe you're descended from that first tribe?"

"Of course not." He laughs. "That was a long, long time ago. And who knows if it's even true? But we started somewhere, didn't we? There must have been a first people at some point in time. Which means that everyone on earth is descended from them and that, in a way, we're all connected, because in the beginning we were one people. One tribe." He looks at me sidelong and smiles. "So you see, we're really not that different after all."

"I guess when you look at it that way," I admit.

"We live different lives," he says, "but we're all human. Our roots are grounded in the same earth."

I stare at him for a long moment. *But what if you're not quite human?*

We end up sitting on the bank for a long while, staring from the river to the sky, from the sky to the river. I think Eio is trying to see it the way I see it, but I don't think he can. I've heard of a condition called sensory overload. I think I'm experiencing it now.

But instead of feeling overwhelmed by all these new sights, I feel a warm, peaceful calm flood me from head to toe, as if I've been coming here all my life. As if this river and these stars were a memory I've always had inside me and am only just now recalling.

As if sitting on the thick, fragrant moss beside a boy as warm and beautiful as the sun were something I did every night. I marvel at how perplexingly new and familiar it all feels.

Before long, I realize that Eio is staring at me more than the river. My cheeks grow warm, just as they did this morning in my room, and I try to ignore him. But soon, I'm staring back. The stars reflect on the river, and the river reflects in Eio's eyes.

"Have you ever thought about running?" Eio asks softly. "Not going back to Little Cam?"

My breath stops, reverses. "Of course not."

"But why? Why would you go back to a place that forbids *this*?" He points at the river. "Why do you choose your cage?"

"It's not a cage. Not . . . not really."

He studies my eyes. "What do they want with you, anyway? What need do scientists have of a *Tapumiri*? Or are there more of you trapped in there?"

"Don't you know? Hasn't your father told you?"

"He doesn't talk about what's inside the fence," Eio replies stiffly.

"Well, I'm the only . . . *Tapumiri* that exists. There are no others. Yet."

Eio lifts his eyebrows. "Yet?"

"Little Cam . . ." I draw a deep breath. This is our most closely guarded secret, but he already knows most of it, thanks to Kapukiri. All the Ai'oans do. *And guess what, Uncle Paolo?*

They haven't locked me up. They aren't invading Little Cam, trying to steal all your research. What do you say to that? My next thought runs through me like a chill. *And what would you do if you knew they knew?*

"Pia?"

"Huh?" I realize suddenly how I must look, stopping in midsentence and staring dull-eyed at nothing while my thoughts crash and collide inside my head. "Oh, sorry. I was telling you that I'm the only one like me. But see, I won't always be. In Little Cam, we're going to make more immortals. More *Tapumiri*, I guess you'd call us. That's why it's not wrong for them to keep me inside the fence, Eio. They need me, and I need them. I need to help them make more immortals, because until I do . . . I'll be alone. The only one of my kind in the world. The only way I'll ever belong anywhere is if I stay in Little Cam and help create more *Tapumiri*. Do you understand?"

He frowns and looks out at the water.

"Eio? What's wrong?"

"You're going to *make* immortals?"

"Well, yes. That's what I just said."

"How?"

"Ah . . . I'm not really sure. They haven't told me yet," I confess. "It's a secret. They don't want anyone to steal their research, so they're very careful about guarding the information."

He studies me with a strange look on his face, as if he can't decide whether I'm telling him the truth or not. He must reach a decision, though, because his expression transforms into sudden comprehension. *What* he's just seen, I cannot make out.

"You don't know, do you?" he says. "About the origin of *yresa?*"

"What?" *Yresa.* My memory retrieves the word. *It's what they call elysia.* "What do you mean, Eio?"

He seems shaken, but he only takes my hand and stands up, bringing me to my feet as well. "It's nothing. Don't worry about it. Listen. They are still beating the drums." He smiles, and the stars fill his eyes again. "Come and dance with me?"

How can I resist?

THIRTEEN

When I open my eyes, it is dawn.

My body freezes as my mind, sluggish with sleep, fights to comprehend what I'm seeing. I expect to see trees through the glass of my bedroom roof. The canopy is there, but no glass. The few specks of sky I can see are pale blue.

Realization seeps slowly through my mind. I am lying on my back, draped in garlands of flowers. Around me I hear the soft patter of bare feet on dirt and hushed voices. There is something narrow and hard under my head.

I sit up and see I was lying on Eio's outstretched arm. He sleeps soundly, his other arm thrown over his eyes. We are lying beside the warm remains of a fire, and several other bodies are stretched out around us. Most of the Ai'oans are still sleeping, exhausted after the long night of feasting and dancing, but a few women are moving around. There is no sign of Alai. The little girl who gave me the plantain last night is sitting a few feet away, weaving palm fronds together and watching me.

Oh, no, no, no . . . I scramble to my feet and yank off the garlands, horror turning my early morning lethargy into a rush of icy adrenaline.

It's dawn. No, past dawn, since the thick foliage of the rainforest prevents any light from reaching the jungle floor until the sun is well up into the sky. Everyone will have already eaten breakfast in Little Cam, and they'll have known immediately that someone was missing.

Me.

Eio wakes and yawns noisily, then laughs. "Pia bird, there is a mantis in your hair."

"Eio, why did you let me fall asleep?" I yell as I brush angrily at my hair. The mantis drops onto my hand and wags his long green antennae indignantly. I ignore him. I am trembling with rage and fear.

Eio frowns. "Let you? *I* asked you if you really wanted to sleep here in Ai'oa, and you said to leave you alone. Then you went back to sleep. *Let* you." He looks as indignant as the mantis.

"I have to go. Now." I drop the last of the orchids to the ground and start for the edge of the village. Several Ai'oans stare as I pass them. "Alai!" I call, but the jaguar doesn't appear.

Eio trots after me, slinging his bow over his shoulder and calling for a boy to bring his arrows. "I'll come with you."

"I don't need you." I know it's not his fault, but I can't help being angry with him. After all, if it weren't for him, I may have never sneaked back into the jungle.

He follows me anyway, and once we're in the trees, he darts around me and leads the way, even though I remember every step. I don't argue, but I ignore him as thoroughly as if he weren't there at all. In this fashion we storm our way through the jungle, making more noise than a pair of howler monkeys. I can tell that Eio is still hurt that I accused him of letting me sleep, but I refuse to apologize. There are too many knots and thorns in my stomach to worry about one native boy's wounded ego.

"Alai, come!" I yell again in panic. "Where is he? Alai!"

My imagination conjures image after image of what might be going on in Little Cam. They're searching my room. They find the map. They trace it back to Dr. Klutz. Now they're locking her up, asking her questions. . . .

I wonder that I can even think these things. After all, I've never seen Uncle Paolo punish anyone, beyond reprimands and maybe docking pay if a worker is consistently stepping out of line. Docked pay makes for very grumpy workers. No one likes to miss out on a chance to buy beer or new clothes when joining Uncle Timothy on a supply run, as nearly everyone does on occasion. But it's not as if we have a prison to lock rule breakers in.

Of course, no one's ever committed a crime worse than, say, stealing candy bars from the warehouse or breaking a piece of gym equipment and not confessing to it. Except for the Accident, of course. But Alex and Marian were never caught. If they were . . . I don't—can't—think about that. For the first time, I think I might understand a little of what they felt. Why they ran. I can't put words to it yet, but I feel, deep down, a spark of empathy where before I only felt pity and even disgust.

Finally Alai responds to my calls and emerges from a stand of heliconias. For an instant, I hardly recognize him for the feral look in his eye and the show of his fangs. But when he sees me, his appearance softens and I see my jaguar once more. I hug his neck, relieved he didn't run off for good to join his wild kin.

"I couldn't lose you, Alai. Don't ever do that again."

We are near Little Cam when Eio stops abruptly and turns to me.

"Will you come back?"

"I don't know," I confess. "I guess it depends on what happens when I get back. They know I'm missing. They must. They'll find the hole in the fence, and then they'll fix it. I'll have no way out."

"I'll climb the fence," he declares. "And bring you out."

"No, Eio! It's electrified. That means when you touch it—"

"I *know* what electrified is. My father *is* a scientist, you know. But I don't care." He takes my hands. "I will climb that fence, if you ask it of me, and I will bring you out."

With a little chill, it dawns on me that this is the nicest thing anyone has ever said to me. All those times I've been called perfect, and this means more than any of them. "Eio, I . . . thank you. But I don't ask it of you. I like my home and the people there. Little Cam isn't evil, no matter what Kapukiri says. One day I'll bring you inside so you can see for yourself. Maybe your father will help me. I wish you would tell me more about him. I'm sure I'd know him just by a description."

Eio's eyelids slide down, his long dark lashes a curtain to block me out. "I told you already. He is ugly, like all foreigners."

"Except me?"

He shrugs. "Go, Pia bird, before you are shot down by an arrow."

"You're so dramatic." But his words are like an arrow themselves, one made of ice. "Good-bye, Eio."

"For the last time?"

I don't know what to say to that. "You better go. If they're scouting around the compound for me, I don't want them to find you."

"Why? I thought there was no evil in Little Cam," he challenges.

"There's not! But you aren't supposed to be here! Little Cam is a secret place, and I'm the most secret part of it. If they found out you knew too much about me, they might . . ."

"Yes?"

"I don't know, Eio, and I don't want to find out." He's making me angry. Why won't he go? Why does he insist on trying to make me doubt the people who raised—and created—me? *And why is it working?* "Go, Eio! Go now!"

Without a word, he turns and vanishes into the jungle. Once he's gone, I feel a fleeting tug at my heart, as if it wants me to follow him.

I make my way through the dense foliage until I see the glitter of the fence and the buildings beyond. I'm near the hole, and since I can't hear any shouts or see anyone scouting the perimeter, I think perhaps I might have a chance of sneaking back in after all.

But when I reach my escape hole, I stop dead and stare in horror, then grab Alai before he can run ahead.

The area is thick with men and women, scientists and workers and uniformed guards. They've discovered the hole, that much is obvious. Do they suspect I found it first?

I slip into the trees, hoping some of Eio's ability to melt into invisibility has rubbed off on me. Hardly daring to breathe, I creep closer to investigate, keeping a tight hold on the jaguar's collar.

Uncle Paolo and Uncle Antonio are both on the scene. Neither looks happy. Their faces are red, and they bristle like the Grouch and Alai when they are facing off in the menagerie. Are they angry at each other or at me? I suspect the latter.

The fallen ceiba tree has been cut up and removed, and several men are in the process of filling in the hole and straightening the fence. They must have turned off the electricity in this section, because they're handling the chain link with bare hands.

When I shift positions, I see more of what's going on. My parents are there, and they look pale and quiet from where they stand on the other side of the fence. Behind them, I see my glass bedroom, empty and, I notice for the first time, extremely open and vulnerable. I can see everything within. The corner where the chair sits, covering the map beneath the carpet, looks undisturbed, which fills me with relief. I'm in plenty of trouble without having to worry about explaining that too.

I have to get closer to find out what they're saying about me. Everyone is probably thinking of the Accident, wondering if it's happened all over again. I start to wish I'd never left last night, that I'd listened to my own sense and stayed put inside Little Cam. But then I think of Eio and the children of Ai'oa, and my spirit rises up stubbornly and crosses its arms. *I'd do it again.*

From the looks of things, though, I might not have that option. I run through my short list of possible next moves.

Walk out now and face them all. Confess everything, even the map, and swear I'll never, ever do it again.

Walk out now and face them all. Confess everything and swear I *will* do it again, whether they like it or not.

Run away. Go native, perhaps, and this time for good.

I don't like any of the options. But there seem to be no more alternatives to choose from. So instead, I opt for stalling. Wait and watch. Something has to present itself.

By staying low to the ground and moving at the speed of a particularly lethargic three-toed sloth, I manage to get within hearing range of the group by the fence without drawing any attention.

"We don't know for sure she went through," Uncle Antonio is saying.

"We have to plan for every possibility. She could be miles from here by now, Antonio. Miles!" Uncle Paolo runs his hands through his hair, looking more agitated than I've ever seen him. "I can't lose her! She means everything to this place! Without her, Little Cam, the research, all of it means nothing! Think of what Strauss will say! Oh god, what will *Strauss* say?"

Strauss? I've never heard of anyone called that, not in Little Cam.

"Calm down, Paolo," Uncle Antonio replies. "She's probably in the compound somewhere. We can't jump to conclusions."

"Conclusions! We searched inside the fence for hours! She sneaked out. It's the only explanation, Antonio. I knew we should never have taken down the cameras in her room. Clarence! What is taking so long? Get a damn bulldozer if you have to, just get that hole filled in!" Uncle Paolo paces back and forth, right and left, never stopping for a moment. "I should have known this would happen. I've made too many concessions. That party was a fool of an idea! She needs a stricter schedule, more supervision. . . . Maybe we should reinstall the cameras. Never mind the fuss she makes, she's spoiled enough. . . ."

Uncle Antonio is stone-faced as he replies, "She's not a *rat*, Paolo."

This time Uncle Paolo does stop pacing, and he and Uncle Antonio stare at each other with venom I'd never even suspected lay between them. I've never known the two to be chummy or anything, but now I realize that there may be much more animosity between them than they normally show. There must be. The looks they give each other now seem much too heavy to be the result of just my disappearance.

Suddenly I'm struck with an idea. All these people outside the fence . . . they surely didn't get there by crawling through the hole beneath it. Which means they must have opened the gate. Which means it might still be open.

Hardly daring to breathe, I begin moving silently around

the perimeter of Little Cam. If I can get to the gate, and it's open, then I can sneak inside and come up with some kind of story . . . maybe I fell asleep beside the pool or got lost in a biology textbook in some dark corner. My thoughts run down three different tracks at the same time, pushing my mind into overdrive.

Maybe that's why I don't notice Harriet Fields until I've walked right into her.

FOURTEEN

"Pia!" She looks as startled as I am, and doubly so when she sees Alai.

I cringe and consider simply running away, but I'm well and truly spotted. I'm only a short dash from the front gate, which is indeed open, as I'd hoped, but I was so lost in my thoughts that I didn't bother checking behind every tree I passed. Dr. Klutz was reclining against one of them, smoking leisurely and apparently enjoying the spectacle my disappearance has created.

"Hello, Dr. Fields," I mumble, not knowing what to expect from her. Likely she'll run yelling for Uncle Paolo like a startled baby monkey for its mother.

"You've caused quite the ruckus," she says, relaxing again and tapping her cigarette thoughtfully to her lower lip. "Where have you been?"

I don't reply. The answer should be pretty obvious. I've been *out*, and that is strictly against the rules. I have no pay to be docked; will they withhold my supper instead? Or something worse?

"Sneaking out, my, my," murmurs Dr. Klutz. "Been a bad girl, Pia perfect."

"Are you going to tell?" I ask, hoping against hope.

She studies me for a long moment and sucks at her cigarette. I steal a glimpse at the gate. There is one guard, but he can't see us through the foliage. Unless, of course, Dr. Klutz were to start shouting. Which is entirely too possible.

"Tell you what," she says finally, flicking ash to the ground. "I've heard you calling everyone else around here *aunt* and *uncle*. Well, I'm as much in this thing as any of you now. Contract, remember? So. You start calling me Aunt Harriet, and I just might help you."

"Just *might*?" I say doubtfully, though I want to weep in relief.

"Say it." A smile sneaks onto her face.

I recall her dangerous birthday present and the trouble I could cause her if someone were to find it, and I give in. "Fine. Aunt Harriet. There. Will you help me now?"

She grins. "Once more. Come on. And not so grudging, girl. I've never done you any wrong."

Except given me a map that could get me in the worst trouble of my life. Well, present predicament excepted, of course. "Please help me get inside the gate, *Aunt Harriet*, and I swear I'll even *think* of you as Aunt Harriet instead of . . ."

"Of what?" She tips her head curiously. "Just what do you think of me as?"

"Uh . . . Dr. Fields, of course."

The look she gives me tells me plainly that this answer is

unconvincing, but I don't offer to amend it. She seems satisfied with my compliance, however, and nods crisply. "Well, then. Inside the gate we go! Wait here a tick."

She tosses her cigarette aside and flounces off through the bushes. Disgusted, I crush the still-burning little cylinder with my shoe, then watch to see what she will do. For all I know, she's telling the guard where I am right now. But no. She's pointing off in the general direction of Uncle Paolo and his crew, and the guard nods and shrugs and starts marching off, supposedly acting on orders Uncle Paolo never gave. Once he is out of sight, *Aunt Harriet* waves at me, and I cautiously emerge from the trees.

"You did it."

"Of course I did," she returns, looking a bit indignant. "I went to a damn all-girls private school. I *had* to learn every trick in the book when it comes to sneaking out, or else die of social deprivation."

Somehow, I can see her doing just that. "Well, thanks, anyway."

"You're welcome. Now are you going to scoot inside or will I have to kill the next person that comes along and sees you on the wrong side of the fence?"

"Kill them?" My mouth drops open. "But—"

"Not literally, Pia!" She throws her hands up in exasperation.

I go through the gate, hardly believing my good luck. After seeing everyone gathered around my secret exit and being so sure I wouldn't be able to sneak back in, I have no idea what to do now. They won't accept a simple explanation for my absence. To say that I was reading in the research library or working out in the gym will never satisfy Uncle Paolo, and having known me all my life, he'd see right through me in a heartbeat. And besides, I'm a terrible liar thanks to the fact that I never *do* lie. Until now, I've never had anything to lie about.

But there *is* someone apparently quite skilled at lying. . . . Though I hate having to go to her for yet another favor. Still, she's all I've got.

"Um, Aunt Harriet?"

"Yes?" She has a look in her eyes like she already knows what I'm going to ask, and it gives her no end of amusement.

Oh, come on, Pia. Swallow your pride and get it over with. "What, uh, should I say when they come in and find me?"

"Hmm. You need a story, and a good one. Several hours and no word or sign, and, let's face it, Little Cam isn't that big. They searched everywhere for you." She nibbles her lip and stares at me thoughtfully. "All right. I've got it. Come with me."

She takes off at a jog across the circular drive, and I follow and hope she knows what she's doing. I've no idea if I can trust her, but under the circumstances, it seems there's no choice. Aunt Harriet knows my secret, so for now, I'm at her mercy.

Once we're out of sight of the fence and anyone who might be patrolling it, she slows and walks beside me. "In situations like this, the best lie is the one that incites sympathy."

"What do you mean?"

"Well, if you were to say you fell asleep in a corner somewhere or were hiding on purpose, that would only make them angrier—and believe me, they're plenty angry already."

I nod, remembering the conversation I overheard between Uncle Paolo and Uncle Antonio.

"So," Aunt Harriet continues, "it's much better to think up a situation that, when discovered, will make *them* feel guilty. For example, a piano fell on top of you, and you couldn't move."

"What!" I stop and stare at her in horror.

"Oh, good grief, Pia, I was only kidding! But you get the idea?"

"I guess," I say, moving again, albeit with much more distance between us, just in case she does decide to drop a piano on me.

"The trick is to get them to feel sorry for you. Sympathy is the best replacement for anger. So," she stops and waves a hand at the building we've stopped at. B Labs, the smaller of the two main research buildings in Little Cam, situated by the northeastern line of the fence. "In we go."

"Why? What's the plan?"

She doesn't answer, but leads me through the white, polished hallways without once looking back. Everyone must be out looking for me; the place is eerily quiet. Our footsteps strike off the floor to echo down the walls, and the tiles beneath my feet are so pristinely clean that when I look down it's as if I'm looking in a mirror. The white doors we pass are all simply marked LAB 114, LAB 115, LAB 116, and they're punctuated with smaller, windowless supply and janitorial closets. Above us, the florescent lights burn as steadily and relentlessly as the sun. Uncle Paolo hates nothing so much as a faulty lightbulb, and whenever one shows the first sign of giving out, he has Clarence change it.

Finally she stops and puts her hands on her hips, staring around with a perplexed look. "Where's that refrigerator room . . ."

"Lab 112?" I say. "It's that way—"

"What's in here?" she interrupts, heading for a door at the end of the hallway.

"Don't go in there," I say.

"Why?" Her hand hovers over the doorknob.

"That's the old wing. It burned years ago. No one uses it; it's just a husk."

"Really?" She studies the door curiously. "Strange. There's no fire damage to the outside of the building."

I shrug. "No one's allowed in there. It's dangerous."

She tries the knob, but it doesn't turn. "Locked."

"Aunt Harriet—"

Before I can stop her, she's slipped her cardkey through the door and the frame, and the door swings open. I almost warn her again not to go in, but my curiosity overwhelms me. I follow her slowly.

The hall beyond is dark and dusty and lined with doors that have little windows in them. Aunt Harriet tries the first one; it opens easily. The room is small and dim, and we can just make out a bench against the far wall. There is no evidence of fire anywhere, but the room looks old and certainly abandoned. It's too small to be a lab or a dorm room and too large to be a supply closet. The wood floor has at least an inch of dust coating it.

Aunt Harriet points wordlessly at the bench. Iron chains, rusty with age, hang over its sides like old bones. Long grooves run down the length of the wood, like marks left by fingernails.

A chill runs down my spine as if it is being raked by those same nails. This room is like none I know in Little Cam. It is too cold and dark and lonely, and there are secrets here I don't want to learn.

"Let's keep looking." Aunt Harriet goes back to the hall-way, and reluctantly I follow. The next room is nearly identical to the first. The one after that has no bench, but it does have more scratches—these ones on the wall, starting at head height and streaking downward. The next room has dark stains on the wood floor and a faint metallic scent in the air.

Every hair on my head seems to be standing on end by now, and when Aunt Harriet starts for the next door, I shake my head. "No more."

Aunt Harriet simply nods. We tiptoe back into the lit hall as if afraid of waking some sleeping monster.

Back in the light, with the door shut securely against the shadows, we stand and stare at each other.

After a minute, I whisper, "I didn't like how it felt. It made me feel . . . cold."

She nods, her face white. "I've seen rooms like those before."

"Where?"

She shakes her head and seems unwilling to speak more of it. "Pia, do you have any idea what that wing was used for?"

"No. They said it was labs and storage, all lost in the . . ." *The fire that never was.* "Why would they lie?" I whisper.

Aunt Harriet doesn't reply, just watches me with a strange, distant gaze. "We need to hide you."

"Oh, yeah." I try to shake off the dark mood that clamped onto me, leechlike, when we entered the hall on the other side of the door. We find Lab 112 and the row of walk-in refrigerators inside—refrigerators that cannot be opened from within. I see Aunt Harriet's plan immediately. It's a good one, but it won't be any fun for me.

With a sigh, I slip into one of them, wishing I could think of a better idea. Aunt Harriet pauses before closing the door.

"Pia . . ."

"Yes?"

"You know, I've been given a small lab near the front gate to do my research in."

"Yeah. So?"

"Well," she lifts her eyebrows meaningfully. "I *could* ask for a certain someone to join me once in a while . . . for educational purposes, of course. Several hours a day, when everyone thinks you're safe and sound with me . . ."

I meet her gaze and understand what she's offering. She can't possibly know what I was up to in the jungle, but she's extending a way for me to go back to it, if I want. But I'm not sure *what* I want right now. So I just give a little, noncommittal nod. She returns the nod and says nothing more on it. "I'll wait an hour or so, then casually ask if anyone thought to check in here. You'd better be prepared with an explanation for getting yourself in such a stupid situation by then, okay?"

I nod.

"Aunt Harriet," I say "Why are you helping me like this?"

She pauses and starts to say something, then covers it in a grim smile. "See you in an hour, Pia."

And she shuts the door.

There's a small window in the door, but it's too frosty to reveal much more than the opening and closing of the lab door as Aunt Harriet leaves. Resigned now to my hour of torture, I turn and survey the little room.

There are two sets of metal shelves on either side of me, filled with plastic containers labeled with complex codes of letters and numbers and even colorful stickers. I chose this refrigerator for a reason, and that reason sits on the second shelf about three feet down from my left arm. It's a container of samples of *Anopholese darlingi*—mosquitoes—which I've been using in my studies of malaria with Uncle Haruto and my father. One of our sessions was scheduled for today; I'll say I wanted to get an early start and accidentally shut the door behind me.

As I sit and shiver on the floor of the refrigerator, I can think only of the intense heat of the Ai'oan fires, so much stronger, wilder, and more dangerous than the electric heaters we use in Little Cam. I'd start a fire in here now, but there's nothing to burn except tissue samples, and they'd hardly last ten minutes.

I wish we had more open fires in Little Cam, just like I wish we had children. No one talks about them here. If any of the workers or scientists here have them, they never mention them. I guess they probably never had any, or maybe they all grew up and moved away; why else would their parents leave them? I already feel like the world is a little darker without their laughter and nonsense games around me. I envy Eio and his life with the children and wonder how my own life would be different if I had had other kids my age to play with as I grew up.

But Little Cam is not a place for children. There is

nowhere for them to run and play, and anyway, Uncle Paolo says anything that doesn't contribute to research here is extraneous and unnecessary. He would say that children only get in the way and break things and distract you from your real work. When I was little, I had Uncle Antonio following me everywhere, keeping me out of everyone's way and making sure I didn't interrupt important experiments. We spent our time in the social center, mostly. He taught me how to swim, read, add, subtract. I imagine all of the Ai'oan children trying to sit for as long as I did with Uncle Antonio, finding square roots and doing long division. It would be a nightmare. They have more wild energy than I ever had—or maybe I did have it, but without other kids, I never learned how to express it. All I knew was how to be an adult, and not just any adult, but a scientist. Even as young as four I was being trained to take my place on the Immortis team.

I tell myself that Uncle Paolo must be right. My enchantment with the littlest of the Ai'oans is only me letting my emotions get out of control. And *there is nothing so dangerous as the loss of control,* Uncle Paolo's voice echoes in my thoughts, repeating one of his favorite sayings.

Deep inside, I know I'm really only thinking about all of this in order to keep a different thought at bay: the thought of that dark hallway and the little rooms, the odd chains and scratch marks on the wooden bench. *What about the fire? Why would they lie to me?*

And one question chills me more than even the refrigerator I'm trapped in: *What are they hiding?*

To stop myself from thinking so much, I start pounding on the door as if I'd been doing so all day. I beat so long and hard against the relentless metal, laced as it is with frost, that I almost begin to believe my own lie. I'm certainly cold enough to be fooled.

When the door opens, I'm half-frozen and so desperate to get out that my fists keep pumping for several seconds after they've wrapped me in blankets. Once I realize that I'm well and truly out and that Uncle Antonio and Mother and Uncle Paolo and Aunt Harriet are all there raining concern down on me, I calm down enough to stammer out my explanation for having been there in the first place. The fake one, of course.

I'm relieved when they don't interrogate me further, and I tell myself that the look Uncle Paolo and Mother exchange is nothing more than coincidence. And that the fierceness of Mother's grip on my shoulder as she escorts me from the room is nothing more than maternal concern for her half-frozen daughter.

Aunt Harriet never so much as blinks.

FIFTEEN

Two days pass. I remain terrified that someone will realize it was all a cover-up, and Aunt Harriet and I will be hauled into Uncle Paolo's office. But nothing happens outside of the usual routine—excepting the box of matches that I steal from the kitchen when Jacques isn't looking.

In the privacy of my room, with my door securely shut, I stand in front of the mirror, pull a match from the box, and strike it. I'm not sure what I'll see, or if I'll see anything at all, but since Ai'oa, I can't get Eio's words out of my head: *"The mark is only seen by fire."*

I hold the match a few inches from my nose and watch for something to happen.

Nothing does.

So I lean closer, until I'm almost nose to nose with my own face, and lift the match higher.

And I see it, just as the match burns to my fingers. I wouldn't have noticed the flame on my skin if it hadn't finally snuffed out. The tips of my fingers are warm, but unmarked by the fire. I strike another match—one, two, three times before it lights—and nearly stick it in my eye, I'm so shaken by what I saw.

It almost looks like firelight reflecting in my eyes. Almost. But the small flame of the match is still and steady, unlike the shifting bursts of gold and violet in my irises. I've never seen them before. Never even suspected. And I'm sure no one else in Little Cam has either. Uncle Paolo has certainly never mentioned the swirling flames. But there they are, tiny lights eddying and blooming against the blue-green of my irises. When I hold the match away, they disappear, but as soon as I bring it back, they're there again. The colors of elysia, trapped in my eyes, blossoming and circling and fading like fire, like water, like smoke.

So this is the mark of jaguar, mantis, and moon. The sign of the Ai'oans' *Tapumiri*. Hand shaking, I blow out the match and drop it into the wastebasket. For a moment, I stand and stare at myself with my now normal gaze. *What other secrets are hidden inside me?* I slowly run my hands down the sides of my face, but I don't know what more I expect to see. Antennae sprouting from my hairline? Scales forming on my cheeks?

In desperate need of a distraction, I decide to go for a swim, though simply walking from my house to B Dorms, where the pool is, could be categorized as a swim. The rain comes down in blankets, and in minutes I'm completely drenched. I strip off my T-shirt and walk in my bathing suit.

The pool is deserted, just how I like it.

I toss my wet tee and shorts on a chair and walk slowly so as not to slip on the tile. The water is blue and still. There is something irresistible about the unbroken, calm waters of a pool. I balance on the edge and relish the anticipation of breaking that serene surface. In the waters below, my own undulating image beckons for me.

My arms stretch out, my hands meet above my head, and I leap into a curving dive that raises hardly a splash. The water is cool and smooth and swallows me whole.

I swim several leisurely laps, alternating between easy breaststrokes and floating on my back. The ceiling above is glass, like my bedroom's, and pebbled with rain.

I have been so preoccupied with *not* thinking about the villagers—lest someone see the truth in my eyes—that I haven't been able to truly reflect on what happened. Now, when I reach for the memory, it comes to me like the remembrance of a dream: hazy, foreign, and impossible.

Did I really do it? Was I there? Was it real? There is an ache in my heart when I think of the wild, vivacious people. I realize I miss them already. Now that the hole in the fence has been repaired, I doubt I'll see them again. There are so many questions I want to ask them. How long have they been here, so near Little Cam? What must they think of us scientists? I think back to what Eio said: *"Why else would the spirits send an undying one?"*

I grab the edge of the pool and wipe the water from my eyes, feeling a chill that doesn't come from the water. *Have there been others like me?*

And do they still exist?

The question is new and unexpected, something no one in Little Cam has ever asked before, at least not to my knowledge. Could the people of Ai'oa know more than anyone here has ever suspected? Has anyone ever thought to ask them? After all, this is their land. If anyone were to know the secrets of elysia, wouldn't it be them? I'm overwhelmed with the questions I want to ask Eio if I see him again.

Eio.

The questions suddenly seem less important than the person, and the chill dissolves into an unexpected warmth.

Eio is nothing like anyone I've ever known in Little Cam. He's my age, for one, but that's not what makes him different. He's not quite Ai'oan, and he's definitely not a member of Little Cam; he seems more a part of the jungle than anything else. Maybe that's just my first impression of him coloring my opinion, since I first met him in the rainforest.

I let go of the edge and float on my back, watching the rain streak the glass overhead, imagining it dripping down the walls into the pool. Me swimming in the same rain that falls on Ai'oa. And on Eio. The boy with nut-brown skin and eyes the color of rain. The boy who showed me the other side of the world. Even now, I can imagine his touch on my skin when we danced and the warmth of his arm under my head as I slept.

I want to see him again. I *need* to see him again. I want to see Ai'oa and Luri and the Three and the dances around the fires, but mostly I want to see Eio. To ask him questions, yes, but also to listen to him talk in his beautiful accent. To hear his stories of hunting anacondas and stalking jaguars through the jungle. His life is so different from mine, I doubt I could ever understand him fully. But that only makes my fascination stronger.

Who is this jungle boy? What is he to me?

Nothing, a sharp, critical voice hisses from within, surprising me with its virulence. *And he must remain nothing. He is a danger. A wild card. An uncontrollable variant. Not for you. Not for you.*

It is my scientist voice, the voice I use when answering Uncle Antonio's quizzes or when describing what I see through a microscope in the lab. The voice makes me angry, makes me want to stamp my feet like a child, but instead I meekly slide into the water headfirst, like an otter, and sink to rest cross-legged on the bottom.

Can an immortal drown?

I don't find out, because as soon as I run out of breath, I press my feet against the bottom and break the surface, breathing deeply of the moist air.

Back in my room, I dry off and change into flannel plaid pants and a tank top, then throw myself across the bed and prepare to laze the evening away. Swimming isn't exhausting—nothing is—but I'm bored with the gym and the lounge and everything else in Little Cam right now. Which isn't a problem I've ever had before. It seems there has always been something to do in Little Cam. One of the things Uncle Paolo is especially careful to avoid is me getting bored. When you have to live forever, it's not a good sign to grow uninterested in life at only seventeen.

After confirming that my mother is out of the house, I retrieve my map from under the carpet in the corner and spread it across my bed.

I am tracing the landmass called Asia with my index finger, memorizing its contours, when I hear a sharp *tat.*

Immediately I crumple up the map, not bothering to follow the folding lines, and stuff it under my pillows. Horrified that my secret is out, I look around. No one at the door. Or in the hall. When I call out, no one answers back from the quiet house.

I go back into my room and have almost decided it was only a nut falling on the roof when I hear another *tat*. Then *tat tat tat*. By the second one I've pinpointed the noise. It's coming from the widest of the glass walls.

When I stand at the window and place my hand on the glass, the next stone hits squarely where my palm is. With a little yelp I leap back and instinctively look at my hand, but of course the pebble bounced off the glass.

"Eio?" I say incredulously, though there's no way he can hear me.

He's standing on the other side of the fence, and when he sees he's got my attention, he drops the rest of the stones in his hand. His mouth moves, but I can't read his lips. I press against the window and shake my head at him, all the while thinking in the back of my mind how glad I am that I changed out of my swimsuit in the closet and not in the bedroom as I sometimes do.

"What are you doing here?" I mouth slowly, but I can see that he isn't understanding. My heart fluttering with trepidation that he'll be seen as well as with excitement that *I* can see him, I hold up one finger, then both hands with palms toward him, until he nods and stands still. *Wait*.

It takes less than a minute to run out the front door, scope the area and find it clear, then navigate around the house to where Eio stands inches from the fence.

"Don't touch it!" I cry out softly when I see him move forward. He pulls away at the last second, and I exhale in relief. I have no desire to see him get fried before he can even explain himself.

"Where have you been, Pia bird?"

"What are you doing here?" I say at the same time.

We each wait for the other to go, then both start again simultaneously. After a moment's confusion, I finally get in, "I couldn't come back, Eio."

"Are you angry with me still?" He looks genuinely concerned.

"No, of course not. It was my fault anyway, Eio, not yours. I should have come home much earlier. Maybe then they wouldn't have found the hole." I point at the recently upturned dirt and misplaced stones around where we stand. "They filled in my way out, Eio. I can't get escape again."

"You must come back!" he insists. "There's so much I want to show you. Waterfalls and caves and—"

"Eio . . ." My heart somersaults with longing, and for a moment, I imagine myself vanishing into the rainforest with him. *An uncontrollable variant,* my inner scientist warns again. *Don't get carried away.* My instincts war with one another. *Run. Stay.* I stare into Eio's mortal eyes, and I feel a tug in my stomach, as if a string has been tied to me and is pulling me back toward Little Cam, away from the unknown. "I . . . I'm not Ai'oan, Eio. My place is here. I'm sorry. I can't come back with you."

He stands back and stares at me for a while. "They've tamed you like a monkey. Trained you to fetch nuts and sit on their shoulders, and now you would rather live on a leash than run free through the treetops."

"That's not true! It's my choice, Eio."

"So says the monkey."

"Eio!" He's so infuriating! Can't he see that more than just a fence divides us? I remember how I lost myself in the Ai'oan dance, those few captivating moments when I felt like I belonged. The sense of forgetting who I was and blending into the crowd was utterly seductive—but the spell was broken the moment my immortality was brought up. "I have no place in your village or in your people's hopes. I told you. I'm immortal. I belong here."

"I don't care about that," he responds. "I want *you*, Pia. You are the first one like me. You belong everywhere and nowhere. Not a scientist, not an Ai'oan. A wild girl. A jungle girl. But still you choose your cage."

I bite my lip, resist the urge to bang my head into the fence in conflicted frustration. "Eio, go home. If they see you here they'll make you leave, and I doubt they'll do it nicely. Please go."

"I can climb these walls and help you out."

"You can't. They're electrified."

He shrugs sullenly.

With a sigh, I say, "It's not that I don't like you or your people. I do. Really, I do. But I can't get out now. The hole is fixed. There's no way out."

"If you found a way, would you come?"

"If I found a way," I promise, wondering why it is that every time he begs, I give in, making promises that tear my reason and my heart in two different directions. *What is your fascination with me, boy, that you won't leave me alone?*

The same fascination I have with him, probably, but I keep that to myself. "Go back now, Eio. Please."

He stares into my eyes for a long while, and I wonder what he thinks he'll find there. Then he turns and melts into the jungle. My heart lurches in my chest as if trying to pull me after him, but the fence is in the way. Always, there's the fence in the way. I want to grab it and shake it, never mind the electricity, but then the alarm would go off, and Uncle Timothy would start asking questions. . . .

When I turn back to the glass house, I feel a raindrop fall down my cheek and onto my lips. It tastes of salt.

SIXTEEN

The next day, I'm supposed to be sketching and then dia-gramming the flowers in the garden between A Labs and B Dorms, but instead, I'm drawing faces. I have an hour to complete the assignment from Uncle Smithy, but it will really only take me fifteen minutes, so I don't worry about the time.

First I draw Uncle Antonio, a square-jawed, hairy face that I've drawn many times. His beard makes him a favorite model of mine, and I enjoy the tediousness of drawing each tiny, individual hair. I also draw Mother and Uncle Will, but grow bored with their portraits before I finish. I'm not as good an artist as Uncle Smithy, who's the best in Little Cam. He says my eye for detail is my downfall; I focus too much on each individual aspect of a person and not enough on the whole of a person's appearance.

For the fun of it, I turn to a blank page and start sketch-ing randomly, with no certain face in mind. Anything's better than drawing yet another leaf or orchid, which I could draw from memory anyway.

My thoughts wander as I draw, until the movements of my pencil become part of the background. I think of Eio standing in the rain outside the fence; it's been three days now since I last saw him. I think of Aunt Harriet helping me cover up my night in the jungle and how angry Uncle Paolo would be if he found out about it. I think about the locked door in B Labs and the mysterious rooms behind it and wonder what the truth about them might be.

When I return from my mental walkabout, I look down at my paper and see Eio's face staring up at me. Shocked, I look over my shoulder to be sure no one's seen. Then, entranced, I study the product of my wandering thoughts.

There is more life in this picture than in any I've ever drawn. Perhaps I've finally discovered what Uncle Smithy calls the "release of tension" and found that artistic groove in which creation is spontaneous and natural. Eio's eyes are nearly as deep and full of life as they were that night in Ai'oa, and I have the sudden, fantastic notion that it's him looking out at me and not a picture at all.

Suddenly I hear voices, and I flip the page over. Uncle Antonio and Aunt Harriet are coming down the covered walkway that links all the buildings in Little Cam together. Aunt Harriet's arm is looped through Uncle Antonio's.

They see me and wave, and Aunt Harriet whispers something to him and then bounces toward me. Uncle Antonio watches for a moment, then continues into the lab building.

"Pia! Hullo, dear! What are you up to?"

"Sketching." I hold the papers close to my chest.

"May I?"

"Well . . . all right." I hand her all of the pictures except Eio's.

She nods and *hmms* over them, taking particular interest in Uncle Antonio's. "They're pretty good. A little . . . dry . . . but good. You've got to add emotion to make them great. Like the Mona Lisa."

"Who is that?"

"Probably someone your Uncle Paolo doesn't want you to meet. What's that?" She points at the paper still in my hands.

"Oh, nothing . . . it's not done yet."

"Let's see it!"

I almost refuse, but then my will weakens. I guess some part of me needs to share him with someone, and of everyone in Little Cam, Aunt Harriet seems least likely to go running to Uncle Paolo with it. *But I won't tell her who it is. Not that. That's too private.*

She takes the paper and nods at it for a while. "Now that's more like it. Emotion."

"You think so?" I look over her shoulder.

"Oh, yes. I wouldn't turn this in to whoever's in charge of you today. Might lead to questions. My, my, he *is* a hunk, isn't he?"

"A what?" The word is new to me.

"A hunk. A . . ." She gestures vaguely at the picture. "A hot guy."

I look at Eio's face again. My cheeks grow warm.

"That's the kind of face a girl wants to wake up to, if you know what I mean," sighs Aunt Harriet. "So who is he?"

"His name is Eio—" I slap a hand over my mouth. *Pia,*

you idiot! What was that? Talk about a lack of self-control . . . I have no idea what made me say it. Maybe the need to share is stronger than I'd thought. If I were alone, I'd smack myself in the head for being so stupid and reckless.

I now have Aunt Harriet's full attention. She turns to face me squarely, one eyebrow raised nearly to her frizzy hairline. "Oh?"

"Please, just give it back. It's nothing. My imagination, that's all . . ."

She hands it back, but a smile is creeping across her face like a red caterpillar on a leaf, slow but determined. "Quite an imagination for a girl who's barely seen a man under thirty."

"Not true," I protest, but the weakness in my voice is unmistakable. *I am seven kinds of idiot, I am.* "You won't tell?"

"I'll add it the box under my bed labeled 'The Secret Confessions of the Immortal Pia.' Good Lord, girl, don't look so mortified. There's not *actually* a box."

I gather up the rest of my drawings and wonder how I can get rid of them. There's nothing incriminating about my father's face, but I'd rather forget this whole episode altogether. Anyone could pull them out of a trashcan. What I really need is fire.

"Here, give them to me," Aunt Harriet commands.

I'm so flustered and paranoid that I give them to her. She casually glances around, but we're still alone. Then she crosses to the fishpond and drops the papers into the water. In moments, the images are blurred beyond comprehension. They might as well be harmless pictures of fern leaves.

"I didn't mean to draw him," I whisper. "I was just doodling. Not paying attention."

"Typical of a daydreamer," she says, gathering up the wet, ruined papers. "I had a friend in school who would stare out the window all through history class, absently doodling curse words across her exams. Needless to say, she failed the class."

"I've never studied history," I comment blandly, though the fact is completely irrelevant to my current predicament. I've never been in so many predicaments in such a short time in all my life. I worry, a little madly, that I'm doomed to live an eternity of rapidly accumulating secrets and dilemmas. How much tension can a person hold before they burst?

"I need a swim," I conclude, but then I remember the plants I'm supposed to be drawing, and my misery doubles.

Aunt Harriet studies me as if I were a jigsaw puzzle missing all the corner pieces. I *feel* like a jigsaw puzzle missing all the corner pieces.

"What you need," she says at last, whispering because Clarence is trundling past with a bin full of dirty towels, "is to think back on the offer I made you a few days ago."

It takes only a second for me to connect the dots. I sum her up warily, wondering where the catch is. "So you still need an 'assistant' to help you with your research?"

"Right-o."

I stare at the tops of my white sneakers, wondering if I'm as translucent as it seems. "How did you know?"

"That the boy in the picture probably has something to do with your disappearance?" She twists her lips wryly. "Oh, Pia, I know how a teenage girl's mind works. It wasn't *so* long ago that

I was a teenage girl myself, you know." She giggles. *Giggles*. Like one of the little girls in Ai'oa. "Once, in high school, I had three boyfriends at the same time. I remember a few nights when I had three dates in a row." She giggles again. "And, you know, not one of them ever found out about the others. I was that good."

"Boyfriends?"

She blinks. "You . . . don't know what a boyfriend is? Oh. Oh, Pia. Darling. You *are* sheltered, aren't you? A boyfriend is a . . . you know . . . a guy that you like and who likes you back. Well, more than likes."

I stare blankly.

"Oh, never mind. That's a lesson for another day."

Boyfriends. Huh. That'll be something to ponder later. I imagine having three Eios and decide Aunt Harriet is definitely nuts. One is hard enough to keep up with. "So . . . if I get permission to spend a few days a week with you . . ."

"And if you were to disappear for the better part of each day . . ."

"They might never even know." I reason it over like any good scientist would. "It would be tricky. I'd have to know exactly what you were doing every minute I was away, in case someone asked. We couldn't even once let an error slip."

"Easily done. As you've no doubt noticed, I'm an excellent liar."

"Would they even let me? After all that's happened . . ."

"There is one thing, Pia, that may always be relied upon when it comes to scientists like the ones in Little Cam."

"Yes?"

She grins and taps a finger to her nose. "Pride."

• • •

According to Aunt Harriet, Uncle Paolo and the Immortis team are so blinded by their success in creating me, they can't imagine me willfully crossing them. They've always been on the lookout for accidental corruptions of my mind and character, outside influences that would distract from my destined role as head of their team. But the thought of me purposefully thwarting their rules is as unfathomable to them as the idea of a paramecium waving its fist at them from beneath the microscope, refusing to be observed any longer, and marching off the slide.

I'm not sure I agree with her, but I go along. After all, her refrigerator idea worked out neatly enough. Perhaps there's more to Aunt Harriet than I initially gave her credit for. Whether I like it or not, she's fast becoming my closest confidant in Little Cam. And also the greatest threat to my future as a scientist—at least that's what Uncle Paolo would say if he found out about all the things she's said and done. Why, then, am I not running straight to him right now, confessing everything?

I suspect the reason has much to do with the fact I unconsciously drew Eio's face on that paper. I dream of my immortals, yes . . . but can't there be room in my heart for more than one dream?

We walk through A Labs, looking for Uncle Paolo. The thing I'm learning about Aunt Harriet is that she backs up her words with immediate and bold action. No sooner did I agree to accept her offer than she started charging off to make it final.

We find him—and the rest of the Immortis team—in none other than my own lab. My mother pores over several spreadsheets on the counter. Dr. Haruto Hashimoto, a severe but brilliant Japanese biochemist, greets us with his characteristic frown. Drs. Jakob Owens and Sergei Zingre smile warmly; they're the nicest of the team. I always feel a little swell of my own pride when I see them all together in their crisp white coats. *My team.* The minds behind my existence. I owe them everything, and one day I will be one of them.

As I look around, I find myself studying the structure of their faces and the colors of their eyes, comparing them to Eio's. *Does he belong to one of you?* My eyes flick back to Uncle Jakob, who is probably the most unpredictable of them all. It's definitely not Uncle Haruto.

"Pia, we were just about to send for you!" exclaims Uncle Paolo. "And Dr. Fields, hello. What brings you to us?"

"I need to talk to you, Paolo, if you please," says Aunt Harriet.

"Of course, what—"

"Alone."

He looks a little stunned, but he nods, and they step into the hall. Meanwhile, I'm left with the rest of the Immortis team. I think of what Eio said the first night we met, about family being more than just blood. I look around at these scientists who raised and mentored me, and I think I know what Eio meant.

Perching myself on a metal stool, I smile and tap Uncle Sergei's clipboard. "So why were you looking for me?"

Uncle Haruto answers in his stern tone, "We should wait for Dr. Alvez."

"Aw, Haruto, give it a rest," drawls Uncle Jakob. "She's as

much one of us as you are. There's no secret here." He turns to me, ignoring Uncle Haruto's disapproving scowl, and winks.

"We're going to have guests," he says.

"Guests? Who?" I sit up straight, heart quickening. "People from the outside?"

Uncle Jakob nods. "From Corpus."

"What's that?"

Uncle Haruto hisses warningly, but Uncle Jakob rolls his eyes. "Paolo was gonna tell her anyway. What's the harm? Corpus is the company that keeps this place running, Pia. They fund the research, send new scientists like Dr. Fields when we need them, stuff like that."

"And now they want to see *you*," Uncle Sergei says. "Corpus has not been to Little Cam for nearly twenty years, and now they are coming. It will be extremely important that we give our best impression. They don't like what they see here, they shut us down"—he smacks the table—"just like that."

"Shut us down?" The room suddenly feels cold. "They would do that? But—"

"Pia, Pia," Mother interrupts. "Don't be ridiculous. Of course they won't shut us down. Because you're going to show them that there is nothing in the world more important than Little Cam." Her eyes catch and hold mine. "Right?"

I know she means *Right, I'm going to show them*, but the look she gives me almost seems to ask, *There's nothing more important than Little Cam . . . right, Pia?*

"When will they get here?" I ask, averting my gaze from her all-too-penetrating stare.

"Three days," Uncle Jakob replies. He looks around the

lab, which is cluttered with old papers and empty coffee mugs, and sighs. "We have a lot of work to do."

"What work?" asks Uncle Paolo, as he and Aunt Harriet step back into the room. I watch her for some clue as to what the outcome of their conversation might be, but her face is blank.

"He told Pia about Corpus," Uncle Haruto says, throwing his hands in the air. "I *told* him to wait for you."

Uncle Paolo sighs and gives Uncle Jakob a hard look, but Uncle Jakob just shrugs. "Fine, then," Uncle Paolo says. "It's told now, and that's what matters. Pia, we'll all be busy the next few days, cleaning this place up and preparing for the guests. We'll need Antonio's help, so your usual lessons will be canceled. Instead, I've decided to assign you to Dr. Fields for now, at least until everything gets back to our normal schedule."

"Oh," I say casually. "Okay, then. If you think that's best."

He nods crisply. "Of course. I'd been thinking about it for a while now, anyway."

Over his shoulder, Aunt Harriet gives the slightest of winks.

SEVENTEEN

"Welcome, Pia!" Aunt Harriet says with a wide smile as I stare at her lab. It's in a building of its own, a small structure hardly bigger than Clarence's gardening shed; it used to hold spare Jeep and truck parts, which they moved to the garage to make room for Aunt Harriet. The place is a wreck. Papers are pinned haphazardly to the wall, cages with mice and rats are stacked in tilting towers in the corners, and nearly a dozen microscopes are lined across a long table in the center of the room. Aunt Harriet appears to be moving from one to the other with the speed of a bee buzzing from flower to flower. I wonder how she can possibly be learning anything of importance in all the clutter and confusion.

"So, what *are* you doing here?" I ask as I pick up a bleached lizard skull I nearly stepped on when I entered the room.

"Here?" She gives the room a frazzled glance.

"No, *here*. In Little Cam. Why are you here at all?"

Aunt Harriet frowns. "I'm a biomedical engineer, Pia."

"Yes, I know that. But what's all . . . *this* for?"

"Ah. Well, before I came to Little Cam, I worked for a company that researched cloning. You know what cloning is?"

"Yes," I reply, a bit insulted. "I know what cloning is."

"Well, how am I to know what they do and don't tell you? I suppose you've never heard of Dolly the sheep—"

"Dolly the sheep. Born the fifth of July, 1996, and died of progressive lung disease on February fourteenth, seven years later—"

"Okay, okay," Aunt Harriet waves a hand. "Enough. I get it."

"*You're* the one who cloned Dolly?" I regard her with new-found awe.

"Well . . . no. Actually, I had nothing to do with Dolly. But I did work in the same facility, and I saw her a few times, so . . . Anyway, I was pretty good at my job, and so they asked me to come down here. They never said exactly what it was I had to clone—at least, not until a few days after I arrived. Since then, of course, I knew all about the true purpose of Little Cam—you. So now they want me to research the possibility of cloning immortals."

"Cloning immortals," I whisper. "Of course. It's the perfect idea. We could—"

"Bypass the five generations of sitting around waiting, yes, yes. Exactly."

"Is it possible?"

She spreads her hands. "That's what I'm here to find out. Of course, my job would be much simpler if someone would just tell me the whole truth behind this place."

"You mean the old wing in B Labs?" I ask.

"That," she replies with a twitch of her brow, "among

other things. For example, what is this 'catalyst' everyone talks about but never produces? If I knew what it was that makes elysia safe to drink, I could progress in my research by absolute bounds."

"They haven't told me, either," I confess. "It's one of the reasons I want to be on the Immortis team so badly. They'll *have* to tell me."

"Well, until old Harriet's likewise proven herself, looks like I'm also to be in the dark. Oh, here, give me that." She crosses the room and takes the lizard skull out of my hands, then perches on the edge of her table—the only place clear enough for sitting in the room—and turns the skull over in her palm. "Don't you find it strange how mysterious all of this is? First this catalyst, then that hallway."

I nod, wishing I could disagree instead. "I'm sure . . . I'm sure it's all for a good reason, though. The secrets and the lies. There must be a reason or Uncle Paolo would tell us both the truth."

She studies me closely, as if curious what *my* skull looks like. "You really think so?"

"I . . . of course." I don't miss the moment of hesitation, and I can see that she doesn't either. But Aunt Harriet just pushes back stray frizz from her eyes and sighs.

"I guess all will be revealed in time, eh? Likely it's all some kind of dramatic display to make them feel important and mysterious. Don't be fooled by all the rigidity and sterilization, Pia. Scientists are showmen at heart—only more boring and with bad eyesight."

I nod uncertainly. "So . . . how exactly am I supposed to get out of here?"

"Oh, yes!" She jumps up, tossing the skull into a half-unpacked box of safety goggles. "I nearly forgot, caught up in all that cloak-and-dagger tripe. Come on, let's see if the coast is clear!"

The gate is only a stone's throw from Harriet's lab, and the stand of trees in the middle of the drive provides an excellent screen between it and the rest of Little Cam. The drive is empty, and the gate is attended by one lonely guard. He sits outside the fence, with his back to us. We stand in the doorway of the little lab, leaning against the frame and trying to look nonchalant.

"What about him?" I ask. "And how will you open the gate?"

"It'll be opened for us," is her confident reply. "Come on."

I follow her across the drive to the spacious tin-roofed carport under which the Jeeps are parked. She walks down the line of vehicles until she reaches the last one, which she taps on the hood. "Here it is. Every day, at lunchtime, one hulking guard will drive out to Falk's Glen to change shifts with another hulking guard. Same thing happens at dusk. Simply be on the Jeep heading out and come back with the afternoon shift, and you're golden. Of course, we can't use this method every time or you're bound to get caught. We'll just have to play it day by day. There's more than one way to skin a tapir." She laughs.

"There's nothing to hide under," I point out. "Do you have some canvas or blankets?"

"Psh! Use your head, Pia. Of course there's something to hide under." She pats the hood of the Jeep again.

Her meaning dawns in a flash. "Oh . . ."

"Oh, come now, it's even better than my refrigerator idea!"

I kneel and peer at the undercarriage of the Jeep. There are certainly plenty of ways I could wedge myself in.

"It'll get pretty hot under there, which would be a problem for most of us. But you shouldn't have any trouble with that." Harriet glances around. "Better hurry. He'll be along soon."

"Just because I can't get burned doesn't mean I can't feel heat!"

She turns a withering look on me. "Do you want to get out of here or don't you?"

With a sigh, I scoot under the Jeep and work my way into the undercarriage, trying to avoid touching more pipes and bars than necessary.

"This is the worst idea you've had yet," I tell Aunt Harriet.

"They're all busy getting ready for Corpus's visit, but it doesn't mean they're blind. Be back by dark. No later, or it will be both our heads on the chopping block. And my neck isn't quite so impermeable as yours."

"I promise."

"And don't get lost. Honestly, I swear, if you do, I'll find a way to chop your head off, immortality or not. He's coming! Got to go. Good luck!" She sticks her hand, thumb extended cheerily, under the Jeep, then dashes off. After a minute, I hear footsteps, see thick black boots, and feel the Jeep sink several inches when the guard climbs in. There's still nearly a foot of space between the ground and me, but it feels much, much closer. The engine starts, and my various handholds begin to rattle, but I grit my teeth and hang on tighter. At the last minute I grab my hair, which was hanging to the ground, and tuck it in my shirt.

I keep my eyes pressed shut so I can focus on holding on, but I can still hear the groan of the gate opening, then closing, and the rev of the engine as the guard driving the Jeep stomps the gas. It's all I can do not to drop to the ground, but then I'd have to explain why there are tire tracks across my stomach. *Better just wait.*

Finally the Jeep skids to a halt and the guard jumps down. After I'm sure he's well into the jungle, I lower myself to the ground and exhale long and slow. I don't think I took a single breath since leaving the compound.

The jungle looms over me as I rub dirt and rust from my hands. It takes me a moment to orient myself. Eyes shut, I mentally retrace the path I walked from Little Cam to Ai'oa and compare the distances and angles to the route the guard took in the Jeep.

"So it must be . . ." I face the direction opposite to the one the guard went. "That way."

I'm not hiking for long when Eio materializes from the leaves. He looks part jungle himself, with leaves tied around his neck, head, and arms. His khaki cargo shorts look as out of place as ever, especially with his face paint and jaguar necklace.

When I see him, a weight I never knew existed lifts from my chest, and I feel, for the first time in the past three days, that I can breathe again. I realize I'm grinning like an idiot, but I can't help it. "Eio!"

"Pia bird. You came." He stands a foot in front of me, staring at me as if he can't believe I'm here. "Burako said I should forget about you. That you'd probably forgotten me."

"Forget you? I couldn't forget you if I tried." *And not just because my memory is infallible.* With my fingers feeling as clumsy and awkward as if they were Alai's paws, I reach out and take his hand. Once I have it, his grasp feels as natural as putting on a glove, and I never want to let go. His touch is fire, sending sparks tingling up my arm. "Of course I came. I told you I would."

He looks at our entwined fingers and smiles. "So you found a way."

"With Aunt Harriet's help, yes."

"The crazy-haired one." He nods knowingly. "She helped you sneak back in."

"Oh, you saw that?" What has he been doing? Sitting in a tree outside Little Cam and taking notes all day?

"I knew you would come. Every day I came here and waited, but you took a long time. Kapukiri said you would come too."

This is the first time I've really been in the jungle during daylight. When I overslept in Ai'oa and had to run home, I didn't take even a moment to look around. Now, however, I stop dead and turn slowly in a full circle, eyes wide and thirsty to drink it all in.

Between mighty kapoks and slender cecropias, narrow vines swoop and drop and tangle over enormous leaves of palulus and anthuriums. The air is thick and damp, even more so than in Little Cam. It's almost like being underwater. Pale, vaporous mist haunts the darkness between low leaves and the forest floor like the ghosts Aunt Nénine fears. Orange and yellow lichen lays claim to anything that's dead and rotting, and where the lichen stops, the moss begins. There are probably a dozen different species of it right here in this spot.

Looking up, the sky is just a speckle of blue here and there, a realm so high above and so obscured by the jungle that it might as well be outer space. In the rainforest, the sky is made of leaves and branches, and instead of stars you have screeching monkeys and birds of every color. It is a living sky.

Most of all—and this is what I missed most during my nighttime wanderings—is the color. The rainforest is green on green on green; the color must have been invented here, and in a thousand different forms. Against the green wash, a shot of purple orchids or orange mushrooms stands out vibrantly, demanding attention. The only thing missing is Alai at my side, but it would have been impossible to sneak him out too.

Despite all the beauty around me, my eyes keep wandering back to Eio. He pushes every branch out of my path, careful not to let them swing back and hit me. Every time he does, water droplets rain down on his shoulders, beading his collarbone and the back of his neck. His dark hair is so damp it hangs in his eyes. My fingers itch to brush it aside.

We reach Ai'oa in less than an hour, thanks to Eio. I could have found it on my own, but it would have taken longer since I'd never been this way before.

The villagers don't flock to greet me this time. Some call out or wave, but there are no garlands of flowers or dances to welcome me into Ai'oa. I wonder if I'm welcome at all. Eio must see my hesitation, because he tells me that once a person's been given their welcome feast, they are forever a part of the village and are treated like one of the villagers.

"They think of me as Ai'oan?"

"In this sense, yes."

"Does every visitor get a welcome feast?"

He meets my eyes steadily. "No. Only you, because you have the mark, and my father, because he loved my mother and proved himself a friend to the village."

I'm not sure whether I should feel honored or frightened. If they think of me as one of their own, what must they expect from me? *Why did I come back here at all? Did I think we'd be dancing and laughing all day long, every time I came? What do I expect from them?*

"Eio," I whisper, "I don't know what to do."

He gives me a funny look, as if I'd asked him what blue smells like. "Just be yourself."

A little girl no higher than my hip runs up to Eio and leaps onto his back. He laughs and tries to tickle her, but she yanks his hair, and he stops. I recognize her from my last visit to Ai'oa; she was the one who hovered by my elbow for hours, watching everything I did with huge, curious eyes.

"Eio!" she squeals. "You brought her back! Like you said you would!" I smile at her. Her English is very good, and her Ai'oan accent softens the consonants and adds a sweet richness to the vowels that I'd never hear in Little Cam.

"If I say I'm going to the river to catch a fish," Eio replies, "I will always bring back a fish. Did you doubt me, Ami?"

"Not for a minute, but Pichira and Akue said you wouldn't, that the lightning fence would stop you." She peers at me over his shoulder. "Hello, Pia bird. Where's your jaguar?"

"Hello," I reply shyly. "Alai couldn't come today. Your name is Ami? It's very pretty."

"It means wicked," says Eio.

"It means perfect child." She looks from Eio to me with a

sly grin. "Eio says *you're* perfect, Pia bird. He says you're the most perfect girl he ever saw!"

Eio turns red and shakes her from his back, roaring that he'll feed her to an anaconda. She runs behind me, screaming and laughing, and, laughing with her, I shield her from him.

"He does?" I ask. "And what else does he say?"

She screws her lips up to her nose, thinking. "That your eyes are like bits of sky seen through the leaves. And that, like the rain washes the mud from the leaves, you . . . how did he say it? Oh, yes. That you wash the darkness from the world."

"He . . . he said that?" Now *I'm* the one turning red.

Eio grabs our hands. "Come on, you awful child. Let's show Pia where we swim."

EIGHTEEN

"**H**ere it is!" Ami announces.

I can already tell I'll never be able to enjoy my pool again, not after this. A crystalline waterfall about twenty feet high drops into a deep, still, turquoise stream. Orchids and heliconias hang over the water as if they're drinking from it, heavy with pink and red and purple blooms.

With a whoop, Eio climbs to the top of the waterfall and throws himself from it. The splash he makes drenches Ami and me.

"He is so dumb," says Ami. "Come on, Pia bird! It's no fun swimming with Eio; he only tries to splash me."

She grabs my hand and leads me downstream, about fifty yards from the waterfall, where the water is shallow and wide, racing over a pebbly bed. The stream sparkles golden in the sunlight filtering through the trees.

"This is our most secret place," she whispers as she kneels on the bank.

"What's so secret about it?" I ask.

"Look in the water."

I kneel beside her and lean over the stream, and I see it. It's not sunlight turning the water gold. It *is* gold. The pebbles at the bottom are flaked with glittering freckles; there must be several handfuls' worth of it.

"Is it real gold?" I ask.

She nods. "We can't tell anyone from the outside. The sight of gold turns *karaíba* into monsters, and they will destroy everything to get to it. That's what Achiri says. So we never tell the *karaíba* about it."

"I'm a *karaíba*," I point out, the Ai'oan word for *foreigner* already filed in my memory.

"Kapukiri says you have the tears of Miua in you, and that makes you one of us."

"But I live in Little Cam."

"You don't have to. You could live with us."

"I can't. Little Cam is my home."

"Then why do you come to Ai'oa?"

I turn away so that she can't see the conflict in my eyes. How do I explain to a seven-year-old that she represents everything I've been denied in Little Cam? *Because you are young and free and one with the jungle. You are mortal, but instead of clinging to the hope of immortality, you embrace each day, one at a time, and never worry about tomorrow.*

She kneels beside me, her feet tucked under her, and stares up at the sky. "Have you ever been in an airplane?" she asks suddenly.

I smile ruefully. "No. Not yet, anyway."

"Oh." She sighs wistfully. "I've always wanted to sit in an airplane. Way above the trees, like a bird."

I look up through the canopy at the flecks of sky. I have seen two planes in my life, one when I was five and one when I was twelve. They were so high and tiny they were almost imperceptible. Uncle Antonio once told me we were too far from any cities to see many planes, but even so, there are enough trees cultivated in Little Cam to cover the compound from any aerial eyes. "Where would you go?" I ask Ami.

"Eio's Papi told us about places where there are no trees. Sometimes it's all buildings made of concrete, for miles and miles. Sometimes it's just sand, so much that you can't even see the end of it."

I try to imagine such a sight, but it seems impossible. "I've never been outside the jungle."

Ami takes my hand and smiles broadly. There's a slight gap between her two front teeth. "We'll go one day. You and me, in a plane. We'll go to China and America and Antarctica."

I stare at her. "How do you know all that?"

"Know what?"

"All those names." I think of my map, recall the words printed on it. "China. That's in . . . Asia?" The names taste strange on my lips, like some foreign food.

She nods. "Papi made Eio and me learn so many names of so many places. He said we should know as much as we can about the world and that . . ." She screws up her face, thinks for a second, then says in the same singsong manner I use when I recite the periodic table of the elements, "That 'ignorance is the curse of God; knowledge is the wing wherewith

we fly to heaven.' That's by some *karaíba* called Shakespeare."
She smiles smugly. "Sometimes I learn quicker than Eio."

"Shakespeare, huh?" He must have been a scientist; it
sounds like something Uncle Paolo would say.

I feel an unexpected bite of jealous anger. Someone from
Little Cam has been teaching Ami and Eio about the outside
world while leaving me sitting in the dark like an idiot. Sure,
I can name all the parts of a paramecium, but a seven-year-
old knows more about the world than I do. If knowledge is
"the wing wherewith we fly to heaven," then I am a bird with
clipped wings.

My fingers dig into the soft soil on the bank, squeezing
it with all the frustration I don't want Ami to see on my face.

Above us, a colony of golden tamarins chatter and laugh
as they chuck berries at our heads. Ami shrieks back at them,
and one comes scurrying down to hop on her shoulder. It
plays with her hair and hisses at me when I try to pet it.

"Ami speaks to monkeys," Eio says, suddenly coming up
behind us and shaking water from his hair, "because she is
half monkey herself."

"Am not!" She holds her arm toward him, and the tamarin runs down it and leaps onto Eio's head and begins pulling
his hair. He yells and swats at it, and Ami and I laugh, my
anger falling away.

When Eio finally rids himself of the little golden monkey,
Ami scoops it up and charges into the pool, startling a pair of
hoatzins who squawk and flutter away, the tufts of feathers on
their heads rippling behind them.

"Her parents died, so she was raised by Achiri," Eio says.
"She is like my little sister. That means I'm her protector."

"She's an angel," I say. "I'd give anything to have a little sister like her."

Eio throws himself onto the ground beside me, stretching his length across the thick layer of leaves that blanket the jungle floor. He stretches his arms over his head, giving me a full display of his abdominal muscles flexing. I feel my cheeks flush, and I swallow, trying not to look like I'm mentally diagramming every inch of his tanned skin.

"How can you believe in angels?" he asks. "You're a scientist."

"I don't." Or Uncle Paolo doesn't, anyway. I pause for a moment. "But I think some of the others do, like Aunt Nénine. She just doesn't say so, or Uncle Paolo gets mad."

"You can't take someone's gods away. You can try, but they'll hide them and pray to them anyway. That's what Kapukiri says."

"You put a lot of faith in what he says." I think of the villagers' reaction to what he said the second time I came to Ai'oa. *Jaguar, mantis, moon.*

"He is our medicine man, our miracle worker. If we are sick, it is Kapukiri who heals us. He sees things before they happen, and sometimes he walks in the spirit world without even using *yoppo.*"

"*Anadenanthera peregrina,*" I say automatically. "A hallucinogen."

He nods. "You wouldn't like it though. *Karaíba* never do. It makes your brain"—he spreads his fingers on either side of his head—"*pyoo!* Like an explosion."

"You're right. I don't think I'd like it." *Yuck.*

My distaste must show on my face, because he laughs.

"We Ai'oans do things a lot differently, yes, but in many ways we are just the same as you."

"How?"

He shrugs and picks a fern frond, pulling one tiny leaf off at a time and rolling them into little beads. "We eat, we sleep, we breathe. We smile when we're happy, and we cry when we're sad. When we swim, we must come up for air. When we work all day, our backs get sore. When we get cut, we bleed."

I look at my pale wrist. *Not all of us.*

"Those of us who are strong take care of the weak, and we live to please those in power over us."

"Uncle Paolo thinks the weak should be culled," I say quietly. "He says that the rest of the world disagrees. That's why the scientists first came here; they had to work in secret because their ideas were too advanced for everyone to accept. They were scorned and discredited because their way of strengthening the human race meant making hard decisions." *They called them monsters, Uncle Paolo told me. And they despised men like Dr. Falk. So Falk came here, to the jungle, where he heard a legend of a flower that could make one immortal. . . .*

Uncle Paolo is angry at the outside world that forced Dr. Falk and his colleagues into hiding. *"They were stupid, Pia, and they still are. They don't understand that taking life can sometimes be a greater mercy than saving life. You have to see the bigger picture, have to look at the whole and not the individual. Once you focus on the leaf and not the whole tree, you lose your objectivity, and your reason is compromised. Always see the tree, Pia. Always be objective. Your reason must rule your heart, not the other way around."*

"And what do *you* think?" Eio asks, rolling onto his stomach and staring me straight in the eye. "Do you agree?"

"Me?" I stare at him. No one's ever asked me how I feel about Uncle Paolo's views. In Little Cam, everyone thinks that way. "Well, I don't *dis*agree. I mean, Uncle Paolo is a scientist. He reaches his conclusions through careful observation and documentation and—"

"Look." Eio says suddenly. He brushes some leaves aside and draws a line in the dirt with his finger. "What is it?"

I look from the line to Eio uncertainly. "Huh?"

"Well, is it a line or a circle?"

"What is this, a trick question?"

"Just answer it."

Guardedly, I reply, "It's a line."

"So it's not a circle? You're sure?"

I give him a flat, unamused stare. "Yes."

"Okay," he says amiably. Then he reaches behind me and picks up a circular leaf—*Tropaeolaceae tropaeolum*, my mind supplies—which he holds lengthwise at eye level, so that it looks like a thin line in the air.

"Line or circle?"

"Okay, smart guy." I roll my eyes. "I get it."

"Line or circle?" he insists.

"It's both. Ha ha." I grab the leaf and hold it upright, my eyes tracing its round outline.

"It's something Papi showed me once," Eio says. "He said that seeing and understanding are two different things. Our eyes show us one side of an object, but that doesn't mean there aren't five other sides we *can't* see. So why trust your eyes? Why live your whole life thinking that just because you can't see every side to something, those other sides don't exist?"

"If you can't trust your eyes then what can you trust?"

He smiles and closes his hand around mine, lifting one finger to tap the leaf. "You trust someone who can see the other sides."

"Like you?" I mean the question in disbelief, but it comes out, to my surprise, completely sincere.

"Well . . . why not?" His smile is wide and cocky, as if he's inviting me to argue with him. "Are you really so surprised we *natives* aren't as ignorant as your scientists say? Do you think you're the only one allowed to be smart?"

I want to say something sharp and clever in response, but my lips stay shut, and I stare at him with slightly bewildered fascination. Still smiling, he yawns and halfheartedly stretches.

"There's a papaya tree over that way. I'll go get us some, and then I'll teach you more smart things." He laughs when I roll my eyes, then stands and heads into the jungle.

"Yeah?" I call after him. "You think you're a proper genius, don't you?"

He turns, gives a short, mocking bow, then disappears into the jungle, laughing.

Shaking my head at his self-satisfaction, I kick off my shoes, roll up my pants, and wade in after Ami.

"What? Too scared to get wet?" She splashes me, and I hold my hands up in defense and laugh.

I notice a dark ripple in the water behind her and point. "What's that?"

"I don't know." Ami wades into the water to get a closer look.

Then I see it. "Ami, no! *Get back!*"

"What—"

She disappears under the water. In mere seconds a snake as thick as my thigh is coiled four times around her little body, and before my horrified eyes, it begins to tighten.

NINETEEN

"Ami!" I scream. "I'm coming!"

I plunge into the water. The anaconda is by far the largest I've ever seen. There's no way to measure exactly, but it is definitely over fifteen feet.

"Ami! Hang on!" I can't see its head, so I grab at its body and pull. It responds by squeezing further. Ami gasps as her face reddens.

"No! You just breathe, Ami! Just keep breathing, damn it!" I pick up rocks and smash them across the snake, and its head rises above Ami's and hisses at me. Its tongue is long and black and forked.

"Get off of her! Let *go*!" I throw a rock at its head, and it strikes true. But instead of dying, the snake moves as fast as the liquid mercury with which Uncle Sergei likes to experiment. It slides off Ami's body, and color returns to her face. I grab her and hold her close.

"It's all right, it's all right."

"Pia!"

I feel something tighten around my leg, and then I'm underwater. It holds me there for one . . . two . . . three minutes. Most people would have drowned by now, but I feel myself enter a strange stasis in which air is no longer necessary. Still, when I thrust upward, plunging my face back into the air, I gulp down one greedy breath before the anaconda pulls me under again. It moves around me like some demonic rope, its skin slick and smooth and cold. It wraps around my legs first, then my waist and chest. On its last pass the snake slides across my neck, slowly this time, almost lovingly, as if trying to soothe me to my death. *Don't you know I can't die, snake?*

But you can be swallowed, a sibilant voice responds, and though I know it's my own, my imagination credits it to the snake. *Swallowed into the wet, dark belly . . .*

I plant my feet on the streambed and use all my strength to thrust myself upward, lifting my head from the water. I suck down air and smell the rotting musk of the snake, and I gag.

Ami is screaming on the bank, and the rocks she throws all go wide. The serpent's head hovers inches from my face, its yellow slitted eyes fixed on mine, its mouth almost smiling.

Suddenly the snake tenses and tightens, and I feel the air squeezed from my lungs. I give a little half gasp, half squeak. I want to tell Ami to run, get help, something besides throwing rocks uselessly, but I can't speak. I don't have the breath. I hate how useless my immortality is at this moment. I would trade it in a heartbeat for the strength to throw this monster off.

The snake draws itself tighter and tighter around me. I'm on my knees in the water, legs scraped and scratched by stones.

Immortality, Pia, aren't you lucky? An eternity in the belly of a snake.

Black patches fill my vision, blocking out Ami. Where the black is not, colors dance vividly, a kaleidoscope sucking me under, luring me into unconsciousness.

I hear a wild yell, water splashing all around, and Ami shrieking. The snake tightens, tightens . . . then releases. Its thick coils fall away like some horrific, scaly garment dropping to the floor. I lunge forward and fall onto the bank. Ami has my hands; she's pulling me out of the water.

I collapse, gasping and coughing and crying, on the mossy bank. I pound my fist on the ground, trying to force air back into my body. When I turn to look back, I see Eio embroiled in battle with the serpent. His eyes are wild, his teeth are bared, and he has an arrow in one hand that he's trying to stab into the snake's head.

"Kill it, Eio! Kill it!" yells Ami.

He's certainly trying his best. When the snake wraps a coil around his chest, he slips a hand under it and struggles to push it off. Muscles strain beneath his tanned skin, his face reddens with effort, but he succeeds in thrusting it off himself. The fight lasts long minutes, and the entire time my heart is in my mouth. *Please, please, please . . .* I wish I knew of a god to pray to. Instead, I can only send the word out like a distress call over the radio. *Please, please . . .*

With a deep, wordless bellow, Eio heaves the snake away from his body. It flips wildly in the air, thrashing and hissing, and lands with a splash in the water. I think it's over, because Eio's free, and we can run now, but he goes after it.

"No!" I croak.

But Eio's not listening; he's in a battle rage. He reaches for the small bow slung across his back, but it broke in the snake's embrace. So he lunges after it with his arrow pointed like a dagger. One lightning-quick thrust, and he's skewered the snake's head right through the eyes.

The body lashes violently for some time, and Eio, exhausted, collapses beside me on the bank. He shuts his eyes and gasps for air.

"Are you okay?" I ask hoarsely.

He doesn't answer, just keeps breathing. But after a moment, he nods once. I take off my tank top, knowing the sight of me in my sports bra won't offend any Ai'oans—many of the women run around topless—and soak it in the river. Then I bathe his face and chest with it, hoping to cool the rush of blood that I can see pulsing in his neck and temples.

After a while, he opens his eyes. They are red-rimmed and tired, but they're open and looking at me, and that's all I care about.

"You saved me," I whisper. "You killed it."

We both look at the snake; it's fallen still at last. Greenish coils loop out of the water. Ami wades in and pokes it with a stick, shrieking when one loop falls over, but the snake is well and truly dead. Its head lies on the opposite bank, the arrow sticking straight out of its skull.

Eio grins at me, the effect of which is a little frightening given that he's covered with mud and leaves and he's just killed a giant snake.

"Dinner," he says.

● ● ●

No matter how they try, the Ai'oans cannot convince me to try anaconda kebab. There is plenty of it, that's for sure. They chop the snake into sections and then skewer and roast them slowly over open fires. I can't watch. There's something about eating a creature that almost ate *me* that ruins my appetite.

When the afternoon begins to wane, I head back to the spot where the guards always park the Jeep. We'll have to figure out a way to explain why I look so rough. My breathing has returned to normal, so I know there's no internal damage, but there's a bruise around my neck and stomach, my hair is a wreck, and my clothes are torn and muddy.

Eio walks me back. He was also silent during the feast, though the villagers were raining praises down on him. Apparently no snake that large has ever been killed by an Ai'oan, at least not in recent history. Eio is the reigning hero now.

"It could have killed you," I say as we make our way up a steep incline, using vines and bushes to pull ourselves up.

He shrugs and extends a hand downward. I grab it, and he pulls me up beside him. "I had to get it off you. You were almost out."

"You might have died for me."

"Maybe," he replies, as if the thought hadn't occurred to him before. "But Kapukiri says the noblest life is the one laid down for another."

I think about that for a while; it's a strange way to look at death. Even stranger is the boy who would risk his life for mine. *If I could die, would I do the same for him?* I know what everyone in Little Cam would say: *"Never, Pia. You are far too important to throw your life away for anyone."* They would remind me that I'm the only immortal and that humanity's hope rests with me. And I would believe them because I always have.

But as I duck under a branch Eio holds up for me, I think of my last visit to Ai'oa and how alive I felt every time our eyes met. How my blood raced beneath his touch. And when I was in danger, he didn't hesitate to risk everything to save me.

Would I do the same for him? The question haunts me because I have no answer. I don't know. To say no would be to betray Eio and the feelings I have for him, but to say yes would be to betray everyone in Little Cam . . . and maybe even my own dream. Would I risk losing eternity with my immortals just to save this one mortal boy?

It'll never come to that, I tell myself. *Surely it won't come to that.*

I notice that Eio put on a black T-shirt sometime during the feast. It says Chicago on it in swooping letters. "What's that mean?" I ask, pointing.

"I don't know, but I think it's a place in the United States of America. Papi was here last night, and he gave it to me. He said sometimes shirts like this get mixed in with the boxes that big man, Timothy, brings back to Little Cam, and they can't wear them there because they're against the rules."

In case I see them, I think, knowing it must be the reason why. "Your Papi was here last night?"

"He comes once a week or so."

"You've never told me who he is." Suddenly I have a terrifying thought. "Eio, you haven't told him about me, have you?" He could be anyone in Little Cam. Maybe he already knows my secret. If so, why hasn't he told anyone? Or he could be Uncle Paolo himself!

"Of course not," he answers, and my heart resumes beating. "I keep your secret, and I keep Papi's. I don't tell him about you, and I won't tell you about him." He shrugs apologetically. "It's only fair."

"I guess so," I sigh, just happy for now that my secret is still safe. "But I'll figure it out sooner or later."

"Maybe," he agrees.

We climb a short roll of land that's draped in ferns. The road is just on the other side, where the Jeep should be waiting.

Eio stops on top of the hill. "You're sure about this plan?"

"No problem. It was a little dusty, but it got me out, didn't it?" I pause beside him. "I guess . . . I'll see you next time?"

He starts to speak, then stops, as if he can't figure out what to say. Then he grabs my hand. "You don't have to go back," he whispers.

"Eio—"

"Pia." His hand runs up my arm to my elbow, leaving goose bumps in its wake. "You shouldn't have to sneak in and out like this, hiding under their cars." He shakes his head, angry crinkles at the corners of his eyes. "You live in fear of these people. Why won't you admit it? It's a cage, Pia. You must see that. You must feel it every time you look over your shoulder. Look, you're doing it now!"

I *am* looking over my shoulder, but it's not because of what he's saying. It's because the spot where my ride home should be—is empty.

The sound of rumbling engines comes from the direction of the river, and I crouch in the ferns with Eio and watch as a Jeep drives past. It's driven by the guard who was supposed to be returning from his shift, and he's carrying two passengers. Strangers: a brunette woman and white-haired man.

"Oh, no," I moan. There's no doubt in my mind as to who they are.

Corpus.

"They're early," I breathe.

"Who is that?" Eio kneels beside me, his hand still on mine.

"They're from the outside. They've come to see me." And when they arrive in Little Cam and ask for me, the truth will be known. Everything—and everyone—will be compromised. Me, Aunt Harriet, Eio.

No. Not Eio. I can't let him get caught up in this. I remember what I told him the morning I sneaked back into Little Cam: *"If they found out you knew too much about me, they might . . ."* I'm still not sure what they would do, but I know I don't want to find out.

More rumbling. Another Jeep is coming. This one, also driven by a guard, is carrying the Corpus representatives' luggage.

"I have to get on one of those Jeeps," I whisper. "Eio, I absolutely must get back into Little Cam without anyone noticing."

He looks like he wants to argue with me about it, but he sighs and nods. "I will help."

"How—"

But he's already gone, ghosting through the jungle after the Jeeps. The second one drives past me just as Eio disappears from view. Then I hear a screech, a shout, and muffled yelling. Following Eio's footsteps, I make my way toward the commotion, then press myself against a Brazil nut tree, out of sight of the Jeeps. By peering around the trunk, I can see everything.

Eio is standing in the middle of the road, arms folded across his chest, blocking the last Jeep. The driver is standing up, yelling, and waving for him to move. This truck has no passengers, just the piled luggage in the back. The other vehicle has gone on; I can see its taillights through the trees. They probably didn't notice what happened.

Eio's eyes flicker to me. He starts shouting back to the driver in Ai'oan. The driver clearly doesn't understand a word, but I've picked up enough of the language to catch most of it.

"Get in, Pia bird, before he runs me over!" he shouts. "You want to go back to that place? Now is your chance. Go, before this idiot does something stupid and I'm forced to put arrows in him!"

Trusting him to keep the driver's attention, I run to the Jeep and vault over its side, landing in a pile of suitcases. I curl up on the dirty mat on the floor and pull a polka-dotted valise over myself. The shouting, mostly consisting of the driver's curses about the stupidity of natives, goes on for a minute more, then finally the Jeep jerks, sputters, and starts rumbling down the road. I poke up my head just enough to peer back. Eio stands on the side of the road, hands at his sides, watching me.

I give him a small wave and a smile, which he doesn't return. Instead, he pulls a passionflower from the quiver on his shoulder and holds it aloft. The message is clear. *Come back soon.*

"I hope so," I whisper. Then the road bends like Eio's bow, and the boy with the flower is lost to the tangled greenery of the jungle.

TWENTY

From under the luggage, I can hear the groan of the gates as we pass into Little Cam, followed by shouts as everyone gathers to greet the visitors. I imagine the smiling faces of the scientists masking their nervousness and the curious eyes of the maintenance workers peering from the back of the crowd. I was supposed to be there. Supposed to be in front, with Uncle Paolo, the first one Corpus saw as they entered the gates of our little compound. I feel like pressing my face into the polka dots of the valise and screaming with frustration. Why are they here two days early? No one whispered a word of this to me this morning. My only conclusion is that no one else knew either.

Perhaps these Corpus people meant to surprise us. Catch us off guard. Like the trick questions Uncle Antonio sometimes throws at me in my studies, designed to make me stumble and backtrack, to reevaluate my hypotheses and even discard them altogether. I hate those questions; they're the only ones that throw me offbeat and mar my otherwise spotless record.

I realize that instead of anticipating the Corpus visitors with excitement, as I have been, maybe I ought to have had more dread. I regarded Uncle Paolo's nervousness with amusement. Perhaps I should have taken it as a warning.

The engines of the Jeeps shut off.

I'm trapped. If I jump out now, everyone will see. If I stay here, they'll find me when they unload the suitcases. That is, if Uncle Paolo hasn't already noticed me missing. What will I say? That this was my first time sneaking out? That I didn't go far? *Ai'oans? What Ai'oans? Never heard of them.* I imagine myself shifting from foot to foot as I say the words, my eyes darting anywhere but to Uncle Paolo's face. Not for the first time, I curse my lousy lying skills.

Just when I resign myself to my doom, I hear a loud, whooping laugh that can only be Aunt Harriet's. It comes from nearby and gets louder; she's walking toward my Jeep.

"I'll help with the luggage!" she says. "No, no, I've got it! I'm sturdier than I look!"

Suddenly the valise is lifted from my face, and there she is. Her expression barely flickers at the sight of me packed under the suitcases. "I'll distract them," she whispers. "You better be quick."

She hauls the valise over the side of the Jeep, chattering on about the humidity and the mosquitoes and the other trials of the jungle, and then I hear a thump. Aunt Harriet swears, and I hear the pounding of feet running to her. Drawing a deep breath, as if I could suck courage into my lungs, I peek over the luggage to scope the scene.

The valise is lying open at Aunt Harriet's feet, its contents—consisting of women's clothes—spread across the dirt.

The brunette woman from Corpus, wearing a white pantsuit totally unsuited to the jungle, is glaring at Aunt Harriet as her colleague tries not to notice the frilly underwear scattered around Aunt Harriet's feet. Taking advantage of the moment and using every ounce of my speed, I roll over the other side of the Jeep and land in a crouch. Everyone on this side of the caravan is too focused on Aunt Harriet and the woman to notice the blur of a girl breezing around the corner of the garage.

Once I'm well out of sight, I sink against the side of the garage and suck down air, hoping to drown my nerves in oxygen. My clothes are a ruin, my hair is in knots, and there's river mud coating my arms and legs and neck. There's no way I can face Corpus like this.

The B Dorms are eighty yards away, and the path to the building is lined with tall shrubs. If I stay low and move quickly, I can make it there in a matter of seconds. I sidle around the garage, then crouch low, draw a breath, and break into a sprint.

I can still hear the sounds of the crowd, which now include the shouts of Uncle Paolo as he tries to calm everyone down. Without missing a step, I slip through the door of B Labs and race down the hall to the pool. In less than a minute I strip and dive into the water. I swim to the other side, leaving a trail of mud swirling behind me, but by the time I climb out, the dirt is sinking to the bottom. I take only a second to slide past the mirror in the locker room to check for any residual mud, then I'm wrapping a towel around me and heading for the door.

By the time I reach the crowd out front, only two and a

half minutes have passed. It's almost as if I never left the Jeep. Soaked, mostly naked, and barefoot, I have no choice but to face everyone.

"There you are," a voice growls, and Uncle Antonio grabs my wrist. "Swimming, Pia? Honestly? I've been searching for half an hour! Paolo said you'd be with Harriet. Harriet said you never showed up. I almost thought you'd climbed the fence and run off into the jungle!"

"Ha!" I bleat. "That—that's crazy, Uncle Antonio! I was . . . swimming. See?" I yank a lock of my dripping hair, then decide it's a perfect time to change the subject. "What's going on?"

He bites. "They radioed us forty minutes ago, said they were standing on the banks of the Little Mississip, waiting for a ride." He shakes his head. "Threw the whole place into chaos. Paolo's been yelling nonstop, I'm pretty sure Haruto had a minor stroke, and now Harriet's gone and dumped their underwear in the mud." Uncle Antonio leads me through the crowd, still muttering. "Damn Corpus *would* pull this kind of stunt."

We emerge between Uncle Paolo and Uncle Sergei, who are apologizing profusely to the scowling woman for Aunt Harriet's clumsiness. But when Uncle Antonio clears his throat and everyone turns to stare at us, they all fall silent.

Feeling extremely self-conscious and clinging to my flimsy towel as if it could somehow rewind this day to its innocent beginnings, I smile my brightest.

"Sir and madam," Uncle Paolo says, a vein in his eyelid pulsing so strongly his whole temple twitches, "here she is. Our Pia."

I know he meant to give me an entire speech to recite at this moment, in order to win Corpus over from the start, but the surprise arrival has thrown pretty much all of Uncle Paolo's planning out the window. So I'm left to my own wits, which are still frayed and raw from the encounter with the anaconda this morning.

Was it only this morning? Resisting the urge to sigh and run straight to my bed, I nod to the visitors. "Hello. Welcome to Little Cam."

I try not to wince at the way their eyes roam my body. Neither says hello back to me or offers their name. Despite the fact their eyes are glued to me, I have a feeling that neither of them *sees* me. They look at me the way Uncle Paolo looks at the lab rats; you can almost see the calculations running across their eyeballs. Summing, subtracting, weighing, and comparing. They don't see a seventeen-year-old girl. They see the result of a particularly long and expensive experiment. And from the intensity and silence of their stares, I can't even tell if they like what they see.

"I'm sure you're hungry and tired," Uncle Paolo says at last. They nod and keep staring as they follow Uncle Paolo and me to the B Dorms, where they'll be put for the duration of their stay. Which is still, as far as I know, undetermined.

Once we're in the dorm and Uncle Antonio helps sort out their luggage, I whisper to Uncle Paolo that I'm going to go change for dinner. He nods distractedly, the tic in his eye still going at full blast. I slip away, glad to be forgotten.

Well, not quite forgotten. The two visitors watch me as I walk down the hall and through the door, as if their eyes were leashed to my heels.

Even as I cross Little Cam, my towel drawn as securely as it can go around me, I feel the weight of those two gazes like chains hung around my neck.

Their names are Victoria Strauss and Gunter Laszlo, I learn during dinner, and together they run the monster of a company that is Corpus. I learn all of this from Aunt Harriet, who sits beside me. The Corpus duo sits with Uncle Paolo and the rest of the Immortis team at their own table. Every five seconds, at least one of them glances over their shoulder at me. I consider sticking my tongue out or picking my nose, but then I remember what Uncle Sergei said about them shutting us down, and I keep my rude gestures to myself.

"They have operations in over twenty countries," Aunt Harriet whispers as she attacks her spaghetti. "Most of them are top secret. There's not a government in the world that can touch these guys. They've got fingers in everything—weapons development, banking, space exploration. But their main focus is biotech research and, more specifically, genetic engineering. In other words"—she chops her noodles so they'll fit on her fork—"*you.*"

"How do you know so much about them?"

"They're the ones who recruited me. It was Strauss who approached me first. The woman's psychotic." The fork stabbing turns vicious.

"Why?" I ask. "Is it a personality disorder? Schizophrenia? I can't imagine that someone who's bipolar or delusional would be given a job as important—"

"She's not literally psychotic, Pia. Good heavens. I meant it figuratively. She's nuts. Don't you think for a minute I spilled *her* suitcase by accident. Oh, no." A meatball suffers a gruesome death beneath Aunt Harriet's knife. "That woman deserves more than just muddy underwear."

"Why?"

"I hear they plan on staying several days. I'm sure you'll figure it out by then."

After dinner, Uncle Paolo suggests the guests retire for the night, but Strauss and Laszlo shake their heads and point toward me. Inwardly, I cringe. After Aunt Harriet's description, I have no idea what to expect from them.

We gather in my lab, which feels tiny once eight people — me, the Immortis team, and the Corpus representatives — are crammed inside of it. I sit on the examination table and hope with every cell in my body that they don't ask me to strip down. They don't, thankfully, but they do comb over every page in my files, which are extensive. Hours go by as Strauss and Laszlo interrogate Uncle Paolo and the rest of the team. What kinds of leukocytes does my body produce against diseases? What are the differences between my chromosomes and those of a normal human? What is my normal level of telomerase? All questions I could answer in my sleep. But no one asks me. Strauss and Laszlo have been here for hours, and not once has either of them spoken a word to me. I have a feeling that if I did say something, they might startle and stare as if an amoeba had suddenly asked them if they enjoyed their breakfast.

After the questions, they want to see demonstrations of my unique properties, starting with my unbreakable skin. Uncle Paolo picks up a scalpel and hands it to Strauss.

I almost refuse, but Mother, without even looking me in the eye, takes my hand and rolls up my sleeve before I can speak. Strauss seems to relish the blade as it presses against my skin, and I think I see a little of the woman Aunt Harriet seems to loathe so deeply.

"Remarkable," Strauss breathes as she hands the scalpel to Laszlo. "Not a scratch on her."

I'm forced to lie back and not grimace as Laszlo runs the blade over my arm and even my cheek. *It doesn't cut, but it still hurts!* I want to scream, but I can't. Uncle Paolo's eyes are on me at every moment, compelling me to comply. So I close my eyes and think about the future. About the first immortal I'll create. *It'll have to be a male. Maybe I'll get to name him. Maybe . . .* Slowly, as if swimming up through water, Eio's face slips into my mind. *Maybe I'll name him George. . . .* Eio, his body arcing into a perfect dive as he leaps from the top of the waterfall. *Or Peter or Jack . . .* Eio's eyes full of stars as we sit by the river. *Klaus or Sven or Heinrich. Good names. They were all scientists here at one time or another. . . .* Eio leading me through the jungle, holding his hand out, urging me to take it . . .

"Open your eyes, Pia," Mother says.

For a moment, I'm disoriented. There are strange faces looming over me, shining lights in my eyes, watching my pupils shrink and retreat. *Fire,* I think. *You really want to see something? Use firelight.* I stare up at Strauss and Laszlo, willing myself not to blink as they pry at my eyelids.

It's two in the morning when they finally run out of questions to ask. Uncle Jakob yawns into the back of his hand, and Uncle Haruto's eyes are bloodshot.

"Well," Uncle Paolo says, his fingers drumming the exam table by my knee. "What do you think?"

Strauss and Laszlo exchange looks, then glance at me.

"We should speak privately, Dr. Alvez," Laszlo says. His voice never seems louder than a whisper, so everyone has to crane to hear him.

Uncle Paolo nods. "All right, everyone. That's it for tonight."

Apparently "privately" means just Uncle Paolo and the two Corpus representatives, but at this hour, no one seems to mind. They shuffle out, yawning and rubbing their eyes.

I trail behind, but when we reach the stairwell, I stop to tie my shoelace.

No one notices that I'm wearing slip-ons.

Once I hear the door shut behind the others, I lightly slip back down the hall. I don't have to go far. My sense of hearing is well above average.

"Yes, yes, there's no denying she's a marvel," Laszlo is saying, his voice severe. "Subject 77 is perfect. Everything we could have hoped for and more. Which is exactly why we're wondering what the delay is, Alvez. We need more of them. She's no good to us on her own."

Subject 77 . . . I have a number?

"We need her if we're to speed up the process," Uncle Paolo replies. I can hear his fingers still drumming the table. "Pia's mind is more advanced than ours could ever be. You've been after a shortcut to immortality for years, haven't you? Well, she's the only one who will discover it, if it even exists. And she's not ready."

I'm ready! I almost yell it out. *I'm ready, oh, am I ready!*

"What exactly are you waiting for?" That's Strauss.

"I've been giving her the Wickham tests right on schedule,

but her scores aren't yet at the level necessary for full induction onto the Immortis team."

"The board is growing anxious," Strauss replies. "They want results."

"Pia *is* a result. The greatest result humanity's ever seen. The board will just have to be patient. Anyway, don't you control the board? If I remember correctly, whatever you say goes. No questions. No complaints."

"Fine. You want to play it straight? *We* want results. Unlike you, not all of us are inspired by terms like 'the good of mankind' or 'building a better future.' We don't want a race of immortals in five generations. We want solutions *now*. Sato's experiments proved that immortality couldn't be attained by someone born mortal. Fine. We've accepted that. But there are those of us who will have children and grandchildren in the coming years."

"But—"

"Yes, we control the board," Strauss continues as if Uncle Paolo had never spoken. "But without more results, without more forward momentum, we'll lose that control. And Paolo. You don't want us to lose control. There are those at Corpus who strongly feel that this operation should be stationed in the States—under a different team."

No, no, no . . . don't shut us down.

"So take Pia to them. Hell, let them all take scalpels to her if they want. Once they see her, they'll shut up about results."

My knees weaken, and I sink against the wall. My hands run up and down my arms as I imagine a hundred scalpels digging into my skin.

"You know we can't do that," Laszlo replies. "Word would

get out. Genisect would start World War III just to get their hands on her. They suspect, you know. They've suspected for years. Why do you think we only risk coming down here once every few decades? They're watching us. Pia is the holy grail of modern science, Alvez; we can't parade her around like a prize pig!"

"All right, point taken. But I'm telling you, she's not ready! We should focus on Dr. Fields's cloning research. It's our best angle."

Silence. Then Strauss: "Dr. Fields isn't going to be cooperating much longer."

"What do you mean?"

Yes, what do you mean?

"The sister. She's dead."

"What?"

"Fields doesn't know. She *can't* know, for as long as possible. The minute she finds out, she'll be gone. We need her research, Alvez. She's the best in her, well, field."

What's going on?! I clap a hand over my mouth to prevent myself from shouting aloud.

"It comes down to Pia," Strauss continues. "When is the next Wickham test scheduled?"

"Three months. And it's not the last one. There are three more—"

"It *is* the last one, and it's happening tomorrow."

"I—Victoria, that's impossible. It's too soon. She's not ready."

"But she will be. After tomorrow."

"Victoria, really, I—"

"*Tomorrow.*" Her voice lowers. I have to strain to hear. "I will speak plainly, Alvez, because we both know what Corpus is capable of. Remember Geneva?"

Complete silence.

Then Strauss continues. "There are at least twenty scientists I can think of who would kill for the chance to have your job. Your job and the jobs of your entire team. Don't make it come to that. I swear, Alvez, if you resist us on this—"

A strangled murmur from Uncle Paolo.

"What was that?" Strauss asks.

"It won't come to that. As you say. Tomorrow."

I hear a rustling of papers and shoes and sense that the conversation is wrapping up.

Heart hammering and skin the temperature of liquid nitrogen, I flee the building.

TWENTY-ONE

I wake up to the familiar glow of sunshine on the glass roof. The light is green, filtered by the drapes of leaves between the roof and the sky, and it falls on me gently. Given the chance, I could easily fall back asleep. But my alarm clock is relentless.

Then I remember the conversation I overheard last night between Uncle Paolo and the Corpus representatives, and I sit up straight, wide awake.

They're going to test me today. My hands grip the blanket until my knuckles turn white. *And it's going to be my last test.*

Someone knocks on my door, and I nearly jump out of my skin, the timing is so eerie. It's Mother.

"There's been a change of schedule, Pia," she says. "You're to meet Dr. Alvez in the menagerie in half an hour." She breezes into the room and whips my blankets away.

"Hey!" I draw my knees up indignantly.

Mother perches on the edge of the bed and leans close to

me. "You must be strong, Pia. This is everything. Everything. You must do all that they ask, or they will take Paolo from us." She grabs the front of my T-shirt. I'm so shocked I don't resist. "I cannot lose him, Pia. Do you understand me? Paolo is . . . I *can't* lose him."

Her fingers are cold and white, her eyes bloodshot from lack of sleep. Did she talk to Uncle Paolo last night? Did he tell her about Strauss and Laszlo's threats? I've always known that Mother worshipped Uncle Paolo, but the intensity in her eyes is stronger than I've ever seen before. She's usually so reserved and controlled. Seeing her like this makes me nervous. I'll be infinitely glad when Strauss and Laszlo leave and everyone starts acting normally again.

"I'm getting up," I whisper. "Everything will be okay. You'll see. I'm ready."

She holds me for a moment longer, then sighs and lets go. Before leaving the room, she looks back and says, "You had better be. Because I'll do *anything* to keep him here."

And I don't doubt a word.

In the menagerie I find not only Uncle Paolo, Laszlo, and Strauss—wearing a different white pantsuit—but Aunt Harriet too. She and the menagerie's supervisor, Jonas Brauer, are watching and discussing a sick marmoset in a wire cage. They see me and wave, but continue in the flow of their conversation.

A feeling of apprehension grows in me as I near Uncle Paolo, but I am determined to succeed, no matter what he asks of me. I think of my eternal people. Of brothers and sisters and friends who will never die. An immortal family, untouched by pain and death, knowing only life and love and beauty. I try to imagine it, try to see their faces in my mind . . . but all I see is a blue-eyed boy sitting by the river, giving me the stars.

So instead I think of Mother and Uncle Paolo and how strong and composed they are. *I can be like them*, I think. *I can do it.* I'm used to them looking at me with pride because of my immortality, but I want them to see that there's more to me, that I am strong and disciplined. A *circle* and *a line* . . .

"Hello, Uncle Paolo," I say with a smile, hoping he can't see how nervous I am. I ignore Strauss and Laszlo. If they aren't interested in talking to me, I'm not interested in talking to them. I'll pass their little test, but I don't have to make any friends while doing it.

"Hello, Pia. Sylvia." He nods to my mother.

"We should get started," Strauss says primly.

Uncle Paolo leads us to the back of the menagerie. I expect the Corpus duo to follow, but they wait until Mother and I go, and then they shadow us like jaguars stalking their prey.

I sense which cage Uncle Paolo is heading for even before he reaches it, and my stomach knots. I hope he'll turn and stop at the tarantula or snake terrariums, but he goes on—and stops at the ocelot cage, just as I feared.

I see Jinx inside, with her new kitten that Uncle Jonas named Sneeze. Jinx is seventy-three years old, our only immortal ocelot. She was bred to a mortal male that had been recently injected with an experimental strain of Immortis, and the scientists had hoped their offspring would have some trace of elysia. But Sneeze was born completely normal, further proving that an immortal must mate with another immortal if they are to pass on their eternality to their offspring.

Jinx and Sneeze are lying by their water dish, Jinx dragging her rough tongue over his back and head. The kitten mews at her in annoyance and then gives his trademark sneeze. They look so peaceful and content that I want to run away right now, before Uncle Paolo can tell me what today's test is. But I can't. I have to keep thinking about the Immortis team and the spot on it reserved for me—if I can only pass this test.

"Pia," says Uncle Paolo, after inspecting a chart on the wall that describes Sneeze's development. "Tell me what we have here."

I read the chart, then sum up what it says. "Sneeze—"

"Subject 294, Pia. Or, if you prefer, juvenile male ocelot. But not Sneeze. Never name your subjects, Pia." He shoots a sidelong look at Strauss as if afraid she'll pounce.

Except for Subject 77. You named her.

"Right. Subject 294 is a male ocelot, *Leopardis pardalis*, two weeks and three days old. Subject 294 tested positive for feline immunodeficiency virus, inherited from the mother, Subject 282, but seems to be tolerating the virus exceptionally well." The feline form of HIV, FIV usually isn't fatal to its carriers, and it might not affect them for years.

"Excellent, excellent," murmurs Uncle Paolo. "Well, Pia, you no doubt suspect what the nature of this test will be."

"Yes," I reply softly. I sense that Uncle Jonas and Aunt Harriet are watching now, but I keep my eyes on Sneeze. He is trying to trap his mother's tail between his paws, but she keeps twitching it away.

"Pia, this is to be your last Wickham test."

"The last one?" I do my best to look surprised. Strauss is watching me like a hawk.

"Yes. If you pass this test, you will be made a fully entitled member of the elysia research team, and you will be told the secret formula to which you owe your existence."

"Immortis," I whisper.

He nods. "That is why this test is so very important. I want you to think about it and be absolutely sure you are ready. There can be no going back after this, Pia."

"Okay."

He hands me a syringe. "Pentobarbital," he says simply.

From down the aisle, I hear a little gasp from Aunt Harriet. My heart falls. I had expected something bad, but not as bad as this. "You want me to . . ." I choke on the words. I can't even look at the kitten. "But the virus isn't *hurting* him! He could live a perfectly normal life—"

"And pass the virus on to his offspring," Uncle Paolo interrupts. "Dr. Zingre has been researching vaccines for FIV, and to do that he needs infected cadavers to examine."

"Is there a problem here?" Laszlo asks sharply.

"No!" Uncle Paolo snaps. There is sweat beading his brow when he turns back to me. "We've all done it at one time or another. We've had to. Little Cambridge isn't like most research facilities, Pia. It's harder. Tougher. More important. While most scientists piddle away with malaria and cancer and a cure for warts, *we*, Pia, we deal with immortality. The eternality of our own species. There is nothing more important than that, Pia. The goal. Remember the goal." He puts his hands on my arms and stares intently into my eyes. "The good of the species, Pia. That's all that matters. The end justifies the means."

This is not about Sneeze or finding a vaccine for FIV. It's not even about Strauss and Laszlo and their threats. This is about me. Sure, this particular test was months, maybe even years off. But it was coming. One day, I'd have to prove myself.

Today is that day.

Am I strong enough? Can I prove myself worthy of my own race? All it takes is a quick plunge of the needle in my hand, a thrust of the thumb to inject the chemical inside. And for Sneeze, it will be like falling asleep.

But when I force myself to look at him, playing with his mother's tail, completely unwitting of his fate, my legs begin to tremble, and I only want to run and hide and cry. Strauss and Laszlo are watching my every move. I can't look at Aunt Harriet. I have a feeling that if I do, I'll lose it completely and start bawling right here.

"We have to be able to make the hard decisions, Pia," Uncle Paolo continues. "If we couldn't, then you wouldn't even be here. This," he points at the needle, "is your legacy and your destiny. You must learn to control your emotions and focus on the goal."

Just a baby, I think, watching Sneeze.

"The final test is always the hardest, Pia," says Uncle Paolo. "You must be absolutely certain. I want you to take your time. Think it through. Take a day. A week. Whatever you need. But you must reach a final decision. Progress or regress. Survival or extinction. Strength or weakness."

"A week?" Strauss interrupts, her voice tight. "Isn't that a bit . . . generous, Paolo?"

Uncle Paolo's reply hisses through his teeth. "I'm already breaking a century's worth of protocol by skipping to the end of the test series, Victoria. This is how the final test is done. Sloppy work makes for sloppy results. Let me do this my way—no, not my way. Little Cam's way. I'm sorry if you don't like it, but some things can't be rushed."

For once, Strauss has no acid reply.

"Pia," Uncle Paolo says. "It's in your hands now. Your dream of an immortal race—it's all in your hands."

I don't reply, but I grip the syringe until my fingers turn white.

"Come, Sylvia," says Uncle Paolo, putting an arm around my mother. "Let's give her some time."

"Be strong," says my mother, the words more warning than encouragement.

Laszlo follows them out, but Strauss lingers. She takes my arm, her nails digging into my wrist, and I realize that she does know I can feel pain. I sense Aunt Harriet starting toward us.

"We created you," Strauss whispers. "We can destroy you. So get on with it."

"*Ahem.*" Aunt Harriet's hand comes down on my shoulder. "I believe she understands, Victoria."

Strauss's eyes rise to meet Aunt Harriet's, and she forces the lines of anger from her face, though her gaze remains as steely as ever. "Harriet. Good to see you again."

Aunt Harriet says nothing.

"Well," Strauss steps back and straightens her white jacket. "I'll be sure to tell Evie you said hello."

Aunt Harriet's lips tighten, but she says nothing.

After she's gone, I sink to the floor and stare at the pair of ocelots. They are so innocent, so unaware that I hold death in my hands, it's nauseating.

"It's a terrible thing to ask anyone to do," says Aunt Harriet.

"Who's Evie?"

"An old colleague of mine. Nobody important," Aunt Harriet replies quickly. "So will you do it?"

"Eventually. Not today." I'm not ready yet, just like Uncle Paolo said. I need time to prepare myself, to steel my nerves and my stomach. And I don't want to give Strauss the satisfaction of seeing me "get on with it" *too* soon.

"I think it's barbaric. What do they want you to prove, anyway? What will they ask of you next, once you've shown you are beyond morality?"

Morality. Not a word oft spoken in Little Cam. It's filed away with words like *love* and *San Francisco.* "I don't know. But it can't be worse than this, can it?"

"How can I know? I know less than you do. I'm new here, remember?"

"He's only a baby."

Aunt Harriet watches me watching Sneeze, then she sits beside me, legs folded, hands knotted beneath her chin. "You don't want to do it."

"Of course I don't!"

"That's good. It means you're human."

I stare at her, feeling the tears redden the rims of my eyes. "If I were truly human, all I'd care about would be the advancement of the species, like Uncle Paolo, and not some stupid kitten."

Aunt Harriet's lips tighten. "That's what they've taught you, I suppose. Ah, well, how can I come in from the wild yonder you've never even heard of, telling you what's right and what's wrong, when you've got all these brilliant scientists to do it already? Still, you don't *want* to listen to them, do you? You wish there was another way."

I nod, unable to trust my own voice.

"That's your moral compass, Pia."

"My what?"

"Moral compass. They're trying to force it to point the wrong way, but it keeps fighting, keeps swinging in the opposite direction. Don't you feel it?"

I do, and I wonder how she knows. It's exactly how I feel.

"Your moral compass," she confirms.

"Are you saying I shouldn't do it?" I ask, holding up the syringe. "That I should give up everything—give up all my dreams—for one insignificant life?"

"You should . . ." She hesitates, and there are things storming behind her eyes that I can't understand. I'm generally good at reading people, but Aunt Harriet closes to me like a thundercloud blocking out the sun. "You should think long and hard about it, Pia," she says at last. "And above all, consider the cost. Ask yourself what it is they are demanding of you. Look at who Pia is now, and ponder who it is they want you to be."

"Perfect," I reply immediately. "They want me to be perfect."

"Perfect," she repeats hollowly, "is in the eye of the beholder."

"Where did you hear that?"

"A man named Plato once said something similar. I don't suppose they've told you about Plato, hmm? Ah, I see not. Should have guessed it. Well, be sure not to mention him to anyone or we'll both be in trouble. I think I've got plenty of potential troubles to deal with for now, thank you, so keep it mum."

She rises and brushes the straw and dust from her jeans. As she begins to go, I call out, "Aunt Harriet?"

"Yes?"

"Everyone who comes to Little Cam has to take a test like this. So what was yours?"

She turns her head so that her frizzy red hair covers her expression. "I don't know what you mean."

With that, she strides hurriedly out of the menagerie, leaving me alone with the animals and the needle in my hands.

TWENTY-
TWO

It's two in the afternoon, which is when I usually hit the gym, but instead I'm stuck shadowing Uncle Paolo as he gives our guests a tour of Little Cam. There's a restlessness tugging at me all day, and I find myself staring longingly at the jungle whenever we go outside. I half hope Eio will appear on the other side of the fence, but he doesn't, which is just as well. Who knows what Strauss and Laszlo would have to say about a wild, shirtless boy knocking on the front gates, asking for Pia?

I'm not the only project that Corpus came to check up on. There are dozens of others run by the scientists who aren't on the Immortis team. Most of them research medicinal uses for the native plants, and some of their projects have even resulted in new medicines. If Little Cam were ever discovered by the wrong people, these are the only projects they would find out about—biomedical research important enough to be kept secret but harmless enough to allay suspicions.

I try to keep as much distance between Strauss and Laszlo and myself as possible. The sight of them reminds me of the syringe tucked in my sock drawer in my bedroom.

Eventually we end up in a room packed with cages of rats. Most of them are descendents of Roosevelt. The thought of that particular rat brings a knot to my stomach. We have dozens of immortal rats in Little Cam, but none of them are as special as Roosevelt was. He was the first, just as I am the first.

The scientists had to put a stop to the breeding of the immortal rats years ago, when it became evident that Little Cam would soon be overrun otherwise. The excess of immortal rats couldn't be released, in case one was found and its unusual abilities discovered. Of course, now that we know elysia is lethal to immortals, we could use it to control the population of rats. I wonder if Uncle Paolo has thought of that yet.

Uncle Paolo is introducing Strauss and Laszlo to a cage of albinos when Laszlo signals for him to be quiet. He pulls a beeping satellite phone from his satchel, but the racket of the rats is too loud for him to hear anything. Laszlo makes his way out of the room and shuts the door.

Seconds later the door reopens.

"We're moving out!" Laszlo yells.

"What?" Strauss's eyes widen. "What's going on?"

"That was Gerard, back in Rio. Several Genisect suits just landed and are sniffing around, trying to pick up our trail. We have to clear out. Now, while we still have time to throw them off the trail to Little Cam."

Strauss rushes to the door, Uncle Paolo and me following.

"So they're leaving? Just like that?" I ask in a low voice as we walk briskly down the hall.

"This is no small matter, Pia." Uncle Paolo's face is white. "It may already be too late. Corpus will have to move fast if they're to lead Genisect away from Little Cam."

"What *is* Genisect, anyway?"

"A rival corporation," Uncle Paolo replies. "Remember when I told you that there are people out there who'd kill everyone in Little Cam just to get to you? That's Genisect."

I imagine men with guns invading our compound and shooting everyone while I stand helpless to stop them, and I shiver. "So that's the end of the big Corpus visit then." Somehow it seems anticlimactic to have worked up such a sweat over a visit that lasted less than twenty-four hours.

"You just need to focus on your test, Pia. This changes nothing."

Once we're outside, he runs to help load the Jeeps, and I'm left alone. I find a place to sit in the shade of a capirona tree by the drive and watch. It's pure chaos. Even Strauss is running, with her polka-dot valise slung over her shoulder like a sack of bananas. I remember what she said about this Genisect starting World War III to get to me, and, strangely, all I can think is: *There have already been two world wars?*

To my surprise, I see Uncle Smithy climbing into the Jeeps with them, carrying his own suitcases. He must be returning to the outside at last. I can't let him go without saying good-bye.

I run to the Jeep and reach over the side, putting my hand on Uncle Smithy's arm.

"Uncle Smithy! You're leaving us already?" I'd expected him to stay for a few more weeks, at least.

The old scientist smiles and pats my hand. His skin is as thin and fragile as a butterfly's wing, and his fingers look

strange without his token paintbrush in their grasp. It's a wonder to think those frail hands could have painted so many
beautiful things in his time here.

"This is farewell, Pia."

"Where will you go?"

"Home. Don't worry about me. Corpus takes excellent
care of its retirees. I plan to sit in a recliner and snooze the
rest of my days away. Don't look so horrified, dear. It's exactly
what I want to do."

It's been a long time since I had to say good-bye to anyone; the last person was Aunt Claire, the medical doctor who
preceded Aunt Brigid. "I'll miss you. I'll miss our painting
sessions."

Uncle Smithy studies my face and slowly shakes his head.
"Forty-three years I gave this place. Forty-three years of this
godforsaken jungle, but I don't regret a moment of it."

"Why?"

"Because," he takes my hand and squeezes it, his grip sur-
prisingly strong for one so old, "it meant I got to touch eternity. You are our hope, Pia. Don't let us down."

Unable to reply for the knot in my throat, I nod. Though
I hate to think it, I have a feeling those words were planted by
someone other than Uncle Smithy. They're just too perfectly
timed with the test given to me this morning. But I don't hold
it against him. Uncle Smithy has never been anything but
kind to me, and I will miss him.

The Jeeps are ready to roll out. Strauss yells for the drivers
to step on it, and the gates creak open. It's been less than an
hour since Laszlo got the call.

The vehicles thunder into the jungle at a breakneck speed,

and in minutes the roar of the engines fades away, replaced by birdsong and monkey chatter.

Little Cam is left dizzied by the whirlwind visit, and everyone looks a little dazed as we stand around the gate, staring after the Jeeps. Yesterday morning, they showed up out of nowhere, and now they're gone, as if they'd never been here at all.

Well, almost. They did leave some evidence of their visit behind, and it's buried in my sock drawer.

When I think about the test, a chill runs down my spine. I want to be glad that Strauss and Laszlo are gone, but all I can feel is overwhelming sadness. How long can I put it off? Or should I go ahead and get it over with?

I try to see the test from a rational, scientific point of view. *It's all for the greater good. Who knows? Maybe Uncle Sergei will find a vaccine for FIV from studying Sneeze's cells.*

But it doesn't help. I still feel sick about the needle, about passing the test, all of it. Maybe Uncle Paolo was right. Maybe I'm not ready after all. I certainly can't see the connection between killing Sneeze and joining the Immortis team; the injection seems completely gratuitous. Maybe if I was going to help Uncle Sergei find a vaccine, the test would make sense, but my future research is totally unrelated to ocelots and FIV and pentobarbital.

But if I don't pass the test, Strauss will fire Uncle Paolo and maybe the rest of the Immortis team as well. Saying goodbye to Uncle Smithy was hard enough; I couldn't bear losing everyone else too. *"You are our hope,"* Uncle Smithy told me. Maybe Uncle Paolo or Victoria Strauss told him to say it, but it doesn't make it less true.

Feeling twisted and torn in every direction, I have to force myself not to scream aloud. I wish Corpus had never come. I wish Uncle Smithy hadn't left. I wish there wasn't a syringe of poison in my sock drawer. I wish . . . I wish . . . *I wish I was with Eio. Right now.*

The urge hits strong and true. I need to get away from Little Cam, at least for a few hours. I have to clear my head, find my rationality. The fence around Little Cam seems to shrink and compress around me, crushing my lungs and leaving no room to breathe. Beyond, the vastness of the jungle beckons.

I realize I'm the only one left standing by the gates. Everyone else has wandered off to labs or dorms, probably to mull over the Corpus visit and what it means for the future of Little Cam. I begin searching for Aunt Harriet and find her sitting in her lab, head bent over a photograph on the table.

"Aunt Harriet?"

She straightens and turns, her hand swiping the picture from the table and into her pocket. Her eyes are red, as if she's been crying. "Oh, Pia."

"Are you . . . okay?" I stand uncertainly in the doorway.

"Of course I'm okay." She rubs the heel of her hand over her eyes. "What do you want?"

"I need to get out for a couple of hours. Do you have any ideas besides using the Jeeps?"

"Pia . . ." She grabs a fistful of her hair and shuts her eyes. "It's really not a good time. Everyone's stirred up over the whole Corpus thing, and that makes them unpredictable. And now they've doubled the pressure on me, saying they want viable clones of immortal rats by the end of the year, and I just can't spare the time right now to sneak you in and out of the compound." She opens her eyes and gives me an exasperated look. "I'm sorry. Wait a few days. Let everything die down."

After a moment of silence, I nod slowly, then back away and head down the hall without replying. Obviously Aunt Harriet's under as much strain as Uncle Paolo.

Fine.

I can get myself out.

I pace the perimeter of the compound, looking for holes in the fence. There are none. In fact, I can see places where Uncle Timothy had the fence reinforced, probably the day my original escape hole was discovered. If I'm going to find a way out, it'll have to be higher up.

The electrified chain link ends about fifteen feet above the ground, though the horizontal iron bars reach higher. Technically, I could climb the fence, since the electricity won't damage me. But it would hurt, and I probably wouldn't make it halfway up before my hands would let go of their own volition. Plus, by that time the alarm in the guardhouse would be set off, and Uncle Timothy's men would be on me in seconds.

Seconds.

The electricity in the fence pulses every 1.2 seconds, which means—theoretically—I could make it out if I was very, *very* quick. But I don't think I could scale those fifteen feet in less than a second even at my fastest speed. *Then again, if I didn't have to climb all of those fifteen feet . . .*

I run along the perimeter of the fence until I find myself behind the maintenance building. This is the most isolated part of Little Cam . . . and the most overgrown. A bucayo tree grows out of the tangled weeds, its branches starting low to the ground and twisting outward, hung with bright scarlet flowers resembling the bills of toucans.

It's perfect.

I hoist myself upward, climbing the way a monkey climbs, using my feet as much as my hands. When I'm level with the top of the chain link, I stop. I could climb higher and aim for the bars above the chain link, but they're too smooth to grab on to, and I'd probably just slip and fall twenty feet to the ground. I'll have to jump, grab hold of the chain link, climb over, and leap to the ground—in less than 1.2 seconds.

The branch I'm crouching on is sturdy, and I grip it in my hands, close my eyes, and breathe in and out as slowly as I can. And I listen.

Uncle Paolo has tested my hearing multiple times, but I've never concentrated on it as hard as this. I block out the wrong sounds—screeching capuchins, wind in the leaves, my own beating heart—and focus on the most subtle noise of all: the almost imperceptible hum of electricity pulsing through the fence. At first, it's only a monotone buzz in my ear, and if I turn my head even a centimeter, I lose it altogether. But the longer I listen, the more distinct the pulses become. *Hum . . . hum . . . hum . . .* My mind catches the pattern: 1.2 seconds, like clockwork.

I open my eyes but keep my ears tuned to the fence. My muscles tense in preparation, I wait for the precise moment— and I leap.

TWENTY-THREE

A tenth of a second after I let go of the fence, the next electric pulse sizzles through the wires. I land in a crouch on the other side and then sprint into the foliage. My heart pounding at my ribs, I lean against a tree trunk and slide to the ground.

I was that close to setting off Uncle Timothy's alarms.

But I made it.

Shakily I stand up and watch the fence, to be sure no one noticed my escape. After several minutes of silence, my pulse finally settles, and I head into the jungle.

The day is warmer than most, and it isn't long before my tank top is damp with sweat. The perpetual buzzing of the cicadas is almost deafening, nearly drowning out the sounds of the birds. The deeper I go, the darker it gets, with the sunlight streaming in golden bars from the sky. Moving from the cool shade into one of these warm cylinders of light is like walking from night into day, from water into fire.

I may be out of Little Cam, but Uncle Smithy's words still follow me, clinging to me like perfume. *You are our hope . . . don't let us down . . . you are our hope. . . .*

I break into a run, as if I could leave all of it behind—Sneeze, Uncle Paolo, the syringe—if I just move fast enough. The trees fly past in a blur, and I move so smoothly across the jungle floor that I have the sensation of *not* moving, that it's the world that's rolling too fast, too recklessly, too out of control.

I am running so fast that when I reach Ai'oa and rein myself in, I skid across the ground, raising dust in a cloud.

Eio is standing with the men and boys, huddled around a fire and holding poison dart frogs with leaves. I barely notice what's going on and head straight for Eio. I grab his hand and whisper in his ear, "Let's go."

"But we're going to hunt. We're about to do the *sapo* ceremony."

I grip his hand tighter. "Please. I need to get away from everything, just for a few hours."

He nods wordlessly and hands the smoldering sticks he's holding to Burako, who regards me with disapproval. We leave them all behind and start walking to the river. The Ai'oans whisper and chuckle as we pass, but I ignore them. Once we reach the edge of the village, I start running again.

"Pia!" Eio calls. "What's going on?"

"Come on!"

It isn't far to the river. I slide down the embankment and stop at the edge of the water, and Eio, trying to keep up with me, nearly tumbles right into the river. I catch him and pull him back.

"What's wrong?" he asks. "Did something happen?"

"No. No, I just . . . needed to get out."

"Did they hurt you? Those strangers, did they do something to you? We saw them leaving. They went down the river an hour ago in their motorboat. I was afraid they'd taken you with them." He turns so that he's facing me squarely. "I thought they'd come to take you away."

"No, they didn't. At least not this time." I stare at the water. It ripples brown and copper in the sun.

"They will come again?"

Not if I do as I'm told and pass this last test. . . . "No. Not for a while."

He nods, then grins. "Did you see what that crazy *karaíba* woman was wearing? All white, flimsy material. It was covered in mud. Almost as stupid as that dress you had on. Remember?"

"I remember." I try to smile, but it doesn't spread to my eyes. I'm still too upset after this morning's Wickham test. *I feel this terrible already, and I haven't even done it yet.*

Eio's fingers gently turn my chin so that my eyes meet his. He takes a strand of my hair and slowly runs his fingers down its length. "I can't lose you, Pia bird," he whispers.

He stands so close, I can smell the jungle on his skin. Bananas and papaya, the smoke of Ai'oan fires, the smell of the earth and the river. It's intoxicating, his scent. It slips into my bloodstream and pounds through my heart, both electric and soothing. I could run the circumference of the earth or I could stand here for eternity with this boy. It doesn't matter which, as long as he's beside me.

What kind of science is this?

"Come with me," he says. "I want to show you something."

He leads me a short distance downriver, where one of the largest kapoks I've ever seen grows several yards from the water. The buttress roots rise at least five to six feet above our heads, and the base of the trunk is as large as my bedroom in the glass house. Eio leads me to the other side of the tree, where a root arches outward before plunging to the ground, creating a shelter. Moss drapes over the root like a curtain, and Eio pulls it aside so we can go in. Even standing up, the underside of the root is several feet above my head. The sunlight filters through the moss, tinting our skin pale green.

"Look," Eio says, running his hand on the underside of the root. Carved into the bark is a heart the size of his hand.

"Did you do that?" I ask, tracing it with my finger.

He shakes his head. "My mother and father."

I press my hand against the heart. "How long ago?"

"Before I was born. But my mother showed it to me not long before she died."

"How did she die?"

The skin on his face grows taut, and his eyes, focused on the heart, turn cold. "Achiri told me it was malaria. But I have seen malaria, and this was not it." He leans against the tree trunk, hands at his sides. "My father stopped coming to visit. I was very young and don't remember much, but I remember her eyes became hollow, and she stopped talking. She went to the village of the scientists and waited outside the lightning fence, but he didn't come. So she wasted away. She died of a broken heart. She died because she lost hope that he would ever come back."

"But he did come back. You said he visits regularly."

"By that time, it was too late. She was dead." He stares

at the ground, the vein in his neck pulsing visibly. "He was very angry when he found out. At first, he wanted nothing to do with me. I didn't care. I was angry with him. I thought it was his fault she died. Then he started coming to Ai'oa again to see me. He told me he tried to come before Míma died but that the scientists prevented it. Still . . . it was a long time before I forgave him."

My hand is still on the carved heart, and Eio covers it with his own.

"He loved my mother," he whispers.

I stare at Eio's hand on mine, then at the taut cords of the tendons on his forearm. I turn my head so I can stare up at his face. "And you're afraid I'm going to do the same thing, aren't you? That I'm going to leave you or that they'll take me away."

He nods, his eyes burning into mine.

"But I won't leave you," I say. "I'll come whenever I can—"

"Is this a game to you, Pia?"

"What?"

"Coming here. Seeing me. What am I to you? A toy? A distraction?"

"Eio—"

"I want you here, Pia. *Here.* Not locked in a cage. Not surrounded by electric fences and glass walls. Not when you feel like it or when you can manage to sneak away, but every day. All the time. Do you think we can go on like this forever? You sneaking out when you can. Me always waiting, wondering if you'll show up or not. Never knowing how long you'll stay. Never knowing if you'll even come back at all."

I stare at him speechlessly.

"Because for me, Pia bird, it's not a game. I don't want to

be a distraction or a toy. I don't want to always be waiting for someone who may not even come. I need to know what you want. Do you want to be a 'scientist,' locked away in there"—he points in the general direction of Little Cam—"or do you want to be free with me? Because you can't do this forever. You can't have both." He takes my hands. "Pia bird, you will have to choose."

"I . . . don't know. I don't know, Eio." I feel tears. I blink them away and try to force words from my lips. "I want both. I want you. I want my immortals. I want . . ." *I want, I want . . . what* do *I want?*

"I want a place to belong," I whisper at last.

"You could belong in Ai'oa. You could belong with me."

"I can't. Why don't you see it?" Frustrated and confused, I stop, breathe, and start again slowly, trying to make him understand. "I will never be Ai'oan. I may live in the jungle, but I am still a foreigner. You Ai'oans are part of this place. The jungle is in your blood."

"That doesn't matter. All that matters is you and me. The rest of it is just a distraction."

No, it's you. You are the distraction . . . only I want *to be distracted. . . .*

"Eio, I—"

He lifts my hand from the root and presses it to his bare chest, over his heart. My breath stops. I wonder if he can feel the pulse racing in my wrist, because it's beating just as quickly as his heartbeat.

"Do you know the Ai'oan word for *heart*?" he asks.

I shake my head.

"It's *py'a*." We're so close, his whisper is right in my ear, and his breath warms the side of my neck. "*You* are my heart, Pia."

I lick my lips. When did they get so dry?

His other hand cradles the back of my head, tipping my face upward. "A body can't live without a heart. And I can't live without you."

I can't think of a single thing to say. Nothing here makes sense. None of this is in Dr. Falk's plan or in Uncle Paolo's syllabus. I don't know what to do, what to say. I wasn't trained for moments like this. No one told me this could happen. Uncle Paolo, Uncle Antonio, Mother—none of them ever breathed a word to me about such a phenomenon. About how standing so *close* could set your skin on fire.

About the urge to be even closer.

I can see every detail of his face. The individual lines of color in his irises. Each fine, dark hair curling over his forehead. The shadow of beard stubble, just visible on his jaw line and over his lips. *His lips . . .*

Eio's eyes slowly wander to my mouth, and he leans down. . . .

"*There* you two are!" a small voice shouts.

Eio and I break apart as if repelled by electric shock. The moss rustles as Ami ducks beneath it, her golden tamarin clinging to her shoulder and looking a little green in the face as she bounces. "We've been looking for you, Eio. The others are ready to hunt, and they sent me—" She stops and stares at us, then a sly grin creeps across her face. "*I* know what *you* two were doing." She starts giggling, then makes kissing noises at her monkey.

"We weren't doing anything!" I say, though I feel the blood rushing to my face as if it's on a mission to betray me. "We were just talking. Come on, we wouldn't want Eio to miss his *hunt*."

I brush the moss aside and blink in the sudden sunlight. Eio and Ami follow, the little girl dragging him by the hand. His eyes follow me, but I can't look at him. I don't want him to see how red my face must be or how I can't seem to stop swallowing. My heart is still playing a tattoo against my ribs, and I avoid his eyes by leading the way back to the village.

Luri, her pregnant belly looking ready to pop, offers me a spear. "You can watch if you want to."

I shake my head. "No, thanks. I should go home."

She narrows her eyes. "Are you okay, Pia bird? These boys . . ." She glances at Eio. "They sometimes get a little too . . . excited, eh? You have to learn how to hit, you know? Teach them to keep their hands to themselves." She holds up a fist and grins.

"What? No. I'm fine. Really. I just need to get home."

She shrugs and tosses the spear to another Ai'oan. I can see Eio trying to get to me, shouldering his way through the villagers. I turn and begin walking in the direction of Little Cam, then stop and wait on the edge of the village until he reaches me.

"You're leaving?" he asks.

I nod, eyes on my shoes, then I slowly lift them to his face. "I'll be back."

"You don't have to leave." A smile tugs at the corners of his mouth, and he steps closer and whispers, "Watch the hunt.

Then, later, maybe we can go back to the river. Without Ami." He raises his eyebrows invitingly.

Trying not to give in to the butterflies, which whirl in my stomach and urge me to say *yes, yes, yes,* I shake my head. "No, I . . . I really should get back."

He stares pleadingly but must see I'm resolute, because he sighs and nods. "Okay. Go on, then. But first . . ." He reaches into the pocket of his cargo shorts and pulls something out. "Here. I've been meaning to give this to you."

He's holding a tiny bird in his hand, carved from the same stone as his jaguar. It's in midflight, with one wing over its head and the other below. A thin cord of tightly braided fibers threads a hole in the bird's upper wing, creating a necklace.

"Oh, Eio. It's beautiful."

He shrugs again. "Just a thing. Nothing special. But it's for you."

"Eio gave the Pia bird a gift!" squeals Ami. She is standing at my elbow, and I hadn't even seen her until she spoke. "That means—"

With a shout, Eio picks her up by her waist and whirls her around. When he sets her down again, he gives her a firm push. "Go! And stop talking! You talk like your mother the monkey, never shutting up!"

She makes a face at him and flounces off, the golden tamarin scampering at her heels.

"What does it mean?" I ask curiously.

"Nothing. It's nothing. Just a stupid . . . You can give it back, you know."

"No, I want to keep it."

"Fine," he says, still surly. "It's nothing."

Despite his nonchalance, he watches closely as I close my fingers around it, then tuck it safely in my pocket. "Thank you," I whisper, then add, "Watch for me."

The look he gives me seems to say *Always*. . . .

TWENTY-FOUR

I sneak back into Little Cam the same way I got out. This time, however, my concentration is so rattled, I'm not quick enough. The electricity sears my hand, and I yelp and fall clumsily to the ground. I'm not hurt, but five thousand volts of electricity and a fifteen-foot fall aren't exactly pleasant, even for me. I groan and lie there for a moment, lacking the will to get up. My hand tingles, but at least the pain drives away some of the panic that's been buzzing in my head, courtesy of Eio.

He was going to kiss me. Kiss me. Another second, and our lips . . . I breathe fast and shallow, not because of exhaustion, but because of terrified wonder. I pull the carved bird he gave me from my pocket and stare at it. *Would I have done it? Would I have let him?* I wanted to, that's for sure. In that moment, when he was so close and warm and vibrant, I wanted nothing more than to feel his lips on mine. But now, surrounded by my familiar Little Cam, I wonder if I really would have gone through with it. The prospect both thrills and alarms me at once.

He was going to kiss me.

I hear footsteps and climb hastily to my feet, tucking the bird back into my pocket. Uncle Timothy comes around the corner of the maintenance building with an automatic rifle slung over his shoulder, and when he sees me, he shakes his head and sighs.

"What are you up to, eh?"

"Sorry. I was taking a walk and got too close." I'm certain he can hear my heart booming. I know *I* can.

Uncle Timothy looks from me to the fence, then studies the jungle beyond. "I walked all this way just because you bumped the fence?"

I swallow and nod.

His dark eyes turn back to me, and I can see he's not completely buying it.

"I said sorry," I tell him. "It's not like no one's done it before. People touch the fence by accident all the time."

He nods slowly. "Yes . . . they do. But you don't."

I shrug, doing my best to look nonchalant, and start walking past him, but he stops me and bends to look in my eye.

"Not doing anything stupid, are you, Pia?"

"No! Let go of me. I have to . . . meet Uncle Paolo. I'm late."

He follows me as I walk, and though he tries to look casual, I know he's still suspicious. So I make my way to A Labs, and as I walk through the door, I turn and see Uncle Timothy watching. Now I'll have to find something to do in here for at least an hour or he'll just get suspicious all over again.

I go upstairs and start hunting for Uncle Paolo. I pass

Uncle Haruto and Uncle Jakob, who are talking quietly in the hall, and they both nod as I go past. Uncle Paolo is alone in the lab next to mine, and he doesn't even hear the door open. He's bent over a table, arranging pictures of people's faces. I come up behind him and watch. The faces are blank and unsmiling; they are all strangers.

"Pia!" Uncle Paolo finally notices me. "What are you doing in here? I thought the door was locked."

"It wasn't."

He glances around like a startled monkey; is there something he doesn't want me to see? But after taking stock of what's in the open and visible to my eyes, he relaxes and doesn't order me out.

"What are you working on?" I ask. "Who are they?"

He looks down at the pictures. "They're the first generation of Project 793."

"Project 793?"

He hesitates, drumming his fingers on the table. "Corpus . . . has expressed a desire for us to move forward with creating more immortals."

"And . . . that's Project 793." *We are going to make Mr. Perfect,* I think, remembering what Aunt Harriet said once. "And them?"

He taps a photograph. "These are the candidates Corpus has selected to begin the process."

"They're coming here? From outside?"

"Soon. When we're ready for them."

"Where will they all fit?"

"B Dorms. Most of the rooms are empty, you know. It was built to hold subject groups like this."

"Will they be here to stay?"

"No, not permanently." He leans back in his chair and props his left ankle on his right knee. His foot bounces as he talks. "The men will be here for three years, long enough to receive three injections of Immortis. Then we'll collect sperm samples from each and send them home. The women, after in vitro fertilization, will stay longer. They'll give birth, and then we'll send them back after they sign contracts ensuring full confidentiality of everything they did and saw here. We can't support a population that size for a length of time, not without attracting attention."

"Is that safe? What if they let something slip?"

"Corpus will deal with that," he says vaguely. "Anyway, they won't ever know what our real work is. Your true nature will be a strictly guarded secret. As far as any of them will ever know, they'll just be providing us the use of their genetic code for some kind of biomedical research."

"Why would they do it?" I stare at the blank expressions on the people's faces. "Why come down here for three years for a project they'll never really know about?"

Uncle Paolo watches me with a frown. "Why are you concerned with their motivations?"

"I'm a scientist." I shrug. "Well, almost a scientist. You always say the only real job a scientist has is to ask questions and find answers."

"All right. Granted." He shuffles the photographs around. "Most of these people are athletes, scholars, and artists who are exceptionally gifted, either mentally or physically, but who have all made bad decisions at some point. They all need something—money, new identities, some just a clean slate to start over with—and we need genetic material. Everyone wins."

"And the children?" My heart leaps. "We'll have lots of children in Little Cam, won't we?"

He nods, sighs, and rubs the bridge of his nose. "Which means we'll have to hire nurses to take care of them. Antonio can't look after them all."

"And the children will have children, and on and on. . . ." I pick up a photo of a brunette woman, very pretty, but her eyes are sad and distant. "And I'll see them all. I'll see them be born, I'll see them grow and learn, and I'll see them die."

Uncle Paolo takes the photograph from me and lays it with the others. "Pia? Is everything all right?"

"I'm fine," I say automatically. "So when will they get here? When will we be ready?"

"That," he says slowly, meeting my eye, "depends largely on you."

"Oh." I know what he's referring to, but I don't want to think about that. Instead, I change the subject to something that's been bothering me the past few days. "Uncle Paolo, when exactly did the fire in B Labs happen? The one that destroyed the old wing?"

He sits up straighter and gives me a sharp look. "Why do you ask?"

"Why not? It's one of the few things about Little Cam I don't know. And how was the fire started? Seems like it must have been an important event; I find it strange I don't hear much about it." Though my tone is casual, I watch him very carefully. I can see the muscles in his neck tense, but there is no change of expression on his face. *Come on. Just tell me the truth.* I want so badly for him to say it: *"There was no fire, Pia."* How hard can it be? If he'd tell me the truth, the uneasiness I've carried with me since Aunt Harriet and I first discovered those rooms would be lifted.

But instead, Uncle Paolo turns the point of the conversational dagger back to me. "Why are you worrying about this? You should be thinking about your test."

Instantly I switch from offense to defense. "You said to take my time—"

"I said I wouldn't pressure you, Pia, I know. But we need you on board for this." He gestures at the photos. "The longer you wait, the more concerned I am that you might not be as ready as we hoped."

"I . . . I'm almost ready." I square my shoulder and look him in the eye, hoping that will convince him.

He nods, but there's still pressure in his eyes. *Then get to it,* they seem to say.

Desperately I ask, "Is it really necessary, though? What purpose does it serve? What does killing Sneeze—ah, Subject 294—prepare me for, exactly?"

"Pia—"

"I just don't see how killing a kitten can show I'm able to mix a formula of Immortis!" I finish strongly, glad to finally have my main frustration out in the open. "Maybe I don't want to do it! Maybe I don't want to pass your test! Who says I have to, anyway?" My temper is rising with every word; they spill out of me like a punctured water bottle. "I'm tired of always doing what you say, Uncle Paolo! I'm tired of staying locked up in this place!"

"Pia—"

"Why does it have to be me? If you need a dead animal for Uncle Sergei to dissect, do it yourself!" I slam my fist onto the table, making the photos flutter into the air. I'm just so *full*. Full of confusion about Eio, full of frustration with Uncle Paolo, full of anger at that Strauss woman and her hideous white pantsuits. I've never had so much emotion locked up in me before. It pours out, and I feel helpless to stop it. "I want . . . I want . . ." *What do I want?* Tears of frustration blur my vision, and I dash them away with my fingers.

Uncle Paolo's lips twitch, and there is a sharp twinge around the corners of his eyes. For a moment, I almost sense he's about to slap me. But he swallows and says calmly, "It's that Fields woman, isn't it?"

"No—"

"She's been putting ideas in your head. I know she would. She has that way about her. If I'd had my say she'd have never . . . Pia. Listen to me." He grips my shoulders and ducks his head so he's looking me square on. There's stubble around his mouth; he's been working so long and hard in preparation for Corpus that he's not even stopped to shave. "You are perfect. *Perfect.* Not just perfect for who you are, but for *what* you are. What you mean to your entire race. You are the pinnacle of human perfection, the dream men have dreamed for millennia. There is no greater good than you, Pia. You are the end to all debates of religion and morality. There is no right and wrong. There is only reason and chaos. Progress and regress. Life and death. We created you for reason, Pia, and for progress, and for life. For *life*. It is the most precious thing of all, and you have more of it than anyone has ever had in history."

His eyes are wild, like Eio's were when he fought the snake, and he starts yelling. "We *gave* you life, Pia, and we *made* you perfect! And we had to make sacrifices to do it. We sacrificed our lives and reputations as prominent men of science in the world. We sacrificed lives of comfort, surrounded by friends and family, to live and work and die in this godforsaken jungle. We sacrificed things that most people wouldn't dream of giving up. We did things—we *do* things—that the people out there call wrong and evil, but they are only ignorant, Pia. Ignorant and weak. But you will put an end to that. You will bring reason and progress and life to a dark, dying world. And where others may point and scream *evil!* we know—we *know*, Pia—that the things we do are really the greatest and most noble form of compassion. We—"

He breaks off, panting, and sits back onto a stool. I rub my shoulders where he gripped them and left them sore and bloodless.

"I'm sorry," I whisper.

He shuts his eyes and pinches the bridge of his nose until he calms down. Then he looks up at me, some of the savagery gone from his gaze. "But do you see, Pia? Do you see what I'm saying? You are perfect, and there is nothing greater than that. Some things must fall by the wayside, yes, including kittens. It is necessary. You don't understand now, but you will. You must do it; you must prove to us that you're ready. That you understand the importance of your own existence and what you mean for humanity. That you can devote yourself to *you* and to the ones who will come after you. They'll look to you, Pia, because you'll be the firstborn of the immortals. One day, long from now, you'll be the oldest creature on this earth. You'll rule over men and women as a queen, an immortal goddess. All of that begins today. It begins the moment you make the choice, when you look in the mirror and say to yourself, 'This is it. I'm going forward, and I'm never going back.' You can't have regrets, and you can't hold on to guilt." He stands again, his face mere inches from mine. "You must kill Subject 294 and be able to leave it in the past, do you understand that? Then, and only then, will you be ready."

I feel as constricted as I had when the anaconda was wrapped around my throat. Uncle Paolo's words are a serpent of their own, frightening and beautiful at the same time.

"I'm sorry, Pia," he says, apparently reading the fear in my eyes. "I never meant to yell. I hoped you would come to see these things on your own. But maybe I was too soft. Maybe I overestimated your strength. Show me how strong you can be. Finish the test."

I nod and, at his wave of assent, flee the room.

I find a quiet spot beneath a low-spreading cinchona tree behind the glass house and kneel there, giving free rein to the tears. They fall over my hands and drop to the ground below, darkening the soil. *What do you want from me? What more do you want? Isn't it enough to be immortal and fast and smart? Why must I . . .* what? What is it they want me to be?

Beyond morality, Aunt Harriet's voice echoes. Isn't that what she said only this morning? *Of course it is, you know it is*, my own voice mocks me. *After all, your memory is . . .*

"Perfect," I whisper, pulling up a handful of grass. *Cynodon dactylon*, I think, studying the slender blades.

I should just *do* it. Get it over with. The pentobarbital is still in my sock drawer; it would take less than a minute to retrieve it. It would all be over then. The frustration, the dread . . .

"Chipmunk?"

I look away, trying to wipe the tears off before he sees them. "Uncle Antonio."

"Are you all right?"

I turn to look at him and do a double take. "Your beard!"

He runs a hand over the smoothness of his chin. "What? Don't you like it?" He actually blushes. "Harriet said she liked it better off. . . ."

But it's not the missing beard that catches my attention. It's what's lain beneath it all this time. I stare in open-mouthed shock at him, eyes tracing the line of his jaw, which I've never seen, the hard line of his lips, the dimple beneath the left corner of his mouth. *I've seen that face before.* I look down at his waist for the final clue . . . and there it is. An anaconda-skin belt. I can only gape at him for a long minute, mind boggling and eyes wide.

"*You're Papi,*" I gasp.

His head rears back, and he jerks a glance over his shoulder, then he's kneeling in front of me, gaze burning as fiercely as Uncle Paolo's. I'm getting a bit weary of all these wild-eyed glares boring into my skull.

"Where did you hear that name?" he hisses.

I'm still shocked. Of all the scientists in Little Cam, I would never have imagined . . . but yes. It does make sense. Uncle Antonio. Quiet Uncle Antonio, who should have been the father of an immortal. Whose purpose in Little Cam has always been uncertain, ever since the Accident. Whose lips twinge whenever someone calls me perfect and whose eyes seem so sad whenever I pass another test.

I'm feeling a little triumphant since I *did* tell Eio I'd probably figure Papi's identity out on my own. And triumph is nothing if not empowering. Maybe that's what emboldens me to speak the truth. "I've been doing it too."

"Doing . . . what?" He's on edge, ready to burst. I've never seen him so tense.

"Visiting." I know he'll understand what I mean, and I see I'm right when he sighs.

"Harriet," is all he says.

I nod. "Harriet."

"The hole in the fence?"

"The hole in the fence," I confirm. It's so wonderfully easy to finally let it all out after lying for so long. I have no fear of Uncle Antonio turning me in. After all, we have the same secret.

"Eio?"

I nod again and whisper, "He saved me from an anaconda. It was twenty-two feet long."

The fact doesn't impress him. He's still too agitated. "Pia, you *can't* . . . you have to stop. Stop sneaking to Ai'oa."

"Why? You do it."

"I'm . . . older. I have less to lose."

"Less to lose?" I snort. "I'm *immortal*. What can they take from me? My dinner?"

"It's more serious than that!" he snaps, and I start to pay more attention.

"Like the empty wing in B Labs?" I ask. "I know it's not burned out. Aunt Harriet and I saw it."

He stares for a long moment. "You . . . Pia, please. Promise me you won't go back."

"I will. You can't stop me. Unless you tell, and then I'll just tell on *you*."

He groans. "How many times have you been?"

I shrug. "Only four so far. You're bad, Uncle Antonio. Really bad. You've been sneaking out for *years*. You even had a baby with—"

"That's none of your business," he says quickly. "And for the record, I loved Larula."

"Why didn't you bring her to Little Cam then? And Eio too?" How different my life would have been if I'd had a friend growing up. And Eio's mother might never have died.

Suddenly I see the irony. If the Accident hadn't happened, Uncle Antonio would have been the father of my immortal Mr. Perfect. Instead, he became the father of Eio. *But Eio can't be my . . . can he?* I think of our almost-kiss, and my heart tumbles.

"I couldn't bring them here," Uncle Antonio replies. "It was too . . . I have my reasons. Pia, you must promise me you won't go back. Trust me. If you were caught . . . they'd take more than your dinner. These people are not to be played with, Pia. They're hell-bent on getting what they want, and anyone who gets in their way is simply collateral damage."

I think of my talk with Uncle Paolo less than an hour ago, and B Labs, and Victoria Strauss's threats about replacing the Immortis team, and I feel Uncle Antonio may be right. It makes me gravely uneasy.

"Promise me, Pia."

"I promise"—*to go back again. A hundred times. As many*

as I have to. I may become everything Uncle Paolo asks of me, but I'll go back to Ai'oa just to remind myself that I am still human.

"How do you get out without being seen?" I ask curiously.

"That's not something you need to know."

"Fine, then. I shared my secret. It's only fair you share yours too." I'm pouting, but I don't care.

"*Pia.*"

"Sorry."

Sooner or later Uncle Antonio will go back to Ai'oa, if only to warn Eio not to come looking for me. When he leaves, I'll be watching. After my conversation with Uncle Paolo today, I have a feeling he's going to put an end to my "studies" with Aunt Harriet and therefore my cover story for my absences. I promised Eio I would come back, which means I need a new way out.

Uncle Antonio is how I'll find one.

TWENTY-FIVE

He leaves that very night.

Does he really believe I'll follow through on my promise not to go back to Ai'oa? If so, the scientists failed miserably at their mission of nurturing above-average intelligence in the elysia subjects.

I watch him from a distance all day. When he leaves dinner, I tell Aunt Brigid and Aunt Nénine, who sit by me, that I want to go to bed early. Hoping that's enough to cover my absence from the lounge or pool tonight, I sneak after Uncle Antonio.

He stops in the dorm where his room is, and I wait in the stairwell for him to go back outside. I'm wearing the necklace Eio gave me, and the neckline of my shirt is high enough to cover it. Now I pull it out and hold it as I wait, the smooth contours of the carving already familiar to me.

After several minutes, Uncle Antonio slips back down the hall, dressed in dark clothes. It's easy to keep an eye on him after that. The many trees in the compound provide excellent hiding places for me as I shadow him.

Several times he looks back to see if anyone's around, but I let my reflexes take over. My eyes register his head turning almost before it happens, and I duck behind a tree or bush before he sees me. Finally he enters the building that stores the power generators. I wait several seconds, then slip silently in after him.

The room is lit with red lights in yellow cages on the walls. The generators are huge cylinders that grind and wheeze night and day, providing electricity for the compound. Even if I were to yell, the rumble of the turbines would prevent Uncle Antonio from hearing me. It takes a minute to find him; he's in the back corner, in the dark, fumbling with a metal storage cabinet against the wall.

I hear a clunk and a long scrape as he pulls the cabinet away from the wall. Behind it is a door, barely visible in the shadows. It's only as high as my belly button. Uncle Antonio opens it and disappears inside, then reappears to pull the cabinet back over the opening.

Great. The thing looks heavy. But I have to try or else risk never seeing Ai'oa again. I wait a few minutes to give Uncle Antonio a lead, then grunt and strain and curse at the cabinet until there is just enough of a space for me to squeeze through. It takes another moment to find the handle of the door, and then more heaving to get the cabinet pulled against the wall.

Once it's done, even my considerable stamina is worn thin, and I have to stop and catch my breath. Really, would it have been too much to make me extra strong as well as extra enduring? I decide that as soon as I'm on the Immortis team,

I'll make it a priority to discover how to genetically enhance strength.

The tunnel is damp and dirty, and I have to feel my way in the dark. I think of snakes and shudder, but I press on. Did Uncle Antonio dig this? Or was it installed years before, when Little Cam was originally built? I imagine that Dr. Falk's paranoia of seeing Little Cam forcefully shut down might have been an impetus for such a tunnel. If so, how did Uncle Antonio find it?

It's not long before the tunnel opens to a trapdoor in the floor of the jungle. It's covered with shrubs and leaves, which I'm careful to replace after I emerge.

Uncle Antonio is nowhere in sight, but that's not a problem anymore. I have my way out, and I know the way from here as well as I know the path from the glass house to the dining hall.

The village is quiet, like the night I first saw it from the trees with Eio. No feasting to greet Uncle Antonio. But then, there wouldn't be. Uncle Antonio is even more a part of the tribe than I am.

He must be meeting Eio, but where? I listen but hear nothing.

Resigned to a long, hard search, I start scouring the jungle around Ai'oa. When I am in the area south of the village, between the houses and the river, I see a light to my left. Cautiously making my way through the trees, using every ounce of my skill to not make any noise, I find a hut tucked into the foliage that I've never noticed before. It's out of view of the village and completely isolated, which is unusual for the Ai'oans. They thrive on close quarters.

There's one small window, and I sit with my back to the wall beneath it and listen.

"I don't care," Eio is saying, and I smile at the anger in his voice. *You're getting the lecture too, huh?* "I want to see her again. And again and again."

"You don't understand the danger you put her in, Eio!" Uncle Antonio shouts. "You can't *possibly* understand."

"I do. I know the story of what happened to you when they caught you trying to run away."

What?

"What they would do to Pia would be worse, and for longer! They can't risk losing her. Me, they just wanted to punish. But Pia is too valuable to risk. They would lock her up like they did me, but instead of a month, it would be years. Years, Eio."

They wouldn't. They'd never do that to me! I swallow, but my mouth is dry. *Would they?*

"She lives in a cage anyway. What difference would it make?"

"You think you're a big man, eh, talking like this? What would you do, Eio? If she was locked away because of you? Would you be able to live with yourself?"

"I would climb the fence and save her."

"You couldn't, it's—"

"I *know* what electricity is!" Eio's voice is getting louder and hotter. "I am *not* an ignorant Ai'oan, Papi! Half of me belongs here in the jungle, yes, but half of me belongs on the other side of that fence with you and Pia!"

"Look, son," Uncle Antonio says, using his most reasonable voice, "I get it. I know what's going on between you two, because twenty years ago, it was me. Me and your mother. And look . . . look how that turned out." His voice grows thick. "It destroyed us both, Eio. Do you dare risk that? I know what you're feeling. Trust me. I *know*. I felt it too. You think that nothing matters as long as you're together, that nothing can harm you two or come between you because you're somehow protected by your feelings for one another."

Feelings. Butterflies in my stomach. Eio's hand over mine, pressing it to his heart.

"You don't know about us," Eio protests. "You don't know anything. I saved her, you know, from the anaconda."

"Very noble. But the men inside that compound are worse than anacondas, Eio. They're a nest of vipers, and they won't hesitate to sink their poisonous fangs into you."

I can't bear it anymore. Eio shouldn't have to take all of the heat, not for me. I stand up and poke my head through the window. "If you'll recall, it was *me* who left Little Cam, all on my own. He had nothing to do with it."

They both stare in shock. Their faces are red from yelling, and their noses are only inches apart. To my surprise, Eio is nearly as tall as Uncle Antonio. The resemblance between them is breathtaking. The same square jaw, hard mouth, dimple, and the same strong build. After all, Eio *is* descended from handpicked, cream-of-the-crop individuals, same as I am. *Not perfect*, I remind myself. *But nearly.*

"Pia, you promised," Uncle Antonio says in his low voice, which is even more dangerous than his loud one.

"I lied. I can do that, you know. After all, I'm *beyond morality*."

"Where did you hear that?"

"Can't you guess?" I return, meeting his gaze squarely, and he sighs.

We say it together. "Harriet."

I climb in through the window and look around. This is no Ai'oan home. It's clearly something put together by Uncle Antonio and Eio.

Pictures of people hang all over the walls, among maps and pictures of cities, oceans, mountains, and places I've never imagined. There are labels and stickers, boxes and transmitters. Radios, cameras, clothes. I pick up a book titled *A Tale of Two Cities* and stare at its picture of a man in strange clothing standing in a wooden cart, surrounded by an angry crowd. When I set it down, I pick up another called *The Complete Works of William Shakespeare* and give a short, bitter laugh. Beneath that book is a black leather one with the words *Holy Bible* inscribed in gold. That one's in tatters—Uncle Antonio's favorite, perhaps?

This is a collection of illegal items that Uncle Antonio would never be allowed to have in Little Cam, a collection with one theme in mind: *outside*. Are these things he had smuggled in through Uncle Timothy, or did he find them on his own? As far as I know, he's never been beyond Ai'oa.

"Where did it all come from?" I breathe.

Uncle Antonio looks about to burst. "You—it's—*aaaagh!*" He throws up his hands. "It's taken a lifetime to collect all of this. And as soon as they discover you've been sneaking out, they'll find it all and destroy it."

"Who dug the tunnel?"

"I don't know, someone showed it to me." He blanches. "Pia! Someone will see the cabinet—"

"Don't worry." I wave a hand. "I pulled it back in place."

"It's not a game, Pia!"

"Isn't it, though?" I'm feeling reckless and wild. There's too much in my head—Uncle Paolo's passionate lecture, the tears, Uncle Antonio's secrets being spilled like stones from a jar, Eio . . . *feelings*. . . . "Maybe it's a game from beginning to end. Birth, life, death. Only, some of us get to play forever." I cock my head and study a picture of a blonde woman trying to keep her skirt down as she stands over an air vent. "Does that mean I win?"

"Pia, you're talking nonsense," Uncle Antonio says nervously.

"So what if I am?" Nonsense is good. It's meaningless, harmless. It's like Uncle Paolo's dreaded *chaos*. Maybe reason is neater and more orderly, but nonsense is freeing. If you spoke nothing but nonsense, no one would ever expect anything from you, right? You wouldn't have to meet expectations. *Wouldn't have to pass tests.*

"Why did you try to run away?" I ask.

He runs a hand through his hair. "I was scared. I knew if someone figured out what I was doing, Larula and Eio would be the ones to pay, and I had to keep them safe. I thought if we ran . . . But I didn't even make it outside the fence. They caught me red-handed, bags packed and everything."

"They locked you up?" I whisper.

"You say you saw the closed wing of B Labs?"

My mouth opens, and for a moment I can't speak. My worst fears, ones I'd never even dared to voice, are confirmed.

"So those rooms are for people? Why would they have such rooms, Uncle Antonio?"

"In case . . . there was ever another incident. Accident."

"Alex and Marian."

"Yeah, Alex and Marian. I was ten when they ran, you know. They were several years late in conceiving; it was something of a joke among the lower-level employees, I recall." He sighs. "They were mad about each other, those two. Even I saw it, and I was just a kid. They were always together, completely inseparable. Then the news came—a baby on the way. Everyone could breathe easier, knowing the plan was still running smooth. Then they ran."

"Why?"

"Good reasons." There is fear in his eyes again. "They almost made it, too. Not like me. Huh."

"What happened to them?" I whisper.

"Mixed stories. Some say their pursuers shot them. Others say they strapped rocks to their feet and jumped in the river. Drowned themselves and the baby girl too."

His intended mate. What went through his head when he heard the news, a ten-year-old boy living among scientists, destined to father an immortal? "Surely they weren't *murdered*."

Uncle Antonio sighs. "I don't know. I don't."

Silence falls. I have more questions, but I'm afraid to get any more answers. The night has already been too revealing for comfort. But I *have* to know one thing.

"Why did they run, Uncle Antonio? What would be worth killing themselves over?"

He doesn't answer for a while, but fiddles with a radio. Nothing comes through but static. Eio watches too, waiting silently and rubbing his thumb absently over his lip. Finally Uncle Antonio shuts off the radio, but instead of answering, he just studies me and scratches his chin as if he's forgotten there's no longer a beard there. I'm about to repeat my question when he finally speaks.

"Pia, I want you to leave Little Cam. For good." He faces me squarely. "And I want you to leave tonight."

TWENTY-SIX

I don't know whether to laugh or run. I look at Eio and find that he's looking at me as intently as Uncle Antonio. It's obvious how he feels about the idea. He said pretty much the same thing to me earlier today.

"Are you—are you serious?" I ask.

"I am extremely serious," Uncle Antonio replies.

"Leave Little Cam? Just like that?" I snap my fingers. "You *are* serious! What in the world—"

"Pia, I need you to understand something," Uncle Antonio interrupts. "This isn't some whim. I . . . I've wanted to say this for a while."

"That I should leave?" I whisper. My stomach flutters from nerves or fear or anger, or maybe from all three.

He nods. "I didn't think the time would come so soon. I wanted you to be older, more experienced. But here we are: you, me, Eio. Alone in the jungle, and the time is ripe. Eio, remember that journey I sent you on? The one you thought was a fool's errand?"

"The city." Eio's eyes widen. "You mean—"

"Yes, I do." Uncle Antonio turns back to me. "Eio is to take you, Pia. He knows the way; he proved that already. He'll take you to Manaus, and after that . . ." He shuts his eyes and rubs his forehead. "There are so many details I haven't planned yet. But you're smart—"

"Uncle Antonio," I start, but he doesn't pause.

"And you'll figure something out. Just get to Manaus for now. You can't stay there long; eventually they'll search there. You have to run, Pia, run far and long. Find somewhere safe—"

"Uncle Antonio—"

"I wonder if I should have told Harriet about this. Maybe she could help . . . I must say, I imagined *I* would be the one to sneak you out, introduce you to Eio. And all this time, you two have—"

"Uncle Antonio, I am *not* leaving Little Cam." I stand with my shoulders high and fists clenched. He finally stops talking and stares at me as I continue. "Why are you saying all of this? You honestly expect me to leave everything behind? My home? My family?"

"Pia." He seems blindsided by my response. "I thought you understood. You saw the cells in B Labs. You know about the terrible tests everyone has to take. And the secrets, the lies—what did you think—"

"Yes, I know all about those things," I reply. "And, okay, I'll admit it: they made me wonder. But are you telling me those are the reasons Alex and Marian killed themselves? They'd rather be dead than . . . what? Be lied to?"

"No." His back is stiff now. Eio watches with silent, heated eyes, his arms crossed over his bare chest. Uncle Antonio presses one fist into his other hand and twists it back and forth as if he wants to punch someone and just can't figure out whom. "That was part of it, yes, but not the reason."

"Then *what was it*? You want me to leave behind everything I have ever known, but you won't tell me *why*?" I pick up the Shakespeare book with one hand and slap it with the other. "'Ignorance is the curse of God; knowledge is the wing wherewith we fly to heaven.' Isn't that how it goes? I can't fly if I'm ignorant, Uncle Antonio!"

His eyes bulge a little. "I—I can't—you don't understand, Pia. If you knew, you . . . I can't *do* that to you. . . .You have to know that nothing good can come of Little Cam! Don't you feel it?"

My own voice chills me when I answer, "*I* came of Little Cam. What does that make me?"

He sighs heavily. "That's not what I meant. Of course you're the only good thing to come out of that place. But, Pia . . . agh! Maybe I *should* tell you, maybe that's what it'll take."

"Then say it! Why can't you say it?" I plead, feeling tears burning the corners of my eyes. "Why did they run, Uncle Antonio? What is Uncle Paolo hiding? What is so terrible about Little Cam that you can't even tell me what it is?"

"Pia—" Eio starts, but Uncle Antonio cuts him off.

"Every time you come out here, you flirt with the idea of leaving forever. Don't you? I know I did."

"Then why didn't you?" I challenge.

"Because of this!" He jerks up the sleeve of his shirt and

turns over his arm. There's a small scar on his forearm that I've never noticed before. "They did more than just lock me up when I tried to run, Pia. They planted a tracking device under my skin, hiding it so deep under arteries and veins that if I tried to gouge it out, I'd kill myself in the process. If I ever disappeared, they'd activate it and hunt me down within hours. That's why I can only visit Eio at night, when they think I'm asleep. That's why I can't run. That's why I have to send my only son to be your guide, to give up forever the only good thing—besides you—that I can account for in my life! Pia, there is evil in Little Cam. The truth would destroy you if I told it to you. I can't put you through that, and I won't. You have to trust me. Would I do all of this—give you Eio—based simply on speculation? I *know* what really goes on behind those lab doors. I've seen it for myself. After you were born, it ended for a while. But now they're starting it again, bringing in new subjects, beginning the whole process from square one. You can't be here for that, Pia. You're *not* who they think you are. You're not one of them. You can't do the things they ask of you."

Trembling, blinking away the tears that bead my eyelashes, I glare at him. It's as if he's been reading my mind these past few days and is now bringing every insecurity I have into the light.

"Papi, stop! Can't you see how upset you've made her?" Eio comes to me and tries to take my hand, but I shake my head.

"What are you saying, Uncle Antonio?"

"You're not their perfect little scientist, Pia. They've done their best to mold you into their image, but you're breaking free. Why else do you come to Ai'oa? Why haven't you killed that kitten yet? But you can't have it both ways. You can't have Ai'oa *and* Little Cam. You've felt it, haven't you? I know, because I've felt it almost my entire life. You try to balance between the two, but sooner or later, you'll just fall. Or you'll end up like me—belonging nowhere."

I laugh. I can't help it. It's as if he and Eio planned it all—this afternoon under the kapok tree, Uncle Paolo's angry lecture, and now this.

"What's funny, Pia?" Eio asks.

"Nothing. Absolutely nothing." Does he not hear how similar Uncle Antonio's words are to the ones he himself told me earlier today? "Anyway, if you have a tracking device, Uncle Antonio, then so must I. I can't go anywhere."

"No, Pia. You don't. They tried implanting one when you were born, but . . . unbreakable skin, remember? They wanted to strap one to your ankle, but I convinced them it wasn't necessary. I told them that as long as you never knew about the outside world, you'd have no desire to see it, and you'd stay safe and secure inside your glass walls. Because I knew the day would come when you would have to run. I've known it for years. But if you're caught, they won't hesitate to use an ankle monitor, and then you will be well and truly trapped."

No! It can't be! I know these people. They're my family. They created me. I could believe it of Victoria Strauss, maybe, but not Uncle Paolo. Not my Immortis team.

But if he's right . . . I close my eyes and imagine going down to the river, climbing into a boat with Eio, and striking off for those distant corners of Aunt Harriet's map. My heart pounds a little faster at the thought. It's possible. We could do it. Simply go and leave it all behind for good.

Leave *what* behind? So Uncle Paolo lied about the fire in B Labs. Would he do that without good reason? Uncle Paolo is the most reasonable person I know. And if I leave, I leave them to the punishment of Corpus. I remember Strauss's words as if she's whispering them in my ear this moment: *"There are at least twenty scientists I can think of who would kill for the chance to have your job. Your job and the jobs of your entire team."* Who knows what will happen to them if I run away? Could I live an eternity with that guilt? *No. I can't do that to them.*

I feel like the set of scales in Uncle Sergei's lab, and each new thought that runs through my head adds weight to one side. I tip this way and that way, but cannot seem to find my balance.

"I don't know how I can believe you, Uncle Antonio," I say miserably. "If there's some terrible secret I don't know about Little Cam, then you would tell me."

"I'm not making this up, Pia." His voice is low. "You know I'm not. You're denying what you know is true."

"I'm not denying anything because I don't know what to deny! You won't tell me!"

He lapses into silence, his eyes a muddle of frustration and sorrow. I envy him; he only has two emotions at war inside him. I have dozens, it seems, but anger is winning out.

"I'm not leaving Little Cam," I say. "I've dreamed my entire life of having someone like me. Someone who knows what it is to live forever and what it's like to never be hurt. Someone who will . . ." I have to force myself not to look at Eio. "Who will stay with me always, who will never grow old and die and leave me alone, while I stay forever young." I hold my hands out, pleading with him to understand. "You're right. I *don't* belong. Not in Little Cam and not in Ai'oa. I'm all alone, Uncle Antonio. I always have been. And if I leave Little Cam, I leave behind my chance of ever belonging to anyone. I'll be alone forever," I whisper.

"You don't have to be alone, Pia!" Eio interjects. "Why don't you see that? *I'm* here."

"Yeah? For how long? How long, Eio? I can't . . . I *can't* have you only to lose you. I can't do it." I look back at Uncle Antonio. "The only place that I will ever have is with my own kind. And they don't even exist yet. This is my dream, Uncle Antonio. It's my destiny."

"Those are Paolo's words," he replies coldly. "Not yours."

"Uncle Paolo made me what I am."

"He's making a monster of you."

That does it. I almost hear a *snap* inside my head. "I'm not going to stand here and listen to this anymore. This is—it's crazy. *You're* crazy. I'm leaving." I turn to the window, then remember there's a door and head for that instead.

"Pia!" His voice stops me just as my hand touches the flimsy wood. "If you knew the truth, would it change your mind?"

I yank open the door and don't turn around to answer. "How can I know that when I don't know what the truth is?"

The jungle seems darker than it was before. I strike out blindly, tripping over rocks and nearly walking into trees, I'm so unsettled. I hear Eio behind me, hurrying to catch up, but I ignore him. It's only when he steps directly in front of me and refuses to let me get by that I am forced to stop.

Eio takes my hand gently. "Come, Pia."

JESSICA KHOURY

"No, I—"

"*Come*, Pia."

"Where are we going?"

"On."

I give in to his will, knowing it's useless to resist. I already saw how his stubbornness held out against Uncle Antonio. Eio's father. That particular revelation is still raw and unexplored. *How could he have hidden you from me all this time?*

Or maybe the question I should be asking is: *Is Uncle Antonio right?* His words terrify me. *There is evil in Little Cam.* But no one *shows* it to me. I see shadows, hear whispers, but none of it is certain. *You tell me to run, but you won't tell me why!* I don't understand why he thinks simply telling me that there is evil—without telling me what it is—will convince me to leave everything I've ever known. If he can't tell me the truth, maybe it doesn't exist.

Be honest with yourself, Pia. You know it does. Despite the warmth of Eio's hand over mine, I shiver. *You know it's true. You've seen the cells. You've seen the look in Paolo's eyes. There's something there, something no one will speak of. . . .*

I shake my head, trying to clear the thoughts that fog it. I used to see so clearly before all of this started happening. Before Aunt Harriet came with her wild red hair and her strong ideas. Before the hole in the fence and the boy on the other side—and his frustrating father. I saw like a scientist. Everything was black and white. Reason and chaos. Progress and regress.

Where am I now? Progressing or regressing? Is this reason, to be out here in the jungle at night, holding the hand of a wild boy with stripes on his face? Surely not. If anything, my life is growing steadily and inexorably more chaotic with each passing day.

"Here," Eio says, pulling aside a thick curtain of vines. Behind it lies the swimming hole, the still water shimmering in the pale moonlight. The moon must be full tonight. I can't see it, but only the light of the full moon ever reaches the forest floor. The waterfall looks like flowing silver, its rumble soft and soothing.

"Wait here," he tells me.

"What—"

"Just wait."

I shut my lips and sit on a mossy log by the pool.

He walks to the edge and leaps into a shallow dive, skimming under the surface like an otter. The water around him begins to shine blue; the pool must be filled with some kind of bioluminescent algae, *Pyrocystis fusiformis* perhaps, that glows when disturbed. I catch my breath, overwhelmed by the ghostly beauty of the scene. I've only ever seen this phenomenon under a microscope in a lab. Out here, beneath the jungle moon, the pale blue light is a hundred times more captivating. Eio swims in light, his body a dark shadow that moves quietly and swiftly toward the waterfall.

He finds a foothold on one of the rocks under the cascade and stands, his body splitting the curtain of water. It splashes off his shoulders and glitters like silver beads when he shakes his hair. My mouth hangs slightly open and I realize I haven't drawn a breath in over a minute. Why are we here again? Am I supposed to be angry? But I can't remember why. It doesn't matter. Nothing matters. My head empties of every thought to make room for the beautiful image of Eio standing in that glowing pool as the jungle anoints his shoulders with its fragrant water.

Eio begins climbing the slippery rocks until he's clinging to the crest of the waterfall, which streams in two silver bands on either side of him and joins together again just below his hips. It pulls at his shorts, threatening to undress him.

I swallow. Hard. And don't blink for a second.

My eyes hardly notice what his hands are doing, they're so fixated on the way his back muscles strain beneath his skin, illuminated by the gentle blue light of the shining pool below. Then he turns, and I realize he's picked a passionflower from a thick vine that hangs over the top of the falls. Eio carefully works his way down and slips back into the water, which shimmers brightly at his touch. He holds the flower above the surface as he makes his way through the luminescent pool toward me. Then he's here, emerging from the water like some kind of myth, some fabled Ai'oan god, his hand smoothing his wet hair back from his face, his chest and shoulders gleaming with water and moonlight. Behind him, a pale, shimmering trail of blue light marks his passage through the water. His wet shorts hang a good bit lower on his hips than they usually do, tempting my imagination. He extends the flower, which I take with trembling fingers.

I hear a soft, strangled *Thank you* and realize it's come from my own lips.

He smiles a small, crooked smile, and I think he knows exactly how tightly he's bound my tongue in knots. I suspect fetching me the passionflower was only half his purpose in swimming through that glowing pool.

"You're welcome," he says as he sits beside me. He's so

close that water from his hair drips onto my shoulder. I don't brush it away. He watches me as I slowly twirl the flower between my fingers, as if waiting to see if it will cheer me up.

"It's beautiful," I tell him.

"More beautiful than your elysia?" he asks.

I realize the question isn't just about flowers. He's simply using them to probe the deeper issue between us: the balance Uncle Antonio warned me about. *The jungle or Little Cam? Eio or Mr. Perfect? Love . . . or eternity?* "Eio, I—I don't know," I confess.

His lips tighten and he looks down at his hands. I feel terrible, keeping him at arm's length but not letting him go. I don't want to give him false hope—but neither do I want to lose him. My fingers absently play with the passionflower's petals as my thoughts wrestle in my head.

The night is filled with nocturnal birds' twittering and the odd howl of a monkey. I remember it was the night jungle that I first fell in love with, when I crawled under the fence for the first time. I find that hasn't changed; the darkness is like a blanket, and the thin moonlight doesn't invade like the sun. It lets me be silent, and it lets me have my secrets to myself.

"He loves you," Eio says after a short while, softly as a breeze. "If he didn't, he wouldn't worry about you so much."

I study his face. "Do *you* think we should run away?"

Eio frowns and runs his hand through his hair again. "I don't know, Pia. I don't know what goes on inside your fence. I'm not a part of that world."

There's a look in his eyes, a kind of evasion, that prompts me to ask, "Do you think he's right, that there's evil in Little Cam? Evil that would destroy me if I knew about it?"

Eio waits a long moment before saying, "I think if he wants you to go, he should tell you why. You're right about that. But maybe you should trust him a little more too. He could be more right than you know."

That's just what I fear.

His eyes are still avoiding mine. "Eio, what do *you* know? Has he told you what he won't tell me?"

Still staring at his hands, he replies, "He has told me nothing."

"He's always been my favorite uncle, you know. He never calls me perfect."

"Then that is his error," Eio says.

I study his face through the paint, which remained perfectly intact despite his midnight swim. "You sound more and more like one of us, the more I hear you speak."

"Us?"

"You know. Scientists. Little Camians or whatever you want to call us."

Even in the darkness, I can see his brow furrow. "I . . . feel less Ai'oan than I used to. Ever since I met you, anyway." He takes my hand and rubs his thumb over my palm. "You've changed me, Pia bird."

You've changed me too. "How?"

"Well, I'm miserable almost all the time."

"What!" I drop his hand.

"*Almost* all the time. That is, whenever you're not here. I can't sleep at night, because all I can think of is you. I meant what I said today. You are my *py'a*. My heart." He picks up my hand again.

"You . . . really feel all those things about me?" I ask, my mouth dry and my heart drumming.

His eyes are serious when they meet mine. "Ever since the moment you first knocked me over, then shone your stupid flashlight in my eyes and set your jaguar on me. I was angry, but mostly because I was terrified."

"Am I really all that scary?"

"Your beauty is," he whispers.

I know what he means, because I feel the same terrified awe when I look at him. It tugs at my heart whenever he looks at me, whenever he grabs my hand and pulls me close. My memory is perfect, yet I can't recall ever not having Eio. I've hardly known him a week, and yet I feel as if it's always been *us*. It's the strangest sensation. In my thoughts, everything is always clear and crisp, defined by numbers and formulas. But with Eio, my mind feels like one of Uncle Smithy's watercolor paintings. Edges blur and numbers jumble and fade until all that is left is wonder. Wonder at how deeply and how quickly I have fallen for this jungle boy. Wonder at how he made my entire world shatter into a million shards, then brought the pieces together again in new patterns, creating a whole new world—and a whole new Pia—that never existed before. The things that were important have fallen into the shadow of new ideas and new dreams . . . and it terrifies me.

"We could go, Pia. We could leave this place. Little Cam and Ai'oa too. I don't care. The boats aren't far from here. I'll take you away." He gently touches a finger to the stone bird around my neck, and I nearly stop breathing. "It can be just you and me. . . . I would be happy. Would you?"

Would I? Inside my head, Wild Pia stands up, lifts her hand, and shouts *yes, yes, yes! Go, Pia!* She is strong and persuasive, and I waver. *Could I?*

His face is very close to mine. I can see every detail—the arch of his eyebrows over blue, blue eyes. That dimple under his mouth. The straight line of his jaw, so firm and stubborn, like Uncle Antonio's.

"Eio . . ."

"Do you feel the same way, Pia? About me?"

"I . . ." Can I? Do I? *Dare I?* When I look at Eio, I see more than just a boy, however handsome and brave he may be. I see Ai'oa, and all the villagers, and Ami laughing and chattering, and Uncle Antonio, and even Aunt Harriet. And the jungle. Always the jungle. Deep, mysterious, beautiful, and irresistible. A place in which I could lose myself forever.

Suddenly Eio hisses, and his hand jerks into the air. Where the water brushes up to the log beside him grows one of the massive water lilies that so fascinate the botanists of Little Cam. *Victoria amazonica*, I think automatically. The underside is covered with tiny, sharp thorns, and it is on one of these that Eio cuts himself.

He holds up a finger bright with blood. I stare at it, transfixed.

"You're bleeding."

With a shrug, he looks closer to see how deep the cut is. All I see is the blood, spilling across his fragile skin, dark and crimson.

No. No, no, no, no, no. "No," I say, jumping to my feet and dropping the passionflower on the ground. "No, Eio, I—I can't. I can't, don't you see?"

He stares at me with wide, shocked eyes. "What do you mean?"

"Eio, I'm immortal. Do you know what that means? I'm going to live forever. I'm never going to die! I'm going to live and live, and you're going to—to—" I choke on the word. "I have a dream, Eio, a dream of engineering my own race, a race of immortals, where I'll truly belong. Not in Little Cam, and not in Ai'oa. In my own place, with my own kind. I'm . . . sorry. But you—I just can't. Uncle Antonio is right. I can't balance between here and there. It's too much." *Love makes you weak. It distracts you from the important things. It can make you lose sight of the objective.*

His eyes are filled with hurt and confusion. He holds a hand toward me, but it's the cut hand, and there's still blood. . . .

I run.

TWENTY-SEVEN

If he's following me, I never know it. I run too fast, leaping logs and boulders as if they were anthills. My feet barely touch the ground; I'm flying. Flying away, flying home, just like the bird Eio thinks I am. But contrary to his words, I'm not flying back to my cage. I'm *not*. Or if I am, it's only for a time. *I must prove to them that I'm ready.*

Yes. That's exactly what I must do. Can't stay here any longer. Should have listened to Uncle Paolo, should have listened to my own head. Not the heart, but the head. He was right. He's always right. The heart leads to chaos. It regresses. The mind is the only way forward to reason and order.

And I almost gave it all up. Weak, stupid Pia! I almost surrendered my dream—my purpose in life—for what? A kiss? And I was so close. Another moment and I would have given in, lost myself to the tidal wave of emotion.

But at the last minute, Eio pricked his finger, and the blood flowed red. *You can bleed, Eio, and I cannot. That is your weakness and my strength. It is the reason I must fly away, and you must forget about me. Please, please forget about me.*

I *am* sorry. Wish I'd never led him on. Wish I'd stayed in my place, on my side of the fence, and kept my eyes glued to a microscope, where they belong.

But now I have the chance to change all that and to do what I didn't have the courage to do before. *I am strong enough, Uncle Paolo, and I will show you. Uncle Antonio was wrong, so wrong. I'm ready. I'll do what you want, be what you want, fulfill the purpose for which you created me. I'll create the immortals, and maybe, years and years from now, I'll find a way to forget everything that happened tonight.*

My destiny is to live. Anger pounds through my veins, propelled by the beating of my wounded heart. Of all people to betray me—Uncle Antonio? If he's so certain of some dark, terrible secret behind Little Cam, why hasn't he burned the place to the ground? Destroyed the research and the immortal rats? Why does he linger, never giving voice to his true feelings? How long has he felt this way? I can't do what he asks of me. Fulfilling my dream means I have to get my hands dirty—so what? Everyone here has had to do the same thing at some point. As Uncle Paolo said, it's necessary. For a moment, back in the jungle, I almost gave in. I imagined getting in a boat with Eio and leaving my world behind forever. That was weakness. I nearly lost my grip on who and what I am—and what I must do with my life—for good. Now I must prove that it won't happen again. I must be strong.

The trapdoor is so well hidden that even *my* memory is

fooled for a moment. Then I see it, and I tear away the leaves and rip open the door. My steps through the tunnel are much surer this time; I reach the other end quickly.

Once I'm outside the powerhouse and in Little Cam again, the wave of adrenaline that carried me here fizzles out. It's still night, and everyone is asleep.

But maybe not everyone . . .

I tiptoe across the grounds to A Labs and peer around the corner of the building. There it is. The window of the elysia labs on the second floor, still yellow. Uncle Paolo is up working late.

Good. I have to keep going. If I stop now, I may lose control again, might give in and go back, beg Eio to hold my hand and take me away. . . .

Stop that thought there. No one is stirring inside the glass house. Mother's room is quiet, but she's always been a soft sleeper.

My room is dark, so I turn on a lamp. I hope Eio's not standing outside, watching me with those big, sad, blue eyes, but I can't think about him. Can't worry about him. Eio is his own person, and he'll have to take care of himself. Let him run to Uncle Antonio.

I yank open my sock drawer more roughly than is necessary. The syringe is still there, the needle as sharp and bright as it was this morning. I pick it up and cradle it gently in my palms. Not much longer now. I can almost feel the fabric of the lab coat brushing against the backs of my legs.

I stop in front of the mirror and stare at myself, a pale, wild-eyed girl with the wind and leaves still in her hair from running through the jungle. With a little face paint, I might pass for an Ai'oan, except for the paleness of my skin. *This is it. I'm going forward, and I'm never going back.*

Setting the syringe down, I stay only long enough to brush my hair and change into a clean pair of clothes. White, wide-leg pants and a simple white tank top. White clothes to go with my white lab coat. White for purity of purpose and clarity of thought.

White for death.

The menagerie is, of course, deserted. Uncle Jonas has left the door unlocked as usual. I flip on the row of lightbulbs overhead, and one by one they flicker and sputter to life. The animals, most of which were sleeping, give grunts and growls of irritation at being disturbed.

I stop at Alai's cage and look in, feeling sorry I've neglected him lately. I've neglected a lot of things that used to be impor-tant to me.

"Hey, boy," I whisper, though there is no one to overhear. "I'm sorry. I promise I'll take you out, maybe tomorrow."

He lifts his spotted head and looks at me, and for a second I'm startled at how human his gaze seems. Is the reproach in his eyes because of my neglect . . . or something else? He stays silent and doesn't come to the door.

My resolve a little shaken, I continue on to the ocelot cage. Jinx is curled up, still slumbering, but Sneeze's little head and bright blue eyes peep open from over her spotted haunch.

Subject 294, I remind myself. *That is all he is.*

The syringe feels as heavy as iron in my pocket as I open the door of the cage and go in. Should I do it in here, where

Jinx can see? Or outside, in front of Alai and everyone else? *That's ridiculous. They're just animals, Pia. They don't have feelings.*

I shut the door behind me, the metal bars as cold as ice in my hands. *And neither should you.*

Sneeze's body is warm and soft. He's used to being handled by Uncle Jonas, so he doesn't mind when I pick him up. Jinx lifts her head and twitches her whiskers, but when she sees it's me, she yawns, baring sharp fangs, and lies back down. So unaware. So innocent.

Just animals.

I decide to take him out of the cage. If his mother senses I'm about to harm her offspring, she'll go berserk.

Against one wall, Uncle Jonas has set a metal table, where he grooms and treats the animals. It's covered with scratches and claw marks, and I even see where something has bitten into the edge. I set Sneeze down and rub my hand along his back. He arches it and purrs, rubs his head against my hand. You'd never even know he had FIV.

I pull out the syringe, feeling Alai's eyes boring into my back. My hand shakes violently, and then my arm. I drop the syringe and it clatters, making me jump. Thankfully it doesn't break. I pick it up and have to hold my wrist with my other hand to stop it from shaking. Instead, my breath begins to rattle, like Roosevelt's just before he died. I feel like one of the maracas the Ai'oans make when they fill empty gourds with dried beans and shake them as they dance.

"It's okay, it's okay," I chant under my breath, not knowing if the words are for me or Sneeze. The kitten blinks, yawns, and stretches, extending his little claws in front of him.

Just do it, Pia; don't think twice. Stop thinking. Just do it and be done.

I hold the syringe and tremble, but my knees are going weak. I can't stand. I scoop up Sneeze and sit cross-legged on the floor.

Have to prove . . . no right and wrong . . . progress, regress, reason, chaos. Life and death.

Sneeze sniffs the syringe, then rubs his head and ears over it, purring, liking the smooth, hard feel of it.

You are the pinnacle of human perfection. . . . There is no greater good than you, Pia . . . really the greatest and most noble form of compassion . . .

He tries to jump away; there's a cricket scuttling by, and Sneeze wants to pounce on it. I hold him back.

You must do it; you must prove to us that you're ready.

I pinch the skin on the back of Sneeze's neck into a roll and fight to steady the violent trembles in my hand. In his cage, Alai is on his feet, pacing back and forth, eyes watching, tail twitching.

You can't have regrets, and you can't hold on to guilt. You must kill Subject 294 and be able to leave it in the past, do you understand?

"I don't," I whisper, and only then do I realize there are tears pouring down my cheeks. "I don't understand." Alai paces, back and forth, back and forth, eyes like Eio's, so sharp and alive and full of knowing.

It is necessary.

"I can't!" I throw the syringe aside and scoop Sneeze up, burying my face in his fur. "I can't do it," I whisper. "I'll never be strong enough.

I hear a thump and look up in surprise to see my mother standing in the doorway, watching me.

"What—what are you doing here?" I stammer. "I thought you were asleep."

"Weak," she says.

"What?" I squeeze the kitten tighter to me.

"You were always weak, Pia. Soft. Emotional. Incompetent."

"I—I'm not! It's just, he's a *kitten*. What's the *point*—"

"The point," she replies, striding toward us. She's still dressed, so I figure she was never in her bedroom to begin with; she was probably working with Uncle Paolo in the lab. "The point is that this is what Paolo asked of you. He is a great scientist, a brilliant man, and you should be honored to work beside him."

"I am—"

She reaches down and lifts Sneeze from my grasp. "You get it from your father, Pia. Certainly not *me*."

"What are you doing?"

She bends over and picks up the syringe. "What you couldn't do. Paolo has poured his life into you, Pia. You mean everything to him. I won't let your weakness cost him his place in Little Cam. Not after everything he's done for us. You *will* become who he wants you to be, but he doesn't have to know that we cut a few corners."

"What do you—*no!*"

It's too late. She drives the needle into the roll of skin and fur. I clap my hands to my ears, trying to block out Sneeze's whimper. Alai growls, and Jinx sits up, her hackles raised. Even the Grouch joins in, starting up his terrible long roar, lips protruding in a wide O. The other animals, roused and

excited by the commotion, begin squawking, barking, growling, chattering. *Too much noise! Stop, stop, stop!*

"Stop!" I cry out to both my mother and the frantic animals. Sneeze is weakening. His tail stops swinging, his paws
stop trying to bat at a lock of my mother's hair, his eyes lose
their curious luster.

He goes still. Mother tosses him to the ground beside me,
the body making a sickening thud, and I recoil in horror.

"There," she says. "I do the dirty work, you get the credit."

"I won't! I'll tell him what you did!"

"You'll do no such thing." She grabs my hand and presses
the syringe into it. "You wouldn't want the little cat to have
died in vain, would you?"

She holds my gaze for a long moment, then turns crisply
and leaves the building, letting the door slam behind her. I
stare after her, wondering if I even know her at all, as a sob
rises in my throat. My heart convulses and tears begin falling
down my cheeks. *How could you, Mother?* I think back to the
night of my birthday party, of how safe I felt in Mother's arms
during that brief, unexpected hug.

Was that moment a lie? I think it must have been. There
was certainly no maternal warmth in her eyes tonight. The
memory of that gentle embrace, which I've carried with me
like a blanket, has been ripped away and shredded.

She said she would do anything to keep Uncle Paolo in
Little Cam, and she proved it. My mother has never been
close to me. Her focus has always been on Uncle Paolo and
the Immortis team, on her figures and sums. But I always
felt I understood her, at least. She is the kind of scientist
Uncle Paolo wants me to be, governed by cool reason and

utterly focused on the task at hand. I've always admired that about her.

But right now I only hate her, and I hate myself for it. I hate myself for so many things at this moment, most of all for the body in my hands.

"Oh, Sneeze," I weep, bending over him. "Sneeze, Sneeze, Sneeze, I'm sorry, I'm sorry, I'm sorry." I look up at Jinx, barely seeing her through the blur of tears. "I'm sorry, I'm sorry. . . ."

I can't stop crying. If this keeps up, someone will hear the racket the animals are making and come investigate. I can't be seen like this. I must be ready, must be strong. After all, I'm one of *them* now. My dream is coming true.

Above all, consider the cost, Harriet's voice haunts. *Ask yourself what it is they are demanding of you. Ponder who it is they want you to be.*

"It's a little late now," I say aloud. "It's done. It was . . . necessary." *But why? No. I can't think like that. It's done; it's over. I have to make myself accept that.* I can't bring Sneeze back, but, like Mother said, I can't let his death be in vain.

I stand up, Sneeze's body much heavier than it was before, and place him on the table. Then I go to the sink by the macaw cages and wash my hands. I cover them in soap, scrub and scrub, then rinse, then do it again. I wash my hands over and over, and I have to force myself to stop.

Then I go back and wrap Sneeze in a blanket, probably the same one Uncle Jonas wrapped him in when he was born. His head peeps out, eyes glazed over and still. Cradling the bundle in my arms, I drop the empty syringe into the trash and head for the door. Sneeze is heavy, so very heavy.

When I flip the lights off in the menagerie, the animals

finally begin to fall silent. Except Alai. Even in the darkness, I can see his eyes glowing, and a ceaseless low growl vibrates in his throat. There is something feral in his actions, something terrifying. He's more like a wild animal than the pet I raised and pampered.

I am glad when the door is shut and it's just me walking quickly across the grounds toward A Labs. Uncle Paolo's light is still on. I'll give him his Subject 294 and be done with it.

As hard as I try to shut out every little thought, especially of my mother, one persists until it slips through my barrier and runs around my head like an escaped and frenetic sparrow.

If this was only the test to prepare me . . . what must come next?

TWENTY-
EIGHT

Today we go to Falk's Glen to get a vial of elysia.

Uncle Paolo and the rest of the team—no one on the Immortis team wants to miss out on a day as monumental as this—make preparations as I sit by and watch. The happy congratulations of the team as they welcomed me into their midst are still fresh in my ears, along with Uncle Paolo's pronouncement last night: in celebration of my new status as a member of the team, we will go to the glen and bring back enough elysia to make one injection of Immortis. A week ago, this would have had me giddy with elation. As it is, my excitement is mingled with dread. I have not seen Uncle Antonio since last night in the hut, and I'm not sure I want to. His words are still parading through my thoughts in bold, capital letters. *Evil in Little Cam* . . . I stare at my hands.

"Are you ready to go, Pia?" asks Uncle Paolo.

"Been ready," I reply, patting my backpack.

"We are loading up in five minutes!" he yells. Scientists

scramble to organize their bags and equipment. Really, I don't see why they need so much *stuff*. It's supposed to be just a quick trip. Go in, get one vial of nectar, and come back.

Ten minutes later, we load up. There are three Jeeps, though we could all fit in two if not for the baggage. The scientists pack as if they're setting up a month-long field operation. My mother climbs up beside Uncle Paolo and gives orders to the others as they load their equipment. I watch her, but she doesn't acknowledge me. She was there last night when I showed Sneeze's body to Uncle Paolo, and she never so much as met my eyes.

Uncle Paolo drives one Jeep, and Uncle Timothy assigns the others to two of his men, who also carry rifles. "For safety," says Uncle Paolo. Uncle Timothy himself is staying behind.

When the gates finally open and we begin rumbling out, I suddenly realize that this is the first time I'm leaving Little Cam with permission. I've been sneaking out so regularly, I'd almost forgotten it was against the rules in the first place.

We turn the first bend in the road, and Little Cam vanishes.

Uncle Jakob gives me a crooked half smile. "Welcome to the jungle, Pia!" he says.

I give him a smile in return, then quickly look away so that he doesn't see how weak it is.

It's only two and half miles to Falk's Glen. We park on the side of the road and have to hike the last mile and a half because the road curves south to the Little Mississip, but the glen lies to the west. The jungle is steamy today, though not too hot. Still, every breath feels damper than the last. The scientists curse and pant, fighting for every step beneath the loads they carry, cursing at my mother when she yells for them to hurry up. Uncle Paolo shakes his head at them and resigns himself to waiting. He's sweating like the rest of them, but he seems infused with an energy that defies the exertion. When I look at him, I swear I can see him trembling with excitement.

It's been eighteen years since the last vial of Immortis was made. The last would have been for my parents, a year or so before they conceived me. Uncle Paolo was here for that, but he wasn't the one in charge. That had been a man named Dr. Sato, who retired not long after I was born. So this is Uncle Paolo's first chance to make Immortis himself, to be the one overseeing it all.

After he announced today's excursion, I asked him why we were going so soon. None of the new subjects have arrived yet, and though I don't know much about Immortis, I know it has to be used within a week of being made or it loses its potency. Uncle Paolo's response was a surprise: "As it stands, Pia, one of the subjects *is* already here: me. Yes, I'm going to be participating in the Immortis project myself, and, as such, I will be receiving the first injection." As far as I know, he's the first scientist to nominate himself for that role. No wonder he is so eager; he has more invested in today's excursion than anyone else—except, perhaps, me.

I know Uncle Paolo has always dreamed of influencing the future of humanity by creating immortals, but he's taking it a step further by inserting his own genetic code into the gene pool that will eventually produce Mr. Perfect. And when one of the female subjects gives birth to what will essentially be Uncle Paolo's son, will that child be treated differently than the others? Suddenly I wonder whether this plan of his is designed not just to have even more influence in the Immortis project, but simply to have a daughter or son. It's a question I've never asked him or any of the scientists: Do they *want* children? All living creatures have the built-in urge to procreate; that's a basic part of biology and one that most of them have sacrificed in order to work here. By the time they retire, it will be too late to have children.

Once again, I'm reminded of how much is invested in me and in the Immortis project, and when I think of how close I came to abandoning this place last night, I feel ashamed.

Yet a little regretful. The hurt in Eio's eyes when I ran . . . But I can't think about that. I have to stay strong.

There's a slender path leading the way, and instead of matching the others' excruciatingly slow pace, I take the lead. As a result, I reach the glen a good five minutes before them. After climbing a small rise drenched in vivid green ferns and red heliconias, I descend again and find myself in Falk's Glen.

For a moment, all I can do is stare. The clearing is no bigger than the courtyard in Little Cam, but it's flooded with purple orchids, like a cup of violet-tinted wine. They're bigger and more elaborately composed than most species of orchid, and the ends of the petals are tipped with gold. They're indescribably beautiful. The sight of the glen, after so many years of wondering, lifts my spirits a little. Surely Uncle Antonio is wrong. Such beauty can't possibly exist beside the evil he imagines, whatever it may be.

I suddenly wonder if the catalyst flower might grow here too, but all I see is elysia.

I'm met by a guard whose name is Dickson, one of Uncle Timothy's crew. He asks where the others are, and when I tell him they're struggling with equipment, he groans and spits on a fern and goes to help them, leaving me alone in the glen.

A smooth rock sits on the edge of the pool of flowers. I sit on it and lean over the flower closest to me, and there, in the small cup formed by the petals, I see a few ounces of the immortality nectar. *Amazing, how death and life can be so closely connected in this one blossom, and the presence of the catalyst makes all the difference between the two.*

"Pia?"

I whirl and see a face framed by fern leaves. Stiffening, I rise to my feet and clench my hands into fists at my sides. "What do *you* want?"

Eio's nearly invisible; he might have stood there all day and gone unnoticed. "I wanted to say I'm sorry. I never meant to make you angry."

"Eio, the scientists will be here any minute. You should go!"

He shakes his head in that stubborn way of his. "Everyone will miss you, especially Ami. She asks for you."

"Just forget about me, both of you—and Uncle Antonio too! I'm where I belong now, doing what I'm supposed to do. *Being* who I really am! Can't you understand that?"

"I understand that I made you angry, and I'm sorry." His face is pained, eyes pleading. It's so hard to maintain my resolve when he looks at me like that. "Punish me if you want, but please, not Ami. Not my father."

Glancing at the path to be sure we're still alone, but knowing we don't have long, I scowl at him and point toward the jungle. "Go, Eio! Leave me alone! I mean it! I don't want to see Ai'oa anymore, or you or Ami or anyone else. Just *go*, will you?"

He looks as if I've shot him with a poisoned arrow. "I came here to deliver a message for Papi. He said that if you must know the truth, you will have it."

"Really?" I eye him skeptically. "He's going to tell me everything? Why Alex and Marian ran? Why he wants me to leave?"

"Yes. No. Well, yes, you're going to learn all of that, but it's not Papi who's going to tell it to you."

I throw up my hands. "Who, then?"

"Kapukiri."

My hands fall back to my sides. "Kapukiri? What does *Kapukiri* know?"

"Will you come? Tonight?"

"I . . ." I remember my anger and Uncle Antonio calling me a monster, and I decide I won't give in so easily. "I don't know. Probably not."

Suddenly I hear voices. The others are coming over the hill; I can see the tops of their heads already.

"Eio! Eio, go!"

He seems on the verge of saying something else, but then he clamps his jaw shut and disappears into the jungle again. I whirl around just as Uncle Paolo descends into the glen, and I hope he can't see a flush in my cheeks or the leaves shaking from where Eio was standing. But Uncle Paolo's eyes are on the elysia, not me, and I exhale slowly and will my heart to calm.

So Uncle Antonio wants to tell me the truth—the whole truth. Will I go? I don't know. I really don't. Maybe it's a trick, and maybe Uncle Antonio is going to force me to leave, since I won't go on my own. Or maybe this is it—my chance to finally find out what all the whispers have been about. But from *Kapukiri*?

The others finally arrive. They immediately begin breaking out cameras and notepads, stepping gingerly through the flowers as they document down to the last speck on each petal.

"Well," says Uncle Paolo, "what do you think, Pia?"

"It's beautiful. Too much for words."

He nods appreciatively. "And to think, in all the world, these are the only flowers of their kind."

"Can I do it?" I ask tentatively. "Can I collect the nectar?"

Uncle Paolo looks at me thoughtfully. "Yes . . . I think that's a good idea."

Trying my best to be the composed, businesslike scientist Uncle Paolo is, I take the small vial he gives me and follow his instructions carefully. Mother, who has a camera in her hands, documents each second of the process.

"Now," says Uncle Paolo, "pick a flower. Any one will do. Good. Put the vial under the lower petal, and simply tip the blossom. Excellent, Pia. Well done."

I hand the vial, half-full of the shimmering clear liquid, to Uncle Paolo. He stoppers it and tucks it carefully into his vest pocket.

"Just one vial?"

"That's all we need today."

It takes thirty minutes for the team to repack their equipment, half of which they didn't even take out of their bags.

I feel regretful when Falk's Glen disappears behind us. It's the kind of place to which you know you'll never find the equal. A place to which memory can't quite do justice, a place so rare and beautiful, it feels sacred.

On the ride back, I find myself emerging from the dark cloud Uncle Antonio pinned over my head. Maybe things aren't going to be so bad. I look around at my team and see smiles, camaraderie, and hope. These aren't monsters. These are my colleagues and mentors. My friends. Even my mother . . . she sits by Uncle Paolo, laughing at something he tells her, and her hand is on his knee. She killed Sneeze, yes. But she did it to save the most important person in her life. Maybe I can learn to accept that.

I feel more and more confident that my return to Little Cam was the right thing. This is my place, and whatever secrets have been kept from me, they can't be as bad as Uncle Antonio thinks.

I consider Eio's invitation to go to Ai'oa tonight and learn the truth. It's tempting, but I don't think I'll go. After all, I'm a scientist now, and Uncle Paolo will soon tell me all the secrets of Immortis, including the nature of the mysterious catalyst. Despite Uncle Antonio's doubts, I *am* one of them—so I should start behaving like one of them. Let Uncle Paolo tell me the truth.

As we rumble through the gates of Little Cam, I'm almost happy again. I made my decision last night when I returned, and I'm sticking to it.

Today is the first day of forever.

At dinner, I sit with Uncle Sergei and Uncle Jakob, who make a checkerboard out of spaghetti noodles on the table, using pepperoni and olives for playing pieces. It's very funny, but I find it difficult to laugh. Over Uncle Sergei's shoulder I can see Uncle Antonio. Every time I look up, he's staring straight at me. I know he wonders if Eio relayed his message.

Later that evening, when I try to go for a swim, I find Uncle Antonio waiting for me. He sits on the edge of the pool, feet in the water. There's no one else here; I know I can't avoid him much longer.

"He talked to you?" he asks as I slip into the water.

I sink to the bottom of the pool and sit for nearly a minute before rising to the surface, where I wipe the water from my eyes and nod.

"And? Well?"

"I'm not going." I float on my back and wish he would just give up and go away.

"Pia, come here."

"No."

"Come *here*."

Reluctant and irritated, I slowly drift his way. When I'm close enough, he grabs my wrist and holds me close, preventing me from disappearing under the water again.

"Uncle Antonio!" I jerk against his grip, but he only tightens it.

"Did anyone ever tell you what happened to your grandparents, Pia? And to my parents?"

"They left Little Cam," I respond angrily. "To start lives in the outside world."

He shakes his head. "Lies. They never left Little Cam. They never had the chance, because after Alex and Marian's 'accident,' they were locked up in B Labs, where they . . ." He draws several short breaths, as if trying to quell some great surge of emotion. His eyes burn with it. "Where they died."

"Died?" I whisper. "How?"

"Sato was in charge at the time. He was less patient than Paolo and wanted to find a way to bypass the five generations of waiting for an immortal to be born. He wanted immortality for himself, and so he . . ." Uncle Paolo closes his eyes, his chest swelling as he breathes in. When he opens them again, the anger is gone, replaced by sorrow. "He used them to test different strains of Immortis. They all died within days of each other, and their bodies . . ."

"Stop," I whisper, because he looks so wretched. And because I don't want to hear it.

But he is merciless. "Their bodies were thrown into the jungle to decompose after Sato was done with them."

"But Mother—"

"Your mother knows the truth, Pia, but she became one of *them* long ago. God knows why. Fear, maybe, that the same thing would happen to her. And then there's Paolo, of course." He shakes his head. "She fell for him the minute he arrived, years ago. She was only fifteen or so when he came, but the moment she laid eyes on him, she was his. Completely. And from that moment on, she hated your poor father. Paolo was everything Will wasn't, and she resented being paired off with Will. Though she'd have done better to choose him. He's a better man than Paolo, he just never lets anyone see it."

The water feels thirty degrees colder, but it's not the temperature that accounts for the goose bumps prickling down my arm. *No. Please, no.* He was right. It *is* more terrible than I ever knew. I think of the rooms in B Labs, the stains on the floors and walls . . . bloodstains. The scratches made by fingernails belonging to my own grandparents, driven insane, perhaps, by pain or claustrophobia. How long did they survive in those dark cells before Sato's experiments claimed their lives? When they did die, was it with relief?

How does my mother live with herself, knowing what happened? My father? He's so quiet and shy . . . maybe this is why. He's always seemed to be hiding from something. I just never knew what.

But even these terrible truths—for though I want to, I cannot doubt they are true, because no lie could produce such anguish on Uncle Antonio's face—are not the worst of it. He still hasn't given me the one answer I've been seeking most of all. Though after what he just told me, I'm not so sure I want to hear it.

"Why did Alex and Marian run, Uncle Antonio?"

"Come with me to Ai'oa, Pia, and you will find out. I swear I will never ask anything more of you. Come with me this once, and if your mind still isn't changed, I'll know you truly are one of them. I'll even hand you your lab coat myself."

His words are hard and clipped, but his eyes are filled with almost desperate pleading.

"If you won't go for me," he continues, "go for Eio. One last time. From what I hear, he risked his life to save yours. You owe him this much."

With that, he stands and slips his sandals on, leaving me free to bury myself beneath the water once more. But I don't. I watch him go and meet his eyes when he pauses at the door and looks back.

"I'll be waiting at the tunnel at midnight." The sadness in his eyes is deep enough to drown in. "It's too late for Alex and Marian, Pia. Too late for me and your mother and your grandparents. It's not too late for you, but you're running out of time."

He leaves, his wet sandals squelching on the tile. I float on my back, drifting to the middle of the pool, thinking of the picture my mother showed me on my birthday and of the blurry form that was my grandfather.

The past seems to float around me, staining the water black, trying to drag me down and drown me. The pool holds no solace for me any longer. When I stare up at the glass panes of the ceiling, I see instead the blurry faces of people I never knew. People whose blood runs in my veins and who suffered terrible deaths. They are frozen in my memory now, and nothing I can ever do will erase them.

TWENTY-NINE

ou came."

"Yes."

Eio looks behind me. "Papi."

"Hello, Eio," Uncle Antonio replies softly. He's said hardly two words since meeting me in the powerhouse. He seems drained, as if digging through the past stole every ounce of his energy and willpower.

"What's Kapukiri got to say to me?" I ask apprehensively.

"He's here, waiting," says Eio. "He said you would come." His eyes drop to my neck. "You're wearing the necklace."

His fingers brush the stone bird as I nod.

Eio leads us toward the center of the village, which is illuminated by half a dozen low-burning fires. Ami comes hurtling out of nowhere and slams into me, arms and legs coiled like lianas around my middle. "Pia! You're here! You're here! Eio said you weren't coming back, but I didn't believe him!"

I hug her as Eio asks, "Why *did* you come back?"

"To see Ami, of course."

She likes that. She laughs and pokes her tongue at Eio.

"Where's Kapukiri, Ami?" I ask.

"Over here, Pia! Come on, come on!" Ami pulls me down the row of huts until we're at the last one, the largest one, where Kapukiri lives. He sits in the center of the hut, cross-legged in front of a bowl of manioc. Burako and Achiri are with him, and the rest of the Ai'oans are gathering outside the hut. I smile at Luri, who smiles back.

Eio motions for me to go in and then follows. We sit across from the medicine man, Uncle Antonio standing behind us. I take some manioc, to be polite, and then, following Eio's lead, I sit and wait. Kapukiri operates according to his own good time, and there's absolutely no use in trying to rush him.

Eio reaches out and takes my hand. I stare at it and then slowly wrap my fingers around his. His skin is warm and a little bit dry, and, as always, his touch is accompanied by an electric thrill that runs up my arm and into my heart.

"I'm sorry," I whisper.

He squeezes my hand. "I know. Me too."

Staring into his steady blue eyes, I feel a tightening of my heartstrings. I had thought I could just forget him—that if I tried hard enough, my feelings for him would vanish. But trying to push Eio out of my heart would be like trying to hide a shadow by turning off the light. The harder I resist, the deeper he falls into my heart.

Fortunately, Kapukiri doesn't make us wait long. I have no idea what to expect from him, but I'm still surprised when he starts speaking in a deep, slow, ceremonious tone.

"The Legend of the Kaluakoa, the Ones Who Were but Are No More," he begins solemnly in Ai'oan.

"The Kaluakoa were a gentle people, like the Ai'oa, and their sign was the jaguar, mantis, and moon. They lived as one with the forest, and even the great anaconda offered himself to their cookfires."

"But over the mountain lived the fierce Maturo, the Face-Eaters. They believed that the more people they killed, the stronger they became, and they took the faces of the ones they killed to make into coats to wrap their babes in. They killed many Kaluakoa."

Kapukiri pauses to take a handful of manioc and chew it. Since he has few teeth, this takes some time. I stare at the fire, imagining a distant past when no *karaíba* had set foot in the jungle and only the Ai'oan ancestors roamed through the trees.

Kapukiri smacks his lips and resumes speaking.

"The Kaluakoa prayed to the gods to send them a protector. So the gods sent Miua, the god-child. Miua saw the cruelty of the Maturo and the dead, faceless Kaluakoa, and she wept many tears for them. From her tears grew the *yresa*, and in the flowers, her tears collected."

I look at Eio. "The origin of *yresa*," I whisper, recalling what he said to me the night he first showed me the river: "*You don't know, do you? About the origin of* yresa?" It's the first time I've thought back to that moment.

Kapukiri clears his throat, and I realize he's annoyed at my interruption.

"Sorry," I whisper.

He keeps his eyes narrowed at me and continues.

"Under Miua's instructions, the Elders drank the tears of the *yresa* and died. The wise man of the village cut the palms of the dead and placed one drop of the Elders' blood on the tongues of the living. This became Miu'mani, the Death Ceremonies. After they drank the blood of the Elders, the people wept and mourned in the valley, and from their tears more *yresa* grew. From then on, no Elder died in his sleep. Instead, he went to the valley of *yresa* and drank their tears, and his lifeblood was given to the people. The lifeblood flowed from mother to daughter, from father to son, and every generation a protector was born. The protectors were mighty warriors, swift and sure. They were called the *Tapumiri*, and they could not die. When the Maturo came over the mountain, the *Tapumiri* defended the Kaluakoa and sent the Maturo away with no faces but their own."

I am transfixed by the fire. The flames take shape, become people. Golden yellow Kaluakoa, rising and falling, giving birth and dying. Brief, fragile lives lived out in seeming obscurity, but now immortalized in Kapukiri's words.

"The *Tapumiri* were so powerful, their bodies did not grow old. But they grew old in their hearts, and when they had lived the fullness of their years, they too drank the tears of Miua and died. For it is said that the great river of lifeblood is not eternal, but must be renewed with blood, just as the great river of the jungle must be renewed with rain. This is why the gods decreed that so many must die for even one protector to be born—there cannot be birth without death. There cannot be life without the shedding of blood.

"But one *Tapumiri* was born to the chief of the Kaluakoa, and he became chief when his father died. This was Izotaza, the Foolish One, for he desired to be the only *Tapumiri* in the world, and the most powerful. So he forbade the Elders from drinking the tears of the *yresa*, and he burned the valley where they grew. The Elders wept for his foolishness, but Izotaza would not be swayed, and no more protectors were born."

The fire burns low, the coals glowing like jaguar eyes. I cannot look away.

"When the Maturo heard of this chief's foolishness, they came over the mountain as never before, women and children too, and they all carried knives and poison darts. Izotaza was not powerful enough to stop them all by himself, and all of the Kaluakoa were killed.

"Izotaza saw what his foolishness and pride had done, and he went to the valley where the *yresa* had been and wept for the death of the Kaluakoa. For three moons and three suns he wept, and when he could weep no more he looked up and saw that the valley was filled with *yresa* once more, grown from his tears. Izotaza drank and died."

Kapukiri pauses. It seems almost as if he's fallen into a trance. He stares into the fire, his eyes glowing with reflected embers. He is as still as stone; not even his chest rises and falls. After a long moment like this, he goes on.

"From then on the valley of *yresa* has been feared by the people of the world. The Ai'oa do not drink, because we are a strong people. We can defend ourselves against tribes like the Maturo, and we have no need of Miua's tears."

He looks up, and his dark eyes, at once so young and so ancient, stare directly into mine, and I feel as if he's looking at every moment of my life, seeing everything I've ever done and hearing every thought I ever had. His eyes hold mine, and they burn.

"But we remember the Kaluakoa, the Ones Who Were but Are No More. And we remember that there must be a balance. No birth without death. No life without tears. What is taken from the world must be given back, and from him who takes and does not give back, who would tip the balance of the river, from him *all* will be taken. No one should live forever, but should give his blood to the river when the time comes so that tomorrow another may live. And so it goes." He closes his eyes, and I exhale for the first time in several minutes, released from his spell. "And so it goes," he whispers.

"And so it goes," repeat the villagers. "And so it goes."

"And so it goes," whispers Eio.

Silence falls.

I feel the strangest sensation. It's as if I'm not me at all. Instead, I'm a disembodied haze suspended in the air above the village, looking down at the cluster of Ai'oans circled around an ancient medicine man and pale, wide-eyed girl. I wonder what she is thinking, to look so still and white. I sense something dreadful has just happened to her, and she doesn't yet understand it. I yearn, desperately, to glide up and away into the canopy of the rainforest, to leave this grim little scene behind me and search for happier company. But I'm pulled down again to the earth, and suddenly I *am* that pale girl sitting on a mat of leaves, and her sorrow is so deep and sharp that I double over and try to suck in breath, but nothing will enter my lungs. As if even the air despises me.

"Pia?" A voice echoes through my head from across a vast distance. Uncle Antonio. I want to hide from him, but there is nowhere to go. I'm open and exposed, like a cell lying spread-eagle on a microscope slide. No place to run.

"Pia, look at me." Eio lifts my chin and finds my eyes with his own. "Are you all right?"

"No," I whisper. "Eio, take me somewhere where they can't see me."

He looks confused, but he acts quickly. The Ai'oans let me go silently, and I avoid their eyes. Uncle Antonio reaches out to me, but I shake my head. I can't face him right now. I need to get away.

We walk into the trees and sink into the dirt at the base of a massive kapok.

"Eio, I can't breathe!"

He pulls me close and lays my head on his shoulder. "Yes, you can, Pia. You're breathing right now. Don't you feel it?"

"I can't feel anything. Have you heard this story before?"

Silence. Then, "Yes."

"Does it mean what I think it means?" I ask.

"I don't know. It's just a story."

I lift my chin so that I can look up at him. "I don't want to believe it. I don't know if I can. But Uncle Antonio believes it, doesn't he?" Of course he does. He said he has seen it with his own eyes: "*I know what really goes on behind those lab doors.*"

"Eio, I have to go back."

"What? Why? He told me that if you heard the story, you would let me take you away."

I sit up and draw a deep breath, let it out. "I have to know if it's true, Eio. I have to go back and see it with my own eyes. Like you said, maybe it's just a story. . . . But I know how I can find out."

"I'll come with you."

"No, please don't. If it *is* true—oh, Eio—if it's true, then Uncle Antonio was right. About everything." *There is evil in Little Cam.* "Stay here. Please. I know where to find you."

He tenses, but finally nods. "Will you be all right?"

"I don't know." I stand and wait until my head stops spinning. "I really don't know."

The walk back to Little Cam is surreal. The jungle might as well be made of paper and string, and me a puppet moving clumsily and unnaturally through it. I go quickly because I don't want Uncle Antonio to catch up to me. I hope he'll stay in Ai'oa a while longer.

I have to put the story of the Kaluakoa to the test. If this legend, told around fires by ancient jungle medicine men, means what I think it means, then Uncle Antonio's worst fears will be realized: the truth will destroy me. I already feel it at work, gnawing like a rat at the end of each thought passing through my head.

Little Cam is nearly as dark as the jungle. I float through it like a ghost come back to haunt. Everyone seems to be asleep. No lights in the windows, no voices in the shadows. I'm alone, which is frightening. I'd rather be locked up in a B Labs cell than locked up in my head with only my own voice for company.

I consider going straight to my bedroom, shutting the door, and crawling into my bed. Hiding under the blankets and never coming out. Simply locking myself in a room where nothing and no one—not any uncles or aunts, not Eio, and especially not the truth—can find me. But I don't. I circle the glass house and go to the cinchona tree where Uncle Antonio found me crying and where I first realized that he was Eio's father.

It's as dark as the night can be, but my elysia eyes can still pick out the leaves on the tree and the blades of grass as I kneel down. I run my hands slowly through the grass, each finger alert and sensitive, in case my eyes miss it. If it's even here at all. I hope with every ounce of will I have that it's not.

After they drank the blood of the Elders, the people wept and mourned in the valley, and from their tears more yresa *grew.*

The grass is already beaded with dew, and soon my hands and clothes are damp. Each blade is soft, unless my fingers brush its edge, and then it feels as sharp as a needle.

For three moons and three suns he wept, and when he could weep no more he looked up and saw that the valley was filled with yresa *once more, grown from his tears.*

It is my eyes, and not my hands, that find it at the last moment, just before I give up and give in to relief. But relief is not to be mine, not tonight, because there it is, in the very spot where my tears fell. Dim and gray in the darkness, but unmistakable. The longer I stare, the more the colors appear. Purple petals tipped with gold, the orchid-like structure, the breathtaking beauty. I hadn't expected a flower. I had expected a seedling, or even a bud, but not a fully developed blossom. *Two days. It grew in only two days.*

What scientific explanation could Uncle Paolo possibly have for that?

The spores that grow elysia are contained in the tears of immortals, in the DNA of people who have elysia absorbed into their genetic code. It makes a kind of sense, in a crazy, scientifically unprecedented way. All this time, and the scientists have never figured it out—and the "ignorant" Ai'oans have known all along.

Back in my room, I lie on the bed and turn the flower over in my hands, careful not to tip it and pour the nectar out. Such beauty. Such terror. All contained in a mere blossom.

I hear a soft knock on the door and Uncle Antonio's voice. "Can I come in?"

"Please," I reply, just loudly enough for him to hear. "Go away. I need some time."

"Pia . . ." I can hear the frustration in his voice. "Okay. Fine. I'll give you time. But you must know there's isn't much left."

"I know."

After he leaves, I study the flower again, feeling the velvet of the petals between my fingers.

The catalyst isn't a flower at all. It's a person, or many people. It's all in the story: one person drinks the deadly nectar of the elysia flower, and when they die, the others drink their blood. *The lifeblood flowed from mother to daughter, from father to son, and every generation a protector was born.* Five generations. It takes five generations of death to produce one "protector," one *Tapumiri*. If nearly an entire village is passing on the genetic influence of elysia, it makes sense that about one child in every generation would be born immortal.

Jaguar, mantis, moon. Kapukiri saw it in my eyes, in the swirling colors visible only by firelight.

In this lovely, deadly flower, I hold the tears of Miua, which would claim the lives of many to give unending life to one.

A mixture of elysia and the blood of a sacrificed human.

That is the catalyst. That is Immortis. That is the secret I was so eager to unveil. The destiny I was so ready to commit myself to.

That is my legacy.

I'm shrinking. The world expands and convolutes around me, a monster that's been sleeping all this time, finally awoken and ravenous to feed. I drop the flower to the floor, not caring if it spills, and curl into a ball on the blankets.

The Wickham tests. Uncle Paolo always said that one day I would understand the necessity of them. Well, now I do. I had to kill Sneeze so that they would believe I could kill a human. Everyone who has come here has had to prove the same thing. We're not a colony of scientists.

We're a colony of murderers.

How many have died that I might live?

And *who* has died that I might live?

They must have had dozens of subjects—no, not subjects. Victims. Immortis must be fresh for each injection. They had to make so many injections: *32 original progenitors; 32 begot 16, 16 begot 8, 8 (minus 2 who ran away and drowned, leaving 1 odd one out) begot 2, and 2 begot me; 3 injections each per lifespan per generation . . .*

"Stop!" I sit up straight in bed, forcing the numbers to dissolve, unable to continue. I'm panting, and there is a thin film of sweat encasing my body.

The injection is scheduled for the day after tomorrow. If Kapukiri's story is at all accurate—they need someone to be the victim. Someone to offer their life to the altar of immortality.

I need to think. Need to clear away the panic and the fog and the horror that paralyzes my thoughts. I run to the bathroom and pour the nectar from the flower into the sink, then run water until every drop of the shimmering liquid is gone. My stomach lurches, and I cling to the edges of the sink as I gag, but nothing comes up.

Terrified—I've never vomited in my life—I walk in circles around the room, do sit-ups and push-ups, jog in place. My blood pumps faster, washing away most of the hysteria. I force myself to swallow the rest. I have to have myself under control or I'll only create a worse mess of things.

I need a plan. And I need an ally.

Finally, I sit on the floor in front of the window and face the jungle, doing all I can to keep the darkness at bay. It looms at the edges of my mind, threatening to swallow me whole if I fail to be diligent for even one moment.

My hands slowly tear the elysia flower into tiny bits as I wait for morning.

THIRTY

As soon as I see sunlight overhead, I go looking for Uncle Antonio. I'm ready to sit with him and talk about what I heard. We need to lay everything out, view it from every angle. Find the cracks and the flaws in the formula. Heat it like water and see what hidden truths rise to the surface.

But it's Aunt Harriet, not Uncle Antonio, whom I find first. She has Alai on a leash outside the menagerie.

"Pia, good heavens, what's happened? You look like death!"

Her unwitting turn of phrase sends a chill down my spine.

I remember that Aunt Harriet is still in the dark. *She deserves the truth. I owe her that much.* I draw a deep, shaky breath. "I . . . I've learned a lot in the past few hours—things you really should know, Aunt Harriet." I look around, and though we're alone, I take her by the elbow and lead her behind the building so we're hidden from anyone who might

310

walk by. "You know how we've been wondering about the catalyst and what it could be?" I whisper.

She nods, her hand tightening slightly on Alai's leash.

"Well . . ." I close my eyes and force the words from my lips. "I've discovered what it is." Then the words rush out like the waterfall where Eio and Ami swim. I hold nothing back. I tell her about our argument in the jungle, Eio's confessed feelings, my intention—and failure—to put down Sneeze, the trip to Falk's Glen, and the legend of the Kaluakoa, which isn't a legend at all. I end by telling her of the elysia grown from my tears.

When I finish, she presses her hands to her mouth and stares at the ground. She stands this way for two, three, four minutes. I count the seconds in my head. Finally she looks up again with pupils constricted to pinpoints. "Are you—are you sure? *Killing* people, Pia?"

"I don't know!" I run my hand through my hair and start pacing to and fro in front of her. "All I know about elysia—besides the fact that I can grow it with my tears—is the Kaluakoa's experience with it. Maybe it isn't necessary to *kill* people to make Immortis. Maybe you can just draw a little blood, mix it with elysia. . . . We're scientists. We have technology and medicine and rats to experiment on. Surely Falk found a way around the killing." *Except for my grandparents.* I stop walking and look at her in desperation. "Right?"

She bites her lip and squints at the ground for a moment before answering. "Well, where would the scientists get people to inject with elysia, anyway? They couldn't be bringing in subjects all the time; someone on the outside would

notice. It's impractical. You're right. There must be a different way." Her voice drops to a whisper. "Surely there must
be. If it's true . . . then it's worse than I imagined. I knew
they were keeping secrets, but I never thought it would be
like this."

"Uncle Antonio tried to warn me. He wanted me to run,
but I didn't believe him—well, I *did*, I just didn't want to."

"There, now, Pia. Like you said, we don't *know* anything
yet." She holds me at arm's length and gives me a stern look.
"You go find Antonio and get the rest of the story. Don't jump
to conclusions."

"Do you think it's true?" I ask. "Do you think they've been
killing people with elysia?"

She shrugs slowly, but I see the fear in her eyes, and I
know she does. "Go," she says. "Find Antonio."

I nod and kneel beside Alai, hand out to rub his ears. But
he hisses and raises his hackles, eyes wild. Stunned, I pull my
hand back and stare at him with dismay. "Alai?"

He shakes his head roughly and stalks away, tail as straight
as one of Eio's arrows.

"He's just skittish," Aunt Harriet says hurriedly, and she
stares up at the sky. "It's this weather. There's a storm coming, and it'll be a big one. I'll take care of him. Find me later,
Pia, and tell me what Antonio says. If the worst is true after
all, well"—she inhales deeply—"you won't be the only one
running."

"Okay." I watch Alai sadly, then, at Aunt Harriet's insis-
tence, leave them there. Try as I might, I can't wash the image
of Alai's hostile glare from my eyes.

I'm searching the gardens when I'm stopped by Uncle

Jakob. When I see him, my mind goes blank. I force myself to breathe and remember that things can't possibly be what they seem. I don't *know* Uncle Jakob is a murderer. Not yet. *There is still hope.*

"Pia, there you are!" He smiles and tucks the pencil he's holding behind his ear. "We've decided to move the operation up a day. The others are waiting in the lab. It's time to teach you about Immortis." His smile fades a little, and a grimness creeps into his eyes. "Come with me."

I panic and nearly flee then and there—*I'm not ready for this. Not yet!*—then frantically reel my emotions into check. I need to talk to Uncle Antonio, need to explore the truth until there can't possibly be any more secrets.

But there's no time. They're waiting for me.

Blindsided and completely unprepared, I follow Uncle Jakob through the courtyard and across the verandas to A Labs just as rain begins to pound the earth. The moment the door shuts behind us, thunder rattles the building.

Uncle Jakob shakes the water from his lab coat. "Gonna be a nasty one, sounds like." He gives me a curious look. "You all right?"

"Who, me?" I ask, a bit too shrill.

"I thought you'd be more excited."

Excited. The thing is, a week ago he would have been right. "I'm just . . ." My voice betrays me again.

"I know." He nods. "It's too much for words."

"Oh. Yeah." I'm relieved when he starts down the hall, apparently satisfied that I'm about to burst with excitement. In truth, I am overwhelmed with apprehension. It's growing in my stomach like bacteria in a petri dish.

I hold my breath as Uncle Jakob opens the door to my own lab.

Inside is the rest of the Immortis team. They are serious and drawn, and my heart falls a little. They don't look like people excitedly anticipating the task at hand. They look as cold and expressionless as slabs of concrete.

I can't help but notice the polished syringe lying on the table next to Uncle Paolo, who turns and greets me with a slow nod. Mother helps me put on my lab coat, with my name newly stitched onto the breast. She squeezes my shoulder and then pats it encouragingly.

Uncle Paolo's earlier energy is muted now, but I can still see it tugging at his face. "Pia, it's almost time."

I nod slowly, then notice that the back corner of the room is curtained off.

"I'm going to let you prepare the Immortis," says Uncle Paolo.

My heart, which has been sinking ever since I entered the room, suddenly climbs up into my throat like a panicked monkey searching for a way out. "What do I do?" I whisper.

He hands me the syringe, then tells me to sit down. Numbly I sit on the nearest stool, surrounded by a semicircle of the most elite—and stone-faced—biologists in the world. Lightning splits the sky outside and whips their faces with streaks of blue-white light.

"Pia," Uncle Paolo begins, voice smooth and even. "You've been tested numerous times over the past few years in ways that perhaps confused and even angered you. Those tests were not random. They were for a particular purpose: to gauge whether or not you were even capable of doing the kind of research necessary to attain our goal and fulfill the original mission of the Little Cambridge Research Facility."

I say the words automatically. "To advance the human species through the grafting of positive eugenics and biomedical engineering in order to create an immortal *Homo sapiens*."

"Precisely. All of that, all of the tests, come to a culmination today. Because of your excellent performance and flawless record, we know that you are entirely capable and suited to the task at hand."

No. Please, no. . . . Surely there's another way. . . .

Uncle Paolo draws a deep breath. "That is, the merging of the catalyst and elysia. A task that falls to you, as our greatest hope and most crowning achievement."

The way he says *catalyst* sends a chill up the back of my neck.

"Come, Pia."

I follow him to the curtain in the corner, with the other scientists behind me. Uncle Paolo takes the edge of the curtain in his hand. It's checkered blue and white, like the blankets we use when picnicking in the courtyard on special occasions.

"The catalyst," he says, and he pulls the curtain aside.

Stretched on my metal exam table, unconscious and dressed in a small white gown, is Ami.

THIRTY-ONE

"**A**re you all right?" Uncle Paolo asks.

The others murmur behind me: "Told you she wasn't ready . . ." "Too much to ask of a mere girl . . ." "Damn it, Paolo, you should have listened to us. . . ."

He hisses for them to be silent. "Pia, you know what you have to do. This is the only way. The good of our species, Pia. That's all that matters. The end justifies the means."

He said those words before, about a kitten.

Nausea churns in my stomach, and my chest feels like it's pressed in a vice. My mother's hands clamp around my shoulders.

"Be strong for us, Pia. Be strong for me. For yourself," she urges.

"Come on, Pia," encourages Uncle Jakob. "You can do it. We have all done it. It's necessary."

"He's right," Uncle Paolo adds, and Uncle Sergei murmurs

assent. Uncle Haruto remains silent, and I can feel his dark eyes boring into my back.

My destiny of death. My legacy of blood.

A wire runs from a patch over Ami's heart to a computer monitoring her heartbeat, which sounds in high, monotone beeps. They've inserted a clear plastic tube into the vein on the inside of her elbow, and a thin stream of blood trickles through it to a plastic bag hung on a rolling hook. Her wrist hangs over the side of the exam table. I can see three bright red drops of blood on the floor; they must have dripped when the tube was inserted in her arm.

Ami's hand twitches. Do the others see it? Is she waking up? How did she get here? Did they kidnap her?

Then I see it, just as a powerful roll of thunder unfurls outside the window, making the glass rattle.

Lying on the Formica countertop by the sink, discarded and forgotten by the Immortis team, is a small stone bird on a woven necklace.

My necklace.

My hand reaches automatically to my collarbone. Bare. It must have fallen off last night, probably while Kapukiri was telling the legend . . . and Ami found it.

And came to Little Cam to give it back.

My mind races, throwing all the pieces together: Eio told me about the Ai'oans who once left the village, who listened when the scientists promised to take them to cities and in airplanes. The Ai'oans who turned their backs on their people and never returned. *More lies, and these ones led to death.*

So this morning, someone must have left Little Cam.

Who? Uncle Timothy? He would have circled the compound, started through the jungle . . . and would never have made it to Ai'oa. I shut my eyes and see the whole scene as it must have played out. *Ami walking quickly through the trees, her monkey trailing her, and in her hands is my necklace. Uncle Timothy or whomever it was stopping and realizing that their job has just become much, much easier, because here is an Ai'oan all alone in the jungle. A defenseless child, no less. Easy prey.*

The horror of it overwhelms me in a cold, malignant wind that sweeps from my head to my feet. Unwitting Ami, on such a gentle, considerate mission, snapped up by monsters.

For me. All for me. All of it, from beginning to end, a list of names and deaths stretching back to 1902, countless lives destroyed—all for me.

I sway on my feet, and Uncle Haruto tenses, probably sensing I'm about to collapse. But I don't. I stand, because the truth I face is so horrible, so devastating, that I won't give myself the luxury of fainting.

I deserve to suffer the truth.

Aunt Harriet's words, spoken only minutes ago, stampede through my brain. *They couldn't be bringing in subjects all the time; someone on the outside would notice.*

Unless the subjects weren't brought from the outside at all . . . because the scientists had an entire village of unwitting prey right here in the Amazon: the Ai'oans. *My* Ai'oans. Deep inside my heart, a fire begins to burn.

How *dare* he reach his bloodstained hands into *my* Ai'oa. How *dare* he harm my sweet, innocent Ami. And how *dare* he put the needle carrying her death in *my* hands, expecting me to execute his unspeakable crime.

Uncle Paolo is talking, describing the process. "The elysia will flow through the subject's veins until it reaches her heart, which is where the catalysis takes place—and which is why we can't draw a few cups of blood and simply mix it with elysia in a petri dish. The heart will absorb the lethal chemicals in elysia, and the blood that flows back out is pure Immortis. Then we draw it out and hurry with the transfusion. We need the blood hot and fresh. If the Immortis cools, it's useless to us."

He's already rolling up his sleeve, baring his forearm, dabbing alcohol on the place where he'll inject himself with Ami's fresh blood, stolen from her veins as she dies.

They are all waiting. Watching. Wondering if I'm strong enough, ready enough.

I look at the needle and look at Ami. Her hand *is* twitching.

I want to say, *You're all monsters, how dare you do this?* But instead what comes out is, "Do you even know her name?" It's a whisper, barely audible.

Uncle Paolo cocks his head. "Name? Pia, you know better than that. This is Subject 334. Nothing more. No *one* more. Just . . . think of it as another kitten."

Those words—*another kitten*—are what snap the thin thread still tying me to Uncle Paolo and his damned *destiny*.

"She is *not* an animal," I hiss. Shock transforms Uncle Paolo's face. "She is a *child*! A human being! *Not* a lab experiment!"

"Pia!" Shock turns into anger. He steps forward. I step back. Behind me, equally surprised scientists move out of my way. Whatever they expected from me, I doubt they expected this.

But my blood is flowing again, hot and wild and reckless and enraged to the point of madness. The sorrow, the guilt, the confusion, the horror, all of the emotions that have rioted in me for the last few days are simply fuel to feed the fire that rages now into an inferno. It consumes and fills me, and I overflow.

"You *monster*! All of you!" I whirl on the others. "How can you do this? How can you—" I choke on my own voice. "Mother! How could you?"

"Pia, calm down," Uncle Paolo intervenes. He's using his soothing voice, sweet and liquid as honey. "Just calm down a minute. You don't have to do it. You're not ready, I see that now. It's too soon—"

"Too soon? Not soon enough! Not soon enough for you to finally give me the truth!"

He starts toward me. I dart behind a table, keeping it between us. "Pia, *listen* to me, will you? You're losing your self-control."

"Monsters in the closet," I say, remembering something Aunt Nénine said once, long, long ago. Inanely, I begin to giggle and tremble all at once. "*Monsters in the closet.*"

"Pia . . ." A worried look comes into his eyes. He thinks I've lost my mind.

Maybe I have.

"Give me the syringe," he orders. The others begin to edge around the walls, getting between me and the door.

"No." I grasp it tightly to my chest. "Not so you can inject her. No. Let her go."

"Pia, you know that's not possible. Damn it, Pia, we've come all this way! You were so close. This is *why* you were created, don't you see that? This is your purpose! This is *how* you were created! Quitting now means quitting on your own existence. You owe your life—your endless life—to what goes on in this room."

"*Murder?*"

"It's not murder, Pia, not really. Think of it not as murder, not as evil, but as the—"

"Greatest form of compassion, I know. You've said it before." I relax, hands lowering a little.

"Good, yes!" He relaxes too.

"The greater good," I say, nodding slowly. "The perfecting of mankind."

"Yes." A smile, small and encouraging, brightens his face.

I hold up the syringe of elysia. "And this is the way."

He nods, watching me carefully, but I see triumph in his eyes.

I nod thoughtfully, studying the crystal liquid. "You know what I say?"

"What, Pia? Tell me."

"I say *screw it.*" I throw the syringe to the tile floor, where it shatters and splatters elysia all over our shoes.

Our eyes meet, his shocked and wide, mine wild and blazing.

"I'm through with you, *Dr.* Paolo Domingo Alvez. Through with all of you. Through with Little Cam, and Dr. Falk, and elysia, and my damn destiny!" I step on the broken glass, grind it with my heel. "And you know what? I *choose* chaos. I choose to regress. I choose *de*volution and extinction and weakness and emotion and my heart, all of it! Because if *this*"—I point at Ami—"is what it means to be truly human, then I don't *want* to be human. And I sure as hell don't want to be one forever. Screw your immortality. Screw your damn ideals and destiny. And screw *you*."

Shaking with rage, I turn and run for Ami, intending to rip the tube out of her arm and carry her all the way back to Ai'oa.

But I only make it three steps, and suddenly Uncle Jakob and Uncle Haruto have me by the arms, holding me still, and Uncle Sergei holds my head from behind so I can't bite them. I struggle, but it's no use. I have unbreakable skin, the sensory perceptions of a hawk, and I will never die—but I am betrayed by my lack of strength. I want to scream with frustration.

Uncle Paolo shakes his head and sighs, long and deep. "I'm sorry, Pia. I'm sorry we failed with you. I'm sorry that after all our hopes and best intentions, you still resorted to the same stupidity and blindness of humans far, far beneath your level."

He reaches into the pocket of his lab coat and pulls out a syringe, the twin to the one I shattered. Horrified, I feel my heart slow and sicken.

"I hoped it wouldn't work out this way, but a good scientist is always prepared." He presses the syringe, squirting a few drops of elysia into the sink.

That's when I notice the metal cart by my left elbow. It's got three trays, and each one is filled with glass beakers.

"I think I taught you that years ago," Uncle Paolo is saying. "Do you remember? Of course you do. Your memory, unlike your decision here today, is perfect."

He walks to the far side of Ami so that he can still see me over her body. His eyes are fixed on me, so he doesn't notice her eyelashes flutter and open, her head turn. Her gaze falls on me, and though confusion clouds her face, she still recognizes me.

"Pia?" she whispers.

I hook my foot around the leg of the cart and jerk it sideways. Glass beakers fly everywhere, smashing into the walls and floor. Everyone ducks, and Uncle Haruto yells. I think a shard of glass landed in his eye. He falls forward and collides with the exam table. His flailing hand catches the tube in Ami's arm, and it comes loose. Blood drains from her like syrup from a bottle, splashing onto the floor. Uncle Haruto slips in it and falls to the tile.

For a moment, everything is chaos, just long enough for me to break free and grab the syringe from Uncle Paolo's hands. I move as swiftly as the lightning outside, pulling Ami off the gurney and dragging her to the door, and I spare a split second to grab my necklace off the counter. When Jakob and Haruto grab me from behind, I stab blindly with the syringe, and they immediately back away from the needle. I keep it raised threateningly and pull Ami with one arm. My shoes track scarlet across the shining white tile.

"Stop, Pia!" orders Paolo as he crashes into the fallen metal cart and steps on the shattered beakers. He shouts and hops sideways, and I hope they've punctured the soles of his shoes. Ami is coming to; we're almost at the door.

I throw it open and pull her into the hallway, slamming the door behind us. Ami is still unconscious, but a small moan slips from her mouth. I shake her, but she doesn't rouse. I let her sink to the floor and look around.

There's a shelf against the wall holding sheets and lab coats, and I grab it with both hands and heave. It crashes to the floor with a loud clatter as an enormous boom of thunder rattles the building and, one by one, the fluorescent lights above us flicker out.

The generators have been hit. It'll take Clarence at least five minutes to get the electricity back on. *Come on, Pia, don't waste this chance. . . .* I shove the shelf against the door. It won't hold them for long, but maybe long enough.

Ami is slumped against the wall, eyes shut and skin pale. Her arm is still bleeding. When Uncle Haruto tore the tube from Ami's arm, it ripped the cut wider, and my dragging her across the floor only made it worse. In the darkness, I can just make out a sticky trail of blood leading from under the lab door. How much has she lost?

I dig through the supplies that fell from the shelf when I overturned it and find gauze and tape. Just when I start to turn back to Ami, my fingers brush something glass, and it rolls across the floor. I snatch it up, hoping it's some kind of antibiotic I can put on the cut. Eyes straining to read the label in the dark, I reach out and grip Ami's upper arm, trying to lessen the flow of blood. From some open window down the hall, lightning flashes, and my eyes catch the label on the vial.

E13.

E13. I remember the bird in the electric cage, its energy spent, the serum kicking in. . . .

A loud crash makes me look up. The scientists must be using something heavy to batter at the door.

Hurry, Pia!

I pop the lid off the glass vial with my teeth; there's nothing to inject it with, and I have no idea how much it will take, but there's no time. I push the vial between her lips and empty half of the contents down her throat, exhaling in relief when she swallows. Then I press the gauze to her arm and wrap tape around it three, four, five times.

Ami's eyes snap open. Another flash of lightning, and I see her pupils are constricted to tiny pinpoints.

"Pia!" She sits up, her entire body trembling. "What happened? Where am I? Why's it so dark?"

"Just hold my hand. I know you're scared, but you have to run!"

Before I even finish speaking, she's on her feet and zipping down the hall, pulling me along behind her. Her movements are jerky and rapid, just like the bird's when it was running on the E13. *Congratulations, Uncle Paolo. Your serum works perfectly.*

Outside, people are yelling and running everywhere, trying to get the lights back on. It'll be only minutes before Clarence has the backup generators on, and then we'll never be able to escape.

I don't bother with hiding. The rain and confusion is cover enough. We head for the nearest portion of fence, and when I look back, I see that Paolo and the others have made it out. They spot us much too quickly.

"Go," I hiss. "Run as fast as you can, Ami, toward the fence!"

"Pia, I brought your necklace," she says. "You dropped it."

"It's okay, Ami! I have it."

"Good. Because it means something special," she yells over her shoulder, "and if you lost it, it would be terrible. Pia . . ." She stops running and looks back. "They're chasing us. Why are they chasing us?"

I take her hand and run along the fence, trying to keep distance between the scientists and us. I have to keep her talking to distract her from our pursuers.

"What's special about the necklace, Ami? Tell me." They're fifty yards behind us and gaining. I try to run faster, but even with the serum spurring her on, Ami's short legs can't keep up.

"It's an Ai'oan symbol," she says. "When an Ai'oan boy gives it to a girl from another tribe, it means she belongs to him and to Ai'oa as long as she wears it."

"Try to keep up, Ami!" We're behind the menagerie now. I glance back and see Uncle Paolo leading the others. Forty yards.

"I couldn't let you lose it," Ami goes on. She hugs my waist. "Because you're one of us."

"Ami, listen to me! You have to run! Run home and tell everyone—" There's no time. I point up. "See that space where the chain link ends? Right under that bar?"

She nods, squinting uncertainly through the rain.

"*Climb*, Ami, and whatever you do, don't stop. As soon as they get the power back on, the fence will be pumping with electricity. You *cannot stop*."

"But what about you?"

"I'll be right behind you! Go!"

She starts climbing with alacrity to rival her monkey's, and I'm close on her heels. She reaches the top and starts navigating over the uppermost bar securing the chain link.

Suddenly a hand grabs my ankle, and I start to fall.

"Pia!" Ami screams, reaching down and grabbing my hand.

"Stop! Let go!" I yank away from her. "Go, Ami, go!"

"Not without you!"

I look down. Sergei has both my ankles, and Paolo has the hem of my lab coat. Looking back up at Ami, I'm forced to make a decision. I let go with both hands, giving me the split moment I need to shove her through the gap. She screams and falls to the ground on the other side, and I fall backward into the arms of the scientists.

I yell for her to run, and she shoots a terrified look at me before racing into the trees. Relieved, I sag limply and let them drag me away.

THIRTY-TWO

They lock me in my glass room, and I run to the bathroom and throw myself on my knees in front of the toilet, retching. I haven't eaten anything today, so all that comes up is stomach acid, but it makes my throat burn.

When I can't choke up any more, I lean back on my heels, gasping and coughing. I notice that there's scarlet streaked on the toilet seat, and I lift up my hands.

They're covered in Ami's blood.

I vomit again, then stumble to the sink, where I wash my hands in scalding-hot water, over and over. Tears fall from my eyes onto my hands, then, stained scarlet with blood, they drip onto the white porcelain. I scrub faster and faster, my entire body shaking.

When the water starts to run cold and my hands are raw, I drag myself back into my room and fall onto my bed, listless and dazed. My throat is on fire from retching, and my hands feel numb. I tuck them against my chest, feel my heart like a sledgehammer against my ribs.

Uncle Paolo and Uncle Timothy stand outside my door for several minutes, discussing security measures. There's a lot of talk of ankle monitors, cameras, and moving me into the abandoned wing of B Labs. Finally I hear their footsteps retreating and the front door closing behind them, but they've left someone behind to guard the door. I can hear him breathing.

I turn to face the jungle and hold my wrists in front of my face, eyes tracing the fine blue lines beneath the skin. *My blood is not my own.* It belongs to Ai'oa, to the many who died that I might be born.

I trace one blue vein with my fingernail, then start pressing down. The skin holds firm, as it always does. My tears sting like acid as I scratch harder and harder at my wrists, but nothing happens. *Not my blood! Not my blood!* My brain screams at me. I can't stop the horrific mantra, can't stop tearing at my wrists. Nothing happens. They've filled my veins with someone else's blood, and I have no way to rid myself of it.

Finally I give up and let my hands collapse to the bed. My wrists are red and sore, but the pain fades too quickly, and once again they are smooth, white, and perfect.

How stupid of Uncle Paolo—*no, not "uncle." Never again. Not him, not any of them*—to have thought that he could train me to be like him and the others. To have thought that, with the right tests and the right lectures, I could be made into a cold-blooded, heartless killer. To have thought that I could ignore the beating of my own heart long enough to stop the beating of another's.

He was a fool, but so was I. I believed it all. From the sparrow in the electric cage to poor, defenseless Sneeze. I believed him when he said it was necessary. It wasn't. None of it was. It was all a waste, a terrible waste of life. Even after I heard the story of the Kaluakoa and I felt in every bone of my body that it was true, I still wouldn't believe. Not fully. I thought, even then, that somehow everything would work out. That the light of day would banish the suspicions of night. That somehow it would all turn out to be a huge misunderstanding.

Yes, Paolo was a fool.

But I was a bigger one.

I think of my virulent outburst and feel not even a shred of triumph that I was finally able to defy him outright. Ami is free, yes, and I wish I could feel some relief at that, but all I feel is defeat and misery and regret and, above all, a terrible, permeating guilt.

What will happen to me? Will I stay locked up, like Uncle Antonio, except that for me it will be forever? How long can they keep me in this glass cage? My mind starts to run calculations, then slows and freezes, reaching for numbers that dissolve like smoke. For the first time in my life, my brain fails me. That should scare me, but I feel too hollow.

Why should I expect to be the same as I was yesterday, anyway? The Pia who was is no more. If I am even Pia at all, I am vastly different. Unalterably changed. The change, I realize, did not happen suddenly. I have been changing for days now, ever since I first stumbled into Ai'oa. The people of the jungle have changed me. Eio has changed me. I haven't been myself for a while, but until now, I hadn't realized it. Until now, I didn't have to. I've been balancing between two worlds that could never coexist, and at last, I was forced to choose. Uncle Antonio knew it would happen and tried to warn me, but instead of choosing the right side, I chose the wrong. I went back to Little Cam. If I had only listened to him then, Eio and I might be long, long gone, safe in some distant land where even Paolo couldn't find us.

But where would that have left the Ai'oans? The killing would have gone on, with or without me. I wonder if Uncle Antonio factored that into his plan. What did he think would happen? That my absence would bring Little Cam to a grinding halt? Far from it. Likely they would have restarted the Immortis project with twice the fervor.

I hear a *tat* at the window, and my heart skips a beat.

Tat, again.

I run to the window and press my hands to the glass.

There he is, in plain view, not even bothering to blend in. Only inches from the fence.

His eyes are feral. He's here because of Ami, I know it. I imagine the rage that must be pulsing through him, equal to the electricity pulsing through the fence. Does he realize the truth now? The Ai'oans know the story of the Kaluakoa. They know my existence must mean the death of many. They just never knew the deaths were their own.

Oh, Eio, I'm sorry, I'm sorry, I'm sorry, I'm sorry. For Ami and for Sneeze and for you and me and for all the others we never knew who died that I might live.

His lips are moving. He has to know I can't hear him. I shake my head.

Suddenly Eio grabs the fence.

"No!" I shout, but he's already jumped backward, hands

held up. I see agony in his face, and I think, *At least he won't try again.*

But he does. He grabs the fence and makes it nearly three feet up before the electricity pulses again and he's forced to release and drop to the ground. He lies in a crumple, and for a moment I think he's dead. The numbers run through my head like the electricity pumping through the fence: *5,000 volts every 1.2 seconds, and if he's wet that drops his resistance level by at least 1,000 ohms, which increases chance of death from 5 percent to 50 percent. If he touches it again, chance of death becomes 95 percent. . . .* I shake off the numbers, force them away until they're pressed against the back of my skull. Even if he's alive, the alarms will already be blaring in the guardhouse. Uncle Timothy will be on his way. If he catches Eio—

My heart stops, my breath stops, and the blood stops flowing through my veins. *No, not Eio . . .*

I can't stand it. I can't watch him kill himself like this, and I won't let him get caught by men who will murder him for his blood. But what can I do? The door is locked.

Your walls are made of glass, Pia.

And what does glass do best? I think of the syringe.

Moving at a speed no other human could equal, I grab the lamp from my nightstand and swing it with all my strength. It bounces harmlessly off the window.

This time I look harder and settle on the piping beneath the sink in my bathroom. I half unscrew, half rip it from the wall, and immediately water begins spraying across the room. Ignoring it, I grip the pipe firmly and smash it with every fiber of my being into the glass.

Cracks don't spiderweb across it, as I expect.

Instead, the entire wall shatters. Glass as fine as drops of rain, even sounding like the rain outside, showers to the floor and the ground outside.

My door bursts open, and the guard named Dickson storms in. He stands for a moment, staring in shock at the opening that used to be a wall, and then he starts toward me. Before my brain can even process my next move, my arms are swinging. The pipe connects with Dickson's knees, and he falls to the floor with a gasp.

I turn for the fence, but he grabs my ankle.

"Let—go!" I try to pull away, but now his hands are around my leg. His face is red with pain and exertion, but he's determined not to let me get away. I glance over my shoulder and see Eio watching, wide-eyed and pale.

"I really don't want to do this," I say to Dickson, holding up the pipe.

At that moment another person comes through my door. Clarence. *You're in on this too?* He must have been in the living room. His eyes connect with mine, and he slowly shakes his head and holds out a hand.

"C'mon, now, Pia. Just hand it over. Everything will work out, you'll—"

I smash the pipe onto Dickson's left hand. He bellows and releases my leg, then grabs the pipe with his other hand, yanking it from my grasp. Weaponless, I stumble backward. Dickson's knees must be smashed, because he can't get up, but Clarence is charging at me now.

"Pia—"

Just as his hands are about to close on my arm, I pivot

and whirl. By the time Clarence even blinks, I'm behind him. Dickson makes a grab for my ankle, but I dance aside. I'm too quick for them, my reflexes too advanced. They are three-toed sloths, and I am Ami's golden tamarin, small and swift and untouchable.

I'm amazed at how slow, how fragile these humans are.

Clarence takes the pipe and tries to land a blow to my stomach, but I simply step aside. The janitor's swing is so strong the momentum causes him to stumble and fall—his head cracks against my shelf of orchids, and he collapses, covered in soil and flowers.

I leap through the opening and run to the fence.

"Eio! Are you okay? Are you breathing?"

Eio nods, eyes fluttering open. "Pia bird."

"Eio, I'm here. I—I can't come to you, but I'm here." The fence is just wide enough for me to reach my arm through. He grasps my hand. His strength is weak, and his fingers tremble. I know we have less than a minute before Uncle Timothy and his men arrive.

"Ami . . . told us . . . they tried—"

"They tried to kill her, Eio. You have to leave or they'll get you too!"

"I will save you. I told you and Papi that I would climb the fence if I had to. And I will."

"No, Eio. Go home and tell your people they must run." Was it just yesterday I was saying something similar to him? But those words were spoken out of pride and anger, from the lips of a different Pia. These words are pleading. Helpless. *We're running out of time. . . .*

He lets go of my hand and, very slowly, stands up. And walks toward the fence.

"Eio, *no!*" I reach both hands through the fence and shove him backward. It shocks and hurts like nothing I've felt before, but I force my mind to overcome the pain because I know it's not really hurting me at all. He's still weak, so he falls to the ground, which is growing soggier by the minute, and he ends up splattered with mud.

"Eio, you *idiot*, it's my fault all of this is happening! They took her because of me, so they could—could use her. . . . You know it's true! You've known all along, because of the Kaluakoa, that in order for me to be immortal, many people had to die. Did you know they were Ai'oans? They were your *people*, Eio, and they died for me!"

I realize I'm kneeling in the mud, hands in my hair, and there are as many tears as raindrops on my cheeks. "I don't deserve you, Eio. Go! Please! Why won't you just *go?*"

His eyes are profoundly sad, as if I'm giving voice to the thoughts in his own head. "Love, Pia. That's why. I love you. That's why I'll climb this fence again and again if I have to. I love you, I love you, I love you. I've been trying to tell you."

Love.

Such a sweet, simple word. A word I've been searching for my entire life—but especially since I met Eio—and I never knew it. Until now. When I hear it on his lips, I know as I can never know anything else—no numbers, no formulas, no scientific names—I *know* it's true. A piece slides into place in my heart, filling a hole I never knew existed.

I breathe out, long and slow, staring at him in wonder.

After everything you know about me . . . the deaths, the sacri-fices, the evil . . .

"You love me," I whisper, knowing this isn't the time, but knowing there may never be another chance.

I need to tell him. I need him to know that I feel the same way, that I *always* felt this way, since the beginning. Since that first night in the jungle, when I felt it—love—but I didn't understand it. *But I understand it now. Oh, do I under-stand. . . .* "Eio, I—"

Suddenly I hear shouting, and the moments we have sto-len are shattered. I turn to see shapes, blurry in the rain, come around the corner of the house and start toward me. *Too late. Just like Alex and Marian. We're too late.*

"Eio, RUN!" I scream as they reach me. Strong arms haul me up, start dragging me away. On the other side, I see more men headed for Eio. *No, no, no. . . .*

"Run, Eio! Please! I promise I'll find you!"

He sees them too, but instead of running, he stands and faces Timothy, who is the first to reach him. I gasp as Timothy throws a powerful punch—but Eio ducks and slams his own fist into the guard's chin. Timothy's head snaps back, but he doesn't lose his footing; he just turns to glare at Eio and swing again. There must still be electricity sizzling through Eio's muscles, because he tries to duck but staggers instead, taking Timothy's blow straight to his stomach.

"Eio!" I scream.

He finds his feet again, but it's too late. Timothy seizes Eio's wrist, yanking him backward. Eio struggles, and even Timothy finds his strength tested against the Ai'oan boy. But other men arrive, and soon Eio is surrounded, held by a dozen hands.

"NO!" I buck against Paolo's grasp.

"Stop it, Pia!" he orders. "Timothy! Take the boy to the lab."

My strength abandons me at those words. I turn horrified eyes on the man I once thought a hero. *To the lab?*

"That's right, Pia. Looks like we're going to make Immortis today after all."

THIRTY-THREE

Eio, yelling threats and insults, has to be picked up and carried across the compound by three men. He twists and struggles, the rain making his skin slippery and giving the men considerable trouble keeping a grip on him, but he can't escape. I feel as if a knife has been thrust into my stomach, and every step makes it twist and dig deeper.

We are led right back into the lab where Ami nearly met her death. Timothy and his men struggle to keep Eio down, while Jakob and Haruto strap his wrists, ankles, torso, and neck to the table. Sergei gags Eio with a towel, stopping his angry shouts.

Paolo says, in a horribly agreeable tone, "Let's try this again, shall we?"

I keep my eyes trained on my muddy shoes and say nothing, resolved to stay silent and expressionless as my mind searches frantically for a way out. But there is nothing. My thoughts are still too full of Eio's words. *"I love you."*

"Haruto." Paolo holds up a hand, and Haruto places a syringe in it. I don't have to ask to know what the clear liquid inside is. Despite my resolution to stand firm, my heart pumps faster.

"Come." He motions to Sergei and Jakob, who prod me. When I refuse to move, they lift me up anyway and push me toward Eio, who's still struggling. I wish I felt the same fighting spirit, but it seems to have been drained out of me.

Paolo presses the syringe into my hand, and when I keep my fingers taut and extended, he forces them shut around it.

"I won't do it. You can't make me." I struggle against him, trying to drop the syringe. He grabs a roll of duct tape and wraps it around my fist. Tears burn my eyes, but I refuse to break down. I have to be able to think clearly.

But I'm starting to lose hope.

"You think by making me do it once you'll change my mind?" I ask, my voice halfway between a whisper and a snarl.

"Of course not, my dear." Paolo whispers in my ear, the stubble on his chin tickling my neck. "But by making you do it a dozen times or five dozen times. However many it takes. After all," he sweeps his hand wide, "we have a whole village to practice on."

"No."

"You seem strangely upset over the fate of people you don't even know," he says thoughtfully. "Or *do* you know them?"

He nods toward the other corner, the one opposite Eio, and I see suddenly that Aunt Harriet is sitting in the shadows, face downcast and arms cradling herself.

"What do you want with her?" I ask.

"Truth, dear Pia. And such truths as we could not have

imagined. Dr. Fields and I had a fascinating conversation while you were in your room, before we were interrupted by your friend's attempt to fry himself on our fence."

"You told him about Eio and me?" I ask her flatly. She doesn't meet my eye, but she nods.

"That . . . among other wonders," Paolo adds. "Apparently you've made a breakthrough discovery of your own? Care to share?"

Cold with horror, I stare in shock and dismay at Aunt Harriet. "You *told* him? About—" I stop, just in case I'm wrong.

But I'm not. He smiles. "Yes, Pia. She told us. After all this time, the secret to reproducing elysia is *you*. It's absolutely incredible. Such a curious life cycle for a plant to have."

"*Traitor*," I whisper. She still won't meet my gaze; she keeps her eyes trained on her shoes. Her shock of red hair hides all expression on her face. If she were close enough, I'd spit on her.

"Can I go now?" she whispers.

Paolo dismisses her with a wave.

As she passes me, Aunt Harriet murmurs, "I'm sorry, Pia."

The door shuts behind her, and Paolo sighs. "People will do anything for the right price, Pia. Discover their deepest desire, and you have them in your power. This wonderful principle applies, my dear, even to you."

He nods toward Eio.

I meet Paolo's eyes squarely, trying to find the uncle I once knew somewhere in that cold gaze. It's impossible. I know the face, but not the man. "This is *me*, Uncle Paolo. Pia. I've known you my whole life. Don't do this."

While we were talking, the others have been at work on Eio. His face has been cleaned of the paint, and even his jaguar necklace is gone. Everything that made him Ai'oan has been stripped away. He looks more like Uncle Antonio than ever. *Do they know who he is? Who his father is?*

It's Jakob who unwittingly answers when he mutters behind me, "Imagine being an immortal beauty like her and falling for some poacher's bastard. Damn shame."

"Don't make me do it. Uncle Paolo," I try to sound reasonable and contrite, "I'll do what you say. I promise. I swear I will, just let him go! Test me, if you like!" It's a lie, of course, but they don't need to know that until Eio is free and far from here.

"But you see," Paolo says, "this *is* the test."

They shove me toward him until I'm only inches away. I can smell the jungle on his skin, wet and fragrant and alive.

A lump the size of a tennis ball lodges in my throat. Tears blind me but don't fall, and my stomach feels as if I've swallowed Uncle Will's titan beetle alive and it's gnawing its way free through my skin.

"You were made for one purpose." Paolo's voice is steel now, hard and unforgiving, a voice I've rarely heard from him before. In a matter of hours, he's become a complete and horrifying stranger. "To create others like you. I don't intend to be the one scientist in Little Cambridge who gets remembered for failing. You are my success, whether you like it or not, and you *will* comply, or you will be forced to. Which is it to be?"

I shut my eyes and stay silent.

"Very well," he sighs.

He grabs my hand, and no matter how hard I strain against him, the combined weight of three men—of whom even one could overpower me—is too much. He lifts my hand, the needle pointed downward, to the level of my face. Eio stares at me, and I'm amazed at how calm he is. He's stopped struggling; now he just looks at me with the whole of the jungle in his eyes. It's almost as if he wants me to do it.

"Remember," Paolo whispers as I feel his arm tensing for the thrust downward. "It didn't have to be this way."

He pushes my hand down and the needle slides into Eio's side, just above his hip. Eio doesn't make a sound, but the muscles in his abdomen clench from the pain. I taste bile on the back of my tongue. As I struggle to keep my thumb raised, refusing to press down on the syringe, I can hardly see for the tears in my eyes. Paolo presses my thumb with his own, trying to force me to inject the elysia into Eio. But I strain against him, wondering at how it all comes down to this—my damned weakness. My one, frail finger is all that stands between Eio and his death. I feel my strength giving way—Paolo is too strong, *too strong*—and the door to the lab bursts from its hinges behind us. Everyone whirls and ducks as bullets pound into the ceiling above our heads. Paolo keeps a grip on me, preventing me from darting away.

"WHERE IS MY SON?" Uncle Antonio bellows, leveling the two AK-47s he's holding at the lot of us. "Get away from him, you bastards!"

I want to cheer. Instead, I bite down hard on Paolo's hand, and he curses and lets go long enough for me to dance to the other side of Eio's gurney. I rip the tape and the syringe from my hand. Trusting Uncle Antonio to handle the scientists, I grab a scalpel and start slicing the straps holding Eio.

"Antonio," Paolo says agreeably, as if they've just met in the breakfast line. "*Son?* My, my . . . any other secrets you'd care to share with the class?" His eyes are bright and hard and angry, so angry I half expect steam to be pouring out of their sockets.

"I *said*, step away!" Uncle Antonio's eyes are blazing, looking as dangerous as the massive guns in his hands. Where did *those* come from? Timothy's secret stash, probably. Uncle Antonio knows more of Little Cam's secrets than I ever even knew existed.

The scientists slowly stand up and walk to the corner where Aunt Harriet sat earlier. Their hands are raised or linked behind their heads, and all of them have eyes only for the guns.

"We don't have long, Pia," Uncle Antonio warns. "The others will be here soon."

The last strap is only halfway cut, but Eio snaps it and jumps to his feet. We run to Uncle Antonio and duck behind him as he begins to back out the door.

"Pia!" Paolo yells. "Come back, Pia. Please. We can work this out. There's still a chance. You can still be a scientist, still live your dream—"

"It was never my dream," I reply. "It was yours. You just made me *think* it was mine. Well, I have a new dream, and, trust me," I stare him straight in the eye, "you don't appear anywhere in it."

"Paolo," Uncle Antonio says, "join us. Now."

He rises slowly, then, at Uncle Antonio's impatient bark, walks briskly to us. Uncle Antonio hands one of his guns to Eio, then grabs Paolo's upper arm and holds him in front as a shield. Paolo is as still as a sculpture, but his eyes follow me like twin lasers.

We leave the rest of them cowering in the corner.

And run like hell.

THIRTY-
FOUR

The first thing I notice when we burst through the doors of A Labs is that it's finally stopped raining. The world is vivid and sharp, as if it's been repainted three shades too bright. I feel exposed and vulnerable, despite Uncle Antonio and his AK-47s. People are already gathering. News travels fast in Little Cam.

So does, apparently, the sound of gunshots.

"Stand back!" Uncle Antonio bellows, swinging his gun like a scythe. Eio keeps his own trained on Paolo's head. I'm surprised at how steady his hands are, despite his distaste for the weapon. But I have a feeling his bow and arrows just wouldn't have the same effect on the crowd closing in on us.

It's one of the strangest moments of my life so far. I'm surrounded by familiar faces, but the eyes that stare out of them are those of strangers. These are the people who raised me, taught me, ate with me, and celebrated my birthdays. Jonas and Jacques and Sergei. Even Aunt Brigid and Aunt Nénine.

They are all looking at us with eyes like ice; some burn cold and some fiery, some with confusion.

Who are you people? What have you done with my Little Cam?

If Aunt Harriet is among them, she manages to evade my eyes. Which is probably just as well; if she appeared, I might ask Uncle Antonio to shoot her.

And where are my parents?

Suddenly we hear heavy footsteps, and Timothy and a dozen of his men shoulder through the crowd. They all hold guns, some even bigger than Uncle Antonio's.

"Stay close to me, Eio," he whispers. "You aren't bullet-proof like Pia is."

We stay in a tight knot with Paolo in front of us, still rigid.

"Get out of our way," Uncle Antonio commands.

"Antonio, my friend," Timothy says softly. "I believe there has been a misunderstanding. Stop all this. Why worry about one wild boy? Tell you what. Put down the guns, and we'll let him go back to his jungle. And we can work all this out."

"Out. Of. Our. Way." Uncle Antonio levels his gun at him.

Timothy spreads his hands, his rifle pointed at the sky. "Easy, friend. Remember all the favors I did you, yeah? The magazines, the maps, the radios . . . We have been in business a long time, no? Today is the same. Put down the gun. We'll work a deal."

"Here's a deal for you," I say, surprising them both. I step in front of my little band, because I am, after all, bulletproof. "How about you get out of the way—and we don't kill you?"

"What are you doing, Pia child?" Timothy shakes his head

at me. "Throwing your lot in with this madman? Did no one tell you? He's been insane for years."

"If he's insane, then so am I. Let us through."

"Do as she says, Timothy." Uncle Antonio shoots the ground in front of the hunter's boots, and Timothy jumps back with a startled cry. "Please," Uncle Antonio adds.

They start to move, and at that moment, Eio's finger unwittingly finds the trigger of his gun. Bullets spray the ground between the crowd and us. I don't know whether Uncle Timothy or Eio is more shocked.

Chaos explodes across the crowd. Everyone starts screaming or shooting, and I'm swept one way by the stampede of scientists running to escape the gunfire. Uncle Antonio and Eio run the other way, losing their hold on Paolo as they do. No one seems to notice when I'm knocked over and into a large bush by the door of A Labs. I crawl behind it and watch as everyone not holding a gun flees the scene and Uncle Antonio and Eio retreat behind the powerhouse. Uncle Timothy orders his men to keep firing at them, then yells, "Where did Pia go?"

Someone points in a direction, and Timothy and the rest of his men charge off. I stand and start for Uncle Antonio and Eio, but then I see Paolo headed in my direction, and at the last minute I crash through the door to A Labs and run down the hall. I burst into the first lab I come to just before Paolo enters the building. Terrified he saw the lab door shut behind me, I shrink against the wall and hold my breath.

The room is dark, but I know from memory that it's Uncle Will's lab. I hear scrabbling in the dark that must come from Babó. Paolo's footsteps pass my hiding place and continue on, and I sigh in relief. But then the door opens, and a head peers around it—and sees me.

Aunt Harriet.

We stare at each other for a long moment, at first in shock, then wariness. There are dark rings under her eyes. She looks like she's been crying ever since she left the lab.

"Pia," she says guardedly.

"Harriet. You going to turn me in? Again?"

She sighs and locks the door. *Lock on the door. Brilliant, Pia. Can't believe you* didn't *think of that.*

"Why did you do it?" I ask. I don't have time, but the moment presented itself. Maybe the truth will too.

She begins slowly, uncertainly. "You once asked me, Pia, what test it was I had to pass in order to get this job."

I nod and wait.

She draws a deep breath before going on. "It was a horse. A black Arabian, the most magnificent creature I'd ever seen. I don't know where she came from or how they knew that of all the creatures on this earth, I love none so much as the Arabian. Victoria Strauss brought me to her and put a gun in my hand and said that if I pulled the trigger, the job would be mine." She looks at her hands. "Under any other circumstances, I wouldn't have done it. But . . ." She sighs and pulls something from her pocket. It's the photograph I saw her crying over yesterday. She hands it to me.

"I lied to you, Pia. Evie isn't a colleague. She's my little sister."

The girl in the picture is not much older than me. She's sitting in a wheelchair and smiling, and Harriet's standing behind her with her arms around the girl.

"Your sister," I whisper. *"The sister is dead,"* Strauss told Paolo. *"Fields doesn't know."* My heart sinks. I don't dare look at Aunt Harriet.

"Evie has cerebral palsy," Aunt Harriet whispers. "It was Strauss who found me, after the diagnosis. She said that Corpus was working on a promising new drug and that it could help Evie if they gave it to her . . . on the condition I came down here for thirty years. The disease was so advanced, and Evie was suffering so much, Pia, I was ready to try or do anything! Even . . . even pass that horrible test. Even so, there's not a day that goes by that I don't wish there had been some other way, some other choice. You remind me so much of her. Before the disease got bad, she had the same curiosity, the same drive. It's why I wanted to help you. It was almost like . . . almost like knowing what Evie would have been, if not for the illness."

My throat feels packed with cotton. I can't tell her that her sister is dead. Maybe I should, but the hope in Aunt Harriet's eyes . . . it's a knife to my heart, and I simply can't turn the blade on her. She'll find out soon, anyway. Strauss can't hide the truth forever; she said as much herself.

For the first time, I understand why Uncle Antonio tried so hard to keep the truth about Immortis from me. The truth can pierce and destroy even the most indestructible of us.

Suddenly we hear footsteps in the hall, and we press against the wall and hold our breaths. Whoever it is, they run past the lab without opening the door—this time.

"Go on," I tell Aunt Harriet. I know there isn't much time, but I need to hear the full story. Otherwise, I may never be able to forgive her.

"When they told you to pass *your* final test," Aunt Harriet continues, "all I saw was myself facing the same decision, the same sacrifice of my soul, and I thought that if only I could stop you, save you somehow from making the same mistake, I could erase my own sin. And for a time, I thought I had. . . . But then Paolo put it all together. He figured out it was me helping you sneak out, and he said . . . he threatened to tell Strauss. And then Evie wouldn't get her treatments and . . . I still had that gun, Pia, and I knew that if I pulled the trigger, I could prove to them that I was still a team player. Still the amoral scientist they wanted. So I did it. I pulled the trigger. I won back their trust, and I bought my sister's life. Whatever humanity I had managed to scrape back together, I shot it all to hell. And you, dear, sweet Pia, you were caught in the cross-fire. I'm sorry. Truly, miserably sorry. But if given the chance to do it all over . . ."

I stare, heartsick, as she starts weeping. "You'd do it again. I know. I understand now, Aunt Harriet." I hand her picture back and hope that Strauss gets eaten by an anaconda. "Uncle Antonio and Eio are pinned down by Timothy's men. I need to get to them and get out of Little Cam. Will you help me?"

She stares at me, sniffling, her red hair looking like some kind of explosion on her head, and then she nods. "I'll see if the coast is clear, then signal for you." She doesn't meet my eyes, but blinks and wipes her eyes, then leaves.

Less than a second later, the door opens again, and she's backing into the room, a gun pointed at her face.

Timothy. And he's backed up by a dozen armed men, Jakob, Sergei, and even my father among them. Uncle Will holds his gun as if it were a snake about to bite him, and he looks at me with large, frightened eyes.

"Enough of this, Pia," says Timothy as he switches on the light. "Just come with us. Let's work this out."

I look at him, look at the others, look at Jakob's frown and Sergei's stormy eyes, and I think only one thing.

Ants.

The terrarium is right behind me. There's a chair right beside me. I glance from it to the terrarium to Uncle Will. He must read what's in my mind, because he starts to turn very, very pale.

"Pia, *no!*"

But I'm already picking up the chair, swinging it, smashing the glass. Ants pour out like living black water. I look straight at Timothy and smile.

Uncle Will runs to the alarm and yanks it down, but he can't get to the insecticide; ants are crawling all over the cabinet. I wonder if the others even know what I've released.

They do. Grown men scream like cornered monkeys and throw their guns down in their haste to flee the room. Timothy tries to keep order, but he's carried out with the tide. Aunt Harriet, her face a mask of horror, doesn't wait around either. I'm right on her heels.

Mass hysteria has broken out across Little Cam. There are people yelling in panic who couldn't possibly know what's going on yet. Maybe it's the sirens screaming at a deafening volume that frightens them. I glance behind just once to see someone—impossible to tell who—disappear under a tidal wave of ants.

I run to Uncle Antonio and Eio. The men who'd been firing on them have abandoned their posts and are stampeding along with everyone else.

"Uncle Will's ants," I say, and Uncle Antonio blanches.

"Ants? They're all scared of some *ants*?" asks Eio.

"They're not just any ants—no time! Let's go!" I grab Eio's hand and pull him along with me. The mass of carnivorous insects has moved toward the center of Little Cam, and I see Haruto yanking off his ant-covered shirt. Everyone is still occupied with escaping the tiny monsters, leaving us free to run for the gate.

Just before we reach the Jeeps, we're intercepted by Timothy, Paolo, and Sergei, all three of them armed. We freeze. They freeze. No one lowers their weapons.

"Stop this madness, Antonio," says Paolo, using his smoothest, most persuasive voice. "It doesn't have to be this way. We'll let the boy go, I swear. I didn't know he was your son. You should have told us. We could have given him a place here. Maybe we still can." Slowly, he bends down and lays his gun on the ground, then extends his hands. "See? I want no violence."

I can't help it. I burst out laughing with disbelief. "No violence? *No violence?* You've killed *how* many people?"

"Pia." He looks at me with reproach. "You may want to look behind you."

I do, and so does Eio. Uncle Antonio tries to turn but is stopped by the prick of a needle against the back of his neck. He goes very still, and so does my heart.

"Mother," I breathe. "*Don't.*"

Her face is an icy mask, and her fingers, delicately holding the syringe of elysia, don't even tremble. "Don't move, Antonio. Don't make me do it."

"Sooner or later, *someone's* going to get injected today," Paolo says. "Timothy?"

Timothy comes forward and takes the guns from Uncle Antonio and Eio, neither of whom object.

"Sylvia," Uncle Antonio whispers. "We grew up together. Remember? You, me, and Will. We used to sneak into the labs and mix the chemicals, make explosions. We stole all the cook's knives and hid them in the nurse's closet. We let out all the animals in the menagerie at once. Remember that day? Old Sato running around, trying to catch that tapir . . ."

"Shut up, Tony," she says and turns to me. "It should have been me," she whispers. "Only one generation removed . . . to think it. Here I am, trapped in this mortal, dying body, and you, you ungrateful, spoiled girl, don't even know what you've got. It should have been *me*. *I* wouldn't have disappointed him."

Him can only be Paolo. I gape at her, stunned once more by the venom I never knew she had. "You're my *mother*. . . ."

"I never asked to be" is her reply, and the words seem to crack the earth between us, creating a chasm no bridge could ever span.

"Well, it seems we've all reached an understanding." Paolo gestures to Timothy and Sergei, and they lower their guns. "There. That's better. We're civilized human beings, after all."

Over his shoulder, through the trunks of the trees planted in the center of the drive, I see the front gate opening. Who is operating it, I can't make out. I glance sidelong and see that Uncle Antonio and Eio have seen it too.

But my mother still has the needle pressed to Uncle Antonio's neck.

"If I stay," I say suddenly, "and swear to do whatever you tell me—will you let Uncle Antonio and Eio go free?"

Paolo gives me a thoughtful look. "Well, let's see now. If—"

He's interrupted by an earsplitting screech. We all look up to see the Grouch go sailing overhead in a magnificent leap from the roof of A Dorms to the stand of trees in the drive, howling all the way. The branches rustle as he claws his way through them, and then he suddenly swings out and through the gap between the metal bars above the chain link, the same gap through which Ami escaped only this morning. The Grouch disappears into the jungle, his wild screech leaving a fading trail behind him.

Someone—probably Uncle Jonas—has released all the animals, probably thinking that the ants might decide to make dessert of the menagerie. Parrots squawk and soar overhead, Jinx slips past like a shadow, and a troupe of monkeys do their best to catch up to the Grouch. Last of all, Alai lopes by, sleek and smooth as the wind, and he spares one golden glance at me before vanishing through the gate.

We all seem to have lost the trail of our conversation, and it is Uncle Antonio who speaks first. He turns his head just enough to see both Eio and me. He gives Eio a long, deep look and a nod, and then he turns his gaze on me. I am terrified by the look I see in his eyes.

"Remember, Pia," he whispers. "Perfect is as perfect does."

He steps backward, and the needle slides into his neck. Mother, shocked, lets go of the syringe, and it falls to the ground, but not before half of its contents are injected directly into Uncle Antonio's bloodstream. He crumples like paper to Mother's feet.

THIRTY-FIVE

The world opens beneath my feet, and I start toward Uncle Antonio, as do Paolo, Timothy, and Sergei. But Eio grabs my hand and pulls me away, and before they can reach us, we are off and running.

Shouts echo after us. We do not stop. Through the stand of trees, across the drive, through the gate — I have only a brief moment to turn and see who has opened it for us.

My father. My meek, gentle, mild-mannered father, who wouldn't contradict someone even if they said the sky was green and the sun nothing more than a big lemon. He gives a sad little wave as we fly past, and there isn't even time to call out to him. When I glance back, I see him being overtaken by Paolo and Timothy.

Please don't hurt him, I cry out inwardly. *He never did anyone any wrong.* The small gesture of help, though feeble compared to the hideous betrayal by my mother, is like a gentle salve on the wound she tore open in my soul. It doesn't heal, but it helps. At least one of them was true, when it came down to the wire.

Gunshots sing by our ears, and I even feel one bite the back of my leg. It stings like nothing I've ever felt before, but of course it doesn't puncture.

"Faster!" Eio yells, pulling me along with him. They can't hope to keep up with us, me with my enhanced speed, Eio with his jungle upbringing.

They can't keep up with us, but their bullets can. Eio stumbles as one slams into his right shoulder, but he doesn't fall.

"You're hit!" I pull on his hand, trying to stop him, but he shakes his head stubbornly and charges on, though at a slower pace, and we cut sideways, off the road and into the jungle.

"Can't . . . stop!" he yells, and I realize there are tears in his eyes. "I promised him I would take you away from here— and I will die before I fail him!"

I cannot argue with that. I see Uncle Antonio fall again, see the life spill from his limbs, see his eyes lose their light. Now I'm crying too, and it makes me clumsy. We've outdistanced our pursuers, but Eio is growing weaker.

"Are you okay?" I yell as I leap over a fallen log. He has to climb over it, and I finally slow to wait for him. "Can you make it? If they catch us, they'll just shoot you again! For good, this time!"

"I'm fine," he insists. "Go. I'm right behind you." To prove it, he picks up the pace.

But only for a few steps. Then he stumbles and collapses. I run back and help him sit up. "Eio, you can't go on like this. You're bleeding too much."

"Mud," he says, gritting his teeth. "To stop the bleeding. Leaves and mud."

I start digging right there, until my hands find the moist soil under the loam. I scoop up handfuls and give them to Eio, who smears them across his shoulder. He gasps with pain and shudders with each touch. I've never felt more helpless.

Once his shoulder is caked in mud, he lies back and shuts his eyes, his chest moving in spasms. My own breathing comes jaggedly, as if my body is trying to mimic his.

"Eio?" I take his hand in mine. "Eio, what do I do now? Should I get Kapukiri?"

"He's gone."

"What? What happened to him?" I involuntarily squeeze Eio's hand in alarm.

"Not Kapukiri." Eio opens his eyes and stares up at the canopy. "Papi."

Oh, yes. That's right. Uncle Antonio is dead. The image replays in my head: Uncle Antonio stepping into the needle, falling to the ground, sprawling unnaturally in the dirt. Chills run up and down my skin. I feel as though I'm covered in the flesh-eating ants.

"Why did he do it?" I ask softly. "I was ready to bargain with them. You both could have been free." But I know why he did it. I know too well. *The noblest life is the one laid down for another.*

Eio shuts his eyes again. I wonder which hurts him more, the bullet or the grief.

"Go, Pia. I'll hide; they'll never find me. Listen. The Ai'oans . . . they're preparing to fight. They want to attack

Little Cam. You must stop them. . . . They'll only get killed."
He winces and pauses to catch his breath. "You have to keep
going. I'll be fine; the jungle is my home. It will . . . hide and
protect me."

"Eio . . ."

"Go," he growls, sounding for all the world like his father.

"Fine," I hiss back. "But don't go far. I'm coming back for
you."

His eyes are shut against the pain, but he nods. I reach out
and touch his cheek, run my thumb down the square line of
his jaw. "Be safe."

"I will. You too."

"I mean it, Eio. You—you're all I have left," I whisper.

"Go, Pia."

I run.

Eio did not lie. The Ai'oans are in an uproar. The men are filling their gourds with curare, and even the women are gathering spears. I stumble down the row between the huts, looking
for Achiri or Luri.

Suddenly a hand grabs me by the back of my shirt and
whirls me around, and I find myself staring Burako in the
eye. His face is slashed with red paint, and his hand holds a
knife—pointlessly, I think—to my throat.

"*You.*" He shakes me and hisses. "*Karaíba!* Have you come
to finish the job?" he asks in Ai'oan. "Come to kill our children, have you? Come to drink their blood? Murderer!"

"No! Of course not! I came to *help*—"

"Liar!" He presses the knife to my skin, and I wonder what
he thinks that will solve.

"Stop!" yells a small voice, and Ami appears at his elbow. "Let her go! She saved me!"

Burako looks from me to Ami with uncertainty, but he doesn't loosen his grip.

Ami puts her hands on her hips and glares at him. "I said she saved me. She's on *our* side, Burako!"

In any other situation, seeing her try to cow the muscled warrior would be funny. As it is, I only breathe in relief when he lets me go. But there is still distrust in his eyes. I can't really blame him.

Ami throws her arms around my waist. "You're here! Pia!"

"Yes," I say. "Your arm, Ami. How is it?"

"I'm fine." Someone has redone the bandage, so it's tighter and neater, and I'm glad to see it seems to have stopped the bleeding. I'm also relieved the E13 didn't leave her unconscious . . . or worse. But I don't regret using it on her; if I hadn't, she might not be alive.

Ami looks around. "Where is Eio?"

"He's coming. He got hurt, but he'll be okay." *He better be okay or I'll kill him.* "Where's Achiri and Kapukiri?"

She leads me to them. The Ai'oans greet me as I pass them, but they don't stop making their preparations. Their faces are grim and angry and smeared with red paint. I have never seen them like this. I see none of their usual tranquility and acceptance. They remind me of Uncle Will's ants: relentless, wild, and deadly.

"Achiri!" When I see the headwoman, I run to her. She is painting Luri's face with frightening jagged lines of paint as red as blood. I call out to her in Ai'oan. "Achiri, you must listen to me!"

She doesn't stop painting, but asks, "What is it, Pia bird? Where is the Farwalker?"

"He's hurt. He's back in the jungle. Can you send someone to find him?"

Achiri nods and snaps at several of the men, yelling for them to go search.

I continue, "He sent me ahead to tell you—you can't attack Little Cam!"

She inspects her handiwork, grunting in satisfaction "Go, Luri." Luri trots off after giving me a fierce smile. Achiri wipes her hands on her skirt and turns to me. "What is this now? First Ami comes to us, speaking of evil men who try to kill her, and you help her escape. Then Eio runs off to find you, and he does not return. Now here you are, telling us we should not defend ourselves against the ones who prey on our children?" She looks down at Ami and scowls. "Even if those children are stupid enough to wander off by themselves!"

Ami scowls back. "I had to give Pia her necklace back!"

"Silly girl," Achiri snaps. "And so you go alone into the jungle? Tsk." She looks up at me again. "Tell me, Pia bird, should we lay ourselves down at these foreigners' feet to be slaughtered?"

Intimidated by her strength—and by the angry red slashes painted across her face—I step back. "No! Of course not! Of all people, I know why you should fight! But they have guns, Achiri, and many Ai'oans will die if you face them like this."

She looks doubtful, and suddenly Burako appears at my right, speaking in Ai'oan. "We will fight! Do not listen to the foreigner girl. Look what trouble she has brought us!"

"Shut up, Burako!" Achiri barks. "Kapukiri! Come!"

The medicine man hobbles over. He alone does not wear face paint. Achiri points at me. "Pia tells us we should not fight. Burako says we should. Eio Farwalker has not returned yet." She throws up her hands. "Fight or do not fight? There are too many voices and too many fingers pointing in different directions! Tell me, Kapukiri, have you seen the way we should take?"

Kapukiri blinks owlishly at her, then looks around. The Ai'oans, aware now of the argument, fall silent and gather close to hear what their leader will say. Ami presses close to me, holding my hand in both of hers.

"I have seen the mark of jaguar, mantis, and moon," Kapukiri says at last, "in the eyes of the daughter of Miua. She who walks with the jaguar as her guardian and who cannot fall to spear or arrow, she has been sent to guide us."

The Ai'oans murmur in agreement, and only Burako scowls.

Kapukiri extends a gnarled hand toward me. "Speak, Undying One, and we shall listen."

He steps back, and I find myself ringed by expectant Ai'oans. Speechless at first, it takes Ami's steady gaze, so hopeful and confident in me, to bring the words out.

"Ai'oa, I am, as you say, a *karaíba*, a foreigner. But you know the story of the Kaluakoa. You know that Undying Ones are only born if many die before them. This was true for the Kaluakoa, and it is true for me." I close my eyes and draw a deep breath, wishing Eio were here, trying not to think of Uncle Antonio falling to the ground. If I can only hold myself together for a few more minutes . . . "I have learned today that many did die—and that they were of your blood. The scientists who created me used lies to deceive your people, and they used elysia—*yresa*—to . . . to kill them. Their blood was taken and passed on, and now it flows in me." I hold up my arms, wrists out, as murmurs ripple through the villagers. "I am a foreigner, but my blood is Ai'oan, and this is a terrible, terrible evil. I cannot give you back your dead, but I can try to stop you from adding to their number. Please, do not attack Little Cam. The scientists have guns, and though I know you are all brave and true, your arrows are no match for them. I agree with you; the foreigners must leave. You must take back your jungle. But this is not the way."

"What, then?" asks Achiri.

"Come with me to where the *yresa* grows." The idea forms as I speak it, and I know it's the only thing we can do. "If we destroy the flowers, we destroy the foreigners' reason for being here. If the *yresa* is gone, the scientists will leave."

I step back to show that I am done speaking. They begin whispering, and the whispers grow louder and louder until Burako has to bellow to make them fall silent again.

"I do not like what the Undying One has said," he announces, and my heart starts to fall. "But her words are true."

I lift my chin hopefully. He nods and gives me a steady look. "We will go to the *yresa*, and we will destroy it all. No more shall die today."

Ami squeezes my hand and gives a squeal of glee.

I want to feel her joy, and I *am* glad the Ai'oans listened to me. But at that moment all I want is Eio and to weep on his shoulder.

• • •

It's approaching evening when we finally reach Falk's Glen. There are five guards here; perhaps Paolo anticipates us. But he hasn't anticipated an entire tribe of Ai'oans. Paralyzing them with curare before they even see us is child's play to these hunters of the jungle.

Then our real work begins. The women empty their baskets of weapons, and we fill them with flowers.

It's strangely difficult for me to do it, even knowing what it costs for the flowers to be of any use. They are stained with the blood of dozens; but they are still tied to my very existence. We share a little DNA, these flowers and I. But I must be merciless. Every last flower must go.

The baskets are soon overflowing, so people begin piling up armfuls. We use shirts and leaves to carry them; some women even thread them in their hair. Purple and gold orchids are turned into garments for the Ai'oa; they are covered in the same flowers that stole the lives of so many of their people.

Luri finds me and gives me a long hug. "You must not bear the burden of another's evil deeds, Pia. It is not your fault. We do not blame you."

I pull away from her. "If it wasn't for me, Luri—"

"If it wasn't you," she says calmly, "it would have been someone else. And who can say? If it had been someone else, perhaps they would not have had such a gentle heart as you do. Perhaps it would have been worse for us. Yet we must not dwell on what is not—but on what *is*. And what is, *py'a*, is that you have proven yourself to be a friend of the Ai'oa. No . . . you have proven yourself to *be* Ai'oan." She's barely as tall as me, but when she looks me squarely in the eye, it feels as if she's much, much taller. "You said our blood is in your veins. Good. We are proud to have you."

The vise around my heart loosens a notch, and I want to throw my arms around her and sob into her shoulder. I want her to hold me the way my mother never did, the way I see her hold little Ami, and I want her to tell me everything is going to be all right. But there is still too much pain in my soul, and instead I clench my hands into fists and stare at the ground.

Luri lifts my chin with one finger. "Little *Tapumiri*, there are monsters in this world." She tucks a stem of elysia behind my ear, then smoothes my hair from my face and smiles. "But you are not one of them. Do not take the weight of the dead on your heart. Leave that to the gods. Death is not always sad—for some, it is the doorway to a world where everyone drinks of the *yresa*, and all are made immortal."

I stare at her, feeling tears in my eyes that do not fall. It's a beautiful idea, but it lifts only a tiny bit of the pain.

Across the glen, I see the warriors who went scouting for Eio return. Eio's not with them. I inhale sharply, and my vision blurs with tears.

Luri gently turns my chin so that I'm looking her in the eye. "Eio is strong, and he knows how to take care of himself. Don't you worry about him now."

My breath still turns to ice in my throat, and it's all I can do not to dash into the jungle myself. But I promised him I would look after the Ai'oans, and after all the evil my life has caused in the world, I won't add to it by breaking that promise.

When we have gathered them all, we march to the river. It's getting late; we need to move more quickly. But I can't rush them. I think, for the Ai'oans, the deed we do is a kind of spiritual rite. Perhaps they will make it a tradition. Perhaps every year the Ai'oans will find a glen filled with some kind of flower that they'll pick and carry to the river. Maybe a hundred years from now they'll still be doing it, still be telling the Story of the Pia-bird, not knowing what really happened, but giving it honor and remembrance all the same.

I am sorry my education did not teach me more of the religions of the world. Who knows? Maybe somewhere out there, the truth behind all of this really does exist. Paolo used to say that truth always finds a way to present itself; I think it might be the only true thing he ever said.

We reach the river and begin tossing the elysia into it. It isn't long before the Little Mississip is drenched in the flowers; a more beautiful sight I have never seen, except perhaps that one afternoon at the swimming hole with Eio and Ami, when we were all smiling and happy and unaware of the evil that haunted our world. I wonder where Eio is and why he hasn't found us yet. He could be alone, bleeding, or even dying—I force myself to stop thinking about it, and I remember what he said: *"The jungle will protect me."*

The last flower is still tucked behind my ear. I pull it down and stare at the nectar inside. *Beauty and death, so closely knit together.* This seems to be the central theme of my life.

I toss it into the water. Unlike the rest, which have already floated out of sight downstream, it sinks and doesn't reappear.

When I look up, I see a pair of yellow eyes in the foliage on the opposite bank. I stand still for a moment, then call, "Alai! Alai, come!"

He emerges from the leaves and stands on the soft mud above the water, watching me. I have seen that look before, after the night I spent in Ai'oa, when Alai ran into the jungle and almost didn't come back. After a long minute, I nod. "Good-bye."

As if he understands, Alai dips his spotted head, then turns. My heart sinks as I see the last of my oldest friend vanish into the jungle, but, after a moment, it lifts again.

It's time for both of us to be free.

THIRTY-SIX

"**A**re you sure he will come?" Burako asks. "How can we know what these foreigners will do? Seems to me one minute they are going this way, next minute they are going that way. No sense. No reason. How can you know?" He mutters and shakes his head.

Achiri responds calmly, "Does not the hunter know the ways of the tapir? So does our Pia bird know the ways of the foreigners. Listen to her."

"He'll come," I say, still trying to focus on the task at hand and not on Eio. *Please be safe, please be okay.* . . . "His work is coming down in shambles around him, and this glen is the center of it all. He will come."

We are hidden around Falk's Glen, or what *used* to be the glen. Now it's just a barren dip in the jungle, a mossy scar that, within days, will be healed over with new growth. The normal orchids and the ferns and the heliconias will cover the wound, and the jungle will forget what once grew there.

Elysia is gone. Forever. Only the Ai'oans and the scientists who manage to make it out of the jungle will remember.

It is getting darker; there is only an hour of daylight left. I'm certain Paolo will come sooner or later to check on the glen, but maybe we'll have to wait until morning before he appears.

I wrap my fingers around the stone bird in my pocket. *Oh, Eio, where are you?*

"Sh. He comes." Kapukiri stands, holding a tall staff in front of him with both hands, eyes shut. My heart flutters, thinking he means Eio, but then I see it isn't so.

I step into the clearing as Paolo emerges from the path at the other end. I don't have to turn around to know the Ai'oans are invisible behind me.

Paolo comes to a slow halt and stares at the ravaged glen. His ice-and-stone façade quivers. Anger flashes through him, hot and virulent as a volcano. Others soon follow: Timothy, the rest of the Immortis team, my mother, assorted scientists and workers. No Aunt Harriet, no Father. I hope those two made it out.

Everyone has guns, of course, and they all look exhausted. Were they able to save anything? Maybe in a few days the ants will be gone, moved on, and they can go back and salvage their belongings and equipment. *Why am I even thinking about this? Little Cam is not my home anymore. Their problems are their own.*

"You have done a terrible thing today, Pia." Uncle Paolo's voice moves like lava beneath rock. "A very, very terrible thing."

"You have done many terrible things. I think I'm entitled to at least one."

He gives an angry sweep of his hand, indicating the ruined glen. "So this is to be your legacy? The one immortal human ever to live—and this is what you give in return? You would cast your own race to the fires of extinction because of a whim. Because of a hormonal attachment to a savage boy."

"I know all about savages," I reply. "I was raised by them."

"Don't try to play pretty word games with me, girl. I made you what you are. You are mine to destroy."

"You will not touch her, *karaíba*," says Luri, breaking cover to join me. Ai'oans fall from the jungle like leaves to gather around us. The scientists step back and raise their guns. But for every one gun, there are five poisoned arrows pointed back.

"*Karaíba*," says Burako, stepping forward, "we of Ai'oa have heard the Story of the Pia-bird. We know now what you did to the brothers and sisters and mothers and fathers who left the village to accept your way of life. We know that they are dead. We have heard these things—"

"We don't have to listen to this!" Sergei yells, stepping forward and lifting his rifle. "They're ignorant, spouting words that Pia fed them. It's ridiculous—"

As if conjured by Kapukiri, a green-feathered arrow bursts into bloom in Sergei's throat. He falls without another word, and the scientists gasp collectively and move back even further. With a cry I start to run to him, forgetting for a moment that he's a murderer. All I see is a man I've known my entire life, someone I thought was a friend. But Luri catches my arm and pulls me back, her eyes solemn. There is no telling who shot the arrow, but Burako continues on, unfazed in the least.

"And we have known them to be true. We of the Ai'oa

do not have much room in our hearts for murderers and liars and thieves. And we have judged you to be all of these things. Now. You will leave this place. All of you will leave this place, today, and never come back. If a foreigner shows his face here, we will shoot it. We will not fall for lies and tricks again. Never again. Go. Go now."

The scientists have mixed reactions. Some look more than ready to obey, but others harden and step forward, guns lifting once more.

Paolo holds up his hands until everyone—Ai'oans included—falls silent to hear what he has to say.

"We will go." The Ai'oans start to cheer, but he waits until they see he's not finished. "We will go," he starts again, "and we will not come back. Whatever reason we had for staying, it's gone." He looks at me. "Now I speak to you, Pia. Listen very, very closely. You *will* come with me. Now."

"Never. I—"

"We have the boy."

My scalp tingles. *That can't be right. Eio said he would hide. The jungle protects him.*

"We have the boy, Pia. And if you do not come, we will kill him. Simple as that."

He spreads his hands, then clasps them in front of himself to indicate he's finished. The Ai'oans mutter about tricks and lies, but I hear only the frantic pounding of my own heart. They have Eio. They must. Even if they didn't, how could I take that chance? Not Eio. Never Eio. I love him—and I haven't even had the chance to tell him so.

"I'll come."

"No, Pia bird!" Luri whispers, but Achiri hushes her.

I walk across the clearing as my body slowly goes numb. Just before I reach Uncle Paolo, I stop and look back at my Ai'oans.

I'm so proud of them. It was really their idea to stand up to the foreigners, to take back their pride. I look at Burako. Achiri. Luri. Kapukiri. Ami. All the rest, whose names are manifestations of the jungle itself. Jungle people. Jaguar people. *Jaguar, mantis, moon.* It's all the same—the Ai'oans and the jungle, the Kaluakoa and the *yresa*, the jaguars and the monkeys and the macaws and the river. A world of beauty and mystery, a world we should never have violated. But we did. And now it is the least guilty who pay the price, while the truly guilty go free to continue their foul work elsewhere. At least my Ai'oans will be safe. *But they were never mine, were they? They are the jungle's as much as the jungle is theirs.*

I turn away, back to Paolo. He puts his arm around my shoulders, and I don't try to stop him. I'm tired of fighting.

His words, whispered in my ear as we walk, make it worse.

"Don't think this is the end, you foolish girl. You may have destroyed it all, but I know your secret, remember?" He grips my chin, pinching hard until tears stand out in my eyes. "There. *There* they are. Hundreds of them, thousands, if I want. All I need is you and your tears. You might have had it all, Pia—an eternity of health, wealth, happiness, power; whatever you could dream, you could have. Instead, you've earned yourself an eternity of sorrow. You will weep, Pia, oh, yes. You will weep. That's your job now. Your purpose. How do you like that? I gave you one purpose, and you threw it in my face. Smashed it on the ground, literally. So what do I do? Kind, generous Uncle Paolo that I am? I give you another

371

one. A life of weeping, weeping flowers, Pia. Doesn't it sound poetic? You should like that, you, with your new emotional morality streak. A pity, really. We'll do better with the next one. Maybe we'll name her Pia too. Maybe we'll name her Antonia. Who knows? The world is full of possibility. I can't *wait*."

We reach the river, where the rest of the Little Cam populace—including my father—is waiting. He gives me a sad look, but I'm just glad they didn't hurt him for helping us escape. "We're not going back to Little Cam?" I ask.

"What? And be devoured by those monsters Will created? I think not, my dear. No, we go on to broader horizons. Maybe Africa. I hear you can see more sky than land in some places there. Wouldn't that be a nice change?"

Everyone begins piling into boats and chugging downriver. Eio was right; there are boats hidden everywhere, safely out of sight of airplanes and helicopters. Always a secret, Little Cam. Right up until the end. Uncle Timothy struggles with the motor on one of the boats, cursing at everyone around him when it doesn't start.

"You don't have Eio, do you?" I ask.

"Of course not," Paolo laughs.

Eio is safe. I can breathe again. That, I can hold on to. That can give me hope.

But not much.

Everything Paolo says is true. Little Cam is finished, yes, but the research lives on in their heads, and my tears give them a future. The Immortis project hasn't ended; it's only just beginning. Which means many more will die. Not Ai'oans, probably, but others.

I was made to bring life into the world. Life in abundance, life overflowing, life beyond the wildest dreams of humanity.

But all I've really brought is death.

"There's one missing," someone says in a random sentence my ear plucks from the air. A missing boat. *Aunt Harriet.* It must have been her. There's no one else. She's safe too, and I'm glad. I hope that whoever does tell her about Evie does it gently and that one day she might learn how to forgive herself. She did everything she could for her sister, but I know perhaps better than anyone that guilt can still find ways to leak into your heart.

The second-to-last boat pulls away from shore with my parents on board. My mother never gives me a second look; my father waves and calls out that he'll see me downriver, earning himself a glare from Sylvia. Only Timothy, Haruto, Jakob, Paolo, and I are left. Timothy cranks the motor, and everyone starts climbing on board. Tears are in my eyes; they gather there quite a lot these days. But they don't fall. Maybe I'm drying out. I still haven't truly wept for Uncle Antonio. Maybe the reality of his death hasn't hit me yet. But if I cry, I don't want it to be in front of Paolo. I don't want to give him that satisfaction, not yet.

The sun's late rays fall on the river, lighting its copper skin on fire. I stare at the rippling water as it laps the shore, waiting to take me away.

A tingle on my scalp. My heartbeat falters, just a little, and I exhale slowly and silently.

There, in the water, bobbing lightly against the side of the boat, is a single blossom of elysia.

THIRTY-SEVEN

The stray blossom must have drifted to the shore while the rest of them floated downstream. I look around and see no others. Just the one, lonely flower, barely noticeable in the shadow of the boat.

"Uncle Paolo," I say. "I need to sit for a moment. To . . . say good-bye."

He frowns and nods distractedly, not really paying attention. He's more worried about the malfunctioning motor on the boat. *Good. That's good.*

I slowly sit down on a mossy rock at the water's edge. I know at last what I must do.

I draw a deep breath. Another. The air in the jungle is wet; I once thought of it as comparable to swimming in the pool in Little Cam. It's like breathing in the jungle itself. Each breath is perfume laced with orchids.

Perfect is as perfect does.

I scoop up the flower and kiss its petals, cool and smooth

as velvet, just as Paolo turns. His eyes widen, and he lunges at me—and a green-feathered arrow slams into his chest.

He stumbles backward into the river, driven by the force of the arrow. The water is up to his ankles, and he sways, staring in shock at the shaft protruding from his chest. The other scientists shout and reach for him, but then suddenly they fall back, eyes wide on something behind me.

A hand grabs mine, pulling the flower from my lips.

I know that touch.

Eio. *My* Eio, pale and ragged, but alive. His shoulder is bloody where the bullet hit, and he's fashioned a kind of bandage out of leaves over it. He's muddy and unkempt, his hair tangled around sticks and leaves, but he's alive, and that's all that matters.

"Did you drink?" His gaze is frantic, searching mine in desperation.

"The others . . ." I point at the remaining scientists, who stand gaping with shock. Paolo falls to his knees, half in the river, his fingers clutching at the soil on the bank, and his mouth gasping and spitting blood.

"Idiot boy," he whispers. "Do you see what you've done?" His hands grapple at the arrow, but his strength leaves him like water leaves a sieve. "No, no, *no* . . . I have . . . I have work to . . . Pia . . ." I can feel the burn of his wild gaze on my skin.

My stomach twists and knots as if I've swallowed a burning torch. I sink to my knees and crawl forward, ignoring Eio's protests. I reach out and touch Paolo's hand.

"I'm sorry," I say, my voice weak. "I never wanted this."

He spits blood and gasps, "You've ruined . . . everything."

I can't help it now. The tears fall freely from my eyes. I feel

Eio's hands on my shoulders, trying to pull me back. I resist. There's something I need to know.

As Paolo turns his hand over, trying to collect my tears in his palm, I ask, "What's Geneva? When Strauss was threatening you, I heard her tell you to remember Geneva. What does it mean?"

His eyes slowly turn to me. I can see the light draining from them, and I know he has only seconds left. "Geneva," I say again.

"Not . . . *what*." His face is turning gray, his breath thin. "*Who*. Geneva . . . was a woman who worked for Corpus." He coughs, and more blood sprays the ground. "She was in line for this job and I . . . I wanted it. I *needed* to be part of the Immortis team, so I . . . I poisoned her."

His body sags to the ground, and the arrow snaps beneath him. "I found out later . . . all along . . . she was my Wickham test."

I back away, and what little pity I had for him is gone.

His eyes roll up, find mine. "All . . . it was all . . . for *you*."

With a hiss, as if it were being released through a metal valve, the air seeps from his mouth. He doesn't inhale again.

He looks unnatural, legs in the water and face planted in the mud, the one eye I can see glaring lifelessly at a pebble on the bank. *Paolo dead?* It seems impossible, like imagining water to be dry or the sun to be cold. Goose bumps run down my arms, and my tongue feels numb.

I'd thought, perhaps, that his Geneva might be like Aunt Harriet's Evie: something good, something noble in his past that might explain why he did so many terrible things. But no. He lived a monster, and he died one. And I find I do pity him, just a little, because it breaks my heart that someone so brilliant and so full of possibility should cast nothing but darkness on the world.

I let Eio help me up. He sits me back on the rock and brushes the hair from my face. Some of Paolo's blood is on my hands, and Eio wipes it away with a leaf.

The other scientists stand still, up to their knees in the river, their eyes locked on the band of Ai'oan warriors materializing from the trees. They carry green-feathered arrows and bows and aim them squarely at the foreigners.

"Did you drink, Pia?" Eio asks again, ignoring the scientists. He grips my wrists so tightly that my fingers start to tingle. Or maybe it's the elysia; I grip the flower in my hand, and its nectar bleeds onto my skin.

"I—I don't know. . . ."

"How can you not know? Pia, *did you drink?*"

"Don't shoot," says Jakob, hands raised. "We're going. See? Into the boat . . ."

They slowly climb in, eyes never wavering from the silent, grim Ai'oans. No one so much as glances at Paolo's body. I wish they would take it with them.

"Go," says Eio. "Don't ever come back. Don't ever speak of this place or of what happened here. Most of all, never speak of Pia."

"Like anyone would believe us," Jakob replies. The others look sick, but say nothing.

After the chugging of the boat motor fades, several warriors go to Paolo's body and shove it into the river. I can't watch, and instead I bury my face in Eio's shoulder. I'm trembling from head to foot and feel tears like drops of fire in my eyes. He strokes my hair and pries open my fingers, letting the elysia fall to the ground.

"I think . . ." I lick my lips, which are tingling, and struggle to meet his eyes. "I think I did drink. A little."

"Why would you do that?" he whispers, and I realize he's crying too. His tears are pure, unlike mine. They shed no death. Only release. "What were you thinking?"

"I couldn't let him hurt anyone else, not because of me."

"Pia, didn't you think for a *minute* that I'd come for you?"

"You were hurt."

"That means nothing! Not when you need me!"

I wait for the convulsions, maybe dizziness, maybe blindness. But nothing happens. Maybe it takes more time? "The noblest life is the one laid down for another, right, Eio?"

Eio presses me to him, rocking me back and forth. The other Ai'oans stay back, watching with still expressions to see what will happen to me. I listen to the drumming of Eio's heart, a sound as familiar now as my own breathing.

"Pia, I came for you. I'll always come for you, always! I promised Papi! Kapukiri will help. He'll know what to do. A remedy—" He turns to the warriors. "Go, run and get Kapukiri! *Hurry!*" They vanish wordlessly, and we're left alone.

For several minutes we sit in silence, Eio rocking me as I wait for the elysia to do its work.

Death.

Such a strange, foreign concept to me. It has permeated the past few days, but I've never felt it so close. So . . . possible. Not for me. Will it hurt? Will I just slip away? And what will come after that? Shouldn't I be more afraid?

"I'm sorry," I whisper.

"Why?" he murmurs into my hair. "Why did you do it?"

"Because I love Ami, and Luri, and Uncle Antonio, and all the rest of them. I love Ai'oa, Eio, just like you do. And . . . I love you too, Eio. I can say it now, you see? I love you." The words are as sweet as elysia. "I can't let the killing go on. No more death, not because of me. This is the only way. You and I both know it. Eio." He tries to look away, but I reach up and catch his chin so he can't. "*I love you.*"

"And I love you," he returns. His tears fall onto my cheeks. I taste their salt on my lips.

Suddenly the world spins sideways and convolutes, and I think, *This is it.* My body doubles over in a spasm, and I gasp and fall to the ground. I feel Eio beside me, his hands trying to lift me up. I wrap my arms around my torso, but the pain is everywhere. I want to scream, and my mouth opens, but all that comes out is a strangled whimper. My voice retreats, trying to escape the pain.

I feel like I'm being electrocuted from the inside out, lighting flaying the underside of my skin. It *hurts*, oh it hurts like nothing I've felt before. I'm not *on* fire—I *am* fire, raging and hot and uncontrolled. I want to scream, but my voice is frozen by the pain. I want them to throw me into the river or bury me in mud, anything to make the pain stop. I can't bear it. Blackness rages across my eyes, stealing Eio from my vision, then it turns inward, devouring my heart and my lungs and my mind. I'm sinking into black waters, and I feel the ghostly hands of everyone who ever died because of me reach out to take my soul. My grandparents, Alex and Marian, the countless Ai'oans—they want their blood back. Their revenge is pain, and my flesh pays the price.

If this is dying, then it is more terrible than I ever imagined.

I grip Eio's hands, hard, clinging to him and to everything he represents: Ai'oa, Uncle Antonio, Alai, the jungle, everything I love, everyone I cannot bear to leave behind. He must see my fear in my eyes, because he holds me so close I can hear his heart throbbing in his chest.

I brace myself for the darkness.

THIRTY-
EIGHT

When I open my eyes, a golden monkey is sitting on my chest and staring straight at me. For a moment, I can't remember anything at all. My head is completely empty, and when I shut my eyes again, I see nothing but white. I don't know where I am. I don't know what happened to me. I'm a blank slate inside. When I reach for the past, I find only empty space, and though I know there must something there, I have the strangest feeling that my life began only today, a minute ago, as if I just popped into existence.

I can't even remember my name.

And then the monkey again. It chatters and grabs my chin, and suddenly it's gone, whisked away by a small pair of hands.

Now there is a different pair of eyes. These ones are dark and vibrant, rimmed with long black lashes, and when they look into mine, they grow very wide.

"She's awake!" shouts a very high-pitched, very excited voice. The eyes disappear, and I'm left staring at a roof of thatch and leaves, and I realize I'm swaying gently, as if in a cradle.

There is noise everywhere. It starts soft, then grows louder and louder. Voices. Monkeys. Birdsong. I want to sit up, but my body resists. It's languid, as if I've been floating on water for days. *Floating on water . . .* a memory slips into my head and skitters away again. *Water, beneath a glass roof.*

More faces. More voices. Many pairs of dark eyes and brown hands. They touch my face and my arms. Who are they? And where am I? I have no memory, none at all. I feel I should be terrified, but instead I have only a vague, permeating sense of content. I lie here, still and quiet, and let them look at me.

Then the faces disappear, and the voices hush. I sense the people all around me, but none of them are talking. They're waiting for something.

Someone new appears. His eyes are different. I stare into them, and I remember suddenly what the color blue looks like. It's the color of this boy's eyes. Blue so vivid and so deep, there may as well be no other colors on the spectrum.

Wait a minute. . . . I know you.

He stares, lips slightly parted, breath held. His blue eyes trace every inch of my face. Then, slowly, he starts to smile. It's a clumsy smile, as if he hasn't practiced it in a while. A dimple suddenly appears on his chin.

My mind reaches upward and outward, as if it's at the bottom of a very deep pool. It swims up, toward light, toward those blue eyes. . . . It's a long way, but I'm determined. . . . Though I lie still, I have the sensation of rising, very quickly and very smoothly, and suddenly—I surface.

My mouth opens wide as I suck in a deep, long draft of air. Oxygen pours in and inflates my empty lungs, making my chest rise. This is the first breath I've taken since opening my eyes.

"Eio," I whisper.

The smile on his face doubles in size. He laughs out loud as he takes my hands in his.

"Pia! Pia, you're alive!" His eyes grow watery. "You're *alive*."

I remember everything. Drinking elysia, Paolo lying dead in the river, me falling into darkness in Eio's arms. *Dying.* The memories rush around my head like leaves in the wind, filling the empty spaces inside me and weighing me down to the earth.

But if I died, why am I here now? Why am I sitting up, being gathered into Eio's arms? He hugs me close, his hands on my back and in my hair.

The legend said the undying ones drank elysia and died. Didn't it? Why is the memory so hard to find? I feel like I'm trying to sculpt a sphere out of water; the words come together, then fall apart before I can make them stick. It shouldn't be this way. Everything is always so clear in my mind because my memory is perfect.

"I feel . . . strange." I study my fingers, then press them to my lips, my throat. My strength is returning. I feel it growing like a fire, warm and steady. "I feel warmer, Eio. Stronger. And . . . lighter."

He pulls away and holds me at arm's length. We're sitting in a hammock in one of the Ai'oan huts. The villagers surround us in a quiet but smiling ring. Ami stands behind Eio, her tamarin hunched on her head like a living, golden hat.

"How long has it been?" I ask.

"It was yesterday," he replies. "We thought you were dead. You stopped breathing, Pia. Right there in my arms, you stopped breathing. I thought . . ." His smile fades. "I thought you were lost to me."

"We tried to take you from him," Luri says in Ai'oan, stepping out of the ring behind Ami. "But he wouldn't let go. For an hour he knelt by the river, holding you and rocking you. We all said you were dead, but still, he wouldn't let you go."

I look back at Eio and shake my head. "So stubborn."

"Finally, we forced you from his arms," Luri goes on. "And he might as well have been dead too, the way he stared at nothing and wouldn't move."

"Then Kapukiri came," Ami says. "And he heard your heart."

"My heart?"

"It was still beating," Eio says. His hand lifts, as if he wants to feel my heartbeat for himself, but Luri steps forward and smacks his hand away.

"None of that," she snaps at him. "There are *children*, Farwalker."

Eio grins and I feel my face flush red.

"But how was my heart beating?" I ask. "I wasn't even breathing." I search the circle of Ai'oans and finally see Kapukiri. He leans on his staff and stares at me with a slight, almost smug smile.

"Who knows?" Eio says. "But all that mattered was that it beat. We carried you back here and put you in this hammock and . . . we waited."

"And waited," Luri snorts. "I'll have you know, little miss, not a one of us slept last night."

"We lit fires and prayed to the gods," Ami says cheerfully. "All night we prayed."

"And here you are," Eio whispers.

I don't know what to think. I don't know where to even begin.

"I want to get up," I say.

Eio helps me stand, and I stumble a bit. I feel odd. There is something not quite right inside, but I can't put my finger on it. It's a little alarming, but for now I just focus on walking.

"Think we can get away?" I ask him. "All these people staring . . ."

He nods, puts his arm around my waist, and leads me toward the jungle. Some of the Ai'oans follow, but he waves them away. I hear more than a few snickers as we leave the village behind.

"Ignore them," he says. "You're alive. *Alive*, Pia. I thought there was a mistake. That your heartbeat was in my imagination. But Kapukiri heard it too. Even still, I thought . . . I thought you'd never wake up. That you'd just slip away."

"I didn't," I say. *Still trying to figure that one out.*

I stumble again and grab onto a palm trunk to steady myself. The bark is sharp, and I jerk my hand away with a wince.

We both see it at the same time and freeze. I hold my index finger up between us and gaze in openmouthed astonishment.

A single scarlet drop balances on its tip.

Eio stares for a long minute before managing to whisper, "Pia . . . you're *bleeding*."

I nod, unable to speak. My pulse pounds in my temples, relentless as Ai'oan drums. The tiny droplet, so simple, so perfectly red, is the most captivating thing I have ever seen in my life. And the most impossible. And the most *wonderful*.

My mind seems stuck in a fog as it tries to make sense of it all. *I drank, I know I did. But I'm alive. I feel fine. Except . . . I'm bleeding. But what about Roosevelt? I thought I was supposed to die. . . .* The answer breaks through like sunlight.

"He was old," I whisper.

"What?" Eio looks panicked. Maybe he thinks I'm dying after all.

"He was old, Eio. That's all it was. He was a hundred years old, and those years hit him all at once." The white hairs on his face and paws—of course. Why didn't Paolo see it? Why didn't *I* see it? Roosevelt didn't die of elysia. *He died of old age.*

And the Kaluakoa?

We continue walking, and my steps grow stronger. Still, though, there's something not quite right about the way I feel. It's almost as if I'm missing something, like a hand or a foot, but all my limbs are intact.

I think back to that night around the fire and Kapukiri's deep intonations as he spoke. The legend said that the Kaluakoa's immortal protectors drank and died like the rest of them . . . *when they had lived the fullness of their years.*

Just like Roosevelt.

It's all becoming clearer, as if I'm looking at the truth through a microscope and only now finding the right adjustment of the lens. I have a suspicion I've been looking at it for a while now; it's just been out of focus.

"They died of old age," I tell Eio in wonder as the river comes into view. "When they drank, they transformed from their immortal prime to their true age, which is why they died. Or maybe not. Maybe they drank and started aging from that day forward. Maybe they lived sixty, eighty more years."

"What?" Eio looks bewildered. "I don't understand, Pia. Are you . . . are you dying?"

"Yes. No. I mean, yes, I died, and no, I'm not dying. Well, I am. I did. It's both. A *circle and a line* . . ." His eyes look ready to pop from his skull. I shake my head, and the fog clears at last. "I mean, I think *Immortal* Pia died. What's left is . . ." Mortal Pia? Someone else entirely?

Finally Eio starts to catch on. Gently, he scoops water from the river with his palm and wipes the blood away and then entwines my fingers in his, staring at them with wide eyes. "So . . . you're saying . . . that you're like me now?"

"I think so," I whisper in amazement. "I think so."

He raises our hands so that his finger can trace my lips. His eyes devour my face as if he were seeing me for the first time. Similarly, I gaze at him, seeing a future I'd never thought possible begin to unfold.

Since the night Eio first showed me the river, I've felt a connection to him, as if we were tied by some invisible string. But at the same time there was always a gap between us that no bridge could span. He was mortal, and I immortal. When he touched me or held me, I felt that one, inescapable difference between us like a cold knife blade. Even when I managed to push it aside and pretend it wasn't there, even when the electric sensation of just being with him drowned all else out, sooner or later, the truth proved too great. How many times did I let his mortality drive me away?

But now, everything is changed. Now, when he touches me, I feel nothing but Eio, pure and whole and constant. Now, when I look into his eyes, I don't see death—but eternity. For the first time in my life, I am looking into someone's gaze and realizing that not only do I understand what's in his eyes . . . *he understands what's in mine.*

The day is brilliant. The sun pours over the river and the leaves, turning everything into white gold. I finally realize what felt so wrong inside me. My senses are dimmer. I can't hear as much or smell or see like I used to. My muscles feel slow. For the first time in my life, I feel clumsy. At odds with my body. When I reach for my memory, it's foggy and vague. Certain moments stand out, still in detail, but so many others are lost to me, as if trapped beneath glazed ice.

And yet . . . the world is no less bright. The breeze on my skin and in my hair is as soft and cool as it ever was. The birdsong in the trees is as sweet. The smoke-and-papaya smell of Eio is as exhilarating as it was before.

It slowly dawns on me what it is, the sensation that has bridged the gap between how I saw the world yesterday and how I see it today. It compensates for my lost keenness and even makes everything around me a little brighter.

Hope.

I reach into my pocket and pull out my necklace. The stone bird dangles between us as I hold it up, and then I give it to Eio. "Ami told me what this means."

He looks from the bird to me. "She did?"

"Apparently, as long as I wear it, I belong to you." I raise one eyebrow at him. "Sneaky of you, Eio."

I turn around and hold my hair up so he can tie it around my neck. Once he's done and I let my hair fall, he holds my shoulders and puts his lips right beside my ear.

"I thought I'd lost you when I saw you with that flower," Eio whispers. "I thought it was all over. I couldn't live if you died, Pia."

"Funny. I was thinking the same thing about you recently."

"There's absolutely nothing funny about it!"

"I know." I turn to face him. "I'm sorry."

His hair hangs into his eyes, and I brush it away. "Eio, I truly *am* sorry. About . . . Uncle Antonio." My throat thickens, and I blink away tears. "I'd give anything to go back. To stop him."

He drops his gaze. "I know. Me too."

The image of Uncle Antonio collapsing, his veins flooded with the venom of elysia, is all too clear in my memory. I fear it will never fade, as so much of my past has.

"He'll be given an Ai'oan funeral," Eio says. "He'd like that."

I nod, and then the tears come. I press my face into Eio's shoulder and weep. We sit on the mossy bank, and he holds me while I cry. There are tears in his eyes too. Eyes so like his father's. I don't know how long we sit like this. I weep sadness for Uncle Antonio, fury at Mother, relief that Eio is alive, and my own guilt for everything that's happened.

"Pia," Eio finally whispers. He presses his lips to my forehead, where they burn like a brand. "It's not your fault. Look at me. It's *not* your fault."

"He'd be alive, Eio, if not for me."

"It was his choice." He holds my face in his hands, forcing me to look him in the eye. "Don't dishonor him by blaming yourself. He gave us the greatest gift he had to give. By feeling guilty, you strip him of that gift and turn him into a victim. And he was not a victim, Pia. He lived a noble life and he made a noble sacrifice. Remember him like that, and you honor his life and his death."

I nod slowly, letting his words sink into my mind. "Okay," I whisper. "But . . . it'll take some time."

"I know." He wraps his arms around me, holding me close. My cheek against his heart, I stare out at the river and swallow the rest of my tears.

"Aren't you scared?" he asks.

"Why?"

"Because, well, you're not immortal anymore. At least, as far as we know; just because you can bleed doesn't mean you'll grow old and die. Maybe you won't."

"How can we know?"

"There's only one way to find out."

"What?"

He smiles. "You'll just have to live."

I stare at him and have to remind myself to breathe.

"I like the sound of that." *I can die. Maybe even grow old.*

I should be terrified. The future, which has always stretched out before me as interminably and reliably as the river beside us, is suddenly uncertain. *I can end. At any moment, I could just . . . cease. No longer be.*

Unless Luri was right, and there is a somewhere else after this, where everyone drinks elysia and lives forever. *We were too greedy, grasping for immortality too soon. Perhaps if we had only been patient, content to wait, we would all have forever in the end.*

"No one should live forever," I whisper. "Isn't that how it goes? 'There must be a balance. No birth without death. No life without tears. What is taken from the world must be given back. No one should live forever, but should give his blood to the river when the time comes so that tomorrow another may live. And so it goes.'"

"And so it goes," he murmurs.

"Eio?" His eyes are still on mine, clear and blue and eternal, and I drink them in as if I were dying of thirst.

"Yes, Pia?"

I slide my hand up and trace the line of his cheek. "I think I can kiss you now."

And so it goes.

EPILOGUE

Four days I drifted on that river. Four days of hiding in the shadows and waiting in dread for someone to find me and shoot me, with gun or arrow or both. I ate what I picked off trees and drank the rainwater that collected at the bottom of my boat. The second day, I found Paolo's body half-submerged in a small inlet, tangled in a mess of roots. It was horrible.

Confident at last that the others had gone, I turned back upriver. If I'd waited one more day, I would have missed them for good. They were packing the last of their possessions, preparing to disappear forever into their jungle, and Pia with them.

When she told me what had happened—how she drank the elysia, how it stole her immortality from her—I was astonished and saddened, though I tried not to show it. Such a wonder, that immortal girl I met in the jungle. She seemed elated with her mortality and almost charmed by the thought of death, albeit a distant and unproven possibility. For all I know, she might still be a vision of a seventeen-year-old goddess, haunting the depths of the Amazon. But somehow, I just don't think so. I think she was right, and Immortal Pia did die that day, along with Paolo Alvez. Creator and creation went down together. It seems almost poetic. When I asked Pia what was left then, she only laughed and said it was Wild Pia.

I stayed with them for three months. I wasn't ready to face the world yet. My time with the Ai'oans healed me in many ways, taught me much about life and death and the struggle in between. But the jungle wasn't for me.

I tried to take her with me. I even told her she could bring that boy, as long he washed off the face paint and put on a shirt. But she wouldn't come. I told her she wasn't really one of them, but that didn't sway her either. She only said she was more Ai'oan than she'd ever thought possible, something about the jungle being in her blood, after all.

She did promise that one day they'd visit and that she dreamed of seeing the places on the map I gave her for her birthday. But even as she said it, I knew it would never happen. I saw in her eyes the fear Paolo drilled into her of the outside world. And perhaps, in this one regard, he was right. The world isn't ready for Pia, and though she is no longer immortal, a part of her will always be tied to elysia. I suspect that the jungle became world enough for her.

I managed to salvage a few blank notebooks from the wreckage of Little Cam before the Ai'oans burned or buried what they could and left the rest to the hunger of the jungle. In them I recorded everything I'd seen and the things Pia told me around the fires late at night. I went to the jungle to find a fortune, but I returned with a story. Even if someone read this account and decided to investigate, they'd find nothing but the bones *of Little Cam and certainly no trace of elysia. Even so, I think I'll burn the notebooks eventually. Maybe on the day I'm also ready to forgive myself. That day feels close, but not quite yet here.*

Every day I think of them. Evie. Antonio. So many Ai'oans. Even Pia, in a way. They all haunt my mind, waiting for me in the shadows of sleep. Reminding me how fragile this life is and how easily it can be lost. Compelling me to live and to live well, while I still can.

Because sooner or later, we must all face eternity.

THE END